D0629182

MAIDEN MURDERS

MAIDEN MURDERS

Mystery Writers

of America

Introduction by
JOHN DICKSON CARR

HARPER & BROTHERS   NEW YORK

For permission to include the following stories in this volume, grateful acknowledgment is made to:

Jerome Barry: "The Fourth Degree" by Jerome Barry. Copyright, 1933, by Liberty Magazine, Inc.

Lawrence G. Blochman: "The Fifty-Carat Jinx" by Lawrence G. Blochman. Copyright, 1929, by Clues, Inc.

Stanley Ellin and *Ellery Queen's Mystery Magazine:* "The Specialty of the House" by Stanley Ellin. Copyright, 1948, by Mercury Publications, Inc.

Joseph Fulling Fishman: "Old Calamity Tries a Bluff" by Joseph Fulling Fishman. Copyright, 1929, by Red Star News Co.

Veronica Parker Johns: "Bezique of Death" by Veronica Parker Johns. Copyright, 1948, by Street & Smith Publications, Inc.

Harry Stephen Keeler: "Victim No. 5" by Harry Stephen Keeler. Copyright, 1914, by Young's Magazine.

Alfred A. Knopf, Inc.: "The Second Sight of Dr. Sam: Johnson" by Lillian de la Torre. Copyright, 1944, 1946, Lillian de la Torre.

Kenneth Millar and *Ellery Queen's Mystery Magazine:* "Find the Woman" by Kenneth Millar. Copyright, 1946, by Mercury Publications, Inc.

Mycroft & Moran and August Derleth: "The Adventure of the Black Narcissus" by August Derleth. Copyright, 1929, by Marazine Publishers, Inc.; Copyright, 1945, by August Dereleth.

Stuart Palmer: "The Riddle of the Dangling Pearl" by Stuart Palmer. Copyright, 1933, by Tower Magazines, Inc.

Popular Publications, Inc.: "A Great Whirring of Wings" by Day Keene. Copyright, 1943, by Popular Publications, Inc. "Room No. 23" by Hugh Pentecost. Copyright, 1925, by Popular Publications, Inc. "Too Many Brides" by Ruth Wilson. Copyright, 1950, by Popular Publications, Inc.

Jerome and Harold Prince and *Ellery Queen's Mystery Magazine:* "The Man in the Velvet Hat" by Jerome and Harold Prince. Copyright, 1944, by Mercury Publications, Inc.

Ellery Queen: "The Adventure of the One-Penny Black" by Ellery Queen. Copyright, 1933, by Ellery Queen.

Georges Simenon and *Ellery Queen's Mystery Magazine:* "The Little House at Croix Rousse" by Georges Simenon. Copyright, 1932, by Artheme Fayard & Cie.; Copyright, 1947, by Mercury Publications, Inc.

Street & Smith Publications, Inc.: "Marksman" by William Campbell Gault. Copyright, 1940, by Street & Smith Publications, Inc.

Lawrence Treat: "Shoes for Breakfast" by Lawrence Treat. Copyright, 1937, by Red Star News Company.

Library of Congress catalog card number: 52-7294

Contents

Preface

This is an anthology without an editor. Or perhaps it would be more accurate to say that the three-hundred-odd members of Mystery Writers of America have acted collectively as their own editor.

The idea for *Maiden Murders*, complete with title, was first proposed by Ellery Queen in "The Biography of a Book," his introduction to *Murder by Experts*, the 1947 MWA anthology. In this introduction, Queen specified that each author should introduce his own first story. That specification has been followed, thus eliminating one of the editor's usual functions. And since there has been no question of trying to get an author's *best* story, but simply his first, the problem of selection, too, has become practically automatic. True, this book does not contain all the "firsts" submitted by MWA authors. Although such a volume would have made surprisingly good reading, with even greater historical interest than this one, the mechanics of bookmaking and the economics of bookselling compelled a more wieldy project. The sole remaining editorial chore of tailoring the contents to meet space restrictions was performed jointly by MWA's Anthology Committee—Ellery Queen, Dorothy Gardiner, and Lawrence G. Blochman—with the valued assistance of Miss Joan Kahn of Harper & Brothers.

Some maiden murders have been left out of this volume because they were good enough to be chosen for previous MWA anthologies—stories, for instance, by Helen McCloy, Kelley Roos, and Fay Stanley. Others squeezed out of this volume will undoubtedly appear in later ones. Still other "firsts" by working authors have yet to be written, judging from the discovery by this Anthology Committee that not a few MWA authors have written full-length novels for years before tackling the trickier short-story form.

Two stories in this anthology deviate somewhat from the general pattern. "Threnody" by Anthony Boucher and "And on the Third Day" by David Alexander have never seen print before. However, since they *are* first stories and since they seem to both authors and to the Committee to be better stories than those which first achieved publication, they are included despite previous editorial repudiation.

To the contributors to *Maiden Murders*, to those authors whose stories were crowded out by the third dimension, to the editors and publishers who have graciously given MWA reprint permissions, to Miss Kahn, and to Past President John Dickson Carr for his wise and witty introduction, the Committee is most grateful.

LAWRENCE G. BLOCHMAN
for the Anthology Committee

Introduction

There are few games more pleasant than those conversations which begin, "Do you remember when—?" Old friends, meeting after an interval of years, can talk happily for hours: usually to the annoyance of those who weren't there in the old days.

But nothing can mar these memories. The sting has been drawn. We forget the times when we made fools of ourselves; when we fell flat on our faces over some task; when we cursed the world and swore the times were out of joint, without even Hamlet's chance to set it right. The light of youth is upon it; and what remains is a smile, a little rueful, as at some good joke.

Something of the same feeling, I think, must be known by any professional writer who—now aged and figuratively bewhiskered —looks back at a long row of books on a shelf, and remembers how he began. Some of us, of course, didn't consciously begin. Some of us simply fell in, as into cold water; and though here I can speak only for myself, I can hardly remember a time when I was not in that same cold water—or in hot.

But there is perhaps a difference in our memories between the days of living and the days of writing. On the one hand we have, say, our first long trousers, our first love affair, the first time we saw dawn over Paris or heard the whistle of a bomb on London. On the other hand we have those first staggering steps at writing, with footprints—appropriate to the detective-story trade—reeling back over many years.

Get up and fall down! Get up and fall down! Then learn to crawl and finally to walk. And, though we may nowadays grin broadly about our first *gaucherie* in the art of living, we are not apt to grin quite so broadly at our first attempt in the art of handling words. That wasn't funny. It hurt.

Please do not think that in saying this I refer to any story in

Maiden Murders, the new anthology of the Mystery Writers of America, to which I have the honor of writing the introduction. On the contrary, my first thought on reading these tales will probably be your thought too:

"Lord, what a lot of practice every one of these writers must have had before he or she even wrote a first-published story! Though this may not be mature work, it sounds like mature work. Though it may not represent the writer at his best, yet it ranges from the competent to the sheerly brilliant. How did they all manage it?"

Well, in these pages each author will tell you. And here is my own problem. Though I have read the stories, I have not seen the biographical notes which tell how they came to be written. It may be, to the dark confusion of your obedient servant, that somebody—or many persons—will say, "It was easy. It was simple. I just got an idea and wrote it."

This, at least, has been said before. A quarter of a century ago there was a popular novelist who called himself Rex Beach. Though a hard cudgeling of memory fails to bring back the title of any book he wrote, Mr. B. *was* popular. And, if memory serves, it was in a series of confessions called *My Maiden Effort* that he stated he found writing easy because he could do the work while he was sitting down.

But experience suggests that this is not altogether a safe criterion. After all, you can fire a revolver while you are sitting down, as Sherlock Holmes did. You can drive a railroad train while you are sitting down. Happily I speculate on the possibilities if some noble-minded railroad official permitted me to be the engineer of a crack train from New York to Chicago. I should accept the offer with pleasure. But I could guarantee nothing except a wreck.

No doubt there are those who began to write, and continued to write, without pain either to themselves or to the reader. In all seriousness we must raise our hats to them. To take a single instance among many, they say Gautier was among the lucky ones.

The trouble is that most of us aren't Gautier, and don't want to be. Gautier never faced the specialized problems which confront the mystery writer. Gautier, engaged in fooling about with

Captain Fracasse and the lady of Maupin, never had to create a
perfect alibi—even in a bedroom. He never had to find some new
form of disguise. He never had to get the murderer out of the
locked room. He never—

Stop! At this point a probably eloquent passage must be interrupted for an apology to the reader. I mention these matters,
alibis and disguises and locked rooms, merely because I happen
to be fond of them and familiar with them. There are those who
declare that the modern detective story should not concern itself
with such toys or baubles, suited to a past age. They declare that
we must have character; we must have psychology; we must, in
short, have a mystery or detective story which has come of age.

And, of course, they are quite right. Mr. Anthony Berkeley said
exactly the same in 1931. True, we must not too much curse alibis
and disguises and locked rooms, or with a resounding bang our
own work will have to suffer comparison with the greatness of
G. K. Chesterton and the glory of Father Brown. True again, we
must not press too hard in the matter of character and nothing
else, or we shall find ourselves saying that the mystery story is a
fine thing so long as there is no mystery in it.

However, the purpose of this meek introduction is not to de-
bate or to lay down rules. Being entirely in agreement with the
Scot who maintained there is no bad whiskey, I enjoy all forms
of sensational literature provided only that they be well written.
The solitary thesis here set forth is one, I hope, with which most
authors would agree: the old saw that easy reading makes damned
hard writing.

Nowadays it is a truism that the short story is the most difficult
form of literary expression. And yet, if we all think back to youth
at twelve or fourteen when we first scribbled or blundered at
a typewriter, the short story is probably what most of us wrote
at the beginning.

We did not want merely to "write." When a person says that,
he often means only that he wants to dream. No; we were more
practical; we wanted to write a story. Since it would have been
too big an undertaking to write a long story, we simply had a go
at what we considered a short story.

Nobody, at that time, told us it was so difficult. No voices of
doom whispered from the ceiling. No mentor said, "Look out!

You must do this," or, "Be careful! No editor would look at that." In our innocence we were as radiantly contemptuous of editors as some of us remain to this day. Perhaps the story never got itself finished. Perhaps, like Mark Twain on one famous occasion, we landed in such a muddle that nobody could have hauled us out anyway. All the same, whether we hacked out battlemented castle or shapeless mud-pie, we had a try at the story.

For, let it be repeated, we meant business. Without doubt we imitated some favorite author, perhaps several of them. Over there on the shelves were the works of someone, supply what name you like, seeming to blaze and glitter with a luster that made all other books look dull. But it was not only that we wanted to be "like" that particular literary hero. It was far more.

A new window had opened. A fiery new idea hummed in our heads. On the beach, say, lay a fine fresh corpse, strangled, with only its own footprints leading out across the damp waste of sand. We might not yet be able skillfully to maneuver with that corpse: no, not yet. But one fine day we would. One fine day, by thunder, we would succeed!

And then one fine day, we did.

That, I hope, is what all the writers represented in this anthology would say to a boy or girl who wants to write: especially one who wants to write a mystery story. Come storm or hobgoblins or broken bones, he has only got to mean business strongly enough, and he will succeed. Does this seem too optimistic a view of the matter? Perhaps it is. On the other hand, if your neophyte really and sincerely means to write, nothing on earth can stop him and thank God it can't.

Should anyone doubt this simple proposition, he is recommended to read the stories of crime, of mystery, of mystery-detection that follow in *Maiden Murders*. This admirable collection, though admittedly not consisting of very youthful attempts such as we discussed a moment ago, at least shows the first story which achieved publication. And, since I had nothing to do with the anthology beyond the pleasure of reading the stories, I am entitled to praise it highly.

Here are the old craftsmen, the serpents, the great masters of the game: Mr. Ellery Queen, Mr. Stuart Palmer, M. Georges

Simenon. Here are those excellent storytellers who are comparative newcomers: Mr. Stanley Ellin, Mr. David Alexander. Here are writers, such as Mr. Lawrence G. Blochman and Mr. Hugh Pentecost and Mr. August Derleth, whose skill can deal with any type of story; and here are such specialists in the *tour de force* as Miss Lillian de la Torre and Mr. Anthony Boucher.

It is not intended that any one story or group of stories shall be singled out for special mention of merit. That is for you who read to decide. But, in a collection of first efforts, the remarkable thing here is the large number of unconventional stories. Your beginner, as a rule, is fairly conventional because he does not want to slip on a banana peel at his very first step. Yet more than half-a-dozen newcomers have dared the banana peel and triumphantly avoided it.

Take, for instance, "The Man in the Velvet Hat," by Messrs. Jerome and Harold Prince. You may like the "film" attack, or you may not like it. But to ignore it is all but impossible. It comes whirling and banging at your head, Dos Passos fashion, defying you to dodge. After the first few pages you have the sensation of one who, on a steeply diving roller coaster, has just swallowed a Bromo-seltzer while listening to an off-key brass band. And yet, when you have emerged through the blare and murk of the unconventional style, you find you have been reading a sound and well-plotted story of straight detection.

Or, in contrast, take what I confess to be one of my own favorites: Miss Lillian de la Torre's "The Second Sight of Dr. Sam. Johnson."

It is possible that you are not an admirer of Dr. Johnson, as presented either by James Boswell or by Miss de la Torre. If not, I am sorry. But, if anyone had told most of us that a writer could turn the Great Lexicographer into a detective and get away with it, I am sure we should not have believed it—until we read the first story.

This, offhand, would seem to be the most slippery banana peel in history. We should imagine Dr. Johnson lumbering down Fleet Street, touching the posts in the soot-drizzle of the eighteenth century, and occasionally turning to snarl over his shoulder, "Elementary!" or, "You know my methods, Boswell." After all, it is a sober fact that both Johnson and Boswell were acquainted with the sermons of a clergyman named Sherlock.

Now it is the triumph of Miss de la Torre that her wit and scholarship permit no unintentional comedy. There is the Great Cham, as large as life, uprearing for the thunderous syllable of, "Sir—" while he solves a sound problem which, in so many of the stories about him, was a real historical problem. Criticism is speechless. But can unconventionality go further?

Or, in still greater contrast, take Mr. Ellin's grisly tale called "The Speciality of the House," in which—

But again let us call a halt. The showman must not beat the big drum too heavily outside the tent, no matter how well he likes the performance inside. It may be that I ought not to say here what I nevertheless believe should be said everywhere. For we all remember where these three stories, by Messrs. Prince and Miss de la Torre and Mr. Ellin, first appeared.

They appeared in *Ellery Queen's Mystery Magazine*. And we know the name of the man who for so many years has labored and fought and inspired to lift the mystery story to its rightful place in American letters; and who with his own two hands has raised it to its present stature of literacy and power. We know the name of Ellery Queen, and to him be all honor.

Here, then, as the showman steals away with what grace he can contrive, are the maiden stories. They are iron maidens, full of sharp spikes and death. Good reader, friendly critic, I wish you joy.

JOHN DICKSON CARR

Villa Mimosa
Tangier, Morocco
March, 1952

MAIDEN
MURDERS

HUGH PENTECOST

Room Number Twenty-three

INTRODUCTION

"Room Number Twenty-three" was written and sold during my sophomore year in college, and there is really some question as to whether or not it is my maiden murder. I became a writer in a great rush, writing two stories and sending them both off to Detective Fiction Weekly *in the same envelope. Incredible as it may seem, both stories were bought for fifty dollars apiece and I was permanently lost. I will never know which one the editor bought first, but "Room Number Twenty-three" was the first one published.*

The character of James W. Bellamy was based on a real-life person and he will probably sue me if he ever reads this. He was a young man in his senior year at Columbia, older than the average senior because he'd served several years in the Royal Canadian Air Force. He was already a writer himself, and a glamorous figure to a young sophomore. The portrait now seems incredibly green and raw, but it grew out of real affection and admiration. Not too many heroes of one's youth stand the test of time, but this gentleman, while he never became a detective, actually has lived a life of adventure and became a renowned story-teller. The admiring sophomore made no effort whatever to conceal the identity of the model for his fiction hero, for he used the same name— almost. The model was James Warner Bellah.

I suppose almost every contributor to this anthology will be painfully aware of a certain imitative and derivative quality in their maiden efforts. Certainly this novice was an unblushing borrower. However, this much can be said. When he stole a formula he stole from the master. Twenty-eight years later he would feel definitely pleased if some new writer found him worthy of imitation.

HUGH PENTECOST

1

Room Number Twenty-three

I FIRST met James Bellamy during the war and was immediately conscious that he was a remarkable fellow. He was young, scarcely twenty-five, yet he had written two novels and was an ace in the Royal Flying Corps.

I had not been as fortunate as some others in my war experience.

When the United States went in, I tried to enlist, but discovered that I had a "leaky valve," or some such tommyrot. I finally got into a Red Cross unit, and it was at a field hospital that I ran across James Bellamy. He had come in to have an infected hand dressed and he was much disgruntled at having to give up flying for a week because of so small an injury.

One afternoon while he was there I had to go to the other side of the town for something, and Bellamy offered to go with me. He was a striking figure as he walked down the shell-riddled street in his handsome uniform, twirling a little cane.

We said nothing, as we scarcely knew each other, and Bellamy was just a little too reserved to inspire loquacity. Before we had reached our destination, a heavy fire of enemy shells began dropping about us and we realized that at any minute we might be blown to bits. I was frightened silly, but Bellamy appeared entirely unmoved.

He sauntered along whistling a little tune and twiddling his stick. He looked at me and his eyes twinkled humorously. If I looked half as frightened as I was I must have been a sorry sight.

"I say, old bean," said Bellamy, "if we've got to die, let's die like gentlemen. Nothing like adopting the proper pose under such circumstances. Pose is all that counts in life." And he offered me a cigarette.

I took one and he held a match for me with steady hands.

"Do you ever read poetry?" he asked.

We continued to our destination discussing poets. Bellamy's utter indifference, at least externally, to the exploding shells was infectious, and I soon found that my pretense of bravery had actually made me forget my fear to a large extent.

2

The next day I had a few hours to myself, and Bellamy and I went to a little wine shop which had escaped destruction. He ordered Scotch whiskey and soda, and I joined him. We continued our discussion of poetry. I found that he was intensely fascinated by all the romanticists in literature, and I confess it surprised me.

Bellamy's air of cynicism had led me to suspect entirely different tastes. I asked him about it. He sat puffing at his pipe for a few moments before he answered.

"It's because I like liars," he said at last. "Lying is dying out altogether too swiftly, and if I get through this fracas I shall devote my time to perfecting the Art of Lying."

"Explain," I said.

"Why, my dear fellow, we can see the hardships and horrors of life on every hand. Why, when we go to literature for entertainment must we read about obvious things? I hate these modern realists. They have no imaginations, so they must write about what they see. But the true artist doesn't care about what he sees, he only cares about what he'd *like* to see. Personally, aside from literature, I believe the truth is a bad habit.

"If you tell the truth you are sure to be found out sooner or later. If you don't tell the truth you amuse your friends a great deal more, and it is much more stimulating to yourself."

"Don't you ever tell the truth?" I asked.

"Only when it is so improbable that no one will believe it," he replied.

The next day Bellamy went back to his post and I didn't see him again. The armistice came and I found myself back in New York. I was fortunate in being able to get back my job on the *Republican*.

I had been reporting for them when war was declared. Donaldson, the managing editor, soon discovered that the war had developed in me a rather keen power of observation and he began sending me out on gruesome leads. I found myself covering all the important and unimportant crimes committed in and about the city.

One morning I was walking up the avenue when I saw the resplendent figure of a man coming toward me from the opposite direction. He was dressed in a smartly cut dark blue suit, with vest and spats of a lighter color. He wore a slouch hat pulled down at a rakish angle, and smoked a cigarette through a long amber holder. He was twirling a malacca walking stick carelessly. Something about the way he carried that stick was familiar to me.

"Bellamy!" I cried, as he came abreast. "How the devil are you?"

He looked somewhat bewildered for a moment.

"I say, if it isn't old Renshaw," he drawled.

We shook hands heartily.

"What are you doing with yourself?" I asked.

"Idling, old bean, idling. It's the only profession left open for a gentleman. And you?"

"Unfortunately I have a bestial appetite," I said, "I must work to feed it. I'm reporting for the *Republican*. I'm a journalist."

"Journalist sounds better than reporter," he drawled. "Always put your best foot forward."

"Idling seems to agree with you," I said. "You look exceedingly prosperous."

"As a matter of fact, I have exactly thirty cents to my name," he said.

"Still lying?" I asked suspiciously.

"No. This is one of the times when it is unlikely that you'll believe the truth."

"You really mean you're that hard up?" I asked.

"Well, I've got some duds, furniture and the like, stored away. I'm looking for some simple soul who will supply an apartment and let me supply the furnishings. Some young fellow ought to jump at the chance to live with me. I would be a liberal education to him."

"Are you serious?" I demanded.

"Quite, old bean."

"Well, I'm your man," I said. "I've been looking for some one to share with me and I should be delighted to have you."

He tapped the curbing with his cane thoughtfully before answering.

"Can't tell when I'll have any money," he said shortly.

"That's all right. When you get it will be time enough to worry about that."

"I shall be devilish cross at times. When I'm writing I'm a bear."

"I understand," I said. "Besides, I shall scarcely be in except to sleep and for breakfast."

"I have a gilt angel in a frame and a set of Casanova that I should insist on having around," he said doubtfully.

"Suits me," I said.

He looked up at me with his rare but charming smile.

"I say, this is bully," he said. "You're sure you mean it?"

"Absolutely."

The next few days were hectic. I was at work all day for the *Republican* and in the evenings Bellamy and I fussed about trying to settle the little apartment on Gramercy Park. Bellamy's furnishings were really lovely, and at the end of the week we had a place that was perfect.

The apartment was in one of those old remodeled houses, and was blessed with a fireplace in the high ceilinged living room. Two great windows looked out over the park, and Bellamy had put a comfortable chair by each window. A heavy oak table stood in the center of the room and a couch was backed up against it, facing the fireplace.

Our first night at home we felt like kings. Bellamy, wrapped in a well-worn dressing gown, sat before a little blaze in the hearth and smoked his pipe thoughtfully. He had just filled it from a red can which bore the name of an English tobacconist.

"What kind of tobacco do you smoke?" he asked, seeing me take my pipe and pouch from the mantelpiece.

"Hampshire," I said.

"Try some of this," he suggested, handing me the red can.

I filled my pipe and lit it. He watched me speculatively.

"How do you like it?" he asked.

"It's very smooth," I said.

"How does it compare with Hampshire?"

"Well, it's much smoother," I said, puffing carefully. "It has a quality which a more expensive tobacco is bound to have."

Bellamy chuckled.

"That shows the unreliability of the senses," he said. "That's

Hampshire you're smoking. I just keep it in this can because there's a little sponge in the top that keeps it moist."

The next morning, when I got to the office, the chief sent me out on a new case. Something had happened at the old Nathan Hotel, and I was to investigate. The Nathan is one of the landmarks of a society which once centered about Washington Square, but which has since migrated uptown.

Nothing of its ancient splendor remains, except the fine courtesy of employees and the clientele of old New Yorkers depressed in fortune. One could still get a delicious chicken and waffle supper there, the fame of which had lasted through a century. It was not the sort of place where one expected to find a crime of any sort.

But there had been a crime at the Nathan, at least the police thought there had been. It was a very odd thing. A Miss Wilson and her brother Robert had put up there for the night. The Wilsons' father had been one of the Nathan's old customers, and his children, who lived out of town, stayed there when in the city.

With the Wilsons on this occasion was a private detective named Herbert Horton. The reason for the detective's presence was this: Miss Wilson had been left a considerable fortune in jewels by an aunt, recently deceased. These jewels had been left with the family lawyer and Miss Wilson and her brother had come to get them.

It seems that they had insisted, against the lawyer's advice, on taking the jewels with them to their home in Stamford. It was late in the afternoon when they left the lawyer's office, too late to deposit them in a safety vault, and too late to get home without being swallowed in the crush.

The Wilsons had decided to stay at the Nathan for the night and take an early train home in the morning. The lawyer, feeling that the whole procedure was a bit rash, had finally persuaded them to let Horton, the detective, accompany them and see that nothing happened to the jewels.

They had no trouble in getting three rooms at the Nathan. These rooms were on the sixth floor, which, by the way, was the top. The rooms were adjoining, though not connecting, and they looked out over the avenue. The numbers of these rooms were Twenty-one, Twenty-three and Twenty-five. Miss Wilson had the center room, with Horton in Twenty-one, and Robert Wilson in Twenty-five.

When they had got settled in their rooms, Miss Wilson had decided she wanted some tea. Her brother had some letters to write and refused to go down. Miss Wilson left the jewels with him and went down to the old bar, which had been converted into a tearoom. Horton remained in his room.

The clerk at the desk saw Miss Wilson go into the tearoom, and about half an hour later he saw her go upstairs again. A chambermaid working in the hall saw her get off the elevator at the sixth floor and go to her room. Almost immediately there was a loud scream, apparently from Miss Wilson's room.

The maid stood terrified, staring at the door of Twenty-three. Horton rushed out of his room and Wilson out of his. They hammered on the door of Twenty-three. They called Miss Wilson, but there was no answer. The door was locked. Horton turned and saw the chambermaid.

He asked her if she had seen Miss Wilson go into her room and she said she had. They redoubled their cries but to no avail. Wilson finally grabbed a fire ax from the wall and soon demolished the door. Horton rushed in, revolver in hand, and stopped on the threshold, amazed. Wilson stared over his shoulder.

The room was absolutely undisturbed. It was empty. Miss Wilson's coat and other articles hung in the closet. Everything was just as it must have been when she left the room. The window was locked on the inside.

Horton concluded that they had made a mistake, despite the chambermaid's evidence, and that the cry had come from someone else. Wilson went down to see if his sister was still in the tearoom.

He came back shortly, white-faced, and told Horton what the clerk had seen. This clerk swore that he had just seen Miss Wilson go upstairs. The Wilsons had often stopped at the hotel, he couldn't be mistaken. Then they questioned the chambermaid.

She had seen Miss Wilson go into her room. She described Miss Wilson perfectly. There could be no doubt about it.

Horton examined the room carefully. He unlocked and opened

the window. There was no means of egress that way. It was a straight drop of six stories to the street. There was no cornice around the building on which any one could walk. Escape by the window was impossible.

There was absolutely no exit from that room except the door, and Miss Wilson hadn't come out of the door. There was no sign of a struggle, nothing to indicate that anything unusual had happened. Yet Miss Wilson had gone into that room, had screamed, hadn't come out, and yet wasn't there.

Horton hinted at foul play, but there was nothing to indicate that such a thing had happened. It seemed that it must have been some peculiar mistake. Miss Wilson couldn't have gone into that room or she'd be there now. They finally concluded that, despite all evidence to the contrary, Miss Wilson hadn't come up, that she had stepped out of the hotel for something.

They waited for her return. But she didn't come back. All night they waited, and during this time the clerk and the maid persisted that what they had said was true. About four in the morning Horton summoned the police.

The police examined the witnesses and the room with the same result. There could be no question of a murder. It was simply a mysterious disappearance. That the girl had gone against her will seemed apparent, inasmuch as she certainly wouldn't have gone off of her own volition without telling her brother.

Immediately a wide-spread search was organized. Every policeman in New York was supplied with a description of Miss Wilson. But nothing happened.

When I finally returned to the *Republican* office to write my story the only additional evidence of any sort was a corroboration of the evidence given by the clerk and the chambermaid. The elevator boy testified that he took Miss Wilson—describing her—up at the time the clerk said he saw her.

He remembered the time because he went off duty at six o'clock. In fact, Miss Wilson was the last passenger he had carried.

But the police obstinately refused to believe that Miss Wilson had ever returned to her room. With a certain sort of stolid logic, they argued that if she had returned she would be there now. No, Miss Wilson was somewhere about the city.

Perhaps some accident, a coincidence under the circumstances, had occurred and Miss Wilson was in a hospital. Every accident ward in the city was searched, but no trace of the missing girl was found.

My own personal opinion was that this was just another of those queer disappearances that always have a logical explanation when the lost person turns up. I could not believe, as the police did, that Miss Wilson's disappearance was involuntary. But then, unlike the police, I believed that the girl had returned to her room.

The evidence of those three people was, to my mind, conclusive. One person might make a mistake, but not three. Therefore, since there was no sign of any sort of a struggle, it seemed probable to me that for some inexplicable reason the girl had left the hotel of her own accord. The only thing I couldn't explain was the scream.

If Miss Wilson wanted to get away unnoticed, why did she scream? What was the cause of that scream? Horton, Wilson and the chambermaid all described it as unquestionably a scream of terror. What was the meaning of it?

I finished my article and walked uptown toward Gramercy Park. Though I was very tired, I wanted some fresh air.

It was after midnight when I got to our apartment and I found that Bellamy had already turned in. I went quietly to bed, but it was not to be for long. I was awakened about three by the frantic ring of the phone. It was the editor of the *Republican*.

"Run over to the Nathan," he ordered. "They've found that girl—murdered," he added after a pause.

"Good God," I cried. "Where did they find her?"

"The body was hidden behind some ash barrels in the basement," said the editor. "The hotel porter discovered it accidentally. Shake a leg and get over there. I'm holding up the presses of the next edition for your story."

I began to dress hurriedly, without making any attempt to be quiet. Bellamy came out of his room, wrapped in his long bathrobe.

"Devil of a thing to wake up a fellow at this hour," he grumbled. "Never can get to sleep again after I awaken. What's up?"

I told him briefly.

"What are the facts of the case?" he asked, stretching himself out on the couch.

I told him, finishing the narrative as I was putting on my hat to go out.

"Are all the police reporters such fools as you?" he asked.

It was his way of asking a question, like the old legal trick of inquiring of the defendant if he has given up beating his wife. An answer either way is an indictment.

There was little to learn at the Nathan besides what the night editor had told me. William Graham, a porter at the Nathan, had made a cache of a bottle of Scotch behind some ash barrels in the cellar. When he reached behind the barrels for his forbidden treasure his hand touched the corpse.

He speedily notified the police, and when I reached the Nathan I found that a special officer had been sent down to question Graham.

This officer was a rather intelligent fellow named Milliken. He got the porter's story from him and was about to dismiss him when Graham, with a puzzled frown, asked if he might add something to the evidence.

"There's something I'd like to tell, sir," he said, "but in telling you I have to confess to a crime myself. If you'll agree not to prosecute me I can tell you something valuable."

Milliken looked at him shrewdly.

"What sort of a crime have you committed?" he asked.

"You won't pull me in?"

"No. Spill it," demanded the officer shortly.

"Well, sir," began Graham, and he actually blushed, "I'm a bootlegger!" Milliken scowled blackly at some of us who laughed. Graham went on, somewhat hesitantly, "I was in the habit, sir, of keeping a case of liquor back of them barrels. The night that the young girl disappeared, last night, I had some customers.

"They came into the cellar for a case of gin I had for them. What I'm getting at is, that I had that case of gin back of them barrels, right where I found the young girl. She wasn't there, sir, yesterday at this time. What's more she wasn't there this afternoon, that is, yesterday afternoon, strictly speaking.

"I put a bottle of Scotch there about five o'clock when I came on duty. She wasn't there then, sir. That girl was put there, sir, some time between five last night and half-past two this morning."

Milliken smoked a cigarette thoughtfully.

"You'd swear to that, Graham? You'd swear she wasn't there last night at five o'clock? That means that the body was put there at least twenty-four hours *after* she disappeared."

"Yes, sir."

"Could anyone get into the basement without you seeing him?" asked the detective.

"Oh, yes, sir. The basement's a big place. I wasn't near them barrels after five o'clock until I found the young girl."

That was all the porter's evidence. But it made the case more difficult than ever. The police now switched their opinion about Miss Wilson's having gone to her room. There never had been any doubt in my mind. She had gone to her room, some one hiding in the room had struck her down, and had escaped himself, *with the body!*

Miss Wilson must have seen her assailant before he struck her, for she had screamed. But how, by all that's wonderful, had they got out of that room? There simply wasn't any way to get out except by the door, and there hadn't been any escape that way.

The chambermaid had been watching, and Horton and young Wilson had come out of their rooms almost immediately as they heard the scream. There had been less than three minutes before they broke in the door. Three minutes in which the murderer escaped with the body. Then, a day later, this murderer had come from wherever he had been hiding and put the body back of those ash barrels.

"The queer part of it is," said Milliken, "that he couldn't have been hiding in the hotel. Mr. Horton and I searched every square inch of it the day after the disappearance. He must have hidden outside somewhere and brought the body back to the hotel last night."

The whole problem was getting too deep for me, and I hurried back to the *Republican* to get an article into the breakfast-table edition. As I reassembled the facts I became more puzzled. A girl is waylaid, probably in an attempt to rob her of the jewels which she didn't have. She screams, and the robber strikes her down.

The cause of her death had been a shattering blow on the head.

Then, in three minutes' time, the murderer escapes with his victim from a room from which escape is impossible. He drags the body somewhere outside the hotel, and then, a day later, brings it back and hides it in the basement.

After writing my article I returned once more to Gramercy Park to freshen up. I found Bellamy still stretched out on the couch. He had been smoking a great deal, for the carpet was littered with ashes.

He looked a little pale from his sleepless night. The coffee percolater was bubbling on the table, and the smell of it made me realize that I was ravenously hungry.

"I was just about to throw together some bacon and eggs," said Bellamy. "You're just in time. What happened?"

I told him between gasps, as I drenched my face and head with cold water from the basin. He lay there, smoking, a queer smile on his face.

"Look here," I said when I had dried my face and hands, "I didn't have time to take up your parting jab this morning. What the devil do you mean by insinuating that I was a fool?"

"Did I insinuate that?" he drawled.

"Yes," I said. "You asked me if all police reporters were such fools as I."

"Did I? Well, perhaps they are. Crime is usually so elemental, the kindergarten of emotions, and you fellows make such a hullabaloo about it. It's ridiculous."

"If you have some brilliant solution to this Wilson business," I said dryly, "explode it. Every poet thinks he knows a devil of a lot about humanity. Suppose you explain this puzzle."

"It looks so simple to me," said Bellamy, "but of course I can't be sure. However, answer these questions if you can."

"Shoot," I said.

"First," said Bellamy, tapping down the ashes in his pipe, "let us get the scene straight. Miss Wilson has a very valuable lot of jewels. They are obviously worth an attempted robbery. But did Miss Wilson publish the fact in the papers that she had them?"

"What are you driving at?" I asked.

"Just this, old bean. Either it was a coincidence, and some

common burglar, a sneak thief hanging about the hotel corridors, chanced into Miss Wilson's room and, being surprised, killed her, or it was not a coincidence, and someone who knew about those jewels was the murderer.

"Now, the people who knew about those jewels were comparatively few. They were her brother and Horton, who were with her, the lawyer who gave them to her, and perhaps one or two of his office force. Now, my dear Renshaw, what do you say? Was it one of these, or was it just a chance burglar?"

"Most likely a chance burglar," I said.

"Very well. Question number two: the police and the reporters have been able to find no exit from that room but the door. Suppose, for the sake of argument, that there is another exit, which I hasten to assure you that I don't believe, do you think that, with Horton and Wilson banging on that door with a fire ax, he would stop to drag off the lifeless body of his victim?

"Remember, we are presuming that it was a chance burglar who knew nothing of the jewels. Someone who knew about the jewels might have thought Miss Wilson had them on her person and made the effort to get the body out with him for further search. But do you think even this is probable?"

I admitted that I didn't.

"Question number three," drawled Bellamy. "Presuming that we are wrong about this and that the murderer did drag the body out with him—out of the hotel, mind you, for the police searched every nook and cranny the day after the disappearance, and she wasn't in the hotel—presuming, I say, that he did drag the body out of the hotel, and concealed it in safety somewhere, which is presuming a great deal, can you by any stretch of imagination conceive of his returning the next day with the body and concealing it in the hotel?"

"No I can't."

"The fourth question is very simple, but to my mind quite pertinent. Presuming that all this happened, can you imagine that in the struggle which took place in Room Twenty-three, the falling body, the dragging of that body out of the room through the unknown exit—which doesn't exist—nothing would have been disturbed—no chair misplaced, no rumpled carpet—nothing?"

"Frankly, I can't," I admitted.

"Now one more point," he said. "We have been imagining that all this was done by a chance burglar. Is it any more likely that one who knew about the jewels would do these things?"

"No," I said, "it isn't."

Bellamy rose from the couch and pulled the plug out of the coffee percolater.

"Me for some breakfast," he said.

"But the solution?" I cried. "All you've done is to make it seem more difficult than ever."

Bellamy smiled. "You'll admit," he said, "that none of these suppositions we have made are possible. Therefore an entirely different set of circumstances must have attended the crime. Use your head, old bean, use your head. I'm for a little bacon and eggs, and then I'm going to write a sonnet about the mayor."

"But you can't leave me in the air this way," I complained.

Bellamy wandered toward the kitchenette to cook his eggs.

"Look up the Wilsons' family history," he suggested. "Family histories are always interesting at a time like this."

And Bellamy would say no more, though I pestered him all through breakfast. I went back to the office then and wrote another article, in which I embodied all of Bellamy's questions.

My chief was much pleased and wanted me to continue with a theory as to what actually happened. I couldn't do that, as I hadn't the vaguest notion about it.

I did follow Bellamy's advice, however, and found out what I could about the Wilsons. When I got home that night I told Bellamy what I had discovered.

"They are a family who once had means," I told him. "The father died about three years ago and left nothing but a mass of debts. The girl took a position as private secretary to some man, and Robert Wilson went on the stage. From what I could find out at his club, he is a man of good habits, though usually rather badly in debt."

Bellamy nodded. "Just as I thought," he said cryptically.

"And you have solved the riddle?"

"Been working on the mayor all day," he said. "I knew the solution this morning."

"Good heavens," I cried, "if you really have any idea of what happened, you ought to tell me. The murderer may be making good his escape."

Bellamy thought for a moment.

"There is just one fact which might scatter my theory to the four winds," he said, "but I'm inclined to think that fact doesn't exist."

"What is that fact?" I asked.

"Were the rooms of Herbert Horton and Robert Wilson searched when the police were looking through the hotel for the body?"

"I see what you are driving at," I said excitedly. "You think the murderer might actually have concealed the body in one of those rooms while Wilson, Horton, and the police were searching the premises!

"Of course the police didn't bother to search those rooms because they knew that they had been occupied by the girl's brother and their own detective when the murder was committed. I think you've hit it," I concluded jubilantly.

"I didn't mean that at all," said Bellamy, "or at least not the way you think I did."

He sat smoking a minute, and then turned to me; and I saw his eyes were unusually bright.

"Renshaw," he said, "you know how absolutely worthless evidence of the visual sort is. I mean one can't count on the eye of a witness. It's been tried over and over again. A whole roomful of men will be asked to describe a pantomime which has been enacted before them, and no two of them will give the same answer.

"You know that a witness may swear to having seen something, swear honestly, that never happened at all."

"That's true."

"Bear in mind, then, old bean, that the chambermaid's testimony was absolutely false, although she thinks she has told the truth."

"What do you mean?" I cried.

"Wait—tell me, Renshaw, why do the police never believe their own conclusions? They say in this case that there is no possible means of escape from Room Twenty-three except the door, yet they are trying to find out how Miss Wilson's murderer got out of that room. Renshaw, if there is no way out of that room but the door, *then the murderer never got out."*

"What do you mean, he was hidden in there? That's impossible, they searched the room immediately they got in."

"I mean," said Bellamy slowly, *"that he never was in that room."*

"Look here," I said, laughing, "I thought you were being serious."

"That's the trouble with you duffers," said Bellamy with unwonted sharpness, "you haven't the brains to accept the truth. You sit by, in this instance, and solemnly assert that the murderer couldn't have escaped from Room Twenty-three, and when I tell you he didn't, you scoff at it. Work out your own solution! You'll never find the truth, if you spend all your time contradicting yourself."

"Oh, come, Bellamy, don't be offended," I said. "I thought you were joking. You must admit it sounds ridiculous to say that the murderer didn't escape from the room in which the murder was committed and then that he never was in that room!"

Bellamy smiled.

"Sorry, old bean. I get awfully bored with pigheadedness at moments. But, see here, I said that the murderer wasn't in Room Twenty-three. The reason he wasn't there was because the *murder wasn't committed in Room Twenty-three."*

"Bellamy!" I ejaculated.

Bellamy paused and filled his pipe.

"Thanks for not laughing at that one," he said dryly as he lit his pipe. "Let me get down to what actually happened," he continued, and I detected an unusual enthusiasm in his tone. His eyes were glowing and he twined and untwined his long fingers nervously.

"Look at the scene, Renshaw. Three rooms stand next to each other in the corridor. A chambermaid is cleaning up in the hall. A young girl gets off the elevator and goes to her room. The maid only casually notices this. But when a loud scream is heard the maid looks up, panic-stricken. For a moment she doubts which room the girl entered.

"There are a dozen similar doors in the corridor. However, she is soon made certain that it was Number Twenty-three since the gentlemen who have the rooms on either side of Twenty-three rush out and bang on that door. Then comes the excitement of breaking into the room. It was found empty. Horton turns to the maid and asks her if she saw Miss Wilson go into Room Twenty-three.

"She swears that she did. But she didn't, Renshaw! She didn't! The thing that made her certain that Miss Wilson *had* entered Twenty-three was that Horton and Wilson came out and banged on *that* door. Could anything be more natural?"

"It still isn't quite clear," I said.

Bellamy smiled tolerantly. "Listen, old bean, Miss Wilson never went into Twenty-three. She went either into Horton's room or her brother's. One of those two men attacked her for some reason and killed her. Just before the attack Miss Wilson screamed.

"The murderer had great presence of mind, a presence of mind bordering on genius. Instead of trying to escape he rushes out into the hall—after pushing the body under the bed, say—and bangs on the door that Miss Wilson *ought to have entered.*

"The guiltless man, I won't say which he is for the moment, naturally supposed that the other fellow was acting on the same impulse as himself. He had heard the scream which he suspected came from Miss Wilson. The guiltless man was completely disarmed, never suspected for a moment.

"The chambermaid might have given the whole game away had she carefully noticed which room the girl entered, but she hadn't noticed carefully. When the two men came out and banged on the door of Twenty-three she thought she was certain, only thought she was certain."

"But, Bellamy," I cried, "which one is it?"

Bellamy leaned forward. He seemed to be thrilled by his own reasoning. He was as excited as a schoolboy.

"What would have made that maid certain about the room?" he asked. "Remember, the evidence of the eyes is not certain, but there is another kind of evidence which is more reliable. The ear, Renshaw, the ear! What might she have heard that would have made her certain about the room?"

"I give up," I said.

"A knock," said Bellamy. "If Miss Wilson had knocked on the door the maid would have looked up, waiting to see who let her in. It was because she *didn't knock* that the murderer has escaped so far and been able to make it seem that the murder took place in Room Twenty-three.

"But it is because she didn't knock that we can pick the guilty man with absolute certainty. Come, Renshaw, surely you see it now? Which is it, Horton or Wilson?"

"I give up," I said. "My mind is whirling round like a pinwheel."

"So simple," chuckled Bellamy. "It was her brother, of course. If she had gone into Horton's room, she would have knocked! Don't you see? But she walked into her brother's room without a word. Have I convinced you, old bean?"

"But why—why would her brother kill her?"

"Ah, that's not in my province," said Bellamy, stretching contentedly. "I have delivered the murderer to you, now you find out why he did it."

Bellamy was right. I took his theory to Milliken and explained the process of reasoning. He was thunderstruck that it had never occurred to him. Wilson, when confronted with the crime, broke down and confessed everything. He had been heavily in debt.

When his sister had left the jewels with him he had decided to extract some of them from the box and pawn them. But the box was locked and his sister had the key. He had been in the act of prying it open when she walked into his room unannounced. She argued with him and in a fit of passion he struck her down with his walking stick, a stout piece of Irish thorn.

She had screamed just before he struck her. He knew this scream would attract attention. His mind worked very fast. He pushed his sister's body under the bed and rushed out into the hall. He was startled when he saw the maid, and still more frightened when Horton questioned her, but his ruse had worked.

The only problem that remained was to get the body out of his room. The police searched the hotel from garret to cellar the first day, all except his room and Horton's. There was no thread of suspicion against them. After this rigorous search and failure to find any trace of the girl, the police activities were largely outside the hotel.

He took a chance on the second night and carried his sister's

body to the freight elevator, which he manipulated himself. He
hid the body back of the ash barrels. He was undetected and
apparently free from danger.

The police force very generously gave me the credit for the
solution which I, in turn, tried to shift to Bellamy. He refused
to take any credit, saying his reputation as a poet would be
seriously damaged if it became known that he was an amateur
detective.

I have written this story now, several years later, since Bellamy's
fame in the field of crime has spread far and wide, and I think
it only right that he should receive his due in the famous mystery
of Room Number Twenty-three.

LAWRENCE G. BLOCHMAN

The Fifty-Carat Jinx

INTRODUCTION

"The Fifty-Carat Jinx" is not my first published story (a little beauty the title of which I have forgotten, published in 1921 in The Occident, *the University of California literary monthly edited by Ralph A. Beals, now director of the New York Public Library); nor is it my first commercial story ("Cholera at Bukit Batu," in* Everybody's, *1927). It is, however, my first successful attempt to write an out-and-out mystery.*

The story was originally called "The Diamond with a Past" and was set in Paris, revolving about the Café des Bijoutiers in the Rue La Fayette where gem-brokers from all over the world, particularly the Orient, used to trade fortunes in precious stones over sidewalk-café tables. The manuscript began its rounds in August, 1927, only to find that editors of American detective-story magazines were not interested in exotic settings. It was almost a year later that I discovered this handicap through a letter from Howard V. Bloomfield of Detective Fiction Weekly *who wrote, "The story is too French. If the author will change the setting to America, make the old murder victim an American beggar or some similar character, and continue the mystery to the end instead of solving it halfway through, I would be interested in seeing the story again."*

In July, 1928, Mr. Bloomfield did see the story again, in a revised and Americanized version, but he still didn't like what he saw. Neither did any of his colleagues.

In August, 1929, having learned something of the mechanics of the detective story from the friendly lips of the late Charles G. Booth (The House on 92nd St.) I rewrote the story again, and gave it its final title. It was bought by Carl Happel, editor of Clues *(now defunct) for $125 —two cents a word—and appeared in* Clues *for January, 1930.*

Lawrence G. Blochman

The Fifty-Carat Jinx

BOLSHEVIKS? Naw, Bolsheviks didn't put that bomb in the courthouse yesterday. Sure, I know the jail is full of Russians and one of 'em will get blamed for it. The real cause, though, don't come from Russia. India, that's where it started. The same thing was to blame for Sarge Taylor getting killed in an auto wreck, and Cap Morton shot by that burglar. It's that hoodoo sparkler upstairs in the D.A.'s safe. Go on, laugh. Maybe it does sound funny for an old flatfoot like me to talk that way, but there's been a lot of funny things happen since that diamond was dragged into court for evidence. That's five—no, six—years ago, and the owner never came back after it. I don't blame him. You know the story, don't you? That's right, you've only been on the force a couple of years.

Well, I'll begin at the beginning, then; a little before the beginning, in fact.

The night things popped started out quiet enough. I was talking to a Hindu jeweler named Domswami. He was one of those little guys that sometimes know more than they're supposed to, and I had him trained to come around with stories of phoney gem rackets or with stuff that might link up with something on the squawk sheet. I liked Domswami and I guess he liked me. He was little and fat, and his skin was dark and oily. His collar was always too big for him and his suits looked like they belonged to somebody else. His mustache and the hair in his ears were gray.

The Hindu was showing me a big scrapbook he used to keep, full of clippings about jewelry. He had stuff pasted in there about crown diamonds and stolen pearls, and famous rocks all over the world—particularly India. He was always telling me about India, and anything he started talking about would always end up with something they did or didn't do back in his old country. This night he was giving me the dope on how Hindus like him never killed anything—not even a mosquito. Out in India, he said, a prince or a rich bird traveling in the sticks where the hotels were lousy wouldn't even kill the things crawling around his room. He'd hire some poor Brahmin to sleep in the bed first so the bugs'd eat their fill of Brahmin and wouldn't be hungry any more by the time the prince turned in.

I laughed when he told me this, but he was serious. That was the way a prince could keep his conscience clean—only Domswami called it "karma." Even if the Brahmin should accidentally kill one of the bugs that bit too hard, it wouldn't count against the prince's record in future lives.

"Sounds silly to you, no doubt," said Domswami when I kept on laughing. "Even my brother laughs."

"I didn't know you had a brother," I said.

"He lives across the bay in Oakland," Domswami answered. "He has a little jewelry store."

Then, just as he was telling me how his brother was very young when he came to this country and was more American than Hindu, bells started ringing and motorcycles went barking and screeching up North Beach way. It seems Chinatown Sam had been found dead.

You never heard of Chinatown Sam, did you? Not many people had up to then, either. His croaking in the back room of Torelli's poolhall wouldn't have rated six lines in any paper in San Francisco, ordinarily. He was a round-shouldered little guy with moth-eaten gray whiskers. He was a kind of guide for Chinatown, and when the tourist game was slack, he'd do odd jobs around Little Italy. He was always dead broke or dead drunk—both, when his credit was good in North Beach speakeasies, which wasn't often. In the off periods, Sam guzzled canned heat.

The night Torelli found him hugging his head on a table in the back room, he says he shook him to tell him for the millionth time that he was running a poolroom, not a hotel. Torelli told us he wasn't surprised to find the old man dead; he always said Sam would corrode his insides with canned heat. But he was annoyed. He didn't like to have cops fussing around his poolhall, with demijohns of red ink cashayed on the premises. He'd been knocked over once before, and we found out afterward that he'd always suspected Chinatown Sam had turned him in to get even for cutting down his credit.

The two cops that finally strolled in were annoyed, too. A lot of bother and not so much as their names in the paper, probably. They fiddled around in the old guy's pockets, but they didn't find anything but on old handbill telling about prices paid for jewelry someplace on Kearny Street, an Oakland transfer, and the grimy card of a stonecutter doing business out by the Lawndale cemeteries. Then, in a chamois bag hanging around his neck on a greasy string, they found a pale blue stone about the size and shape of a big almond, cut flat the way they used to cut diamonds once.

The cops said that Torelli's eyes nearly popped out of his head when he saw the stone. He got all excited and spouted Italian at 'em while he tried to get the stone into his own hands and look at it close. They backed him off and calmed him down enough to quiz him. After Torelli had explained that Chinatown Sam didn't figure either in the social register or Dun and Bradstreet's, he had to agree with the cops that the rock must be phoney. So the coroner got it when he showed up a while later.

The coroner wasn't so sure it was paste, and brought the rock to the station. Captain Morton turned it over to me, as ranking dick on the three-ball detail. I was to get the thing appraised, and if it was the real McCoy, to find out where it came from.

It was the goods, all right. The first time I asked the question I got the answer in about twenty seconds. The guy that told me didn't even have to twist a microscope into his eye to see it was real. So when I started out to make the rounds of the hockshops and ask more questions, I felt kind of funny to know that I had fifty carats worth of sparkles in my pocket.

That funny feeling got stronger and stronger, even though I didn't find out a thing from the pawnshops. And I wasn't altogether surprised when I got back to the station and saw the coroner's report. The autopsy showed that Chinatown Sam hadn't been croaked by canned heat, but with a sharp, thin blade about a quarter-inch wide. Somebody had pushed the knife into his back, between two ribs into his heart, and then slipped it out again. There was almost no hole, and practically all the bleeding was done inside.

When I finished reading the report, that diamond seemed to burn my pocket. I hurried it out and into the safe, my head all the while buzzing with questions. Who was this old soak, usually without a dime, who made his drink money telling tourists about Chinatown and Barbary Coast before the fire, all the time he

had on him a rock worth a fat fortune? Why had he been bumped
off? Who was the killer that didn't steal, that ran off without
touching a little piece of loot that would have bought his kids
shoes for the rest of their life?

Well, the homicide squad got busy right away and dragged
Torelli down from his North Beach poolroom to do a little
talking. Captain Morton had me sit in on the party so I could
keep up with developments.

Torelli was pretty much excited. He threw his hands around
quite a bit while he insisted that Sam's death must have been
from natural causes. A murder in his respectable poolroom?
Never. Impossible. Canned heat killed Chinatown Sam.

"Canned heat hell!" said Morton, rubbing the paunch that
always made his vests wrinkle. "Sam was stabbed in the back."

Then Torelli quit yelling. He kind of sulked, as he sat there
twisting his black mustache half off. No, he didn't remember
seeing anyone with Sam that night. Sam didn't have many friends;
he was broke too often. It was only as a special favor that he
allowed Chinatown Sam to stay in his poolroom. He never spent
much . . .

"Lemme refresh your memory," said Cap Morton, giving him
a deep frown. "Lemme tell you about a red-headed newsboy
called Pinky. I happen to know that there was a queer sort of
friendship between old Chinatown Sam and this nineteen-year-
old kid. People say they were pals. Now did Pinky—"

"Ah, yes; Pinky!" broke in Torelli, going after his mustache
with both hands. "Pinky. I know him. He is there in my place
same night Sam is died. I know now. He come just after Chinaman."

"A Chinaman? To see Sam?"

"Yes. I forgot. He come say few talk to Sam, then go."

"Damn it, Torelli!" shouted the captain, leaving off rubbing
his paunch to pound the desk. "You're holding out on us. Now
tell us what you know and quit stalling. Quick. Did you ever see
this man before?"

"What man? Chinaman? Oh, yeh. He calla himself Foo Wang.
He got bootcha shop Grant Avenue."

The Cap's eyebrows went up half an inch, and he scribbled
something on a piece of paper.

"What else do you remember about Sam's actions that night?" he said, none too polite.

"Tha's all. I don' know nothin'. Lossa people there, talk, yell, I can't remember," was the Italian's comeback.

"When the Chink left, Pinky came in. That right?"

"Yeh. Tha's right."

"Do you remember what Sam and Pinky said to each other?"

"No. I don' lissen."

"Did they fight or argue or . . ."

"Fight? Yeh, they fight like hell."

Cap Morton slid up to the edge of his chair and leaned across his desk.

"What were they fighting about?" he wanted to know.

"Oh, they fight like hell," said Torelli. "Pinky calla Sam big names, get mad, when big talla man come stop him."

"Who's this big tall man?"

"I don' know. First time I see him in my place. He come up and say, 'Hey kid, don' get so fresh with olda man. He got a white hair. Be more kinder.' So Pinky go away. Talla man sit down and buy cup coffee for Sam, then he go too."

"Did Pinky come back?"

"Pinky come back? Yes. No. I don' know. Maybe. I don' remember."

Captain Morton plugged away for another half hour, but he couldn't get any further. Torelli kept pulling at his black mustache and looking out the window. He said he couldn't remember. So Cap sent him home and turned to the detective sergeant sitting next to me.

"Taylor," he said, "send up that red-headed kid Pinky Malone. Then I want you to find a Chinaman named Foo Wang who has a butcher shop on Grant Avenue. Bring him right down here. I want to talk to him."

Pinky Malone was supposed to be nineteen, but he didn't look it with his cap off. The way his light red hair straggled down over his freckled forehead made you expect to see him with bare feet and a fish-pole over his shoulder. Even when he pulled his cap down over one ear, he looked just like a grammar school kid playing tough with other kids in the back yard.

As soon as Cap Morton started to shoot the questions, I could tell he had the kid sized up as the killer. Pinky admitted he had a runin with Chinatown Sam and said he was sorry he got sore. He didn't want to tell what the row was about at first, but Cap Morton pounded his desk and got hard until the kid opened up.

"Money," he said at last.

Cap Morton settled back in his chair and began rubbing his paunch, ready to gloat because he'd got the kid to talk.

"Whose money?" he wanted to know. "Yours?"

"Well . . . no," said the kid.

"Whose, then?"

"Well . . . it was money he might have made if he hadn't been such a fool. You see, the Chink—gosh, don't say I told you this, or they'll nick me, too."

"Go on," said Morton.

"Well, the Chink promised Sam a nice piece of change if he'd pack a sack of cans from the dock up to Chinatown. Sam said he would, and the Chink gave the address and directions, and everything. Then Sam changed his mind. Decided he was too old to get mixed up in any smuggling racket. When I heard what he'd done, I told him he was batty. 'Not only are you losin' the jack,' I says, "but you got the dope cold on the poor Chinks. They'll think you want to double-cross 'em, and they'll snuff you out.' 'No, they won't,' says he. But they did."

"So you were arguing with Sam over his business connections," said Morton, kind of sarcastic. "Nothing else?"

"That was enough," the kid comes back. "He was sore as hell at me for criticisin' his virtue."

"Who was this fellow that sat down with you during the argument?"

"What d'ya mean?" asked Pinky. "There was only the two of us."

"Come on, come on!" Morton raps out, leaning over the desk again. "We know all about this tall guy that came in and sat down with the two of you. Who was he?"

Pinky's face got so red you couldn't see the freckles.

"I wasn't tryin' to hold out on you," he stammered. "I forgot all about that guy. Honest I did. I never saw him before."

"What did he say to you?"

"Aw, he handed out a Sunday school line about young fellas bein' kind to the aged."

"Then you left."

"Yeah."

"And when you came back, he was gone?"

"I . . . I didn't come back."

"Yes, you did!" Morton was staring at the way Pinky grabbed the edge of the desk. "Come on, kid. Tell us what you did with the knife you stuck in Chinatown Sam?"

The kid got up slowly and looked from one pair of eyes to the other. His freckles were showing again now—against a pretty pale face. He finally managed to squeeze out a few scared words.

"Honest to God, mister," he said in a ghastly voice. "I didn't have nothin' to do with it. I wish I knew who did. I wish I could help . . . Gee whiz, mister, what makes you think I done it?"

Morton took a bunch of dirty papers out of the drawer and spread them out. He asked, "Chinatown Sam owed you some money, didn't he?"

"Yessir. I used to lend him a quarter or fifty cents once in a while."

Morton tapped the papers with his fist.

"He gave you these IOU's, didn't he? We found 'em in your room. About twenty dollars' worth. That was one of the reasons why you were so anxious about Sam making a little dough from the Chinks—so you could get your loans back."

"No sir, it wasn't."

"Wasn't? Well, how about this. Ever see it before?" Cap Morton tossed a grimy envelope toward the kid.

"Yeah," admitted Pinky. "Sam brought it to me about a month ago. Says I should open it if he should ever croak."

"It was sealed when we found it. How come you didn't open it when you heard Sam was dead?"

"Why . . . I . . . I don't know. I forgot. I was kinda cut up over Sam kickin' in like that . . ."

Morton laughed. I could see he didn't believe the kid.

"You didn't rush to open it," said Morton, "because you knew what was in it. You'd already read it and sealed it up again. You knew that Sam was leaving you a thousand bucks."

"Where the hell would Sam get the grand?" demanded the kid.

Then Cap Morton unfolded the paper, and ran his fingers over a paragraph of shaky writing telling about the sparkler, and how it was to be sold to pay his debts, to give a big hunk to Pinky, and the rest to go for carving a fancy monument for his grave.

The kid sat down again. His mouth twitched a little and there were tears in his eyes when he said, "No, I didn't know about that."

"That's just too bad," said Morton. "Too bad you couldn't have waited till the old man got ingrown dandruff or something to die of naturally. Because after what's happened, the will might be busted. Lock him up, sergeant."

The kid didn't say anything for a minute.

"That Chink . . ." he started. Then he went silent again.

"Any charge against him?" asked the bull that was taking him downstairs.

"None—yet," said Cap Morton. "Book him: Held as material witness.

"It's funny anyhow," he said to me when Pinky was gone. "A Chinaman came and looked at Sam's body in the morgue the night of the murder. But I guess he was just checking up, to see if it was the same guy that was in on their smuggling secrets."

Before I could make any comment, the phone rang. Morton answered.

"Can't find Foo Wang? Why not? . . . Hasn't been seen in how long? . . . Two days? . . . I know, I know, Chinks won't talk. . . . Well, dig him up anyway. . . . Keep looking till you pick up a trace."

I talked to Pinky for about five minutes that afternoon. The kid swore up and down he hadn't anything to do with the murder. He kept saying over and over, "Why should I kill my best friend?" The logic of the will and the thousand bucks as Cap Morton explained it, didn't seem to register with him.

I asked him more about this stranger who sat down with them the night of the murder, but all he could tell me was what the fellow looked like.

"Aw, he didn't have nothin' to do with the killin,'" said Pinky. "He was just one of those meddlesome guys that thinks he's got to do a good deed every hour. What would he want to kill poor old Sam for? He didn't steal nothin' and Sam didn't have any more enemies than he had friends. Now, you dicks better keep lookin' for the Chink. That's your bet!"

The early editions, though, said the police were looking for the tall stranger in connection with the Chinatown Sam murder. It wasn't much of a yarn yet, because we were holding back the dope on the sparkler until we knew a little better where we stood. But the papers hadn't been on the street an hour, before the tall stranger himself came around to the station. He drove up in a shiny new car with an out-of-state license and a chauffeur.

He introduced himself as Reginald Cole, from some little town in Oregon. He'd been reading about the murder in the papers and wanted to help us all he could. He was just a tourist in 'Frisco, he said, and was looking around where the old Barbary Coast used to be—just popped in to Torelli's by accident, and butted in over to Chinatown Sam's table because he was sorry to see the way the old man was being raked over the coals by the red-headed kid. His story checked with the way Pinky and Torelli told about it, and he said he felt kinda guilty for not taking the old man away with him when he saw how hot the kid was getting. He peeled off a brand new century from a fat wad of bills and said it was to keep Chinatown Sam from being planted in Potter's Field. If he could help us any further, he said, we'd find him at the Palace Hotel.

When Cole left, Morton called the Palace and found out that he was registered there all right. I asked for the junk that had been found in Chinatown Sam's pockets, and copied the name and address off the stonecutter's card, and then went out to see him.

The man in question was a round, red-faced little Frenchie named Daffot, who looked like he ought to be wearing a chef's cap instead of fussing around out there with marble crosses and wreaths. Daffot remembered Sam from my description, and when I told him the old man was dead, he said, "Impossible," just as though it wasn't people dying that keep him in business. Then he slapped his knees and said, "Ah-h-h" as though a doctor just asked him to stick out his tongue. "He must have suicided himself," he said. "He just ordered a fine tombstone from me a few days ago."

I told him that only a contortionist could have stabbed himself in the back the way Sam was croaked. So Daffot told how Sam had been around to order the finest thing in the cemetery, with marble angels on each corner, and in the middle statues of him and his wife.

"Wife?" I yelped, surprised.

Then he told me how Sam had brought an old picture of a beautiful blonde with big eyes, for the sculptor to copy. She'd been dead for years. The whole story came out when Daffot began to talk finances, and Sam produced the diamond and a customs receipt showing he paid duty on the stone when he brought it to this country eighteen years ago.

It seems that Sam was crazy about this beautiful wife of his and went to the Orient to make a lot of money quick so he could give her all the swell things she was so good at thinking of. Well, she came out and met him in India and saw this diamond as big as your eye. Nothing would do but she must have it, so Sam got it for her. A week later she was dead from cholera.

Daffot said Sam was nearly nuts from the shock, and started to drink like a fish. He let his business slide, and lost piles of dough. He came back to San Francisco and tried to drink himself into a state of joyous forgetfulness. Believe me, 'Frisco was a place where you could forget a lot of things easy in those days, but not Sam. All he got out of his serious sprees was an empty pocketbook and a taste for liquor. That's why he was always tight up in North Beach, Daffot says. But drunk or broke or both, he wouldn't separate himself from the diamond his wife made such a fuss about just before she died. That was the last kick she got out of life, so he wouldn't think of selling it.

Then one day when he was sober, according to Daffot, Sam looked in the mirror and found out he was an old man. In a little while he would be dead. Why not convert the souvenir into a great memorial to his wife, with a spare room for himself whenever he kicked off?

"I told him a monument like that would be expensive," said Daffot, "but he was sure he'd get plenty for the diamond. But he never came back."

Daffot looked sad enough to be mourning his only brother, instead of just a customer. He brightened up a little when I told him that maybe he could go ahead and make the tomb anyhow. I'd let him know.

He gave me the customs receipt, and I took it back to the station to show that Chinatown Sam was really the owner of the diamond, and that his name had been Samuel Bentley. I suggested that this sort of validated the last will and testament, and that the sparkler ought to be liquidated and the money put into a swell tombstone like the old man wanted. So Cap Morton called up the public administrator and started wheels turning to sell the stone at auction.

Well, the stonecutter's story started me thinking on another track. The murder looked to me to be tied up with the Orient. There wasn't much back of my theory but a hunch that came while Daffot was telling me about Sam getting that diamond over in India. I wondered about the Chink that the homicide squad couldn't locate . . .

I went to the safe and dug out the diamond to give it the once over. It sure was a beautiful boulder. It kinda gave me the creeps while I held it in my hand. I don't know why, but it was shaped something like a man's eye, and it lay there winking at me with pale blue flashes like electric sparks. I said to myself, a rock like that must have a history, so I took a run up to Domswami's place to look through his scrapbook.

I spent a couple of hours reading over the clippings before I came to a yellow old article that clicked. It was cut out of some jewelers' journal that got it out of an English paper that clipped it from the Madras *Mail*. Complicated, eh? Well, the clipping was dated fifteen years back, and wondered what had become of a famous diamond called the Evil Eye, which had disappeared from India after being a jinx for generations.

It seems the rock once belonged to a rajah who was killed by a tiger. The rajah's son got fired by the British, and sold all his jewels to go to Paris on. Some rich Hindu in a place called Pondicherry bought the Evil Eye and the jinx along with it. He was so tickled with his bargain that he forgot the day was a festival of some elephant god, when Hindus aren't supposed to look at the moon. Well, he looked at the moon by mistake, and had to go and get the curse knocked out of him by Brahmins. It seems he got everything knocked out of him but the jinx, and next day he died. Well, the old man had a son of his own who was a rich gem broker and got all excited over inheriting such a fine rock. He inherited the jinx, too. He got sick, and lost his old cunning. He made a bunch of bum deals and went into debt. An American forced him into bankruptcy. The Hindu wanted time, having a family to look out for, but the American had his eye set on the sparkler, and crushed the Hindu who died of the disgrace. That was the last ever heard of the diamond, the clipping said.

I showed the clipping to Domswami, who immediately got excited. The Evil Eye was in San Francisco, he said. That was one of the things he had come to tell me the other night, but I had been called away before he had a chance to say so.

"How do you know the stone is here?" I asked.

"A man tried to sell it to my brother in Oakland," said Domswami. "He recognized it. All Hindus know that diamond."

Well, Domswami's clipping pieced together with the stone-cutter's story gave me another idea. That night I spent several hours in the identification bureau, looking up Oriental criminals. I could find only three Hindus in the region with records. One of 'em was hung for murder, another had been deported. But the third was a fellow named Lal Bannerji, a kind of Indian Bolshevik who'd been arrested for hiring thugs to beat up the British consul once. The thing that got me all aflutter was a note on the card that Bannerji was born in Pondicherry—the town where the jinx diamond was last heard from. Suppose Chinatown Sam was the American mentioned in the clipping—which he seemed to be—as forcing the rich Hindu into fatal bankruptcy. Suppose the rich Hindu, not named in the clipping, had been Lal Bannerji's old man . . .

Next morning, when I went down to tell my new theory to Captain Morton, Torelli was waiting to see me.

"Catch murder fellow yet?" he asked.

I said we hadn't.

"Gonna catch pretty soon?"

I told him yes, and he said that was fine and that I was a smart guy. When he went away pulling his mustache, I wondered for a minute if he was spoofing me or what . . .

When I started to tell Morton what progress I was making in

solving the Chinatown Sam case—on paper—he pulled me up short.

"I think you better drop it," said Morton. "We got a pretty complete case against Pinky Malone by now. We found the stiletto he killed Sam with."

"Where'd you find it?" I asked.

"Some of the boys found the canvas sack Pinky used to put his papers in. There was a detective-story novel in it, and a narrow knife."

"Blood on it?"

"No. In fact, the kid says it's a paper knife. But it could kill a man, all right. The coroner is ready to testify that it could have made the wound that killed Sam. Then, finding it like that with a book on crime looks like cause and result, don't you see? These detective stories are a bad influence on our younger generation, besides making fun always of all police departments."

"How about the Chinaman the kid talks about?" I asked.

"The homicide boys are looking for him," said Cap Morton. "They'll find him, I guess, but he won't add anything much to the case."

Then I told Morton I'd like to round up a few Hindus, on a hunch. I explained I'd only have to interview a few, because circumstances limited the people I wanted to see. Chinatown Sam had gone unnoticed for eighteen years. It was only when he had tried to dispose of his diamond that he was recognized and killed. My trail, then, led to one of a dozen Hindu jewelers in San Francisco proper and in Oakland, Alameda, and Berkeley across the bay. Lal Bannerji's name was among them. I cut off Domswami's, because he was with me the night of the murder. But Domswami's brother in Oakland I left on. I went to Oakland first, because the streetcar transfer in Chinatown Sam's pocket indicated that he'd been across the bay.

I found Domswami's young brother down in the south end of Oakland where the city begins to change color. He wasn't anything like the older one. He looked like an American kid that had got all sunburned at the beach—nothing Oriental about his getup. He had a big pearl stickpin in a red tie, his hair was slicked back and smelled nice.

Of course he remembered Chinatown Sam and the big diamond.

"He was an old miser," the younger Domswami said to me. "He dressed like a tramp and packed a diamond worth a fortune. I thought I'd put one over on him and get it cheap. I told him to see a few Hindu jewelers I knew wouldn't touch the stone. There's supposed to be a curse on it. I told him that if they wouldn't buy, he should come back and I'd see what I could do. He never came. Now I wish I'd bought it outright."

I told him he could still buy it, as they were going to auction the thing off. He wanted to know where and when. I told him. Then he wanted to know why. I told him that too. He kind of jumped at the news.

"Killed?" he said. "My brother would say the old curse on the stone is still working."

He wanted to know more, but I finally got in my question. I asked him if Lal Bannerji's name was on the list of jewelers he'd given Sam. He gave me a funny look before he answered.

"Yes," he said. "His name was first on the list. Do you know him?"

"Only by reputation," I said. "He's the Bannerji from Pondicherry, isn't he?"

Young Domswami said he was, so I ran out to see him.

Bannerji practically snapped at me when I started to quiz him. He was suspicious and surly, and told me his business was to sell jewelry, not to answer questions. He finally admitted he'd seen the diamond, but said he wasn't interested in it—or in me either. Well, I didn't like the way he talked and acted, and chalked it up against him. But I still didn't have anything on the guy. Hell, you can't hang a man for looking at a sparkler.

When I got back to the city, I told Captain Morton what I'd found out, and mostly what I didn't find out.

"Well," said the captain, stroking his paunch, "did Bannerji kill Chinatown Sam?"

I said I couldn't tell yet.

"He didn't," said Morton, "because I got a complaint from the district attorney this afternoon, charging Pinky Malone with murder in the first degree. We're going to arraign him tomorrow morning."

This news kind of jolted me up. I knew Morton had the kid spotted as the killer, but he looked and talked so damned innocent to me that all of a sudden I knew that all this running around I'd been doing was just business to back up my own idea that Pinky didn't kill Sam. And I decided to stage a last-minute rush.

"Hell, Cap," I said. "Have you got enough evidence lined up? How about the Chinese angle?"

"That's just the point," said Morton. "The kid has been banking all along on shifting the blame to this Chink Foo Wang. Well, we found Foo Wang today. The federal narcotics squad had him booked over at the county jail under a different name. He's been in jail since half an hour before the murder. So I guess that knocks the props out from under that yarn of the kid's."

It did, all right. And I didn't have anything definite to offer in its place. I didn't tell Cap Morton so, though. I told the Cap I was pretty hot on a new development, and that I'd work hard to bring it to a head before morning, so as not to have him embarrassed by arraigning the wrong man. I asked for six men to shadow some Hindu jewelers. It was a stall, of course, but I thought I could go back and see Bannerji again at midnight, and work on his superstitions by using some of the diamond hocus-pocus I'd read about in Domswami's clipping. Morton hesitated a minute.

"All right," he said after a while. "Take the men and stick 'em where you want, if it'll make you any happier. But even if you showed that the King of Siam did the killing, it wouldn't save me any embarrassment now. I already gave the story to the papers."

The papers played it, too, because Morton had finally handed out the dope about the diamond. It made a good yarn, the pauper murdered, and a diamond found on him, untouched, worth a fortune instead of being phoney like people thought at first. I guess every sheet in town used it on page one, and some of 'em made it the big story, with a tie-up on the story of the auction.

After I glanced at the papers, I stopped in at the jail to see Pinky. He was a pretty forlorn-looking kid, and didn't cheer up much when I told him that I was working like hell to clear him.

I spent the afternoon tearing around, trying to pick up some clue that the homicide gang might have passed over. I saw Torelli again, but he didn't do any good—just got excited. I went around to the Palace to see if Reginald Cole could remember any more than the story he told us at the station. But the clerk at the Palace said Cole checked out the day before and had gone back to Oregon. Well, I planted the guys I wanted to shadow the Hindus, went out for a bite of dinner, and came back to figure out just how I was going to work on Bannerji's superstitions. Since his house was shadowed, I thought I'd give him a little mystery call on the phone and watch what happened. I was just looking at the phone, ready to pick it up, when the damned thing rang.

It was Domswami calling—the older one. He was all worked up into a lather, and talked English in bigger hunks than he'd ever done before. I had to pull him up and make him start over before I got the story out of him.

He said his brother had bought the Evil Eye, the hard-luck sparkler, at auction. And since the young Domswami wasn't going back to Oakland that night, he brought the stone to the older brother to keep in his safe.

"I don't want it, sir. I don't want it in my family or in my house," Domswami yelled in his funny tenor voice. The phone vibrated in my ear while he was shouting at me he didn't want the curse to fall on him.

"Don't be a damned fool!" I told him. "You're not in the jungle now. You're in the U. S. A."

"Damned fool if you like," he came back. "And since you don't believe, will you help me? Will you keep the stone in your safe tonight? I'll send for it in the morning. I want to get rid of it right away."

He seemed so downright scared that I told him to come on, but to make it snappy because I had a big night ahead of me.

Domswami didn't live far away. A taxi would bring him in seven minutes. A streetcar would take fifteen or twenty. When he didn't show up in half an hour, I figured he'd walked. I tried to read the newspaper, but didn't make any sense out of it. I just sat there waiting, wondering what the hell had got into me to be getting the creeps from just looking at a telephone. It's a funny thing, but I couldn't keep my eyes off the mouthpiece, and all the time little shivers running up and down my back like they did a couple of days before when I took that jinx sparkler out of the safe to look at it.

Well, sure enough the phone rang, just like I was expecting it to. I answered, all keyed up to hear something big—but I didn't. It was Torelli, wanting to know if we'd caught the murderer yet. I was sore. What was it to him if we caught him or not?

"No!" I yelled back at him. "We haven't pinched anybody yet, but we know who did it."

"Who?" he wanted to know.

"You did!" I shot back at him.

Well, of course he went off into Italian, spluttering and fussing, so I hung up before he short-circuited the phone with his damned language.

Still no Domswami, though. I began to think he was spoofing me, with his diamond yarn. I went back to the phone to call him, but the bell rang before I took up the receiver. I guess I answered kind of short.

"This is Captain Morton," said a voice. "Come to the morgue at once."

"What's up?" I asked. No answer. The morgue! I jiggled the hook. No use. Morton had already hung up. I'd have to go down to find out what he wanted.

I violated a dozen traffic ordinances getting there.

Captain Morton met me at the door.

"I want you to identify this stiff," he said, leading me down the aisle between the marble slabs.

It's funny how a fellow's brain works. I stared down at the face of the corpse a full minute before my mind could form the name of the person I was looking at. Of course, death had somewhat changed the familiar features, but that wasn't really what made me hesitate. It was unexpected, the refusal of my subconscious or whatever you call it, to grasp the fact that this corpse I was looking at was a living man talking to me not a helluva while before, that sort of drew a veil over my thinking apparatus.

The dead man was the elder Domswami.

Then, all of a sudden while I stood there with my mouth open, the whole business cleared up in a flash. It was just as though some cog clicked into place and the wheels in my brain started grinding out thoughts. I remembered what Domswami told me about rich men in India getting poor Brahmins to sleep in their beds, to get them out of the blame for killing bugs. Domswami was the rich man, and Sam was the bug. It must have been Domswami's father that Sam had ruined and disgraced to get the diamond, years before, and Domswami was avenging the family honor. Being a Hindu, he must have hired someone to do his killing for him. The slip had come when the professional killer saw the afternoon papers about the diamond, thought Domswami had double-crossed him, and had probably come back for a settling of accounts all over again.

"What's the matter?" says Morton to me, when I didn't bust out with a single word. "Don't you know this bird?"

"Sure, I know him," I said. "He's the guy who arranged the murder of Chinatown Sam. His name is Domswami."

"I thought you were looking for a Hindu named Bannerji," Morton said.

"I changed all that," I answered.

"Whatever it is," said Morton, "this Hindu got killed the same way Sam did—a narrow stilleto in the back between the ribs."

"The same guy did it. Domswami was only murderer by proxy. The operating murderer did this job because he figured he got a bum deal on the other. Did you find the diamond on Domswami?" I asked.

"Didn't find a thing. Every mark of identification gone."

So the jinx diamond had changed hands again! I wondered how the new man was going to get along with the so-called curse, whether we'd ever get our hands on him. Suddenly it came to me that I'd planted a dick to shadow Domswami.

"How about the killer himself?" I asked the captain. "Taylor was supposed to be camping on Domswami's trail. Have you heard from Taylor?"

"I expect the killer over here any minute now," said Morton, yawning and rubbing his paunch. "He's over in the emergency hospital now, but I don't imagine they'll keep him long. Taylor pumped him too full of lead when he jumped out of Domswami's taxi and started to run."

"And he is . . . ?"

"He *was* a guy who called himself Reginald Cole when he came down to offer a brand new bank note toward burying Chinatown Sam. Taylor phoned that when he knew he was done for he confessed to a couple of paid murders in Chicago. He said that new auto of his was part of his fee for killing Sam. Come on, let's go over and let Pinky Malone out of jail."

As soon as he passed out of the big-barred door, Pinky changed from a worried, pinched-faced chap to the happy freckled kid he was before he was locked up.

But the man who changed the most in this whole business was young Domswami. When he heard his brother had been bumped off, his American manner dropped from him like an old coat. He had old Domswami cremated in regular Brahmin fashion, with a fire of sandalwood and rice and gold dust and melted butter in his mouth. He took the ashes back to India himself. Said he was going to throw 'em in the Ganges. And he never did write for the diamond, which was tied up as evidence in case Cole, who was shot full of holes, should recover and make the state stand the expense of a trial. Cole died the day after Domswami left town, and the diamond's been up in the D.A.'s safe, ever since, working its jinx right through the steel door.

There goes the bell, sonny. They want a motorcycle. Well, hop to it.

VERONICA PARKER JOHNS

Bezique of Death

INTRODUCTION

I wrote "Bezique of Death" because I hate to go to the Post Office, where dreadful things always happen to me. For example, last Christmas an attempt was made to deliver a package to me when I was not at home. In its stead the postman left a summons to appear at the P.O. in person to pick it up. Well, you may not believe this but the clerk who had my present was also in charge of alien registration and I had to stand in line fifty-five minutes.

Until late in '47, when I wrote "Bezique," I'd done only novels—three of them—and a novelette, all of which involved me deeply with the U. S. mails. Especially the novels. There are usually revisions, and there are always galleys. I was becoming a nervous wreck, and yet I just didn't have the strength of character to swear off writing completely.

When Oliver Claxton, then editor of Charm, turned to me at a party and suggested that I let him see something between three thousand and five thousand words long it seemed a happy solution. I figured twelve cents postage would amply cover that amount of paper and a manila envelope, which I could cram into the corner mailbox.

So I wrote the story, the details of which had been loitering in the back of my mind for some time. The mise-en-scène had been kicking around since a round-the-world tour I made at the impressionable age of seventeen. I'd met the model for my chief protagonist's physical characteristics in Halifax a few years later, and the concept of his bizarre hobby had come to me as I killed beetles in my Connecticut garden.

They all added up to something Charm printed in March of '48. Ellery Queen's Mystery Magazine reprinted it in December of '50. I'm running low on stamps, but I managed to scrape together enough to mail it in to this anthology.

Is anyone going to the Post Office? Hey, while you're there . . .

VERONICA PARKER JOHNS

Bezique of Death

OF COURSE I assumed he was joking, in a nasty, macabre way. It was scarcely a subject for humor, but this was a humorless night and the setting was unsuitable for comedy.

I was standing on the top deck of the steamer *Princess Charlotte Anne* because there, if anywhere, there might be a breeze. The *Princess* was noble in name only. She was a down-at-the-heels cargo ship, the seagoing equivalent of a one-and-a-half-ton truck which had suffered indignities at the hands of many owners. She reeked of curry and imponderables, but she offered the only means of my getting to Bombay at the time I wished to be there. My friends in Ceylon, who had reluctantly arranged the sailing, considered it folly for a woman alone. They cautioned me against speaking to strangers or even stewards, stocked me with provisions, packed a delicious supper which included a thermos of Singapore gin-slings, and deposited me in my cabin, where they advised me to remain as long as possible.

They were wise, perhaps, but not infinitely so. They could not foretell the excess of oppression I would feel in that tiny, box-like space; and the smell, how could they guess at that? The amalgam, almost tangible, of the odors of old citrus fruits, rats, salt, something with an affinity to ether which had been used tentatively to clean the place, and the curry—the age-old, ante-diluvian curry. It was like being shut up in a coffin with offerings selected by an enemy, and I chose the open air.

The air was still; if we'd carried sail we'd not have been moving. As it was, we plowed through the night with effort, the engines straining, the vibration like the pounding of an aching temple. Below me, on the afterdeck, the off-watch crew members were massed. A hiccuping phonograph played "Tipperary" unceasingly, reminding me that it was a long, long way. In counterpoint, some of the sailors chanted to themselves—tunelessly, it seemed to my Occidental ears. The scene was set in sepia and somehow blurred, a tawny light dulling the contrast between the lascars' brown skins and the washed-out, sun-bleached robes they wore.

As I watched, an enormous rat scuttled across the deck and, within seconds, a rifle cracked. The rat dragged itself a few inches and dropped; a sailor, with the gun under his arm, descended from the starboard railing and crossed over to the animal. He picked it up by the tail, babbling boastfully, and tossed it overboard. There was a murmur of approval from his wakeful associates, and a mutter of curses from those who were attempting to sleep. And then I heard the voice, a British one, at my elbow.

"Good shot," it said, but dolorously, not as one says, "Well bowled," at cricket. "But such trivial combat," it added.

I turned in amazement, having felt myself alone at this Olympian height, observing the microcosmic show below being put on solely for my benefit. The man beside me stepped a little bit more into the light and I caught my first glimpse of him.

He was scarcely more than a skeleton with paraffin-like skin stretched over it. He wore khaki shorts and a shirt with cut-off sleeves, from which knees and elbows were bony protuberances. He removed a cigarette in a long holder from his thin-lipped mouth, and his face was a skull grinning at me. But his eyes—his eyes didn't go with him.

They were not moribund. They were quick and darting, like a fox's, like those of a juvenile delinquent who has secret and devious meanings for the things he does. There was no decay in them, rather an ever-eager questing; one could only hope that the mind behind them was a competent censor.

His name was Jemison, or Jamison—I wasn't quite certain which, because he threw it away in that dry-as-chaff voice. He lived on the outskirts of Colombo, and he was going to Bombay to sign some legal papers. He would head directly back to Ceylon, to something—he made me feel its magnetism—which held him there. He had an active distaste for civilization, and a bottle of Scotch in his cabin. Would I join him there for a drink?

"Not," I said, "if your cabin is anything like mine." I wasn't being coy. The way he looked at me I knew he didn't think of me as a woman, that all sex had ended within him. It was merely that if his cabin duplicated mine I could not bear the thought of tandem entombment. We compared notes, decided his quarters were no better, and he left me momentarily, to return with the bottle, a carafe of boiled water, and two glasses. We sat in a lifeboat, believing that in view of the way the engines were heaving that might prove to be the safest place; at any rate, it was moderately comfortable, and the slight motion as it swung upon its davits had the soporific effect of a summertime hammock. As I sipped his Scotch, which was of the best, his speech went on like a bedtime story.

He had been to the United States, he told me, had lived for a while in Connecticut. "Jolly spot," he said. "Trim little house, fine garden. I left when the Japanese invaded it."

"The Japanese?" I repeated, wondering if the man were mad. He'd already said that he'd lived in the East throughout the war. Had the onsweeping hordes of our little yellow brothers unhinged him, made him believe they had covered the earth?

"Yes," he said. "They made lacework of my roses."

Then I understood. He meant the beetles, those irridescent, gimcracky creatures which look like things sold in Japanese stores five for the penny, innocent-seeming and gaudy, but lethal to lovely flowers.

"Filthy little beggars," he went on. "Breeding constantly, and eating the while, deficient both in morals and manners. They so upset me that eventually I spent all my time exterminating them. I'd put them into a Mason jar, I believe you call it, which was half-filled with water with an inch of kerosene on top. I used to count them, compulsorily. One day I killed three hundred and forty. You should have seen them fighting for air, scrambling all over their fellows in an effort at survival. It was exciting."

He said the last in that same dry tone, the voice of a man who could no longer be thrilled by anything, and I knew that the excitement he mentioned was not the sort I would choose to experience. Killing the beetles, evidently, excited him as a frog is stirred by an electric shock, but certainly no more dramatically.

"But it soon began to pall," he was saying, "because, you see, I always won. Try as they would they could never crawl out of the jar; they would skid on the glass sides and plunge down, their wings and their hapless heads heavy with kerosene.

"I wonder," he mused, sucking his empty cigarette holder, "about the theosophy of beetles. Do you fancy they are Buddhists?" He chuckled dryly, and I made some noncommittal reply. "Not," he continued, "that I feel professions of any organized religion an essential to respect for death; a boy who has never read Dante may have a superior image of hell. Or should I say 'inferior'?"

He chuckled again, but I did not join in his acrid merriment. I was not liking this. In the sinister night, threading through the raucous and jaunty tune on the phonograph, his reminiscences were becoming unbearable. I tried to change the subject.

"When did you move to Ceylon?" I asked.

"I shall come to that," he assured me. "First there was Africa. Then India." He was not to be hurried, I could see; I settled back.

"As I was saying," he resumed, "to appreciate death one needs no blueprint drawn by a master. Each aware being has his own notion of what comes next, even though some believe it only to be nothingness, the end of all that is. But, alas, beetles do not impress me as being especially aware. True, they experienced some discomfort in the kerosene, but I at last decided that they could not possibly know that that would be the end of them, that life was about to cease. They no more sensed extinction than does a candle flame the second before I snuff it out.

"You asked when I moved to Ceylon. Now we start eastward. Africa first, for game. Big game, bigger than beetles. Smarter." He sighed and continued, "But the same thing eventually occurred there. Inevitably, again, I won a hollow victory; I killed, but the beasts did not know what death was. Once, face to face with a lioness, I thought I saw fear which went beyond immediate danger, a hint of the knowledge of finality, but it rapidly passed and she died insensitively.

"Then someone recommended tigers, Bengal tigers. A magnificent creature, I was told, with a nobility of intellect. So I went to India about ten years ago, my heart high with hope of finding a worthy adversary. It is no more good to kill without rapport than it would be so to love. If I were to kiss you—" I drew back, although he had not altered his position in the boat— "think how dull for me it would be if you did not know you were being kissed, if it produced in you no emotion of pleasure or of revulsion."

There was an erotic purr in his voice now, but he wasn't trying to entice me. He was in love with his topic, his hobby of creation in reverse. In the heat, the cloistering heat, I shivered.

"And with tigers?" I whispered.

"Same story," he stated. "I won handily, and the first two or three knew only a moment of terror but no prescience. It occurred to me that their marvelous intellects might be in low gear, that they needed some time for understanding, so I began to take chances, giving them plenty of time before I fired the telling shot. I got clawed badly once in the process, and I realized that that wasn't any good either, for the beast would not know what he had done to *me*. At best he would see me as a menace averted, at worst as a tasty meal, but he would never know that he had worked a miracle, that he had suddenly stopped all the living organism of me.

"So tigers, too, proved unsatisfactory. You could prolong killing only with a creature so small and ineffectual that it presented no threat to you. With a more formidable animal, prolongation is merely a dressed-up suicide, meaningful merely to you; in short, a game of patience. If one wants a two-handed game, a bezique of death, there is only one possible antagonist."

I didn't want to ask the question, but it formed itself without my direction. "And that is?" I prompted.

"Human beings," he said, quite calmly.

I stood up in the lifeboat. My cabin seemed the most inviting spot in the world.

"You're not going?" he asked, and I told him vehemently that such was my intention.

"But I'm just coming to the interesting portion of my story," he protested.

"You don't mean you actually tried—murder?" I said.

"But of course."

I stumbled while getting out of the boat, and his hand on my arm was shockingly cool.

"I can manage," I said. "You stay here. Don't bother to see me to my cabin. Perhaps you can find somebody else to listen to your little jokes."

"You think I'm joking?" He sounded hurt.

I did. I hoped so. We had been in almost total darkness, but the light from the radio operator's room now caught his eyes and they seemed to be laughing at me.

"Of course you are," I said, ashamed of my sudden panic. "Good night, Mr. —er, Jemison."

"Good night. And, as you Americans say, I'll be looking for you."

He didn't find me for some time. No stowaway could have hidden more completely than I. I breathed the stench in that cabin long enough to accept it as my natural atmosphere. In fact, I added the redolence of Sterno and the canned foodstuffs I had brought aboard. I wasn't afraid that Mr. J. would push me overboard, after first specifically explaining what the action would mean to both of us. At least I don't think I was. Consciously, I thought he was a little crazy and pent-up, with a desire to capture somebody's attention. I wanted no part of him.

Three hours before we were due to dock I decided to desert my hermitage for a venture onto the fringes of society; there would be doctors in Bombay to cure the consequences of a meal in the dining salon. The food wasn't too bad, I found, and Mr. J. was nowhere to be seen. I wondered idly if another listener had taken him more seriously than I and had had him put in irons.

After dinner I went above to what was euphemistically called a lounge, a dingy little cubicle amidship. I ordered a gin-sling, and got a surprisingly good one. I sat at a table near the porthole. There was a pack of cards on it, and as I sipped my sling I started to play one of my favorite brands of idiot's delight. My bags were all packed and I was ready to disembark. I didn't have a thing to worry about.

So I'd thought. I had reckoned without Mr. J.; he stepped into the lounge and made straight for my table.

"I'm glad to see you using my playing cards," he said, and I dropped them as if they were acid. "I've been playing patience all voyage. May I join you in a game of bezique?"

I looked at him sharply. In the skull of his face his eyes crackled as breakfast cereals are supposed to do. Surely he was laughing.

"I don't play," I said, in as surly a manner as I could summon. I didn't ask him to sit down, I didn't have to. He did so, and told the bar boy to bring me another of whatever I had been drinking.

"I've missed you. Were you seasick?" he asked solicitously.

"Yes," I lied. It seemed simplest.

"Poor girl," he said. "I hope no remarks of mine contributed to your distress."

"Not at all," I told him. "You were, of course, only joking when you talked to me."

"Not necessarily," he contradicted.

I thought he might start the whole business over again and I was determined to ward it off. I looked straight at him. "Nonsense, Mr. J.," I said. "I know that you have never murdered anyone. Anyone with such a predilection for confiding in strangers could never have done so and remained at large. So please spare me any post-mortems of your bezique of death."

He looked at the table; with his lids down he more than ever resembled a death mask. "It is a very difficult game," he said. "Impossible to enjoy if one of the players cheats."

He picked up the cards and shuffled them, starting to deal two hands. "There's an old saw," he said, "that the cards never forgive. It's true. If one doesn't play them well at the first opportunity, one rarely gets a second chance."

He arranged one of the hands, frowning, biting the corner of his thumb. I got up. "I've got to see to my packing," I said.

"Of course," he muttered, from some deep crevice of thought. He didn't say good-by.

A week or so later I was at a cocktail party in Bombay. A Mrs. Heath arrived late, with the excuse that she'd been seeing a friend off on a ship for Ceylon. Such a dear man, she said, Harold Jamison.

My ears pricked at the name. I asked Mrs. Heath if that could be the Mr. J. who had come on from Ceylon a few days before.

"I'm sure it is," she said. "A slender man?"

I nodded.

"Well," Mrs. Heath said, "if he lost an opportunity to renew a shipboard acquaintance, I'm doubly sorry that I could not persuade him to stay over. The poor man does so need a holiday, but he came here solely to attend to some legal matter and insisted upon taking the next steamer back."

She sighed, in palpable sympathy. "Harold's is such a sad story," she said. "I've been close to much of it. I went to his wedding. He was a bachelor for most of his life, and you know how they fall when they do. Her name is Irene; she's red-haired and beautiful. They met when he first arrived in Ceylon about nine years ago, and it was love at first sight for both of them.

They were married almost immediately, and were so enthralled with each other that they didn't want other people around. They built a cabin up in the hills, beyond Kandy, miles from anyone, and I believe they would have lived there the rest of their lives if it had not happened."

"If it had not happened?" I picked up.

"Yes, a most shocking thing and quite unexplainable. Irene must always have been a little skittish, I expect. Harold hated to talk about it, of course, but as closely as we can figure it out this is what occurred: Irene and Harold were walking through the jungle one day, searching for orchids for their dinner table. I suppose they had a lovers' quarrel or something of the sort—anyhow, Irene got the wind up and started running. She lost her balance and fell off a ledge, about eighty feet down, the deepest drop around there.

"You can imagine how he felt. Somehow he got to her. By some miracle she wasn't dead, but there lay his beloved Irene, unable to move and babbling like a child, not even recognizing him. The poor man picked her up and carried her to the nearest village. There was a rest house there with a telephone, and he fetched up the ambulance from the hospital in Colombo. For months, while Irene was in a cast, he stayed beside her day and night. About all the doctors could do was to set the broken bones and ease her over the initial agony. When she was finally discharged she was hopelessly paralyzed and," she touched her forehead, "unable to understand the simplest thing.

"I think it would have been more merciful for all concerned if she had died, but Harold took her to a bungalow near town and has made it his life's work to help her to recovery. He keeps saying that some day she will be well enough to return to their cabin. When I left him just now he seemed almost apprehensive that she might have recovered in his absence, for he should hate to miss a minute of Irene as she used to be. God knows how the man maintains such faith, because she has the mind of a baby. A baby, did I say? It's more like the mind of an animal, unable to co-ordinate thoughts, to comprehend anything said to her. Every once in a while she looks at him in the strangest way, as if all things were known to her, and the poor man is so pathetically encouraged. He tries then to converse with her—you should hear the mad way she laughs when that happens—but then the curtain comes down again and she's as remote as ever. Sometimes you almost feel that she could help herself if she'd only try."

She was much sorrier, I could see, for Mr. Jamison than for his wife, as if she felt that Mrs. J. were deliberately being a burden, had chosen to be immobile and stupid purely to spite her doting husband. I walked away from the woman resenting her deeply, and amazed to find myself such a violent partisan of Irene Jamison. Certainly Mrs. Heath knew the pair better than I, and her estimate of the affair was no doubt accurate; I had nothing to go on but a mistrust of Jamison's crackling eyes and the brain I detected behind them, the twisted psyche which could joke about death and the pleasure of its infliction.

And then it struck me, shaking me. Maybe he wasn't joking.

Irene would have thought he was joking also, at first, loving him, living with him in the jungled hill. She might even, in the manner of wives, have found the joke becoming tiresome, but she would never for a minute have believed it, until one day he found new words and a ledge at her back to give them credence. They'd been hunting for orchids for their dinner table, pushing their way through the tangled ferns, ducking beneath the low-hanging branches, precariously keeping their footing on the slippery dark-brown soil. The green smell, the snake smell, the chattering and the danger all around, and the precipitous plunges —but beside Irene the man she trusted; until he said it believably, and for the first time she believed and knew that the gravest danger in the world for her was her husband. The realization must have startled her so that she fell, before he was ready, down the deepest drop around.

And since then what had gone on between them? He had devoted himself to her, trying to heal her body and to clear her mind so that they might return to the cabin. So that they might start the ghastly game over again?

I could almost see them, the man, and the faceless, mindless, red-haired beauty; the man shuffling the cards and waiting for the wife who wasn't well enough to play. And I thought: Irene Jamison, is that the only way you know how to beat him, to retreat into your incomprehension as I retreated into my cabin?

The world is larger than a ship. You could get away, if you cured
yourself.

Or (I began to wonder) is that your idea of getting even, of
punishing him for the game he played before, when something
in his calculations went wrong and he did not quite win? As he
said, the cards never forgive; perhaps you are even less placable.

I remembered vaguely how bezique is played; in the first half
of the game you draw and discard, building a hand which you
play in the latter half, to the end. Kibitzing is onerous; however
I must say this: although it's not the way I'd have played it, Mrs.
Jamison was certainly winning.

GEORGES SIMENON

The Little House at Croix-Rousse

INTRODUCTION

I am not positive that "The Little House at Croix-Rousse" was the first short mystery I wrote, but it was certainly one of the first—part of a series that I turned out in 1927 on commission for a Paris periodical called Detective. *The stories were all built to the same design—to be stopped a few paragraphs before the end so that the reader could have a chance to guess the solution. The contest proved so successful that it was continued for some forty stories which were later collected in three volumes entitled* The Thirteen Mysteries *(in which "The Little House" appeared),* The Thirteen Enigmas, *and* The Thirteen Culprits.

The story was written aboard the fishing schooner Ostrogoth, *anchored in Dutch waters, the year before I began to write the Inspector Maigret stories. I had fitted up the* Ostrogoth *as my home and lived aboard her for nearly two years. Prior to reaching Holland and turning to the short story form, I had cruised the Mediterranean and the Aegean, and sailed through the Dardanelles into the Black Sea. Between standing wheel watch and shooting the sun, I managed to write several novels during this period.*

The English translation of The Little House *(by Anthony Boucher) appeared in* Ellery Queen's Mystery Magazine *twenty years after it was written and—symbolically, perhaps—at about the same time I came to the United States to live.*

Incidentally, I was captain of the Ostrogoth *when I wrote the story, and still have my master's papers. So if the writing business ever takes a turn for the worse—*

GEORGES SIMENON

The Little House at Croix-Rousse

TRANSLATED BY ANTHONY BOUCHER

I HAD never seen Joseph Leborgne at work before. I received something of a shock when I entered his room that day.

His blond hair, usually plastered down, was in complete disorder. The individual hairs, stiffened by brilliantine, stuck out all over his head. His face was pale and worn. Nervous twitches distorted his features.

He threw a grudging glare at me which almost drove me from the room. But since I could see that he was hunched over a diagram, my curiosity was stronger than my sensitivity. I advanced into the room and took off my hat and coat.

"A fine time you've picked!" he grumbled.

This was hardly encouraging. I stammered, "A tricky case?"

"That's putting it mildly. Look at that paper."

"It's the plan of a house? A small house?"

"The subtlety of your mind! A child of four could guess that. You know the Croix-Rousse district in Lyons?"

"I've passed through there."

"Good! This little house lies in one of the most deserted sections of the district—not a district, I might add, which is distinguished by its liveliness."

"What do these black crosses mean, in the garden and on the street?"

"Policemen."

"Good Lord! And the crosses mark where they've been killed?"

"Who said anything about dead policemen? The crosses indicate policemen who were on duty at these several spots on the night of the eighth-to-ninth. The cross that's heavier than the others is Corporal Manchard."

I dared not utter a word nor move a muscle. I felt it wisest not to interrupt Leborgne, who was favoring the plan with the same furious glares which he had bestowed upon me.

"Well? Aren't you going to ask me why policemen were stationed there—six of them, no less—on the night of the eighth-to-ninth? Or maybe you're going to pretend that you've figured it out?"

I said nothing.

"They were there because the Lyons police had received, the day before, the following letter: 'Dr. Luigi Ceccioni will be murdered, at his home, on the night of the eighth-to-ninth instant.'"

"And the doctor had been warned?" I asked at last.

"No! Since Ceccioni was an Italian exile and it seemed more than likely that the affair had political aspects, the police preferred to take their precautions without warning the party involved."

"And he was murdered anyway?"

"Patience! Dr. Ceccioni, fifty years of age, lived alone in this wretched little hovel. He kept house for himself and ate his evening meal every day in an Italian restaurant nearby. On the eighth he left home at seven o'clock, as usual, for the restaurant. And Corporal Manchard, one of the best police officers in France and a pupil, to boot, of the great Lyons criminologist Dr. Edmond Locard, searched the house from basement to attic. He proved to himself that no one was hidden there and that it was impossible to get in by any other means than the ordinary doors and windows visible from the outside. No subterranean passages nor any such hocus-pocus. Nothing out of a novel. . . . You understand?"

I was careful to say nothing, but Leborgne's vindictive tone seemed to accuse me of willfully interpolating hocus-pocus.

"No one in the house! Nothing to watch but two doors and three windows! A lesser man than Corporal Manchard would have been content to set up the watch with only himself and one policeman. But Manchard requisitioned five, one for each entrance, with himself to watch the watchers. At nine P.M., the shadow of the doctor appeared in the street. He re-entered his house, absolutely alone. His room was upstairs; a light went on in there promptly. And then the police vigil began. Not one of them dozed! Not one of them deserted his post! Not one of them lost sight of the precise point which he had been delegated to watch! Every fifteen minutes Manchard made the round of the group. Around three A.M. the petroleum lamp upstairs went out slowly, as though it had run out of fuel. The corporal hesitated. At last he decided to use his lock-picking gadget and go in. Upstairs, in the bedroom, seated (or rather half-lying) on the edge of the bed was Dr. Luigi Ceccioni. His hands were clutched to his chest and he was dead. He was completely dressed, even to the cape which still hung over his shoulders. His hat had fallen to the floor. His underclothing and suit were saturated with blood and his hands were soaked in it. One bullet from a six-millimeter Browning had penetrated less than a centimeter above his heart."

I gazed at Joseph Leborgne with awe. I saw his lip tremble.

"No one entered the house! No one left!" he groaned. "I'll swear to that as though I'd stood guard myself; I know my Corporal Manchard. And don't go thinking that they found the revolver in the house. There wasn't any revolver! Not in sight and not hidden. Not in the fireplace, nor even in the roof gutter. Not in the garden—not anywhere at all! In other words, a bullet was fired in a place where there was no one save the victim himself and where there was no firearm! As for the windows, they were closed and undamaged; a bullet fired from outside would have shattered the panes. Besides, a revolver doesn't carry far enough to have been fired from outside the range covered by the cordon of policemen. Look at the plan! Eat it up with your eyes! And you may restore some hope of life to poor Corporal Manchard, who has given up sleeping and looks upon himself virtually as a murderer."

I timidly ventured, "What do you know about Ceccioni?"

"That he used to be rich. That he's hardly practiced medicine at all, but rather devoted himself to politics—which made it healthier for him to leave Italy."

"Married? Bachelor?"

"Widower. One child, a son, at present studying in Argentina."

"What did he live on in Lyons?"

"A little of everything and nothing. Indefinite subsidies from his political colleagues. Occasional consultations, but those chiefly gratis among the poor of the Italian colony."

"Was anything stolen from the house?"

"Not a trace of any larcenous entry."

I don't know why, but at this moment I wanted to laugh. It suddenly seemed to me that some master of mystification had amused himself by presenting Joseph Leborgne with a totally unlikely problem, simply to give him a needed lesson in modesty.

He noticed the broadening of my lips. Seizing the plan, he crossed the room to plunge himself angrily into his armchair.

"Let me know when you've solved it!" he snapped.

"I can certainly solve nothing before you," I said tactfully.

"Thanks," he observed.

I began to fill my pipe, I lit it, disregarding my companion's rage which was reaching the point of paroxysm.

"All I ask of you is that you sit quietly," he pronounced. "And don't breathe so loudly," he added.

Ten minutes passed as unpleasantly as possible. Despite myself, I called up the image of the plan, with the six black crosses marking the policemen.

And the unlikelihood of this story, which had at first so amused me, began to seem curiously disquieting.

After all, this was not a matter of psychology or of detectival flair, but of pure geometry.

"This Manchard," I asked suddenly. "Has he ever served as a subject for hypnotism?"

Joseph Leborgne did not even deign to answer that one.

"Did Ceccioni have many political enemies in Lyons?"

He shrugged his shoulders.

"And its been proved that the son is in Argentina?"

This time he merely took the pipe out of my mouth and tossed it on the mantelpiece.

"You have the names of all the policemen?"

He handed me a sheet of paper:

Jérôme Pallois, 28, married

Jean-Joseph Stockman, 31, single

Armand Dubois, 26, married

Hubert Trajanu, 43, divorced

Germain Garros, 32, married

I reread these lines three times. The names were in the order in which the men had been stationed around the building, starting from the left.

I was ready to accept the craziest notions. Desperately I exclaimed at last, "It's impossible!"

And I looked at Joseph Leborgne. A moment before his face had been pale, his eyes encircled, his lips bitter. Now, to my astonishment, I saw him smilingly head for a pot of jam.

As he passed a mirror, he noticed himself and seemed scandalized by the incongruous contortions of his hair. He combed it meticulously. He adjusted the knot of his cravat.

Once again Joseph Leborgne was his habitual self. As he looked for a spoon with which to consume his horrible jam of leaves-of-God-knows-what, he favored me with a sarcastic smile.

"How simple it would always be to reach the truth if preconceived ideas did not falsify our judgment!" he sighed. "You have just said, 'It is impossible!' So therefore . . ."

I waited for him to contradict me. I'm used to that.

"So therefore," he went on, "it is impossible. Just so. And all that we needed to do from the very beginning was simply to admit that fact. There was no revolver in the house, no murderer hidden there. Very well: then there was no shot fired there."

"But then? . . ."

"Then, very simply, Luigi Ceccioni arrived with the bullet already in his chest. I've every reason to believe that he fired the bullet himself. He was a doctor; he knew just where to aim ('less than a centimeter above the heart,' you'll recall) so that the wound would not be instantly fatal, but would allow him to move about for a short time."

Joseph Leborgne closed his eyes.

"Imagine this poor hopeless man. He has only one son. The boy is studying abroad, but the father no longer has any money to send him. Ceccioni insures his life with the boy as beneficiary. His next step is to die—but somehow to die with no suspicion of suicide, or the insurance company will refuse to pay.

"By means of an anonymous letter he summons the police themselves as witnesses. They see him enter his house where there is no weapon and they find him dead several hours later.

"It was enough, once he was seated on his bed, to massage his chest, forcing the bullet to penetrate more deeply, at last to touch the heart . . ."

I let out an involuntary cry of pain.

But Leborgne did not stir. He was no longer concerned with me.

It was not until a week later that he showed me a telegram from Corporal Manchard.

AUTOPSY REVEALS ECCHYMOSIS AROUND WOUND AND TRACES

FINGER PRESSURE STOP DOCTOR AND SELF PUZZLED POSSIBLE CAUSE STOP REQUEST YOUR ADVICE IMMEDIATELY

"You answered?"

He looked at me reproachfully. "It requires both great courage and great imagination to massage oneself to death. Why should the poor man have done that in vain? The insurance company has a capital of four hundred million . . ."

STUART PALMER

The Riddle of the Dangling Pearl

INTRODUCTION

Our good friend(s) Ellery Queen really dreamed up a perfectly fiendish idea for this year's MWA anthology. A first short story is apt to be as fumbling as a first kiss or a first dive, and it is a somewhat disconcerting experience for an author to reread something he wrote twenty years ago.

This story was written in one evening, when I was living in a little furnished apartment on a side street in Manhattan. It was truly a street to inspire a young writer—in the house next door Joseph Elwell the playboy bridge-teacher had been found with a bullet through his head some years before, and across the street in the big brownstone house called "Sandalwood" Mr. Fulton Oursler was in the midst of writing his early Anthony Abbot yarns.

I had spent that afternoon up at the Metropolitan Museum on Fifth Avenue, and had found my way into the room where was and is displayed the Cellini Coupe, perhaps the most valuable single art object in the world. It amused me as a sort of mental exercise to try to work out a way in which it could be stolen.

A few months after the story appeared in print I dropped in again at the Museum, and discovered that the curators had read the thing and then had hastily revised their entire security regulations! No longer were students of sculpture allowed to work in clay in the halls, and a relay of guards had been stationed in the room where the Cellini cup was displayed, with orders never to leave that post whatever the alarm. An associate curator told me ruefully that in his opinion the device used in my story would have worked, without question. And I noticed that a gimlet-eyed guard hovered around me from then on whenever I visited the place.

"The Dangling Pearl" was the first of some fifty short stories about Miss Hildegarde Withers. For all of its imperfections I am fond of

it—fonder than I was of the movie version made by RKO some years later. It was far from my best story, but it was fun to write and there was some satisfaction in knowing that it scared hell out of the Museum officials.

STUART PALMER

The Riddle of the Dangling Pearl

RUSHING through the wide doors of the Cosmopolitan Museum of Art came Miss Hildegarde Withers, out of the blinding sunlight of Fifth Avenue in August into a hushed, dim world. Pausing only for a moment to sniff the musty odors which cling to the vast treasure house wherein men have gathered together the objects saved from vandal Time, the angular schoolteacher went on, sailing serenely past the checkroom to be halted by a gray uniformed guard at the turnstile.

"Have to check your umbrella, ma'am."

"Young man," she advised him sharply, "can't you see that I need it?" She leaned on the umbrella heavily, and the guard, with a shrug of his shoulders, let her through. She was not lying, even by implication, for this day she was to need her only weapon as never before in all her assiduous, if amateur, efforts at crime detection.

It had been some months since Miss Withers had last found occasion to visit the museum, and today there seemed to be fewer guards and more visitors, particularly juvenile visitors, than formerly. She threaded her resolute way through the crowd, entering the Hall of Sculpture and pushing on toward the staircase at the rear of the building. In this hall the visitors were fewer, and only a solitary art student here and there was copying a painting, lost to the rest of the world.

"You'll find Professor Carter somewhere in the Florentine Wing," the Inspector had told her over the telephone. "You can't miss him, he's a tall, dried-up old fossil with a big round head bald as an egg." But at this moment Miss Withers had no idea how, and where, she was to find Professor Carter, associate curator of the Cosmopolitan. For all her haste, she paused for a moment beside a crouching marble nude labelled "Nymph—by Hebilly West." Using her dampened handkerchief, Miss Withers frowningly removed a penciled mustache from the classic stone face, shaking her head at the laxity of the guards. Then suddenly she looked up.

From somewhere came the patter of light footsteps—the quick steps of a small man or perhaps a woman—fading away down some distant corridor. As they passed, she heard a hoarse masculine scream, thin with surprise, which set a thousand echoes ringing in the vaulted halls. After the schoolteacher turned and ran on down the hall, turning toward the stairs, she stopped short.

A man was coming, slowly and horribly, down the hundred marble steps—a man whose hoarse scream had almost become a bellow, and who clutched unavailingly at this air. His body was bent forward almost parallel with the slope of the steep steps. . . .

Miss Withers was frozen with horror, for at the foot of the stairs loomed a gigantic statuary group upon a granite base. As she watched, powerless to move, the plunging man collided headlong with the base of the statue, and his screaming stopped.

There was no doubt in Miss Withers' mind as to the identity of this man. Inspector Oscar Piper had told her that Carter, the man she had come to see, was a tall and dried-up "fossil" with a head like an egg. And like an egg the round hairless skull of Professor Carter had cracked against the implacable stone.

Almost instantly the hall was filled with gasping, curious onlookers. Here and there a guard began to push his way through. But Miss Withers turned swiftly away, and moved up the stairs. She was looking for something, and when she reached the top step she found it. Then, and not until then, did she rejoin the murmuring, excited group at the base of the stairs.

A small, almost dandyish man in morning clothes was approaching from the opposite corridor, and the guards made a path for him. Miss Withers heard one of them whisper, "It's the curator!"

Willard Robbins, chief curator of the museum, resembled a young and bustling business man more than the custodian of a large share of the world's art treasures. He was not one to waste time upon adjectives. "Quick, Dugan—the canvas and stretcher." He looked around, through the crowd, for a uniformed figure which was not there. "Burton! How did this happen? Where is Burton?"

"Probably studying art again," said one of the uniformed men, softly.

But the curator went on. "Please move back, everybody. Back, out of the hallway. Everybody. . . ."

Miss Hildegarde Withers stood her ground. "Young man, I want a word with you!"

Curator Robbins looked annoyed. Then one of his men whispered something to him. His face cleared. "So you're the lady who saw the accident? Won't you step this way, to my office?"

They faced each other across a bare mahogany desk. "Well?" said the curator.

"It wasn't an accident," said Hildegarde Withers. "Someone tied this—" she produced a loose ball of twine—"across the top step. That was murder."

"Impossible," gasped Robbins. He handled the string gingerly. "And you mean to tell me that poor Carter stumbled over this, and plunged to his death—you expect me to believe that?"

"I expect you to believe what I say," she told him tartly. "Because the police will, if you don't. You may not know that Professor Carter was afraid of something like this. He telephoned Inspector Piper at Headquarters this morning, asking for police help. The Inspector was busy, so he called me and asked me to drop in, because I live just across the Park, and I've been of service to him at times in the past. Now do you believe me?"

Robbins nodded slowly. "All except that Carter phoned for police protection for himself. The old man never thought of his own safety. He lived for the Cellini Cup, which as you perhaps know is the most valuable single art object in the world. He was always dithering for fear bandits would grab it, although we have a burglar-proof system here to protect it. He'd been reading reports from France that a gang of super crooks stole the Mona Lisa from the Louvre, substituting a copy. Why, he even used to spend most of his time in the Florentine Wing, watching over his Cup. . . ."

Miss Withers nodded. "Then there was some reason behind his dithering!"

But the curator shook his head. "Carter had outlived his usefulness here. He had ceased to distinguish between major and minor matters. Indeed, his chief worry was that small boys would do some harm to the Cellini. He used to drive them away from the Florentine Wing religiously, and in turn they teased him. . . ."

The curator smashed his fist against the desk. "That's it! This was no murder plot. Anyone wanting Carter out of the way could have managed it without going to this extreme. Don't you see? It was only a thoughtless prank on the part of some of the little hoodlums who play about here on free days. They tied the cord there to give him a bad fall, as a joke, never dreaming of the possible consequence. . . ."

Miss Withers remembered the light, running footsteps. Yet she was somehow surprised that she could not agree with the curator's easy explanation. Perhaps—and yet it was too pat.

"I'm going to find Burton, the guard who was supposed to be stationed near the head of that staircase," explained Robbins. "Then we'll have every child in the building searched to find the rest of that string. It was probably taken off a kite string."

"Probably," agreed Miss Withers. "I have two favors to ask. First, please don't let anybody know that I'm anything but a visitor here. Second, let me go in search of this Burton. I think I can guess where he is."

Robbins bowed, twice. "You'll probably find Joel Burton around a skirt," he advised her. "He's a new guard, but highly recommended. Only he has this one vice. . . ."

"That you know of," said the school teacher. "What does he look like?"

Tall, blue-eyed, and Irish as a thatched roof, Joel Burton stood near the end of the second floor corridor which leads to the Florentine Wing of the museum.

"Sure, I ought to be getting back to my post," he was saying. But he kept on obediently squirting water from an atomizer upon the clay figure which was beginning to take shape under the slim, deft fingers of the girl.

"Then go," said Dagmar. Her voice was slow and rich and throaty. She looked at the young and handsome guard through lashes as tawny-yellow as her hair. All the same, he knew that she didn't want him to go. It had been five weeks now since Dagmar, one of a dozen art students permitted to copy in the halls, had been at work on her version of Rodin's "Satyr," and for four and a half weeks of that time he had been her slave. The slave of hair and eyes and hands and the tall, smooth body. . . .

She tweaked a clay ear into pert life. "That's enough water," she said. "Do you want to drown it? Now you can go back to your work."

But Burton lingered. "Just the one trick I'm going to show you," he said. From Dagmar's fingers he took the braided bit of wire with which she cut the damp clay. Then with all his strength he flung it down the corridor. The girl heard it strike tinklingly against a distant window. Then Burton leaned over and neatly extracted it from her curving ear.

She clasped her hands excitedly. "Wonderful!"

Burton persisted. "That's nothing. See this. I used to wow them with this when I was on Pantages time." From his pocket he took a small roll of string, and handed it to her. "Take hold of the end, and pull." He took back the ball, and Dagmar pulled. She pulled until the floor around her was a tangle of string, and then from his cupped hands, came half a dozen silken flags of the Entente, knotted into the cord, followed by a birdcage containing two celluloid canaries.

Dagmar laughed, and clapped her hands again. The applause was echoed from behind them, and the young couple suddenly became aware of their situation, and sprang apart. Peering benevolently at them was an angular, schoolteacherish person in a Queen Mary hat. "Splendid, young man!" said Miss Withers. "You've missed your vocation." She came closer.

"If you don't mind an old woman's butting in, you've also missed something else. There's been an accident on the main staircase and unless I miss my guess, the curator is looking for you. You'd better start thinking up an excuse . . ."

"Huh? Thanks!" muttered Joel Burton, fervently. He scooped up his string and the rest of his props and flew.

"That was a kindhearted thing to do," said Dagmar, coolly, after there had been a moment's silence.

Miss Withers stared at the lovely art student. "I'm not so

old but that I can remember when I was young," she said. She waved a thin yet graceful arm. "Romance . . ."

Dagmar flushed a little, and bent over her modeling. But Miss Hildegarde Withers was not to be got rid of so easily. "You have talent," she observed critically. "That's an excellent copy you're doing. The flair, the feeling of the original—and something added . . ."

Dagmar bowed, almost formally. Then she looked up and faced the intruder with a complete change of subject. "He really isn't meant for this sort of thing, you know." Her tone was almost defiant. "He may be only a museum guard, but he belongs in a different place from this."

Miss Withers cleared her throat. Then—"I'm inclined to agree with you," she said. If her tone was grim, the girl did not sense it. "Then you didn't hear the noise a few minutes ago, either of you?"

Dagmar shook her head. "Oh, yes—I heard a man shouting. But the echoes distort sounds here so much that I didn't pay much attention. I don't know, if Joel heard it or not—he was—"

"Oh, he wasn't with you all the time?" Miss Withers noticed the pail of fresh water beside Dagmar's stool. "Did he go on an errand?"

But the girl was quick. "Joel was with me for the last half hour," she announced. "If it makes any difference . . ."

"It might—who can tell?" said Miss Withers softly, and then withdrew.

There was a guard outside the door of the curator's office. "You can't go in there," he told Miss Withers.

"I can and I may," she retorted, and plunged through, umbrella clutched firmly in her hand. Inside she found Robbins, flustered somewhat, facing fifteen or twenty youngsters of ages assorted from six to twelve.

"I want the boy who did this wicked thing to come forward and confess!" the curator was thundering. Behind him stood a perspiring and bulky guard. The urchins scratched and shrugged and kept their silence.

"Perhaps," suggested a voice from the doorway, "perhaps you'd let me help, Mr. Curator. I'm used to boys of this age in my own classes . . ."

But Robbins was out of temper. "Thank you, madam," he said, shortly, "but I'm confident that one of these hooligans caused the death of Professor Carter, and I'm going to find out which one it was. Search them, Cassidy."

Miss Withers stood back and watched the process, which was not without its difficulty. "Put everything out of yer pockets here on the table," ordered Cassidy.

One boy hesitated, and Robbins leaped forward. "There! In that pocket. What have you got hidden there?"

He inserted his well-manicured hand swiftly, and withdrew it holding a gummy mass of old butterscotch. The guard continued the search, bringing to light several balls of kite string, but none which matched the sinister cord which lay across the curator's desk. He stepped back, his face perplexed.

Then there came a knock at the door. It opened, and in came Joel Burton, clinging to the arm of a resisting red-headed gamin who had been discovered, he said, lurking in Armour Hall. "This is the last of them," he announced.

The urchin grinned widely, showing the lack of a front tooth. His head was a mass of red curls, and his dress consisted of a ragged sweater and worn overalls. "Leave me alone," the lad insisted. "I done nothing."

"Search him, Cassidy, and see if you find any cord to match this," ordered the curator.

The prisoner submitted without resistance, his hard, young-old face defiant. But Miss Withers was not watching the boy. Her keen eyes were upon Joel Burton, who stood by the door with his eyes upon the cord which lay on Robbins' table. Automatically his hand went to his side pocket—closed around something—

"What have you there, if I may ask?" said Miss Withers swiftly. All eyes turned on her, and then on the guard.

He never blinked an eye. "Nothing at all," he said. The muscles of his wrist flickered, and then he extended his open palm. "What would I have?"

Miss Withers remembered the exhibition in the hallway. "Never mind," she said. And the search went on, with the result which Miss Withers had known would occur. The boys were released, with a general warning to behave themselves for the good of their souls, and poured out of the office, the red-haired lad in the lead. Miss Withers and the curator looked after them.

"I told you so," said the lady. "No child planned that diabolical scheme." Robbins did not answer. He was smiling at the red-headed urchin, who was walking fast down the hall, away from the others, with his cap perched on one side of his curly poll and his feet turned out, Charlie Chaplin fashion.

"Fathers of men," observed the curator, sententiously.

"Fathers of men and sons of Belial," Miss Withers told him, from bitter experience. Then she faced Robbins. "I still feel that this mystery, if it is a mystery, has something to do with the Cellini Cup you spoke of. I wonder if you'd send one of the guards with me to look at it—preferably one of those whose duty it is to watch it."

The curator hesitated. "That would be Joel Burton. From his post at the head of the stairs he commands a view, down the long corridor, of the Rodin Hall and the Florentine Wing which holds the Cellini. The Cellini case is placed beneath a skylight, so that he could check on it every minute—when he is at his post. He's wandered away once too often, so I've demoted him to the check-room downstairs, and put Cassidy in his place. Will he do?"

"Splendidly," said Hildegarde Withers. A few moments later she was following the broad gray back of Cassidy down the hall, past the Rodin statues and the pale-haired girl who worked busily in her corner with the mobile clay, and on into a large, airy room whose walls were lined with glass cabinets filled with glittering old-encrusted glass.

But she had no eyes for the walls. Set squarely in the center of the room, upon a solid metal pedestal, was a square case of heavy glass. Its base was a polished mirror, and upon the mirror rested an object at once so beautiful and so decadent, so opulent in its color and design, that Miss Withers almost shuddered.

It was small, this Cellini Cup—not more than eight inches in diameter and perhaps seven inches high. But she knew it to be worth the ransom of seven kings.

Its base, resting on the mirror, was a turtle—the legendary tortoise who holds the world upon his back, according to mythology. But this turtle was of crusted gold. Upon the turtle rested a winged dragon of shimmering green and yellow and red enamel, and upon the wings and neck and tail of the dragon rested a wide and richly curving sea shell of hammered gold.

Crouching on the lip of the shell was a sphinx, with the head of a lovely woman modeled in pure gold, and a serpentine, animalistic body of ardent, opulent greens, blues, whites, and yellows. From the ears of the sphinx depended two miniature pearls, and from her breast, hanging over the bowl in which the Princes of Rospigliosi were wont to keep their salt, hung a great white pearl larger than a pea. This pearl swung back and forth, back and forth, endlessly.

"Vibration of the building," said Cassidy, the guard. "Professor Carter used to say it showed perfect balance."

Miss Withers nodded. "And this cup is left here, protected only by a glass case?"

Cassidy laughed, and then turned to make sure that they were alone. "Not on your life, ma'am. The Professor used to hang about all the time, but he didn't need to. This case is safer than a vault. Look down the hall where we came. See the stair? Well, that's where one of us is always stationed. Now look this way, toward the other end of the Florentine Wing. See Schultz watching us? One or the other of them has his eyes on this case every minute. But that ain't all. Come here."

With a thick finger he traced out the almost invisible wires which ran through the glass. "If one of them is broken, it sets off all the alarms. Instanter, every door and window in the place is double-locked. This wing has no doors and no fire escapes leading out—and the only exit is back through the Rodin Hall to the main stair. What chance do you think a burglar would have, even if the guards did slip? The police would get the alarm direct, and surround the place in two minutes . . ." He beamed at Miss Withers, proudly.

She was forced to admit that the protection of the priceless treasure did seem thorough. But hadn't she read somewhere that anything one man devised could be outdone by some other man?

Miss Withers thanked Cassidy, and returned to the stair, pausing on her way to note the slow but steady progress of Dagmar's satyr. She found, on reaching the main hall, that she was just in time to have missed the undertakers as they removed the body of Professor Carter, canvas and all. Full well she knew that it was her duty to telephone Inspector Piper that this was a job for the whole homicide squad. But that was one of the advantages of having no official standing. She could do exactly as she saw fit, as long as the results justified the means. For the time being she was content to have the death put down as simple misadventure.

She was surprised to notice that the building was gradually emptying— not because of the "accident" but because it was time for lunch. Thoughts of a sandwich began to fill Miss Withers' busy mind, until she started down the main staircase and saw two white-clad porters mopping the floor around the statuary group at the foot of the stair, and she lost her appetite.

Hildegarde Withers would never have counted this minor loss as an evidence of the good luck which more often than not attended her amateurish efforts as a detective. Yet otherwise she might have stepped out of the building, and missed one of the most exciting hours of her life.

She was sitting on a stone bench in the vast main hall of the lower floor when it happened, trying unavailingly to put in their proper positions the various characters in this mad drama. But she leaped to her feet as there came, from somewhere on the second floor, an unmistakable shot followed by two more in rapid succession.

The few straggling visitors who remained within sight milled about like cattle, but Hildegarde Withers was going up the stairs three steps at a time. She passed Curator Robbins near the top, and both of them went galloping down the hall toward the American Wing, from which sounds of a scuffle were arising. All the alarms went off hideously.

In the doorway they came upon brawny Cassidy and two other guards, a wiry, swarthy little man grasped firmly in their thick red hands. He was mouthing incoherent cries, and making efforts to regain the cheap nickel-plated revolver which Cassidy had taken from him.

"Nobody hurt, Mr. Robbins," announced Cassidy. "Just a bloody anarchist who wants to destroy the paintings that Mr. Morgan loaned us. All he did was to crack a molding."

The curator drew a long breath. "Good Lord I thought it was —well something worse. This day has been a nightmare. Take him downstairs and turn him over to the cop on the beat. I'll prefer drunk and disorderly charges against him later."

Robbins walked back toward the head of the stair with Miss

Withers, who was thinking fast. "Funny how things happen all at once," he observed. "Six months go by, and this is the sleepiest place in town. Then in one day we have a fatal accident and an anarchist. I hope this is the end."

But Miss Withers did not answer him. She was standing stock-still. "Prepare yourself," she advised him. "This is far from the end of things."

Somehow she had known all along that this would happen. She was staring down the Rodin Hall, toward the distant showcase which stood beneath the skylight. Even from that distance, both could see that the light glinted on smashed glass, and that the brilliant, jeweled setting of the showcase was gone.

"Come on," shouted Robbins, unnecessarily, and began to sprint.

Miss Withers followed, but this time she did not run. She walked slowly, staring at the floor. It was too late to hurry. This was the time to be sure and careful. Halfway down the Rodin Hall she paused, finding the clue, the discrepancy, for which she was looking.

She could hear the agonized voice of the curator as he came face to face with the shattered case which had held the Cellini. But Miss Withers was bending over the sprawled body of a tall girl in a black smock, a girl who tried weakly to sit up as the school teacher grasped her shoulder.

At least this wasn't another corpse. Dagmar pushed aside the proffered aid and stared down the corridor. "Where did he go?"

"Where did who go?"

"The man in the trench coat, blast him!" Dagmar's red lips curled in anger. "Slamming into me that way, and knocking me headlong. And look—look what he did to my model?" The satyr did show signs of maltreatment.

Hastily the girl smoothed the profaned clay. "Five weeks' work —ruined!"

"It's not ruined beyond repair, child," said Miss Withers. "But this man. Did you see his face?" The curator was coming back, and she beckoned to him. "We have a witness, Mr. Robbins."

"Of course I saw his face," said Dagmar. "It was—well, just a face. No whiskers or anything. About thirty, or maybe forty. He had his mouth open. And he wore a cap or maybe it was a hat. Anyway, he had on a trench coat."

"Good enough," the curator told her. "The doors and windows locked instantly when the case was broken. All we have to do is to round up the fellow . . ."

That was all. It was easy enough. Three men of early middle age were apprehended without difficulty in the lower halls carrying trench coats. One wore a cap, the other two had hats. Each gave as his only reference the particular relief organization which happened to be maintaining him among the ranks of the unemployed, and none possessed any string or any sign of the Cellini Cup.

Worst of all, Dagmar, when confronted with the trio, was unable to point out any one of them as the man who had crashed into her in the hallway. They all looked familiar, but she couldn't be sure. She tried, desperately, to remember. But, after all, she had got only the briefest glance of the man on his mad flight, and the subsequent crash and its resulting dizziness had erased everything but the memory of the trench coat. Dagmar thought that the man of mystery had been holding something bulky beneath the coat, but even this was hazy.

Even now the tall, blond girl clung to her satyr, and as soon as Robbins permitted her, she went resolutely back at smoothing out the signs of its rude handling as the vandal rushed by. Miss Withers gave her a long mark for pluckiness.

Outside, the police were already hammering at the double-locked doors to be let in. Three carloads of the burglary squad and four cops from the local precinct station were admitted, and then the doors made fast again.

"A cup worth at least several millions of dollars has been stolen," announced Robbins. "It's here, in the building. Find it."

From a polite distance, Hildegarde Withers watched, for two hours, while every person in the building was searched, every nook and cranny and corner pried into. Mummy cases were opened, vases plumbed, fountains drained. Bundles of towels were turned out in the washrooms. Stew from the building cafeteria was poured out into the sink, and garbage sorted on newspapers. All to no avail.

Robbins and his guards took the lead in the search, but the

actual fine-toothing was done by the officers under the leadership of Captain Malone of Centre Street. He recognized Miss Withers, and would have passed her up, but she requested quickly that the matron search her as well as the rest. "The quarry is too important for you to consider persons and personalities," she told him.

But after all, the search finished where it had begun. A snarling incoherent anarchist languished in handcuffs, loudly advocating the destruction of the paintings which Mr. Morgan had loaned to the museum for an indefinite showing. Three sad, bleary men holding trench coats over their arms waited hopelessly and patiently in Robbins' office, also handcuffed. But the Cellini Cup, the only remaining creation of the roistering genius of the sixteenth century, Signor Benvenuto Cellini, had vanished as if into thin air.

Robbins gave up in disgust and spent twenty minutes in browbeating Cassidy and Schultz, the two guards whose duty it had been to keep the Cellini in view all the time, and who had been lured away by the decoy shots. The police promised to get something out of the self-styled anarchist, but it was Miss Withers' private opinion that he had been hired for the job by an intermediary, and would have little enough to tell, even in a third degree. The crowd clamored to be released; the art students took down their easels and their modeling stands and also demanded their freedom, and still the blond Dagmar smoothed and worked and patted at her satyr. Miss Withers shrewdly guessed that the girl had no intention of leaving until she had seen her young man.

It was at this stage of the game that Inspector Oscar Piper came battering upon the main doors of the museum until he was admitted. The wiry, gray little man, a dead cigar clenched, as always, in his teeth, made straight for Miss Withers.

"Hildegarde— I sent you here to calm down a fussy old man, and you've set off plenty of fireworks. What's coming off?"

The spinster who had almost married him once now transfixed him with an icy eye. She told him. Not everything, but almost everything. "That's how matters stand," she finished. "And the Cup has vanished like morning dew."

"Vanished my eye," said Piper, ungallantly. He whirled around and stared toward the checkroom, where poor Joel Burton still stood, with nothing to do. Then the Inspector smashed his right fist into his left palm. "Blundering idiotic numbskulls," he accused, genially. He spoke loudly enough, so that not only the police captain but also Curator Robbins approached.

With his cigar the Inspector indicated the checkroom. "Anybody look there for this wandering soup-plate of yours?"

"But Inspector," protested Robbins. "The checkroom is outside the turnstile. Nobody but a magician could get down from upstairs, cross the wide lobby, and hide a package there without somebody seeing him."

But Piper was already vaulting the barrier. Miss Withers tagged along behind, feeling unnecessary.

"It wouldn't be hidden, it would be in plain view," said the Inspector. He poked at a top coat or two, tore open a bundle which contained nine packages of flea soap for dogs—Miss Withers often wondered why, afterward—and finally came to a square package, neatly wrapped and sealed, at the end of the package shelf.

It bore the seals of a midtown drug store, and a label—MEDI-CINES—BREAKABLE. A check attached bore the number 41.

He turned on Joel Burton. "When was this box checked?"

Burton shrugged. "It was here when I came to duty at about eleven. Ask Bruce, the regular checkroom man."

Bruce, easily discovered, admitted that the package had been checked early that morning by a man whom he did not remember.

"Rats," said the Inspector. "Are you all blind? This package was checked like fun. One resembling it was brought in here, and while you were all gawping at this so-called anarchist, the Cellini Cup was wrapped up, brought here, and substituted. Maybe the other box was crumpled up as waste paper. Anyway, the thieves planned on your being too stupid to put two and two together —and by heavens, you were!"

"Nobody could have substituted boxes without my knowing it," cut in Joel Burton.

The Inspector stared at him. "That's what I was thinking," he said, gratingly.

The police and guards crowded around as the Inspector took out his pocket knife, carefully lifted off the seals, and opened the box. There was a quantity of tissue paper—and then, to Miss Wither's utter amazement and chagrin, the delicately enameled sphinx came into view. Beneath were the glowing curves of the shell, the dragon, and the turtle. There were excited cries from the crowd inside the gates.

Curator Robbins exhaled noisily. But the Inspector lifted out the glowing chalice and stared at it. Then he whirled on the curator.

"This the missing cup? Sure of it?" Miss Withers found herself nodding eagerly.

"Of course I'm sure," said Robbins. "There couldn't be two like it in the world. Of course, I don't know the piece as thoroughly as poor old Carter, but it seems genuine to me."

"We'll make sure," said Piper. He beckoned to Captain Malone. "Got anybody here from the Jewel Squad?"

"I was on it for two years," said that worthy. Piper indicated the masterpiece, and Captain Malone bent over it. He tapped the shell. "Twenty-one carat, at least," he said. He ticked at the enamel. "True-blue," he decided. "They don't mix colors like that today." Last of all, he bent over the pendant pearl which hung from the breasts of the sphinx, and looked up, grinning. "First water, and a real honey," he gave as his final verdict.

"O.K.," said the Inspector. He handed the Cellini Cup back to the curator. "Now hang on to it," he said. "As for me, I'll hang on to him."

Moving catlike across the floor, he suddenly pinioned the arms of the guard, Joel Burton. "And this washes up our case."

But Hildegarde Withers did not join in the congratulations. "It was easy as falling off a log," Piper told her as they moved toward the stair. "I'll check over this sculptress' testimony just to make sure which one of the three dopes with the trench coats was hired to play messenger and deliver the Cup to Burton at the checkroom. Then we're through."

"Easy as falling off a log," Miss Withers repeated. That was just the trouble. Something in the back of her mind clamored for attention, but she could not reach it. Something—

"I'd like to know what that fool of a guard thought he could do with the thing if he did get away with it," Piper was saying. "Melted down it wouldn't bring more than a thousand or two. It's the craftsmanship and the associations that make it so valuable. And it would be unsalable. I guess the poor guy just went nuts looking at it day after day."

"Nuts enough to kill poor Professor Carter when it wasn't necessary?" Miss Withers wanted to know. She stopped suddenly. Suppose—suppose it was necessary?

"Wait," she said. "You're holding Burton downstairs until you all leave, aren't you? May I have a word with him?"

"All you want," Piper promised her. He was glowing with achievement. So it was that Hildegarde Withers faced a sullen, handcuffed man across a desk in an anteroom, with a policeman looking out of the window and another at the door.

She wasted no time in beating around bushes. "You're in serious trouble, young man. Attempted grand larceny is one thing, but murder is another. Were you with Miss Dagmar whatever her name is when Carter plunged to his death."

Burton stared at her, and shook his head. "I was getting a pail of water for her," he said. "But you won't believe me."

"I won't—until you tell me what happened to the ball of string," Miss Withers ventured. But Joel Burton only turned his face away, and refused to answer. There Miss Withers left him.

The Inspector and Robbins were waiting. "Before you go," said the latter, "I'd like to show you something. The electricians have been busy—and the new showcase has been brought up from the basement and installed." He led them up the stairs and through the Rodin to the Florentine Wing. Dagmar had finally given up work, and sat sadly surveying her clay satyr.

She caught Miss Withers' eyes. "I'm going home," the girl announced. "And I'm never coming back. I hate this place and everybody in it!" She bent her sensitive face above her work. This had been a hard day for Dagmar.

As they came into the room containing the Cellini, an urchin or two disappeared through the far door. "Tell the cops that those kids can be released," Robbins ordered a nearby guard. Miss Withers recognized with some amusement the curly red head of the little fellow with the ancient overalls and the toed-out, Chaplinesque feet. This must have been a memorable day in that lad's life.

The Cellini Cup, restored to its rightful place, shimmered as brightly as ever. The turtle held his everlasting burden as cheerfully, the winged dragon hovered as balefully, and the golden lady whose body was that of a reptile smiled forever. Only the pearl which hung from her breast was still.

"This is not the first time that murder has been done for the possession of that Cup," said Robbins. But the Inspector cut him short in his lecture.

"Come on, Hildegarde. A word with the little sculptress outside, and then we'll write finis to this."

"Finis" was very nearly written to another history as the three of them lingered beside the modeling stand in the hall. As Piper questioned the girl in regard to the mysterious man in the trench coat, and as Miss Withers idly rubbed her fingers against the cool wet clay of the sculptured satyr, a globule of lead came twisting past her head to clip away a strand or two of brown hair and flatten itself against the wall. It happened so simply, and with so little noise, that the four of them stood aghast for nearly a minute before they could move.

There was only one direction from which the shot could have been fired, and to Robbins' eternal credit let it be written that the dapper curator was abreast of the Inspector in the race down the corridor.

Robbins shouted to guards at the stairhead, and in a moment the entire wing was blocked off. From that time on it was only a matter of steady advance until every human being in the Florentine Wing was corraled.

The captives consisted of five little boys, most of whom Miss Withers remembered having seen here and there throughout the building during the hectic day. One of them was the grinning lad with the red hair and the Chaplin feet.

Two of the boys had been found playing with an automatic pistol equipped with a Maxim silencer, though they stoutly denied having fired it at all. They had found it underneath a showcase, they maintained, but a moment before.

"Hold these two, and let the others go," decided the Inspector. But Miss Withers gripped his arm.

"I want to speak to that one," she said. "The little boy with the red hair. Oscar, I've taught thousands of children, but while many of them toe in, I never saw one before that habitually toed out!"

She stepped forward, and suddenly the gamin wheeled and started to run. Miss Withers' lunge missed his shoulder by a fraction of an inch, but caught at his curly red hair. She screamed a little as it came away in her hand, leaving a shiny bald head.

The running figure turned, disclosing the mature, seamed face of a grown man. "Lord Almighty," said Piper. At last he saw the reason for the oddly turned feet. What they had thought was a child of nine or ten was a midget—and a midget whose face was now a mask of hate and defiance! The loose overalls had hidden the bowed legs. . . .

Miss Withers turned away, acutely ill, as the abortive escape was halted and the hideous, frustrated creature dragged back by guards and police.

"Let me go, you canaille," screamed the creature. "Take your hands from Alexius! I would have succeeded but for the fault of that worthless gun. But still you are fools, fools!" Spitting, cursing, the midget was dragged away. His eerie laughter echoed through the place for minutes after he was gone.

The Inspector returned and faced Miss Withers. "The shoe is on the other foot," he said. "I knew there was a master-mind behind this, but it was you who saw through his disguise. I've heard of Alexius—the police of Budapest dubbed him 'the Gnome.' There were rumors that a mad dwarf was the brains of a gang operating in the large cities of Europe and stealing art treasures by sheer black magic, but I thought it was newspaper talk."

Robbins nodded. "I heard the rumors, and evidently so did poor Carter. He feared that the gang were after his pet treasure, and so they were. But why they had to kill him—"

"I can answer that," said Hildegarde Withers. She turned to stare, almost compassionately, at the tall girl who stood behind them. "But by the way, I think here is a young lady who would very much like to go home, now that she knows her boy friend is innocent of wrong-doing."

"But is he?" cut in Piper. "How about the checkroom?"

Miss Withers hushed him. "Is it all right for Dagmar here to leave, and take her copy in clay?"

"Of course," said Robbins. "By all means."

Gratefully, the girl began to throw wet cloths around the statue. But Miss Withers was quick and cruel.

She wheeled, so that almost by accident, the sharp point of her umbrella slashed into the soft clay. Dagmar cried out, but Miss Withers pointed like an avenging figure of justice. "Look!"

They all looked—and saw, beneath the concealing clay, the gold and enamel of the true Cellini! Quickly Miss Withers laid more of the treasure bare.

"It might have been hidden there when I was knocked over. . . ." began Dagmar wildly, but she stopped, for she saw that no one believed her. Her greenish eyes turned a flaring yellow, and she reached for a palette knife, but the Inspector gripped her in time. Silently, like a condemned Juno, she was led away after her master, the dwarf.

"You see," explained Miss Withers later, "I knew that there must have been a real reason for killing Carter. He was the one man who could tell the true Cellini from the copy which had been made by some unknown but marvelous craftsman. The thieves were willing to pay the price of offering a substitute made of genuine gold, jewels, and enamel, in order to have the genuine Cellini. It fooled everybody—even myself—until I saw that the pearl in the spurious cup did not swing back and forth. It wasn't balanced exactly as in the original.

"Carter was trapped. The midget found that the Professor had been annoyed by small boys, so he tied the cord across the stair and then lured the old man into chasing him for some minor infraction of the rules. That got him out of the way. Dagmar, at the time, was taking care that Burton, the guard at the stairhead, was out of the way. She even found opportunity to snip a length of the cord which he carried about with him to do magic tricks with, to further incriminate him."

"The spurious cup, then, was checked in the checkroom and left to be found, just as I found it?" Piper was crestfallen.

Miss Withers nodded. "Exactly, if we hadn't found it, a hint would have been dropped somehow. Alexius, in his role of urchin, kept tabs on that. Then at noon, when the place was nearly deserted, he planted a fake anarchist in the American wing, and while the alarm was on, smashed the showcase, lifted the Cellini, and immediately slipped it into the yawning statue of clay which

Dagmar had ready just outside the door. She was thrown flat on the floor to cover her failure to identify the man properly—and probably she noticed the men with trench coats and gave us that as a blind."

"Then, with the Cup supposedly found, there'd be no difficulty in her getting out with the genuine one?"

"Not at all," Miss Withers continued. "The only danger was that some one would get inquisitive about the girl's statue. The midget lurked nearby, saw me touch it, and lost his nerve and fired."

"I don't suppose you'd mind telling me where he got the gun?" Piper wanted to know. "Remember, the midget has been twice searched—and the building, too."

"Elementary," quoted Miss Withers smilingly. "The gun was waiting in the receptacle provided under the clay for the Cup. Just in case something went wrong. As something did. He picked up the gun when everything was clear. And very nearly sent me to Kingdom Come with it, too."

They were sitting on a marble bench in the main hall. The three men with trench coats were being released, and hopelessly shambled out into the sunlight again. Joel Burton stood unhappily staring after the figure of Dagmar, the girl whose talent had been turned to such strange uses, as she was led away between two buxom policewomen. She never glanced in his direction.

Then Robbins rushed up to Miss Withers. "My dear lady," he beamed. "I have just consulted with our Board, and to show our appreciation we would like to give you as a souvenir of this day the imitation Cellini, provided the police do not want it to try and check up on its artisan. . . ."

"I hope I never see it again," said Oscar Piper fervently.

"Nor I," said Hildegarde Withers. "Instead, I wonder if you'd grant me just one thing—let me have the remains of the clay satyr which Dagmar copied so painstakingly from the original Rodin?"

That crumbling clay satyr leers today from Miss Withers' living-room table, the marks of her umbrella still gouged deep in the smoothly molded body. Strangely enough, the thing has about its eyes and mouth something of the twisted malevolence of Alexius, the red gnome.

LAWRENCE TREAT

Shoes for Breakfast

INTRODUCTION

My maiden murder was a massacre. Six dead, including a dame. But, by popular clamor of the nineteen other writers who appear in this volume, the work was declared ineligible. It was a five-part serial, and left no room for anybody else.

Following the serial, I wrote sporadically for several years, chiefly adventure stuff and detective puzzles, and then decided to tackle the short mystery story. I lit into the field with a schedule of a story a day, and kept it up for almost a week.

I can still remember the horrible Thursday or Friday of that week when I sat in front of my typewriter in a complete blank. Not a word, not an idea. I had writer's block, I was through. Then I took myself firmly in hand and, by way of challenge, set myself the toughest job I could think of—concocting a story from three outlandish and unrelated clues. I picked a pair of fried eggs, a bicycle pedal and some eyeglasses. If I could do that, I could do anything.

My background of detective puzzles helped, and "Shoes for Breakfast" emerged. It was not, however, acclaimed as a work of genius, or even as worth a buck. The best editors turned it down without comment.

But my pride was involved. I'd written the piece to kill a dragon of the mind, and the only effective poison was printer's ink. The story had to get published. I took it back for revision and I worked hard, although I no longer recall what was involved. Early in 1937 it went to market for the second time, and was bought by Detective Fiction Weekly, *to whom I had made several previous sales.*

"Shoes for Breakfast" is important to me. It is the story that made me a professional writer, dedicated to discipline and sweat, and leaving inspiration to the dabblers and the lucky.

LAWRENCE TREAT

Shoes for Breakfast

JOE McPHAIL parked his car, picked up his lawyer's briefcase and stepped out to the sidewalk. He noticed the guy at once. He looked tall because his neck was long and his head was high and narrow. But he was nervous and pasty and about half the size of Joe McPhail.

When Joe saw him staring up at the tower building, he thought of the story about the crowd peering at the sky because somebody had a stiff neck. So Joe didn't bother looking up. He crossed the street, entered the lobby of the apartment and asked for the Crosby penthouse.

He was nervous on the way up in the elevator. He hadn't seen Tony since her marriage, except for those few tense moments when she had pleaded with him to stay away. And here he was walking into her home.

It wasn't his fault. Crosby had insisted, with a crotchety, senile impatience, that Joe come himself.

"And don't send up one of your fool clerks," the old man had warned.

Joe had tried to get out of it. "Just a matter of a signature. The codicil's in order, so you won't need me."

Crosby had flared, "You come here yourself, hear me? Otherwise I'll take my business where they pay me a little respect!"

Joe had assented. Crosby's business was worth too much to risk, and if Tony didn't want to see Joe she could keep out of the way. So he had glanced over the codicil that left ten thousand dollars to a son who previously had been disinherited, stuffed the document in his brief case and drove uptown.

Joe stepped out of the elevator into the luxurious private foyer, pushed the doorbell and waited. He was a big man, built hard and straight and rugged, like the trunk of a tree. His hair was dark, thick, curly, and matched the mahogany color of his wide steady eyes.

He was shaky now, and his throat was dry. If he saw Tony alone, he knew he'd grab her in his arms and say, "You never wanted to marry him and you're only staying from a sense of loyalty. The hell with him and the hell with his money. Tony, we're the only things that count—you and I!"

From inside the apartment, he heard a phone tinkle twice and stop. Joe rang again and began to get impatient. Maybe the damn thing wasn't working.

He took a deep breath, pressed the bell button and listened carefully until he heard its jangle. A moment later the door opened a few inches and a quiet wiry man with thin lips and sharp eyes poked his head into the crack and asked, "What do you wish, sir?"

"Mr. Crosby. He's expecting me."

The butler's body came into view. He was wearing a dark sack suit and a wing collar. "Mr. Crosby isn't interested in insurance," he said with a contemptuous glance at the brief case, and tried to close the door.

Joe wedged a foot solidly against the jamb. "I'm a lawyer and I have an appointment. What's the idea?"

"I'm sorry, sir. Mr. Crosby left no instructions about you."

Joe noticed the butler was holding one hand in the side pocket of his suit. The arm was bent stiffly and uncomfortably.

Joe didn't see the advantage of a discussion. He grunted, put one shoulder to the door and shoved. The butler went backward and Joe went forward. As far as the arched entrance to a vast, paneled living room.

"Now I'm in," he observed. "You may as well announce me. Mr. McPhail."

The butler disagreed. He glared, grabbed Joe by the arm and tried to rush him out. He was much stronger than McPhail had expected. Joe rocked back on his heels, jerked his body and thrust.

The two men locked for a few seconds. Joe saw something glint and flash out of sight as they swayed and jarred against the wall. Honors were about even when the pair of them stopped suddenly and stared at each other.

It came from right behind them. A long thin wail of terror. It began on a high note and stayed there, without a break, until Joe and the butler rushed in.

A parlor maid was holding aside the red curtains of an alcove and pointing to the floor. On the floor lay Silenus Crosby, flat on his stomach. The top of his head showed bald and shiny above the whitish fringe of neck hair. But Joe's eyes traveled down instead of up.

From the back of the neck protruded the thin delicate point of a knife. The blade was red.

McPhail snapped, "Stop it!" at the maid. She closed her mouth so hard that her teeth clicked. It must have hurt, because she looked surprised and forgot about Crosby.

Small rapid footsteps thudded from another part of the house. Joe gulped and thought of Tony. The maid started to cry. He snapped at her again, "Stop it!" paused and added, "Get a doctor! Must be one in the house." She stopped crying and went quietly out of the room.

Then Joe began to notice things.

First of all, there was the footstool. It had overturned and lay under one of Crosby's shins. The telephone wires trailed from a carved stand. The wires were long and they were tangled in the footstool and around Crosby's legs. The phone itself was resting on top of a pair of thick, gilt-bound volumes.

Two daggers were lying on the floor and one of them was propped, point up, by a book. They were shiny and sharp and had jeweled hilts. Apparently they were companion pieces to the weapon that had killed Crosby.

McPhail stooped and read the titles of the two books on the floor. Gibbon's *Decline and Fall of the Roman Empire*, volumes three and five.

He stiffened when he stood up. "Where's Ton— that is, where's Mrs. Crosby?"

"She rides in the park at this hour," answered the butler. "I daresay she'll be somewhat upset. I'd better telephone the police."

Joe heaved a deep sigh of relief. In any case, Tony was out of it. He hated to think of what it would have been otherwise. A young, beautiful wife, former actress—a cranky old millionaire—police grilling—tabloid publicity.

He thrust and slapped an arm at the butler as he was reaching for the phone. "You damned fool—don't you know enough not to touch anything? Every dust speck may be evidence. What's your name?"

"La Farge, sir. Albert La Farge. I'll use the other phone."

Joe watched him glide from the room and wondered whether he'd come back. But if he were guilty, he wouldn't give himself away by disappearing. And why suspect him anyhow? Just because he'd been nasty before? Joe thought momentarily of the object that had fallen from La Farge's pocket. He crossed the room and looked at the carpet where it had dropped. There was nothing.

Two more servants had entered. They were wailing and making themselves useless. The bell rang and a doctor hurried in. He turned Crosby over, gave him a cursory examination and let him flop back.

"Nothing to be done," he remarked, closing the curtains of the alcove. The butler returned. A phone rang at the back of the apartment. The maid who had jarred her teeth left to answer it. When she reappeared, she said, "It's the doorman. He wants to know whether you have a red coupé with the license HP-27-34. There's some trouble about parking."

Joe said, "Yes" and got up. He didn't understand what could be wrong with his car. He wondered whether this was a trick to get him out of the room. But three people and the doctor were there and it seemed safe. As he passed the place where he had struggled with La Farge, he looked carefully at the rug. There was still no sign of the shiny object.

As soon as he stepped out of the downstairs lobby he knew it was a gag. The pasty man with the stiff neck was sitting in the red coupé and smoking.

McPhail strode up angrily. "What's the idea?" he demanded.

"I'm Ed Crosby—Silenus's son. You're from his attorney's office, aren't you?"

"What about it?"

"Did he sign?"

"Sign what?"

"The will—the codicil leaving me ten thousand—my father promised it—he didn't change his mind, did he?"

Joe leaned one elbow on the door. "Why so worried? If he doesn't sign today he'll sign tomorrow, won't he?"

"He might change his mind. He always does, for no reason at all. He's beginning to show his age."

"How's your neck?" demanded Joe unexpectedly.

Crosby rubbed it and looked surprised. "Nothing's the matter with it. Why don't you answer me?"

"Your father's dead."

"Dead! Then—they got him! But the will?"

"I got there too late. Who killed him?"

Crosby leaned forward and spoke in a low voice. "Listen, they're desperate—they'll get you too! I was afraid to go upstairs —that's why I made up the parking story, so I could speak to you. They'll kill you if you don't keep your mouth shut!"

McPhail grabbed Crosby by the lapels and shook him. "Who'll kill me if I don't keep my mouth shut about what?"

"I can't tell! I'm doing you a favor warning you, but it's as much as my life is worth to say more."

McPhail released his grip. "Stick around, Crosby. I just thought of a way of getting you that ten thousand. Come down to my office tomorrow."

Ed Crosby seemed dubious. "There's nothing crooked about it, is there? If he didn't sign . . ."

Joe shot him a withering glance. "When I do something crooked," he thundered, "I'll disbar myself. Until then, go easy on cracks like that. You want the ten thousand, don't you? Well, be at my office tomorrow. Now get out of my car."

Joe drove downtown. He realized the Crosby business would keep him most of the day and he wanted to clear up some matters on his desk.

A few hours later he returned to the big apartment house. A crowd was milling around the entrance. They had seen the police cars siren up to the marquee but they didn't know what it was all about. They were milling around a little man who acted as if he had inside information, and he was giving it out for what it was worth. Joe caught a phrase or two. Vice raid—three women. He elbowed through and gave his name to a cop. He was sent up an once.

The Crosby living room had changed considerably. It was a bustle of activity now, with uniformed and plain clothes police puttering and talking and shouting, measuring and examining and moving tripods, while the quick dazzle of a flash-bulb explosion flared between the red curtains of the alcove.

A big jovial man in a stiff collar saw McPhail and bellowed at him. "Joe, come on over!"

It was Inspector Bush. McPhail grinned and crossed the room with his hand out. "You promised me once I could watch you work. Have a cigar?"

"Never use 'em!" roared Bush, a foot away. "Dulls my brain. Can't afford to take chances with it."

"Delicate, like the rest of you? Listen, Bush, I'm the guy that practically discovered the body. I had an appointment with Crosby."

"I know it. Just been calling your office. What was it about?"

Joe thought of Tony and thought fast. If he mentioned the unsigned codicil, he'd be dragging her into it. She'd stood to lose ten thousand. "Just a legal form," he remarked casually. "I had to notarize a signature on a title deed. The butler tell you about the scrap we had?"

"Yeah," bellowed the inspector. Joe turned to see to whom Bush was shouting at on the other side of the room, saw nobody and realized it was himself.

Bush thundered on. "So he thought you were selling insurance. That's a good one on you! Show me how the body was lying when you found it."

They stepped toward the alcove. The body had been removed and the rug was a puddle of blood. Joe shivered as he bent down. Stiffly he explained and answered questions. Bush was particularly interested in the telephone wires. When he had it clear, he walked out of the alcove.

"It's a funny setup. Butler, two maids and the grocer boy all in the kitchen when the phone rang. They all check each other. La Farge got bawled out by the missus this morning and was grumpy, so he wouldn't answer the phone. Old Crosby took the call, tripped over the footstool and stabbed himself in the neck. Obliging old codger. What business did you say you had with him?"

Joe repeated his story. A plain-clothes man came over and said, "Not a print in the place. Looks as if somebody wiped everything with a cloth."

Bush remarked, in a sort of public meditation that echoed through the room, "Butler. He said he'd been dusting in there. Come on, Joe. Somebody said there was a nice view from the terrace."

Bush hooked an arm through McPhail's and led him to the terrace door. The green motley of Central Park stretched out twenty floors below. Bush made himself comfortable in a wicker chair, rubbed some of the fierceness out of his eyes and spoke in a whisper that didn't carry more than fifty feet.

"What do you think of it, Joe?"

"He fell on the daggers, of course. Must have tripped over the phone wires and impaled himself on one of the blades."

"Obliging of him, wasn't it? Murderer says, 'Si, old boy, trip for me and you'll get a dagger through the jugular.' So Si trips and gets it in the neck. Any better ideas?"

"Somebody may have pushed him."

"Who? All the servants were together when the phone rang. The phone rang twice and then stopped, so that fixes pretty well the time. Notice the mark on his nose?"

"No, I didn't. What kind of a mark?"

"From glasses. Was he wearing 'em when you saw him?"

Joe thought back and said, "No."

"Check. Glasses were lying under the body. And it took intelligent glasses to get there. They must have bounced off when he fell, slid down the telephone wire, whistled 'Annie Laurie,' caromed off the leg of the table and wriggled under his stomach. Joe, somebody put those glasses there *after* he fell!"

"La Farge could have done that. He didn't open the door for me until I'd been ringing a couple of minutes."

"Maybe it was suicide. Crosby was funny up here." Bush screwed up his ruddy face and tapped his forehead significantly. "He tried it twice."

"Killing himself?"

"Yeah. With a bottle of poison once. The maid caught him just before he swallowed it and he pretended it was a mistake. The other time he jumped out of bed and tried to dive through the window. He had bad aim. And if he couldn't hit a window, how the hell could he hit a Toledo dagger? He had a temper too. What's Mrs. Crosby like?"

"She's nice," said Joe quickly. "She couldn't possibly—" He saw Bush watching him closely, and he broke off. "There'd be no motive, anyhow. She had everything she wanted."

"Except somebody her own age. Fifty years between 'em. Or was it only forty-nine?"

Joe started to figure it and stopped. "I wouldn't know," he remarked.

Bush leaned back and looked at the sky. "What was it you came to see Crosby about?"

"I told you before. Forgotten?"

"No, not me. I thought maybe you had. You'd better come clean."

Joe felt like a fool. The most natural question for Bush to ask McPhail's office was what he'd been doing at the Crosbys'.

"Maybe I'd better," he admitted, running a big hand through his thick curly hair.

Bush listened while Joe told about the codicil, and about Ed Crosby. When he was through, Bush yelled through the door, "Hey, what the hell's the matter with the phone company? Haven't they traced that call yet? Send the butler out here."

La Farge glided through the terrace door with the clatter of a ghost. Bush glared.

"Hear you had a scrap with my friend McPhail."

The butler coughed slightly. "I hadn't been told Mr. McPhail was expected, and Mr. Crosby's strict orders were to let no one in except by appointment. It was one of his peculiarities."

"One of 'em? What were the others? Think he was bughouse enough to commit suicide? Fall on his sword like a Roman? He'd been reading Roman history, two volumes at a time."

"I don't know whether I could say, sir, but he wasn't quite right in his mind."

"For instance?"

"This morning when I brought in his breakfast. I always bring it with the morning paper. He carries the tray into Mrs. Crosby's room and they have breakfast together.

"About five minutes after I'd left the tray, Mrs. Crosby rang for me, very furiously. She accused me of putting a pair of shoes on the tray instead of the eggs. You see, sir, that was the way Mr. Crosby had brought in the breakfast—a pair of shoes on the egg plate." Albert coughed again. "They were baby shoes."

"Where were the eggs?"

"In Mr. Crosby's bureau drawer, on top of his canary yellow shirt."

Bush went livid. "What the hell does a guy of seventy-three wear canary yellow for?"

"He liked to appear young, sir. The very old often do."

"He usually in bed when you bring in the breakfast?"

"Yes, sir. I wake him, draw his bath and leave the tray."

"Shoes for breakfast, huh?"

"He behaved oddly. On a previous occasion he brought her a bicycle pedal on her breakfast tray."

Bush's grunt exploded like a clap of thunder. "Bah! Maybe old Crosby starved to death. Leave the door open, Albert."

Albert's departure was like a wraith. Joe saw him leave, but if he hadn't been looking he would never have known.

Bush scowled, moved his chair to face McPhail and bellowed, "Yates! Go get Mrs. Crosby!"

Joe gripped the arms of his chair as hard as he could and observed in a controlled voice, "I thought she was out riding when it happened."

Then he pushed himself up and gaped.

She cried, "Joe!" in a startled voice. Her blue eyes that used to be as placid as a summer sky had no calmness now. She clutched at her hair to smooth it and she dislocated a hairpin. For about ten seconds there was absolute silence. A draft was blowing through the door and her gown and her hair were rippling. Her skin was the color of milk, her lips were bloodless. Then Joe stepped forward and put his arm around her. He felt her recoil and come to him in the same motion. Bush spoiled it all.

"So," he rasped in his stage whisper. "You know the widow Crosby!"

Joe turned hotly. "Lay off that, Bush! You know damn well we . . ."

It occurred to him that maybe Bush didn't know at all. "What are you trying to pull off, anyhow?"

"Not a thing," remarked the inspector. "But isn't it a nice setup for a murder?"

"If you have any questions," declared Tony in a frigid voice, "you can ask them."

"No questions at all. Any statement?"

"No statement at all," she replied, and swept back to the house.

Joe rose. "Work to do at the office. If you want me, you know where to find me."

He felt ridiculous as he stalked off.

But he did no work the rest of the day. He sat back in his chair and smoked, most of the time. He saw what a nice case was shaping up for Bush. McPhail, who'd been in love with Tony Sorelle, the actress. A lover's quarrel, a broken engagement, and Tony married on the rebound. To a seventy-three-year-old millionaire. McPhail meets her again, they find out that after all they were just a pair of obstinate fools who took a scrap too seriously. Fact, every word of that, and capable of proof.

The rest was inference, but none the less credible. Joe rehearsed it as Bush might figure it, and realized how damning it all looked. Assume a plot to kill Crosby for his money and Tony's freedom. On the day Crosby was to change his will, to take ten thousand and leave it to his son, he is murdered. McPhail is there at the time, Tony has gone about a half hour before. How prove that she didn't plant the three fatal daggers?

Joe was a worried man when he went home. He'd invented and discarded a hundred theories. The one that came nearest to standing up had the biggest hole in it. Suppose Ed Crosby and La Farge had conspired to kill Crosby. Suppose when Crosby was staring up at the sky he'd actually been gazing at the penthouse for La Farge's signal that the coast was clear for the phone call which would bring Crosby to his death. Bush's checkup from the telephone company would make or break that particular theory, but the rest of the facts were easy to fit in. The time it had taken La Farge to answer the bell—that was the period during which Crosby had been killed by a push.

But—and here was the bit that knocked the theory into a cocked hat—what motive? If Ed Crosby had waited ten minutes, he'd have been ten thousand dollars richer. A murder after Silenus had signed was completely logical; a murder before was insane.

And yet, Joe clung to the idea and felt there was something in it.

He decided to sleep on it. He'd see Ed Crosby in the morning. If Joe McPhail was any judge of men, Ed would sell his soul for a chance at cash.

Joe undressed thoughtfully. As he took off his trousers and held them upside down to fold over a hanger, something dropped to the floor. He stooped and picked up a pair of glasses. They were gold pince-nez, like Silenus Crosby's.

McPhail examined them. One lens was broken, the other was plain glass, like a window pane. So they couldn't be Crosby's after all. He'd had weak eyes.

Joe tossed the spectacles into a bureau drawer but couldn't forget them. They must have been dropped by someone and fallen into his trouser cuff. He remembered a quarter he'd lost once and found in the evening in the same place.

Joe lit a cigarette and puffed hard. The object La Farge had been holding in his pocket when he'd opened the door—the object that had glinted and disappeared during their argument —the glasses!

Joe put out his cigarette, switched off the light and lay back, thinking. For a long while he couldn't sleep. Then, abruptly, he tensed up.

The screen in the corner of his room was moving. Joe blinked, told himself he was imagining things and knew he wasn't.

The figure of a man slipped from one wing of the screen. The man wore a dark suit and a mask over his face. He held a gun in one hand.

Joe thought of Ed Crosby's warning. "They're desperate— they'll get you too!" But who were they? Who was this, and what did he want?

McPhail's back began to itch furiously. He held himself rigid, wondering how long he could hold out. What would he do if the intruder pointed the gun at him?

The man was gliding across the room. Joe felt as if he'd go crazy if he didn't scratch. He moved his arm cautiously. The bed creaked and the masked man whirled. Joe kept his breathing steady and his eyes shut. When he opened them again the man was searching silently in a bureau drawer. The drawer in which he'd slipped the glasses.

Joe couldn't stand it any longer. He was scared, but the suspense was worse than his fear. He noticed the revolver was on top of the bureau. He tensed, tightened his muscles and hurled himself from the bed in a dive of desperation.

The figure wheeled and seized the gun. Joe remembered something he had heard once, and his outstretched hand gripped the cylinder and clamped. He felt it push as fingers squeezed on the trigger. But the cylinder couldn't turn and so no shot could be fired.

Joe grabbed for the other arm and tried to wrench the glasses loose. He hooked one finger under the nose piece. It bent, snapped suddenly and filliped behind the bureau. He stopped, uncorked a short uppercut.

The hold on the gun relaxed suddenly. He didn't realize he'd been tugging at it until he was staggering backward. The big humidor on the bureau flew at him. He spun sideways, lowered his head and charged.

The door slammed in his face and a key turned. He hammered at it, heard footsteps. Then the front door banged shut and he stepped back.

La Farge. Joe hadn't seen the man's face, but he was sure. The build was right, the slinkiness of movement was right. La Farge must have gained entrance some time during the afternoon and waited for his chance to redeem the window pane glasses. But why were they so important?

Joe dropped onto the edge of the bed and rubbed his forehead. He was sweating, and now that it was over he felt weak as a cat. And more bewildered than ever.

He switched on the lights, picked up the gun and the glasses, and freed himself by removing the hinges from the door. And while he worked his mind was busy with a flock of new ideas.

As soon as he was free, he went to the phone and dialed Tony's number. She answered it herself.

"Tony, this is Joe."

Her voice was cool. "Joe? But why at such an hour?"

"I want to know something. It's important to both of us. Tony, why did Silenus act queer?"

"I don't see what right you have to ask a question like that. He was a little peculiar, that's all. Perhaps old age—I don't know."

"You're stalling! We're in this together, Tony, and when we're out of it I'm taking you away You know that, don't you? When I saw you this morning I realized—"

"This is ridiculous. I told you long ago that it was all over, that

I didn't want to see you. And now you pester me at midnight with a lot of fool questions."

"Tony, you know perfectly well—"

He hung up and stared at the wall. The wire was dead.

Ten minutes later when the front door bell rang sharply, he jerked up, took the captured gun from his pocket and strode to the door. This time he was armed, the door was bolted as well as locked and he was taking no chances.

"Who's there?" he barked.

"It's me—Ed Crosby."

Joe leveled his gun through the crack as he opened the door. Crosby was alone. He didn't see the revolver at first, but when he did he became more nervous than usual. "Why—that?"

McPhail put it back in his pocket. "Just jittery these days. What did you want?"

"You told me to come to your office, but I couldn't wait. You see, I'm in a jam and I need money bad."

"What kind of a jam?"

Crosby stalled. "Not really a jam, maybe, but well—it's over a woman."

"So you want to know your chances. I said tomorrow at my office. Still, listen, Crosby, I usually get a retainer in advance. I might waive it, for reasons of my own, if you can assure me nobody else is in on this. That you have no commitment of any kind with any other lawyer."

"And if I have?"

"Then tell me his name and I'll speak to him."

"Purcell. Charlie Purcell. He sort of represents me, sometimes."

"Thanks. I'll see you in the morning."

Ed fidgeted with his watch chain. "I sort of thought, maybe, you could put me up for the night. I have no place to go, and I'm broke."

McPhail handed him a dollar. "You can sleep on that. Now—get out!"

Joe reached his office late the following morning. He found Yates, the big detective whom he'd seen at the penthouse, waiting for him.

"Morning, McPhail. I just dropped around. The inspector wants you up at the Crosby place."

"Later on. I have work to do."

"It'll keep." Yates smiled lazily, but there was no doubt as to what his instructions had been. Joe shrugged and accompanied him.

When McPhail reached the apartment he saw Tony first, even though she was sitting in the far corner and was partly hidden by a table. She had no makeup on and she looked like a tired, defenseless child. McPhail started for her but Inspector Bush blocked the way.

"Morning, Joe!" he bellowed. "Sleep well?"

"Pretty good. I had a couple of visitors."

"I know all about them. Had your house watched." Bush changed suddenly. His big energetic jovial face darkened, his eyes flashed and his voice lashed out like a whip-stroke. "I'm cracking down on you!"

Joe tensed. Mentally, he felt as if he were facing a hurricane wind. "Meaning what?"

"The key! The key to this apartment that Mrs. Crosby gave you! *Hand it over!*"

He saw Tony dart forward and utter a little gasp. He gave Bush a vicious shove aside, strode past him and took Tony's hand. "Don't worry, kid," he said quickly. "We'll get out of this together."

She smiled up at him. "Joe dear—last night—I spoke that way because somebody was listening in on the extension."

His laugh was forgiving and almost gay as he wheeled and faced them. He noticed Yates had a hand in his pocket and that the uniformed patrolman at the doorway was fingering his holster.

"Let's have it, Bush! Go ahead and make a fool of yourself."

Bush parried it. "Have what, Joe? What are you expecting me to do?"

"First of all, your insinuation about my having a key to this apartment and carrying on an affair with Mrs. Crosby. It's a damned lie!"

"I said nothing about an affair. You used that key to sneak into this place yesterday morning and you shoved Crosby as he was walking to the phone! Then you beat it outside and rang the bell. You did that at ten o'clock sharp. And Mrs. Crosby arranged the daggers point up and went out for her daily ride—after telling Crosby *she'd call him at exactly ten o'clock!*"

"But I rang the bell as soon as I left the elevator. I rang three times before the door was finally answered!"

Bush's words clipped out like a death sentence. "You rang once! Four people were in the kitchen and heard it. Once!"

"They're crazy!"

"Sure." The inspector's voice dropped to a soothing tone. "It's a crazy world."

"The bell must have been out of order—there's got to be something wrong with it. Bush, I rang three times. I say it now and I'll say it the rest of my life. Either there were four liars in the kitchen or the bell didn't work!"

He was scared now, and he knew he showed it. Maybe it was just a trick of Bush, a trick to break his nerve and force a confession. But on the other hand, maybe the bell hadn't worked and he was just in for a rotten break.

He studied Bush and the other people in the room. His words had impressed them, and he followed up his advantage. "Besides, he'd have seen the dagger contraption and jumped away from it. There'd have been some evidence of resistance, of a fight."

"If he'd had his glasses on, he would. But he didn't—he was holding them in his hand—that's why they were under his stomach. And Silenus Crosby was practically blind without glasses!"

Joe sat down suddenly and covered his eyes. It was coming clear now. He was mixed up in a horrible series of accidents. Because he loved Tony and because Silenus Crosby had been killed, Bush naturally suspected Tony and him. The rest of Bush's case was just a bad dream.

"Tony," asked Joe slowly. "All this so-called queerness of Silenus—could it all be explained as the behavior of a man who was temporarily blind? Who didn't have his glasses, for example?"

"Yes," she said, and her blue eyes gleamed. "But Joe—Joe dear —he had his glasses on."

"Glasses," he cried out. "Glasses—but not his glasses! Not

lenses, but window panes!" He rose and threw the broken piece of the pince-nez toward Bush. "There they are," he snapped. "Trace 'em!"

"Where'd you get hold of that?"

"La Farge's pocket! It dropped in my trouser cuff yesterday and he broke into my apartment last night to recover them. But he only got half, and I took away his gun. You might trace that, too. Here it is!"

The effect was electrical. Yates and the patrolman at the doorway snapped up revolvers. At the same instant a crushing blow paralyzed Joe's arm. He yelped and dropped the weapon. A detective whom he hadn't even noticed was standing next to him. "No you don't!" he was muttering, while he covered McPhail.

Joe leaned back and started laughing. "You traced that call, Bush. Who made it?"

"The call had nothing to do with it. Just an accident it happened to ring then. That's what set me wrong yesterday."

"Who made it?" Joe wet his lips. If the guess he was about to make proved wrong, within two hours he'd be in jail and charged with a murder. And Tony too. As accomplice.

"That phone call," he shouted in a voice that made Bush's seem like an invalid's, "was made by Ed Crosby! He was staring at the building when I came in and waiting for La Farge's signal. La Farge switched Silenus' glasses and La Farge planted the daggers, and that's why he took so long to answer the door for me!"

"Yeah," drawled Bush sarcastically. "And Ed Crosby's motive was to gyp himself out of the ten thousand he'd have gotten if he waited ten minutes. Yeah!"

"Ed Crosby's motive," retorted Joe in a low quiver, "was to get the whole damned estate! He just pretended he was after the ten thousand so that nobody'd suspect him. Only he pretended it too hard, and that's what made me suspect him. He even pretended to retain me to get the ten thousand. But it was all made up, to hide his real purpose."

"Prove it!"

"That's your job, but I'll give you the clues. They fit together like a nursery rhyme. Under Silenus' will before he married Tony,

Ed was the sole heir. Silenus didn't get along with his son and he cut him out after the marriage, making Tony sole heir. All the funny behavior dates from the time of that new will, and the scheme was to contest the probate on grounds of testamentary incapacity. If the will was knocked out, then the earlier will leaving everything to Ed would be valid.

"Ed pretended he was innocent, made up a story about being threatened, and figured nobody could guess his real reason. And all the things Silenus did—the bicycle pedal and the shoes for breakfast, the apparent suicide attempts—they were the actions of a blind and thoroughly confused man, who couldn't see and was ashamed to admit it. But the point was to make him look loony and thus prevent him from executing a valid will. And the chief witnesses were supposed to be La Farge and Tony. And the man who can clinch it all is Purcell, who gave Ed Crosby the legal advice on which the scheme was founded!"

Bush's laughter exploded in a great bellowing roar. "You've got it, Joe! I knew the will was mixed up in it, but I didn't know how. So I figured if I got a smart young lawyer like you with his back to the wall, he'd do my work for me. All right, boys—La Farge and Ed Crosby—that's the pair we want."

Joe rubbed his forehead and wondered whether he was dreaming. And years later, when he and Tony began to have Inspector Bush for dinner, the two of them were still wondering whether the jovial inspector had figured it that way from the beginning, or whether he'd merely thought fast and said it to cover a boner.

As for Bush, he let them guess.

KENNETH MILLAR

Find the Woman

INTRODUCTION

This story was written underwater, somewhere between San Francisco and Kwajalein, in the early fall of 1945. I was a Communications Officer aboard the U.S.S. Shipley Bay, an escort carrier, and my cabin was below the waterline, in that charming situation known as Torpedo Junction. The Japanese war was over, the ship had been converted into a troop transport, and there were no more sixteen-hour days in the coding room. The first night out, I pulled the opening chapters of a novel out of a box. I had written them the previous year, after my first book was published. They failed to excite me. Perhaps I needed some kind of a warmup before going on with the novel. The night before, over drinks in a San Francisco hotel room, Tony Boucher had told me about Ellery Queen's first annual short story contest and suggested I enter a story in it. I started to think about plots.

My wife Margaret was working for Warner Brothers that year, writing a screenplay for "The Iron Gates." A few weeks before, I had spent a ten-day leave with her in Hollywood. (Transport duty on the pineapple run was good duty.) The contrast between the comparative simplicity of life at sea and the complexity of human relations on shore must have struck me forcibly. Anyway, it gave me the outlines of a plot. The final twist in the plot occurred to me as I wrote. With Boucher's encouragement and a year's accumulation of frustration behind my pen, the story wrote itself in two evenings. Three weeks later, when the Shipley Bay wallowed into port again, the novel was finished, too. Those were the days.

The original title of the story was "Death by Water." Ellery Queen gave it a better title and a four hundred dollar prize. I still like it pretty well, in spite of its obvious stylistic debt to Raymond Chandler. I suppose you could describe it as Chandler with onions. But then

Chandler himself is Hammett with Freud potatoes. As Dostoevsky said about Gogol (I think), we all came out from under Hammett's black mask.

Kenneth Millar

Find the Woman

I HAD seen her before, and made a point of noticing her. I make a point of noticing people who make a thousand a week. I do that because a thousand a week is fifty thousand a year.

Mrs. Dreen did the national publicity for Tele-Pictures. She was forty and looked it, but there was electricity in her, plugged in to a secret source that time could never wear out. Look how high and tight I carry my body, her movements said. My hair is hennaed but comely, said her coiffure, inviting not to conviction but to suspension of disbelief. Her eyes were green and inconstant like the sea. They said what the hell.

She sat down by my desk and told me that her daughter had disappeared the day before, which was September the seventh.

"I was in Hollywood all day—we have an apartment there—and left her alone at the beach house, about ten miles north of here. When I got home to the beach house last night she was gone."

"Did you call the police?"

"It didn't occur to me. She's twenty-two and knows what she's doing, and apron strings don't become me." She smiled fiercely like a cat and moved her scarlet-taloned fingers in her narrow silk lap. "Anyway it was very late and frankly I was a trifle stewed. I went to bed. But when I woke up this morning it occurred to me that she might have drowned. I objected to it because she wasn't a strong swimmer, but she went in for solitary swimming. I think of the most dreadful things when I wake up in the morning."

"*Went* in for solitary swimming, Mrs. Dreen?"

" 'Went' slipped out, didn't it? I told you I think of dreadful things when I wake up in the morning."

"If she drowned you should be talking to the police. They can arrange for dragging and such things. All I can give you is my sympathy."

As if to estimate the value of that commodity, her eyes flickered from my shoulders to my waist and up again to my face. "The Santa Barbara police are what you might expect in a town of this size. You see, I've heard about you, Mr. Rogers."

"My initial fee is one hundred dollars. After that I charge people according to how much I think I can get out of them."

From a bright black bag she gave me five twenties. "Naturally, I'm conscious of publicity angles. My daughter retired a year ago when she married—"

"Twenty-one is a good age to retire."

"From pictures, maybe you're right. But she could want to go back. And I have to look out for myself. It isn't true that there's no such thing as bad publicity. I don't know why Una went away."

"Una Sand?"

"I assumed you knew." She was a trifle pained by my ignorance of the details of her life. She didn't have to tell me that she had a feeling for publicity angles.

Though Una Sand meant less to me than Hecuba, I remembered the name and with it a sleek blonde who did more justice to her gowns than to the featured parts she had had during her year or two in the sun.

"Wasn't her marriage happy? I mean, isn't it?"

"You see how easy it is to slip into the past tense?" Mrs. Dreen smiled another fierce and purring smile, and her very white fingers fluttered in glee before her immobile body. "Her marriage is happy enough. Her ensign is a personable young man, I suppose, handsome, naïve, and passionate. He was runner-up in the State tennis championships the last year he played. And, of course, he's a flier."

What do you expect of a war marriage? she seemed to be saying. Permanence? Fidelity? The works?

"As a matter of fact," she went on, "it was thinking about Jack Ross, more than anything else, that brought me here to you. He's due back this week, and naturally—" like many unnatural people, she overused that adverb—"he'll expect her to be waiting for him. It'll be rather embarrassing for me if he comes home and I can't tell him where she's gone, or why, or with whom. You'd really think she'd leave a note."

"A minute ago Una was in the clutches of the cruel crawling foam. Now she's gone away with a romantic stranger. Who's she been knocking around with?"

"I consider possibilities, that is all. When I was Una's age—" Our gazes, mine as impassive as hers I hoped, met, struck no spark, and disengaged.

"I'm getting to know you pretty well," I said with the necessary smile, "but not the missing girl. My conversation is fair for an aging 4-F, but it isn't worth a hundred bucks."

"That gray over your ears is rather distinguished. Sort of a chinchilla effect."

"Thanks. But shall we look at the scene of the crime?"

"There isn't any crime." She got up quickly and gracefully, a movement which at her age required self-control. An admirable and expert slut, I said to myself as I followed her high slim shoulders and tight-sheathed hips down the stairs to the bright street. But I felt a little sorry for the army of men who had warmed their hands at that secret electricity. I couldn't help wondering if her daugher Una was like that. When I did get to see Una, the current had been cut off; I learned about it only by the marks it left. It left marks.

I followed Mrs. Dreen's Buick convertible north out of Santa Barbara and for seven or eight miles along the coast highway. Then for a mile and a half along a winding dirt road through broken country to her private beach. The beach house was set far back from the sea at the convergence of high brown bluffs which huddled over it like scarred shoulders. To reach it we had to drive along the beach for a quarter of a mile, detouring to the very edge of the sea around the southern bluff. The blue-white August dazzle of sun, sand, and sea was like an arc-furnace. But there was some breeze from the sea, and a few clouds moved languidly in-land over our heads. A little high plane was gamboling among them like a terrier in a hen yard.

"You have privacy," I said to Mrs. Dreen when we had parked.

"One tires of the goldfish role. When I lie out there in the afternoons I—forget I have a name." She pointed to a white raft in the middle of the cove which moved gently in the swells. "I simply take off my clothes and revert to protoplasm. *All* my clothes."

I cocked an eye at the plane which dropped, turning like an early falling leaf, swooped like a hawk, climbed like an aspiration.

She said with a laugh, "If they come too low I cover my face, of course."

Almost unconsciously, we had been moving toward the water. Nothing could have looked more innocent than the quiet blue cove, held in the curve of the white beach like a benign blue eye set in a serene brow. Even while I thought that, however, the colors shifted as a cloud passed over the sun. Sly green and cruel imperial purple veiled the blue. I felt the primitive fascination and terror of water. The tide had turned and was coming in. The waves came up toward us, gnawing eternally at the land like the toothless jaws of a blind unsightly animal.

For a moment Mrs. Dreen looked old and uncertain. "It's got funny moods, hasn't it? I hope she isn't in there."

"Are there bad currents here, or anything like that?"

"No. It's deep, though. It must be twenty feet under the raft. I could never bottom it there."

"I'd like to look at her room," I said. "It might tell us where she went, and even with whom. You'd know what clothes were missing?"

She laughed a little apologetically as she opened the door. "I used to dress my daughter, naturally. Not any more. Besides, more than half of her things must be in the Hollywood apartment. I'll try to help you, though."

It was good to step out of the vibrating brightness of the beach into shadowy stillness behind Venetian blinds. "I noticed that you unlocked the door," I said. "It's a big house with a lot of furniture in it. No servants?"

"I occasionally have to knuckle under to producers. But I won't to my employees. They'll be easier to get along with soon, now that the plane plants are shutting down."

We went to Una's room, which was light and airy in both atmosphere and furnishings. But it showed the lack of servants. Stockings, shoes, underwear, dresses, bathing suits, lipstick-smeared tissue, littered the chairs and the floor. The bed was unmade. The framed photograph on the night table was obscured by two empty glasses which smelled of highball, and flanked by overflowing ashtrays.

I moved the glasses and looked at the young man with the wings on his chest. Naïve, handsome, passionate were words which suited the strong blunt nose, the full lips and square jaw, the wide proud eyes. For Mrs. Dreen he would have made a single healthy meal, and I wondered again if her daughter was a carnivore. At least the photograph of Jack Ross was the only sign of a man in her room. The two glasses could easily have been from separate nights. Or separate weeks, to judge by the condition of the room. Not that it wasn't an attractive room. It was like a pretty girl in disarray. But disarray.

We went through the room, the closets, the bathroom, and found nothing of importance, either positive or negative. When we had waded through the brilliant and muddled wardrobe which Una Ross had shed, I said, "I guess I'll have to go to Hollywood. It would help me if you'd come along. It would help me more if you'd tell me who your daughter knew. Or rather who she liked, I suppose she knew everybody."

"I'd love to. Go along to Hollywood, I mean. I take it you haven't found anything in the room?"

"One thing I'm pretty sure of. Una didn't intentionally go away for long. Women usually just have one razor, and hers is in her bathroom."

"You notice things. Also Jack's picture. She only had the one, because she liked it best."

"That isn't so conclusive," I said. "I don't suppose you'd know whether there's a bathing suit missing?"

"I really couldn't say, she had so many. She was at her best in them."

"Still was?"

"I guess so, as a working hypothesis. Unless that hundred can buy evidence to the contrary."

"You didn't like your daughter much, did you?"

"No. I didn't like her father. And she was prettier than I."

"But not so intelligent?"

"Not as bitchy, you mean? She was bitchy enough. But I'm still worried about Jack. He loved her. Even if I didn't."

The telephone in the hall took the cue and began to ring. "This

is Millicent Dreen," she said into it. "Yes, you may read it to me."
A pause. "'Kill the fatted calf, ice the champagne, turn down the
sheets and break out the black silk nightie. Am coming home tomorrow.' Is that right?

"Hold it a minute," she said then. "I wish to send an answer.
To Ensign Jack Ross, USS *Guam*, CVE 173, Naval Air Station,
Alameda—is that Ensign Ross's correct address? The text is:
'Dear Jack join me at the Hollywood apartment; there is no one
at the beach house. Millicent.' Repeat it, please. . . . Right. Thank
you."

She turned from the phone and collapsed in the nearest chair,
not forgetting to arrange her legs symmetrically.

"So Jack is coming home tomorrow?" I said. "All I had before
was no evidence. Now I have no evidence and until tomorrow."

She leaned forward to look at me. "How far can I trust you,
I've been wondering?"

"Not so far. But I'm not a blackmailer. It's just that it's sort of
hard, so to speak, to play tennis with the invisible man."

"The invisible man has nothing to do with this. I called him
when Una didn't come home."

"All right," I said. "You're the one that wants to find Una.
You'll get around to telling me. In the meantime, who else did
you call?"

"Hilda Karp, Una's best friend—her *only* female friend."

"Where can I get hold of her?"

"She married Gray Karp, the agent, and resides, as they say,
in the Karp residence."

Since Mrs. Dreen had another car in Hollywood, we drove
down in my car. It was just over a hundred miles: just over a
hundred minutes. En route the temperature rose ten degrees,
which is one reason I live in Santa Barbara. But Mrs. Dreen's
apartment in the Park-Wilshire was air-conditioned and equipped
with a very elaborate bar. In spite of the fact that she was able to
offer me Scotch, I tore myself away.

Mr. and Mrs. Karp had made the San Fernando Valley their
home. Their ranch, set high on a plateau of rolling lawn, was
huge and fashionably grotesque: Spanish Mission and Cubist with
a dash of paranoia. The room where I waited for Mrs. Karp was

as big as a small barn and full of blue furniture. The bar had a brass rail.

Hilda Karp was a Dresden blonde with an athletic body and brains. By appearing in it, she made the room seem realer. "Mr. Rogers, I believe?" She had my card in her hand, the one with Private Investigator on it.

"Una Sand disappeared yesterday. Her mother said you were her best friend."

"Millicent—Mrs. Dreen—called me early this morning. But as I said then, I haven't seen Una for several days."

"Why would she go away?"

Hilda Karp sat down on the arm of a chair, and looked thoughtful. "I can't understand why her mother should be worried. She can take care of herself, and she's gone away before. I don't know why this time. I know her well enough to know that she's unpredictable."

"Why did she go away before?"

"Why do girls leave home, Mr. Rogers?"

"She picked a queer time to leave home. Her husband's coming home tomorrow."

"That's right, she told me he sent her a cable from Pearl. He's a nice boy."

"Did Una think so?"

She looked at me frigidly as only a pale blonde can look, and said nothing.

"Look," I said. "I'm trying to do a job for Mrs. Dreen. My job is laying skeletons to rest, not teaching them the choreography of the Danse Macabre."

"Nicely put," she said, as who should say: you win the one-pound box of chocolates and a free ticket to the voluptuous hula fiesta. "Actually there's no skeleton. Una has played around, in a perfectly innocent way I mean, with two or three men in the last year."

"Simultaneously, or one at a time?"

"One at a time. She's monandrous to that extent. The latest is Terry Neville."

"I thought he was married."

"In an interlocutory way only. For God's sake, don't bring my name into it. My husband's in business in this town."

"He seems to be prosperous," I said, looking more at her than at the house. "Thank you very much, Mrs. Karp. Your name will never pass my lips."

"Hideous, isn't it? I hope you find her. Jack will be terribly disappointed if you don't."

I had begun to turn toward the door, but turned back. "It couldn't be anything like this, could it? She heard he was coming home, she felt unworthy of him, unable to face him, so she decided to lam out?"

"Millicent said she didn't leave a letter. Women don't go in for all such drama and pathos without leaving a letter. Or at least a marked copy of Tolstoi's *Resurrection*."

"I'll take your word for it." Her blue eyes were very bright in the great dim room. "How about this? She didn't like Jack at all. She went away for the sole purpose of letting him know that. A little sadism, maybe?"

"But she did like Jack. It's just that he was away for over a year. Whenever the subject came up in a mixed gathering, she always insisted that he was a wonderful lover."

"Like that, eh? Did Mrs. Dreen say you were Una's best friend?"

Her eyes were brighter and her thin pretty mouth twisted in amusement. "Certainly. You should have heard her talk about me."

"Maybe I will. Thanks. Good-by."

A telephone call to a screen writer I knew, the suit for which I had paid a hundred and fifty dollars in a moment of euphoria, and a false air of assurance got me past the studio guards and as far as the door of Terry Neville's dressing room. He had a bungalow to himself, which meant he was as important as the publicity claims. I didn't know what I was going to say to him, but I knocked on the door and, when someone said, "Who is it?" showed him.

Only the blind had not seen Terry Neville. He was over six feet, colorful, shapely, and fragrant like a distant garden of flowers. For a minute he went on reading and smoking in his brocaded armchair, carefully refraining from raising his eyes to look at me. He even turned a page of his book.

"Who are you?" he said finally. "I don't know you."

"Una Sand—"

"I don't know her, either." Grammatical solecisms had been

weeded out of his speech, but nothing had been put in their place. His voice lacked pace and life.

"Millicent Dreen's daughter," I said, humoring him. "Una Ross."

"Naturally I know Millicent Dreen. But you haven't said anything. Good day."

"Una Sand disappeared yesterday. I thought you might be willing to help me find out why."

"You still haven't said anything." He got up and took a step toward me, very tall and wide. "What I said was good day."

But not tall and wide enough. I've always had an idea, probably incorrect, that I could handle any man who wears scarlet silk bathrobes. He saw that idea on my face and changed his tune. "If you don't get out of here, my man, I'll call a guard."

"In the meantime I'd straighten out that delightful marcel of yours. I might even be able to make a little trouble for you." I said that on the assumption that any man with his pan and sexual opportunities would be on the brink of trouble most of the time.

It worked. "What do you mean by saying that?" he said. A sudden pallor made his carefully plucked black eyebrows stand our starkly. "You could get into a very great deal of hot water by standing there talking like that."

"What happened to Una Sand?"

"I don't know. Get out of here."

"You're a liar."

Like one of the clean-cut young men in one of his own movies, he threw a punch at me. I let it go over my shoulder and while he was off balance placed the heel of my hand against his very flat solar plexus and pushed him down into his chair. Then I shut the door and walked fast to the front gate. I'd just as soon have gone on playing tennis with the invisible man.

"No luck, I take it?" Mrs. Dreen said when she opened the door of her apartment to me.

"I've got nothing to go on. If you really want to find your daughter you'd better go to Missing Persons. They've got the organization and the connections."

"I suppose Jack will be going to them. He's home already."

"I thought he was coming tomorrow."

"That telegram was sent yesterday. It was delayed somehow. His ship got in yesterday afternoon."

"Where is he now?"

"At the beach house by now, I guess. He flew down from Alameda in a Navy plane and called me from Santa Barbara."

"What did you tell him?"

"What could I tell him? That Una was gone. He's frantic. He thinks she may have drowned." It was late afternoon, and in spite of the whiskey which she drank slowly and steadily like an alcohol lamp, Mrs. Dreen's fires were burning low. Her hands and eyes were limp, and her voice was weary.

"Well," I said, "I might as well go back to Santa Barbara. I talked to Hilda Karp but she couldn't help me. Are you coming along?"

"I have to go to the studio tomorrow. Anyway, I don't want to see Jack just now. I'll stay here."

The sun was low over the sea, gold-leafing the water and bloodying the sky, when I got through Santa Barbara and back onto the coast highway. Not thinking it would do any good but by way of doing something or other to earn my keep, I stopped at the last filling station before the road turned off to Mrs. Dreen's beach house. It was about a quarter of a mile from the turning.

"Fill her up," I said to the woman attendant. I needed gas anyway.

"I've got some friends who live around here," I said when she held out her hand for her money. "Do you know where Mrs. Dreen lives?"

She looked at me from behind disapproving spectacles. "You should know. You were down there with her today, weren't you?"

I covered my confusion by handing her a five and telling her, "Keep the change."

"No, thank you."

"Don't misunderstand me. All I want you to do is tell me who was there yesterday. You see all. Tell a little."

"Who are you?"

I showed her my card.

"Oh." Her lips moved unconsciously, computing the size of the tip. "There was a guy in a green roadster, I think it was a

Chrysler. He went down around noon and drove out again around four I guess it was, like a bat out of hell."

"That's what I wanted to hear. You're wonderful. What did he look like?"

"Sort of dark and pretty good-looking. It's kind of hard to describe. Like the guy that took the part of the pilot in that picture last week—*you* know—only not so good-looking."

"Terry Neville."

"That's right, only not so good-looking. I've seen him go down there plenty of times."

"I don't know who that would be," I said, "but thanks anyway. There wasn't anybody with him, was there?"

"Not that I could see."

I went down the road to the beach house like a bat into hell. The sun, huge and angry red, was horizontal now, half-eclipsed by the sea and almost perceptibly sinking. It spread a red glow over the shore like a soft and creeping fire. After a long time, I thought, the cliffs would crumple, the sea would dry up, the whole earth would burn out. There'd be nothing left but bone-white cratered ashes like the moon.

When I rounded the bluff and came within sight of the beach I saw a man coming out of the sea. In the creeping fire which the sun shed he, too, seemed to be burning. The diving mask over his face made him look strange and inhuman. He walked out of the water as if he had never set foot on land before.

"Who are you?" he shouted to me when I stopped the car.

I walked toward him. "Mr. Ross?"

"Yes." He raised the glass mask from his face and with it the illusion of strangeness lifted. He was just a handsome young man, well set up, tanned, and worried-looking.

"My name is Rogers."

He held out his hand, which was wet, after wiping it on his bathing trunks, which were also wet. "Oh, yes, Mr. Rogers. My mother-in-law mentioned you over the phone."

"Are you enjoying your swim?"

"I am looking for the body of my wife." It sounded as if he meant it. I looked at him more closely. He was big and husky, but he was just a kid, twenty-one at most. Out of high school into the air, I thought. Probably met Una Sand at a party, fell hard for all that glamour, married her the week before he shipped out, and had dreamed bright dreams ever since. I remembered the brash telegram he had sent, as if life were like the people in slick magazine advertisements.

"What makes you think she drowned?"

"She wouldn't go away like this. She knew I was coming home this week. I cabled her from Pearl."

"Maybe she never got the cable."

After a pause he said, "Excuse me." He turned toward the waves which were breaking almost at his feet. The sun had disappeared and the sea was turning gray and cold-looking, an antihuman element.

"Wait a minute. If she's in there, which I doubt, you should call the police. This is no way to look for her."

"If I don't find her before dark, I'll call them then," he said. "But if she's here, I want to find her myself." I could never have guessed his reason for that, but when I found it out it made sense. So far as anything in the situation made sense.

He walked a few steps into the surf, which was heavier now that the tide was coming in, plunged forward, and swam slowly toward the raft with his masked face under the water. His arms and legs beat the intricate rhythm of the crawl as if his muscles took pleasure in it, but his face was downcast, searching the darkening sea floor. He swam in widening circles about the raft, raising his head about twice a minute for air.

He had completed several circles and I was beginning to feel that he wasn't really looking for anything, but expressing his sorrow, dancing a futile ritualistic water dance, when suddenly he took air and dived. For what seemed a long time but was probably about twenty seconds, the surface of the sea was empty except for the white raft. Then the masked head broke water, and Ross began to swim toward shore. He swam a laborious sidestroke, with both arms submerged. It was twilight now, and I couldn't see him very well, but I could see that he was swimming very slowly. When he came nearer I saw a swirl of yellow hair.

He stood up, tore off his mask and threw it away into the sea with an angry gesture. He looked at me angrily, one arm holding the body of his wife against him. The white body half-floating in the shifting water was nude, a strange bright glistening catch from the sea floor.

"Go away," he said in a choked voice.

I went to get a blanket out of the car, and brought it to him where he laid her out on the beach. He crouched over her as if to shield her body from my gaze. He covered her and stroked the wet hair back from her face. Her face was not pretty. He covered that, too.

I said, "You'll have to call the police now."

After a time he answered, "I guess you're right. Will you help me to carry her into the house."

I helped him. Then I called the police in Santa Barbara, and told them that a woman had been drowned and where to find her. I left Jack Ross shivering in his wet trunks beside her blanketed body, and drove to Hollywood for the second time that day.

Millicent Dreen was in her apartment. At noon there had been a full decanter of Scotch on her buffet. At ten o'clock it was on the coffee table beside her chair, and nearly empty. Her face and body had sagged. I wondered if every day she aged so many years, and every morning recreated herself through the power of her will.

She said, "I thought you were going back to Santa Barbara. I was just going to go to bed."

"I did go. Didn't Jack phone you?"

"No." She looked at me, and her green eyes were suddenly very much alive, almost fluorescent. "You found her," she said.

"Jack found her in the sea. She was drowned."

"I was afraid of that." But there was something like relief in her voice. As if worse things might have happened. As if at least she had lost no weapons and gained no foes in the daily battle to hold her position in the world's most competitive and unpredictable city.

"You hired me to find her," I said. "She's found, though I had nothing to do with finding her—and that's that. Unless you want me to find out who drowned her."

"What do you mean?"

"What I said. Perhaps it wasn't an accident. Or perhaps somebody stood by and watched her drown."

I had given her plenty of reason to be angry with me before, but for the first time that day she was angry. "I gave you a hundred dollars for doing nothing. Isn't that enough for you? Are you trying to drum up extra business?"

"I did one thing. I found out that Una wasn't by herself yesterday."

"Who was with her?" She stood up and walked quickly back and forth across the rug. As she walked her body was remolding itself into the forms of youth and vigor. She recreated herself before my eyes.

"The invisible man," I said. "My tennis partner."

Still she wouldn't speak the name. She was like the priestess of a cult whose tongue was forbidden to pronounce a secret word. But she said quickly and harshly, "If my daughter was killed I want to know who did it, I don't care who it was. But if you're giving me a line and if you make trouble for me and nothing comes of it, I'll have you kicked out of Southern California. I could do that."

Her eyes flashed, her breath came fast, and her sharp breast rose and fell with many of the appearances of reality. I liked her very much at that moment. So I went away and instead of making trouble for her, I made trouble for myself.

I found a booth in a drugstore on Wilshire and confirmed what I knew, that Terry Neville would have an unlisted number. I called a girl I knew who fed gossip to a movie columnist, and found out that Neville lived in Beverly Hills but spent most of his evenings around town. At this time of night he was usually at Ronald's or Chasen's, a little later at Ciro's. I went to Ronald's because it was nearer, and Terry Neville was there.

He was sitting in a booth for two in the long, low, smoke-filled room, eating smoked salmon and drinking stout. Across from him there was a sharp-faced terrierlike man who looked like his business manager and was drinking milk. Some Hollywood actors spend a lot of time with their managers, because they have a common interest.

I avoided the headwaiter and stepped up to Neville's table. He saw me and stood up, saying, "I warned you this afternoon. If you don't get out of here I'll call the police."

I said quietly, "I sort of am the police. Una Sand is dead." He didn't answer and I went on. "This isn't a good place to talk. If you'll step outside for a minute I'd like to mention a couple of facts to you."

"You say you're a policeman," the sharp-faced man snapped, but quietly. "Where's your identification? Don't pay any attention to him, Terry."

Terry didn't say anything. I said, "I'm a private detective. I'm investigating the death of Una Sand. Shall we step outside, gentlemen?"

"We'll go out to the car," Terry Neville said tonelessly. "Come on, Ed."

The car was not a green Chrysler roadster, but a black Packard limousine equipped with a uniformed chauffeur. When we entered the parking lot he got out of the car and opened the door. He was big and battered-looking.

I said, "I don't think I'll get in. I listen better standing up. I always stand up at concerts and confessions."

"You're not going to listen to anything," Ed said.

The parking lot was deserted and far back from the street, and I forgot to keep my eye on the chauffeur. He rabbit-punched me and a gush of pain surged into my head. He rabbit-punched me again and my eyes rattled in their sockets and my body became invertebrate. Two men moving in a maze of stars took hold of my upper arms and lifted me into the car. Unconsciousness was a big black limousine with a swiftly purring motor and the blinds down.

Though it leaves the neck sore for days, the effect of a rabbit-punch on the centers of consciousness is sudden and brief. In two or three minutes I came out of it, to the sound of Ed's voice saying, "We don't like hurting people and we aren't going to hurt you. But you've got to learn to understand, whatever your name is—"

"Sacher—Masoch," I said.

"A bright boy," said Ed. "But a bright boy can be too bright for his own good. You've got to learn to understand that you can't go around annoying people, especially very important people like Mr. Neville here."

Terry Neville was sitting in the far corner of the back seat, looking worried. Ed was between us. The car was in motion, and I could see lights moving beyond the chauffeur's shoulders hunched over the wheel. The blinds were down over the back windows.

"Mr. Neville should keep out of my cases," I said. "At the moment you'd better let me out of this car or I'll have you arrested for kidnapping."

Ed laughed, but not cheerfully. "You don't seem to realize what's happening to you. You're on your way to the police station, where Mr. Neville and I are going to charge you with attempted blackmail."

"Mr. Neville is a very brave little man," I said, "Inasmuch as he was seen leaving Una Sand's house shortly after she was killed. He was seen leaving in a great hurry and a green roadster."

"My God, Ed," Terry Neville said, "you're getting me in a frightful mess. You don't know what a frightful mess you're getting me in." His voice was high, with a ragged edge of hysteria.

"For God's sake, you're not afraid of this bum, are you," Ed said in a terrier yap.

"You get out of here, Ed. This is a terrible thing, and you don't know how to handle it. I've got to talk to this man. Get out of this car."

He leaned forward to take the speaking tube, but Ed put a hand on his shoulder. "Play it your way, then Terry. I still think I had the right play, but you spoiled it."

"Where are we going?" I said. I suspected that we were headed for Beverly Hills, where the police know who pays them their wages.

Neville said into the speaking tube, "Turn down a side street and park. Then take a walk around the block."

"That's better," I said when we had parked. Terry Neville looked frightened. Ed looked sulky and worried. For no good reason, I felt complacent.

"Spill it," I said to Terry Neville. "Did you kill the girl? Or did she accidentally drown—and you ran away so you wouldn't get mixed up in it? Or have you thought of a better one than that?"

"I'll tell you the truth," he said. "I didn't kill her. I didn't even know she was dead. But I was there with her yesterday afternoon. We were sunning ourselves on the raft, when a plane came over flying very low. I went away, because I didn't want to be seen there with her—"

"You mean you weren't exactly sunning yourselves."

"Yes. That's right. This plane came over high at first, then he

circled back and came down very low. I thought maybe he recognized me, and might be trying to take pictures or something."

"What kind of a plane was it?"

"I don't know. A military plane, I guess. A fighter plane. It
was a single-seater painted blue. I don't know military planes."

"What did Una Sand do when you went away?"

"I don't know. I swam to shore, put on some clothes, and drove
away. She stayed on the raft, I guess. But she was certainly all
right when I left her. It would be a terrible thing for me if I
were dragged into this thing, Mr.—"

"Rogers."

"Mr. Rogers. I'm terribly sorry if we hurt you. If I could make
it right with you—" He pulled out a wallet.

His steady pallid whine bored me. Even his sheaf of bills bored
me. The situation bored me.

I said, "I have no interest in messing up your brilliant career,
Mr. Neville. I'd like to mess up your brilliant pan sometime, but
that can wait. Until I have some reason to believe that you haven't
told me the truth, I'll keep what you said under my hat. In the
meantime, I want to hear what the coroner has to say."

They took me back to Ronald's, where my car was, and left me
with many protestations of good fellowship. I said good-night
to them, rubbing the back of my neck with an exaggerated gesture. Certain other gestures occurred to me.

When I got back to Santa Barbara the coroner was working
over Una Sand's body. He said that there no marks of violence
on her body, and very little water in her lungs and stomach, but
this condition was characteristic of about one drowning in ten.

I hadn't known that before, so I asked him to put it into sixty-
four dollar words. He was glad to.

"Sudden inhalation of water may result in a severe reflex spasm
of the larynx, followed swiftly by asphyxia. Such a laryngeal
spasm is more likely to occur if the victim's face is upward,
allowing water to rush into the nostrils, and would be likely to
be facilitated by emotional or nervous shock. It may have happened like that or it may not."

"Hell," I said, "she may not even be dead."

He gave me a sour look. "Thirty-six hours ago she wasn't."

I figured it out as I got in my car. Una Sand couldn't have drowned much later than four o'clock in the afternoon on September the seventh.

It was three in the morning when I got to bed. I got up at seven, had breakfast in a restaurant in Santa Barbara, and went to the beach house to talk to Jack Ross. It was only about eight o'clock when I got there, but Ross was sitting on the beach in a canvas chair watching the sea.

"You again?" he said when he saw me.

"I'd think you'd have had enough of the sea for a while. How long were you out?"

"A year." He seemed unwilling to talk.

"I hate bothering people," I said, "but my business is always making a nuisance out of me."

"Evidently. What exactly is your business?"

"I'm currently working for your mother-in-law. I'm still trying to find out what happened to her daughter."

"Are you trying to needle me?" He put his hands on the arms of the chair as if to get up. For a moment his knuckles were white. Then he relaxed. "You saw what happened, didn't you?"

"Yes. But do you mind my asking what time your ship got into Frisco on September the seventh?"

"No. Four o'clock. Four o'clock in the afternoon."

"I suppose that could be checked?"

He didn't answer. There was a newspaper on the sand beside his chair, and he leaned over and handed it to me. It was the late night final of a San Francisco newspaper for the seventh.

"Turn to page four," he said.

I turned to page four and found an article describing the arrival of the USS *Guam* at the Golden Gate, at four o'clock in the afternoon. A contingent of Waves had greeted the returning heroes, and a band had played "California, Here I Come."

"If you want to see Mrs. Dreen, she's in the house," Jack Ross said. "But it looks to me as if your job is finished."

"Thanks," I said.

"And if I don't see you again, good-bye."

"Are you leaving?"

"A friend is coming out from Santa Barbara to pick me up in a few minutes. I'm flying up to Alameda with him to see about getting leave. I just had a forty-eight, and I've got to be here for the inquest tomorrow. And the funeral." His voice was hard. His whole personality had hardened overnight. The evening before his nature had been wide open. Now it was closed and invulnerable.

"Good-by," I said, and plodded through the soft sand to the house. On the way I thought of something and walked faster.

When I knocked, Mrs. Dreen came to the door holding a cup of coffee, not very steadily. She was wearing a heavy wool dressing robe with a silk rope around the waist, and a silk cap on her head. Her eyes were bleary.

"Hello," she said. "I came back last night after all. I couldn't work today anyway. And I didn't think Jack should be by himself."

"He seems to be doing all right."

"I'm glad you think so. Will you come in?"

I stepped inside. "You said last night that you wanted to know who killed Una no matter who it was.

"Well?"

"Does that still go?"

"Yes. Why? Did you find out something?"

"Not exactly. I thought of something, that's all."

"The coroner believes it was an accident. I talked to him on the phone this morning." She sipped her black coffee. Her hand vibrated steadily, like a leaf in the wind.

"He may be right," I said. "He may be wrong."

There was the sound of a car outside, and I moved to the window and looked out. A station wagon stopped on the beach, and a Navy officer got out and walked toward Jack Ross. Ross got up and they shook hands.

"Will you call Jack, Mrs. Dreen, and tell him to come into the house for a minute?"

"If you wish." She went to the door and called him.

Ross came to the door and said a little impatiently, "What is it?"

"Come in," I said. "And tell me what time you left the ship the day before yesterday."

"Let's see. We got in at four—"

"No, you didn't. The ship did, but not you. Am I right?"

"I don't know what you mean."

"You know what I mean. It's so simple that it couldn't fool anybody for a minute, not if he knew anything about carriers. You flew your plane off the ship a couple of hours before she got into port. My guess is that you gave that telegram to a buddy to send for you before you left the ship. You flew down here, caught your wife being made love to by another man, landed on the beach—and drowned her."

"You're insane!" After a moment he said less violently, "I admit I flew off the ship. You could easily find that out anyway. I flew around for a couple of hours, getting in some flying time—"

"Where did you fly?"

"Along the coast. I didn't get down this far. I landed at Alameda at five-thirty, and I can prove it."

"Who's your friend?" I pointed through the open door to the other officer, who was standing on the beach looking out to sea.

"Lieutenant Harris. I'm going to fly up to Alameda with him. I warn you, don't make any ridiculous accusations in his presence, or you'll suffer for it."

"I want to ask him a question," I said. "What sort of plane were you flying?"

"FM-3."

I went out of the house and down the slope to Lieutenant Harris. He turned toward me and I saw the wings on his blouse.

"Good morning, Lieutenant," I said. "You've done a good deal of flying, I suppose?"

"Thirty-two months. Why?"

"I want to settle a bet. Could a plane land on this beach and take off again?"

"I think maybe a Piper Cub could. I'd try it anyway."

"It was a fighter I had in mind. An FM-3."

"Not an FM-3," he said. "Not possibly. It might just conceivably be able to land but it'd never get off again. Not enough room, and very poor surface. Ask Jack, he'll tell you the same."

I went back to the house and said to Jack, "I was wrong. I'm sorry. As you said, I guess I'm all washed up with this case."

"Good-by, Millicent," Jack said and kissed her cheek. "If I'm not back tonight I'll be back first thing in the morning. Keep a stiff upper lip."

"You do, too, Jack."

He went away without looking at me again. So the case ended as it had begun, with me and Mrs. Dreen alone in a room wondering what had happened to her daughter.

"You shouldn't have said what you did to him," she said. "He's had enough to bear."

My mind was working very fast. I wondered whether it was producing anything. "I suppose Lieutenant Harris knows what he's talking about. He says a fighter couldn't land and take off from this beach. There's no other place around here he could have landed without being seen. So he didn't land.

"But I still don't believe that he wasn't here. No young husband flying along the coast within range of the house where his wife was—well, he'd fly low and dip his wings to her, wouldn't he? Terry Neville saw the plane come down."

"Terry Neville?"

"I talked to him last night. He was with Una before she died. The two of them were out on the raft together when Jack's plane came down. Jack saw them, and saw what they were doing. They saw him. Terry Neville went away. Then what?"

"You're making this up," Mrs. Dreen said, but her green eyes were intent on my face.

"I'm making it up, of course. I wasn't here. After Terry Neville ran away, there was no one here but Una, and Jack in a plane circling over her head. I'm trying to figure out why Una died. I think she died of fright. I think Jack dived at her and forced her into the water. I think he kept on diving at her until she was gone. Then he flew back to Alameda and chalked up his flying time."

"Fantasy," she said. "And very ugly. I don't believe it."

"You should. You've got that cable, haven't you?"

"I don't know what you're talking about."

"Jack sent Una a cable from Pearl, telling her what day he was arriving. Una mentioned it to Hilda Karp, Hilda Karp mentioned it to me. It's funny you didn't say anything about it."

"I didn't know about it," Millicent Dreen said. Her eyes were blank.

I went on, paying no attention to her denial. "My guess is that the cable said not only that Jack's ship was coming in on the seventh, but that he'd fly over the beach house that afternoon.

Fortunately, I don't have to depend on guesswork. The cable will be on file at Western Union, and the police will be able to look at it. I'm going into town now."

"Wait," she said. "Don't go to the police about it. You'll only get Jack in trouble. I destroyed the cable to protect him, but I'll tell you what was in it. Your guess was right. He said he'd fly over on the seventh."

"When did you destroy it?"

"Yesterday, before I came to you. I was afraid it would implicate Jack."

"Why did you come to me at all, if you wanted to protect Jack? It seems that you knew what happened."

"I wasn't sure. I didn't know what had happened to her, and until I found out I didn't know what to do."

"You're still not sure," I said. "But I'm beginning to be. For one thing, it's certain that Una never got her cable, at least not as it was sent. Otherwise she wouldn't have been doing what she was doing on the afternoon that her husband was going to fly over and say hello. You changed the date on it, perhaps? So that Una expected Jack a day later? Then you arranged to be in Hollywood on the seventh, so that Una could spend a final afternoon with Terry Neville."

"Perhaps." Her face was complexly alive, controlled but full of dangerous energy, like a cobra listening to music.

"Perhaps you wanted Jack for yourself," I said. "Perhaps you had another reason. I don't know. I think even a psychoanalyst would have a hard time working through your motivations, Mrs. Dreen, and I'm not one. All I know is that you precipitated a murder. Your plan worked even better than you expected."

"It was accidental death," she said hoarsely. "If you go to the police you'll only make a fool of yourself, and cause trouble for Jack."

"You care about Jack, don't you?"

"Why shouldn't I?" she said. "He was mine before he ever saw Una. She took him away from me."

"And now you think you've got him back." I got up to go. "I hope for your sake he doesn't figure out for himself what I've just figured out."

"Do you think he will?" There was sudden terror in her eyes.

"I don't know," I said from the door, and went out.

WILLIAM CAMPBELL GAULT

Marksman

INTRODUCTION

I had been writing (and selling) some sport stories and syndicate stuff in the late 1930's, but my agent, Harry Altshuler, had always been after me to try the detective field, which seemd to be fairly solvent, whereas the sport market, then as now, was erratic. I was just a part-time writer and couldn't see taking any of my limited time to study detectives. I had a new baby and I was afraid of the dark and I was going through some emotional turmoil at the time; so why not be hardboiled about it all? Why not make some money out of my trouble? And maybe if I killed the man, fictionally, I wouldn't be so inclined to slap him in the chops actually. (He was shorter than I was and what kind of trouble he was giving me you'll have to guess; I'm not washing all my linen in public.) So I wrote this emotional thing and got to within three paragraphs of the end—and no gimmick to turn the plot on. The development was logical, but I lacked the mechanical device to reveal my climax.

Well, we had a little amateur writing club in Milwaukee at that time, and there was a guy in there who had more gimmicks than Edison, a guy who even then had the least channeled approach to plotting of anybody I'd read. I went to him—it was Fredric Brown, of course—and he gave me the tool gimmick and everything fell nicely into place.

So I took it home and wrote it, and three nights later read it to a meeting of the club (Allied Authors, Milwaukee) for approbation or disdain. I finished it; nobody said nuttin. The hell with 'em. I went out to the kitchen to stir the cocoa (my wife was out with that guy). Footsteps, and Fred Brown stood next to the stove. "Damn it, I wish I'd written that," he said, and went back to the living room.

Nanovic bought it for Clues *(then a Street & Smith pulp) and when it appeared in the September, 1940, number, gave it the following puff: "In this issue we give you* Marksman *by William Campbell Gault, a brand-new writer to these pages. . . . This is not a detective story according to standard rules and regulations. However, it is one of the best short stories we have read in ages and the fact that it has no detective in it does not, in our opinion, keep it from being a detective story in its true sense."*

After the terrific build-up which went on for another paragraph, the editor paid me thirty-seven dollars.

WILLIAM CAMPBELL GAULT

Marksman

I AM very ordinary. I am of medium height, medium income, average intelligence—strictly middle class. In fact, I'm a little less than ordinary because I lack physical courage.

Still, I murdered a man! My neighbors all know it. The whole country knows it. And when my eighteen-month-old son grows up, he will hear about it. And that hurts more than all the rest. But I couldn't help it. I had to—

I was sitting in my living room. I was reading about the Finns' gallant stand against the Russians and feeling the admiration that weak men feel for the brave. I admired them particularly for the beautiful way they were handling their rifles. I could appreciate that, because in this one way I am a little above the ordinary. I am president of the local rifle club, and last year I won the Southern States Championship.

I was sitting there alone because Alice had gone out to her bridge club and I had to stay home with Buster. There were just the two of us in the house. Buster was in the back bedroom, asleep in his crib. I was in the living room reading about the Finns and I began to feel nervous.

I began to feel nervous because I am afraid of the dark, and if you think that's funny in a grown man, let me correct you. It's sad and damnable and maddening; but it's not funny—not at all.

I put the paper down. It was a gloomy night outside, and the light from the street lamp was haloed in a late spring fog. It was a hell of a night for a man afraid of the dark to be home alone.

I decided to put Buster into the big bed and climb in with him. I am just ordinary enough to enjoy that. I turned out the lights in the living room and was halfway to the bedroom when the phone rang.

I had a premonition as I picked up the receiver. Or perhaps I was just scared. Perhaps, if it had been Alice, I would have had the same chilled feeling. But it wasn't Alice. It was a man's voice, low, muffled.

He said, "It's important that I see you tonight, Mr. Johnson. Where can you meet me?"

I hesitated. "Who is this?"

"It's about the Reform League," he said. "I can't give you my name over the phone."

I knew him for a phoney then. Because if he could say "Reform League" over a phone, he could give his name. There was nothing secret about that. All of us were listed on the league stationery.

My heart began to hammer and I fought to keep my voice calm. I said, "You can see me at my store in the morning."

"No!" the voice said. "I'll be over in about ten minutes."

I started to object but the line was dead.

I was scared. I went into the baby's room and closed the window. I latched it. I looked into his closet. Then I watched him for a second, and I was close to tears. He was lying flat on his back, his hands above his head. He was smiling faintly. I turned off the light and looked out the window into the back yard.

But all I could see was mist and shadow.

From the shelf in my closet, I took out the Camp Perry model Colt that Alice had given me for Christmas. It had a long barrel, but the pockets in my corduroy house jacket were ample. I turned on the porch light and sat down to wait.

This Reform League was the latest attempt to clean up our town. And it wasn't having any more success than its predecessors, because whoever controlled the graft in this rotten little metropolis was in absolute control.

The police dragged in hoodlum after hoodlum and turned on the heat. They even pulled in one poor snowbird and kept him off the stuff for a week. He was about ready for the asylum then, but it did no good. Nobody would break.

All the law could do was sentence them; squealing would mean certain suicide.

I had been made an honorary member when I won the Southern States and had promptly forgotten all about it. But evidently somebody else hadn't.

I shivered a little and looked out the window. I hoped against hope that Alice wouldn't come home early. Then, as I fingered the Colt in my pocket, the doorbell rang.

I could feel the hair on my neck bristle, and my hand on the doorknob shook. The man standing on the porch was about my height, but broad.

I said, "Come in."

He didn't say a word as he walked into the living room. He was foreign-looking, with a bluish cast to his beard stubble, and dark, murky eyes. He sat down on the room's biggest chair and tensed on its edge.

He didn't give me a chance to open my mouth. He said, "You're a good shot with a rifle? An expert?"

I nodded.

"We've got a job for you—to kill a man!"

I was plenty scared. But I took out the Colt. I said, "What's to prevent me from doing that right now?"

I was the only frightened person in that room. He said, "Put it away. You could kill me all right. But your wife—and the kid—" He shrugged "The boss never makes a mistake. You'd better just sit and listen."

I thought of Alice and Buster. I sat down shakily.

He said, "Bruce Barnum is going to give a surprise talk at the band concert in the city park. He's got some names to name and dirt to spill. You will be in the loft of that garage across the street. You will kill him from the window with a rifle. The boss thinks it should put an end to all this reform stuff. The boss is getting annoyed with all these reform movements that keep popping up."

Bruce Barnum was head of the league. He was fearless and a bachelor. That's why they'd picked him for the job. And he was my friend. I told Bluebeard that.

He shrugged again. "Even if I felt sorry for you, it wouldn't make any difference. I work under orders."

I said slowly, "There's quite a bit of money represented on the league board. It would be worth all we could raise to learn the name of the boss."

He smiled faintly. "I'm one of the few guys who know that. And there isn't enough money in the world to buy my life." He paused. "We've tried to get Barnum a couple of times. But he's pretty well guarded. That's why we have to do it from a distance. And you just happen to be the unlucky guy."

"And if I refuse?"

For the third time he shrugged. "Maybe you, maybe your wife or the kid—"

I almost went for the Colt again. But it would do no good. As he said, he was only working under orders.

As he rose to go, he said casually, "Don't look so sick. Murder's a little tough the first time. But you get used to it." His eyes fell on the paper. "They're sure getting used to it in Russia."

The whole thing was like something out of a gangster movie, one of those wild B pictures. But this was no movie. This was happening to me, George Johnson, citizen. I tried to get a grip on myself, reason sanely. But my mind was numb.

At the door, Bluebeard said, "We'll get in touch with you again, probably tomorrow."

I only nodded.

I went back to the living room and sat down again. I was still sitting there, staring dumbly at nothing, when Alice and Fred Lock came in.

Alice said, "Why George Fraidy-cat Johnson! Don't tell me you saw another ghost?"

I tried to smile. Fred Lock was looking at me curiously.

Alice sensed, then, that this was something more than my usual home-alone nervousness. "What happened?" she asked.

I hesitated. It was Fred who had nominated me for the league. If I told anyone, I could tell him. But I shook my head. "Nothing happened," I said. "I don't feel so well."

Fred left then, and Alice said, "You're not jealous, are you, George? I mean . . . I know he's been around a lot lately, but—"

That was almost funny. Alice and Fred had been practically engaged all through college. Then Fred went to law school and I stepped in. Fred just couldn't keep away from her, now, and I wouldn't have liked that if I hadn't trusted Alice a hundred per cent.

"I'm not jealous," I told her. "I'm a little fagged out. There's been a lot of trouble at the store lately, spring inventory and all." I knew then that I'd never be able to tell her.

I remembered Bluebeard's comment, and I tried to tell myself that mass murder was going on in Europe; that I had to do this for my family. But I couldn't. I'd never even been able to go hunting, and, now, I was expected to kill a man.

I wasn't worth anything at the store next morning. I thought of taking the family out of town. But I would probably be trailed, and I didn't have the money to re-establish myself in another town.

There was a luncheon meeting of the league at noon. I had to stay active to keep from going crazy so I attended.

When Bruce Barnum got up to speak, I kept my eyes averted. I kept seeing a bullet hole in his high forehead, blood in the grayish-black of his hair. Nausea stirred in me. Fred Lock was sitting next to me, and he whispered, "What's the matter, George? You still sick?"

I nodded.

Barnum was saying, "I want you all to understand that the police are one hundred per cent behind us. There have been rumors—and one of the papers has hinted—that a corrupt police department is partly responsible for this town's criminal record. I have investigated this thoroughly for the past month and have proved to myself that the rumor has no basis in fact. I wish you would give this information all the publicity within your power. I know an—"

I couldn't listen any more. I mumbled something to Fred about explaining to the others; then I slipped out the door.

But, outside, there was no place to go. I could have gone back to the store; but it's a sporting-goods store, and I feature a complete line of rifles. I didn't want to look at any rifles this afternoon. I got into my car and headed for the country.

It was beautiful. The mist of the evening before had brought out all the sleepy beauty of our southern spring. The sun was hot, but the sun could never get too hot for me. I love it too well. Which is just another way of saying I hate the dark.

I think, if Bluebeard had approached me in the daytime, I would have shot him.

My mind went back to the luncheon. I remembered Barnum's words regarding the police department. Perhaps—just perhaps—the police had uncovered something new. I turned the car back toward town.

My association with the league gave me a few privileges and I had known the chief of police since boyhood. He shook his head at my question.

"Nothing new, George. It's the same old story, and it will continue to be the same story until we get the headman." He shook his bushy head hopelessly. "Terror rules this gang. If we could get the boss, the organization would dissolve. I know that as well as I know my name. I'm willing to admit that we've hit a new low in the viciousness of our third degrees; but not a man will break. They're scum, every last one of them, but their fear of the boss is greater than their fear of us."

I knew that too well. Because here I was, three feet from the law, and I was no criminal. Still, I couldn't say what I wanted to say. I couldn't tell an old friend about Bluebeard, I couldn't go to the law which I was pledged to uphold. It was like living under a dictator—a criminal dictator! It wasn't American.

Oh, I cursed myself silently. And I was thoroughly ashamed of my yellow streak. But I didn't say anything. That, really, is what is important. I left, and again I had no place to go.

Then I remembered I had to go one place. Fred Lock had borrowed my Varminter a few weeks ago for a local meet. It was the gun I intended to use. I drove over to the boulevard.

There was a black sedan in the drive. If it was Fred's, it was a new one. But it wasn't Fred's. A little man in a loud suit was sitting in Fred's study when the butler ushered me in.

Fred was saying, "And you can tell your boss that I have no price. You can tell him that it's only a matter of weeks, now, before we bust his rotten ring wide open. Now, get out of here!"

The little fellow growled something, shot me a scornful glance and walked out.

Fred was smiling grimly. "One of the big boy's stooges trying to buy me off. I'd have thrown him in jail if I thought it would do any good."

I said something about his courage, and he shook his head.

"It's not courage. I have all the money I need and enough love for my home town to fight for it."

I asked for my gun, and he lifted it from the rack in one corner of the room.

"It's a beauty, George. If you ever want to sell it—"

After I used it, I would be glad to give it away. But I didn't tell Fred that.

It was late enough now to go home. And I dreaded it because the more I saw of Alice and Buster now, the more I would miss them later. For I knew, despite my weakness, that I could never again face them unless I confessed. And that would mean a life sentence, at least.

Buster was in one of his playful moods. For a half-hour I tried to share that mood; tried to hide the sickness and the fear within me. But it was hopeless. I went down into the basement to load some cartridges. As I passed through the kitchen, Alice looked at me curiously. But she said nothing.

I have all the paraphernalia for making my own cartridges, including a mold of my own design. It would be possible for me to make a bullet which would hit Bruce Barnum between the eyes and still not kill him.

For a moment I toyed with the idea. It would be possible, but the results would not be a certainty. And if Bluebeard's boss should suspect—I shivered.

I heard Buster's feet on the floor above; heard Alice moving about the kitchen. I was a weak man, but I could commit murder for them.

I compromised then. Two of the cartridges carried the regular load; the third I loaded lightly.

I put the gun in a machine rest and fired it with the light load. Then I examined the pine board I had used as a target. If I were to use a load that light, I would have to compensate for the comparatively short distance from the garage loft to the bandstand. And Bruce Barnum would be blind for life, even if I didn't kill him!

I made another of the light cartridges before Alice called me to dinner. I would take it along, tomorrow night, and perhaps I would have the nerve to use it.

Bluebeard called at ten o'clock. "Tomorrow night's the band concert," he said. "I'll pick you up in front of your store at eight."

I mumbled something and hung up.

Back in the living room, Alice put down her paper. She said, "I want to know what's wrong, George." Her blue eyes were filled with worry. "Don't tell me it's business. And it's not your health. It's something a lot more important than either—and I want to help."

I was silent for seconds. Finally, I said, "You'll know by Saturday. It's about the league and I'm pledged to secrecy. But I promise you'll have all the details by Saturday. Everything will be clear by then."

Quietly, she asked. "Is it dangerous George?"

I nodded. "It's dangerous, honey. But I have to go through with it." I looked at her squarely. "Remember, honey, that whatever I do, I do for you and Buster. I'm not the cinema type, but you can believe that no one could love you more than I do."

She smiled then, and there was more than love in that smile. There was admiration, and that was something I didn't deserve. I kissed her humbly.

That night was sleepless of course. And I will never remember the next day. I was going through the mechanics of my regular routine. But behind the front, I was a jumbled mass of nerves, and I knew that without some form of opiate, I would be a poor marksman that night. All the long day I fought myself, and by six o'clock I had regained some semblance of normalcy.

I had brought my rifle down in the morning; so I didn't need to go home for dinner. I decided to eat at a restaurant, and then come back to the store to meet Bluebeard.

I called Alice.

"This business," she asked hesitantly, "Is it coming off tonight?"

"It is," I said.

The line was quiet a moment. Then, "You took your rifle this morning, George—that new one."

"I did," I said.

Her voice was almost a whisper, now. "I'll wait up for you, George. And—I'll pray."

I was physically sick for the next fifteen minutes. I decided not to eat. I locked the store and turned out the lights. And for the next two hours, I walked the streets.

I don't know what streets. I walked and cursed. I cursed myself and the criminal boss. I even cursed Barnum for starting the league. But, mostly, I cursed myself.

I was in front of the store at eight o'clock. And a big black sedan was waiting. The front door was open. Bluebeard was behind the wheel. I got my gun and came out again.

Without a word I climbed in. Bluebeard just nodded; then he swung the big car away from the curb and up toward the city park.

The park was nearly filled when we pulled into the alley alongside the garage. The huge bandstand was brilliantly lighted; the shell behind it looking like an inverted sea shell, magnified thousands of times.

Bluebeard said, "You've got a good white background there, and the lights in the garage will do."

I said nothing.

Only one man was in the lower part of the garage. He watched us as we silently climbed the stairs to the loft. He may have been an accomplice or he may have been another me. I didn't know, and I didn't care.

The loft smelled of oil and rubber and dust. At one end, the window was open toward the park. The light was all right, and it was an easy shot. And my nervousness was gone. I was an inanimate piece of flesh at the moment. A murderer!

There were three men on the bandstand, three men in evening clothes. Their black suits stood out against the shell of the rostrum. The middle man was Barnum. The man on the left, the man who was rising to speak, was Fred Lock. He said over the public address system, "We have a surprise for you tonight—"

I didn't listen; Bluebeard was talking. "We thought you might try to pull a double cross; so I brought along a cartridge that we know will do the trick. I'll have those you have in your pocket."

I handed him the three I had brought along. He took a stand against the opposite wall. The muzzle of his automatic was on me and it didn't waver a bit.

I broke open the breech. From force of habit, I weighed the cartridge in my hand; glanced at it. For a second my heart stopped beating.

That mark on the rim! Was it— It was, beyond a doubt. And the bullet had been cast in my own mold. The taper was unmistakable, and so was that mark that had been made when my tool slipped—the J-shaped mark that wouldn't be duplicated in a million shells.

It was one of the cartridges I had given Fred Lock!

All the incidents of the past turbulent days came to my mind. The car in Fred's drive, the same that had carried me tonight. I had caught him unawares, and he had covered his windy speech to the little fellow. And tonight's talk was to be a secret among the members of the league. Yet, Bluebeard had known the night he first came to call. And I remembered that Fred had been a poor credit risk two years ago; while today he was wealthy. And he had always coveted Alice. He would want me out of the way!

I snapped the gun shut and laid it on the sill. I wasn't afraid. I wasn't nervous. I was something far worse than that. I was filled with hate!

I knelt behind the rifle, my hands steady. I caught Fred's forehead in the scope. I pulled the trigger gently.

It was an easy shot.

It wasn't courage that filled me when I turned to Bluebeard. I was beyond courage. I wasn't even fully conscious.

"I missed Barnum," I said.

His face was stoical as he crossed the room toward me. He had the automatic jammed in my ribs as he looked out the window. The people were streaming onto the stand, but he saw what he wanted to see.

Then he turned to me, and still I felt no fear.

"Maybe," he said softly, "you didn't miss. You'd better git; nobody's coming this way, yet." .

I said, "You mean you're not going to—"

"Nobody wants to kill," he said. "Not even me, unless there's money in it. And who'd pay me, now?" He threw the automatic behind a pile of tires and clomped down the stairs, out of my sight and out of my life—

I was cleared of course. Especially after a police search of Lock's papers. And our town is clean. But I killed a man! And it doesn't help to know I had to. My guns are sold, my beautiful guns. And fishing isn't in it with target shooting.

But I suppose I'll learn to like it after a while.

HARRY STEPHEN KEELER

Victim No. 5

INTRODUCTION

The short story destined to become entitled "Victim Number 5," and also the skeleton structure of a mystery novel, popped into my head at one and the same moment, while crossing the State Street Bridge in Chicago one sunny summer morning long ago.

Why this amazing happening should have taken place is quite beyond me—for the lugubrious view from the bridge was but the greenish sluggish Chicago River flowing backward out of the Lake, a dilapidated freighter tied up at the docks, a street just off the river filled with excitedly screaming Italian banana peddlers getting their previous day's stock from ramshackle commission houses.

The short story was immediately written up, and it sold—on its very first trip out—to Courtland Young, publisher of Young's Magazine, putatively a "magazine of realistic stories"! And Mr. Young rendered the writer of it the munificent sum of ten dollars.

But a really satisfying sum, at that! For it enabled this scribe to pay up four week's room rent that was in arrears, and to take out to dinner and the theater his gal, Hazel Goodwin, also a short-story writer, and destined years later to be a novelist in her own right, also a collaborator with this scribe in many mystery novels published in Britain and America—destined, even, to be his wife!—and also, as today, a member of Mystery Writers of America.

But how all this—on ten dollars?

Ah me! The main-floor theater seats then were three dollars a pair. Table d'hote dinners—with even free red wine thrown in!—were sixty-five cents each. Taxicab fare for a swain and his gal from home to Loop was thirty cents each way. And the rent of a cubicle of a broom-closet hall-bedroom looking down on North State Street was one dollar a week. And—

Oh, the novel whose skeletal structure popped into head at same

131

instant? Well, it was many years before it was destined to be meticu-
lously set out in manuscript form. For, like all novels, it did a bit of
maturing. But the most curious feature of this revelation is that that
novel is now being published at the same time as this anthology.

HARRY STEPHEN KEELER

Victim No. 5

THE Strangler was broke again!

That is, to Chicago police and crime reporters who had co-
ordinated his past four gruesome and widely separated crimes—
more or less hypothetically, to be sure—he was known as The
Strangler.

Though his name was, of course, Ivan Kossakoff.

Even though he had been in America for twenty-three of the
twenty-seven years comprising the span of his life, and spoke as
fluent and glib "Americanese" as any native-born American, he
never called himself The Strangler. Inordinately proud as he
was, too, of his calling. As a matter of fact, he never analyzed
himself at all; he did not even know that he liked to kill in the
particular manner he did, partly because, possessing hyperdeveloped fingers that were as powerful almost as steel talons,
the use of those fingers, at least in the individual way *he* used
them, gave him a tremendous sense of superiority over other
people. That is, they compensated for a certain terrible infer-
iority, deep within himself, due to his smallness of stature. Nor
did he know, either, that he liked also to kill in the way he did,
because—Well, had anyone told him that, held within his complicated Russian make-up, was the mind and soul of a true sadist,
he would have just gazed at such a person pityingly for talking
another language than English.

In fact, he would have naïvely told such a person—that is, were
it possible to reach such a stage of frank discussion about cold-
blooded murder—that he, Ivan Kossakoff, strangled in order to
eat! And would have believed it himself. Because, after all, what
is more important than to be able to eat? Though Ivan would
have admitted, if pressed, that when he "gave somebody the

works," he no longer minded, for some months after, the tall men who gazed condescendingly at him on the street; and that, moreover, his "nerves" got very peaceful—after a good "choke-off" job!

But murderers keep their own counsel. And tell no one—unless, perhaps, it be the priests who attend them on their way to the electric chair—anything.

And tonight, as it has been said, The Strangler was broke. That is, not "stony" broke. For he *did* have four dollars. No—three dollars and fifty cents—thanks to paying twenty-five cents tonight, in the Restaurant Russki on West Chicago Avenue, for that huge bowl of borsch, and twenty-five cents for the plate of herring chopped in sour cream.

So—bowl of borsch and plate of herring—had reduced Ivan's total worldly wealth to three dollars and fifty cents. Some people would have termed that condition merely one of "relative impecuniosity"; but Ivan Kossakoff, fluent wielder of phrases "Americanese," called it being plain "lousy broke." And nothing, he knew, would relieve such a precarious state, whatever one might call it, except another "job"—like the previous ones. For there was, he'd long since found, really no need to work for a living. He had tried that in the long, long ago—and only got hyperdeveloped fingers for doing it. For he'd been a wrought-iron worker, wielding heavy tongs and heavy hammers all day. Making countless ornamental iron palings to go in equally count-less sections of tall spiked iron fences for millionaires' residences. And grillworks to go over gateways. A dull sort of an existence, at best. Now, he had a new way to live. A vastly superior way. A way in which ten minutes' easy work brought as much, sometimes, as ten months' work, at twenty-five dollars a week, *used* to bring—at the forge. For it was really so, so easy to come silently through an open first-floor rear window, approach a bed in stocking feet, and fasten one's steel-like fingers about the neck of a lone sleeper. A judiciously and previously selected sleeper, that is. To be sure, it required a bit of nerve—"guts," Ivan called it—during the couple or so minutes of the short struggle which always ensued in the darkness; but there was little or no chance to fail—at least, not with *his* fingers!—particularly if that powerful right thumb of his were pressed like an ore-crushing plug against the

"patient's" windpipe. Just a question, at most, of holding the
pressure—two—three—four minutes—till the victim went limp
—"wilted," as Ivan termed it!—then waiting a minute or two
further, with grip still unrelaxed, then turning on his tiny pocket
electric flashlight to make sure that the face staring up from
the bed was purplish-black. That always meant conclusively that
the job—at least the troublesome stage—was finished. After that,
nothing ever remained to be done but to scrape together the
valuables—and particularly the money. And get out.

Either this simple way of existence—or else working eight
hours per day.

And *if* you worked, who were you? And what were you? Just
one of a stinking, lousy mob of bastard nobodies. Conscious of
your small stature. Conscious of being browbeaten by your fore-
man. Conscious of the weekly humiliation that lay in taking a
paycheck made out for you by a man bigger in size than you.
For all employers—damn them!—seemed to be big, tall men.
And all foremen, moreover, were—

Such, in general, were the thoughts which constituted the
reflections of Ivan Kossakoff—professional strangler—as he
leaned against a convenient lamp post on Chicago's Near North
Side, this pleasant evening of October 20th, his cap pulled down
over his low forehead, shielding thereby his narrow-set eyes,
and his "valuable" hands sunk deep in his pockets. The darkness
of late autumn had fallen over the entire city, and the lamp on
the iron post against which Ivan leaned had been lighted, now
for over an hour. And though he leaned against the post with
exceeding nonchalance, it is not to be inferred that he was idly
loafing. On the contrary, he was strictly on the job, and waiting
expectantly.

Waiting, in fact, for her who was to be—a little later on
tonight, that is—Victim No. 5!

Questioningly, his eyes glanced toward the clock, visible
through the window of the corner tavern.

8:05 P.M.

She certainly ought to be along soon. For her life, so he'd found,
was as regular a thing as a train timetable. It was right here, in
fact, that he had first seen her, a number of evenings before, as
she strode briskly home after her dinner. Which dinner, he'd

found, was invariably eaten in the little basement French tearoom a half block or so up the street. An expensive dump, too. A
buck for a "table de hoat"—with wine! She was a tall dark girl
—twenty-eight years, perhaps, in age—maybe more. Either she
was disregardful of Chicago holdup men—or else, as was most
probably the case, she knew she was perfectly safe on a well-
lighted street at eight o'clock in the evening. For the diamond
that glistened in each of her earlobes was the real thing—and
Ivan prided himself that he knew scintillations—when he saw
scintillation! For hadn't Aunt Sonya Vointskaya, when he'd been a
boy there on Goose Island, had at least a half-dozen real diamonds
—and given them all to the Russian Church, too, when she died,
the damned old bitch? No, these earrings were, as Ivan put it,
the "McCoy"—showing that he knew the argot of his native-born
criminal brothers as well as he knew jewelry. The eardrops were, in
fact, as "good stuff" as the dinner ring—the "hoop," as Ivan called
it—that always reposed on the middle finger of this girl's ungloved
right hand. To be sure, she had Ivan more or less puzzled. But
because the big first-floor rear room to which she always repaired
after eating her dinner—and immediately went to bed in, and
alone, moreover!—was in a theatrical rooming house just a few
blocks further south on Washington Square, Ivan guessed that
she might be a kicker—a burleycue gal, that is—or maybe a
chorine—now at leisure—but one whose "daddy," during some
previous affair—had "iced her" generously. And even "padded
her purse" as well. Though she might be a principal, at that. An
actress. A "warbler" maybe. Ivan couldn't guess. He had heard,
however, that "frogs" always ate dinner late—and went to bed
right after. And she could well be a "frog" at that. That dark
hair! However, chances were plenty good that there was more
jewelry. For when they wore that much on the street, there was
bound to be more in their bureau drawer. Or in their trinket
case. Plain logic! And besides all of which, those who had jewelry
always had "mazuma." It had never failed yet to be the case. But
the getting of it all had better be tonight, Ivan concluded. For she
might, at that, catch an engagement—join up with some troupe
—maybe a nightclub act—and be out of the city in the wink
of a gnat's eye. No use to risk that. And, having all the data now,
neither was there any more use of following her any longer,

night after night. To check up on her movements. And besides
—the three dollars and fifty cents!

No, tonight was the night!

Tonight was the night to—ah! here she came!

On time as usual.

8:16—by the clock in the tavern.

Eardrops sparkling.

Dinner ring on her finger.

Everything "jake"!

Ivan lighted a cigarette nonchalantly, as she passed.

She vouchsafed him not even a sidewise glance. No flirt, she!
Though Ivan's ego was not, thereby, in the least hurt. For he had
no use for women. That is, in the customary relationships. But
strangling!—ah—there was *something* in strangling a person—
man or woman—it didn't matter—that partook of—of—of
ecstasy. "Had a kick to it," was the way Ivan put it!

A half block behind her. Ivan fell into step. Curious, he reflected, that this was to be the last time he would be trailing her
home. To that three-story and basement dump of red brick which
fixed her status in things histrionic. And that it *was* a theatrical
rooming house, he knew absolutely. For one thing, a kid had
told him so, that afternoon two days ago, while he had been
snooping around there to get "a line on the dame"; and besides
he, Ivan, had that very day seen trunks going in—and trunks
going out—from a huge Parmalee Express wagon—and some
were marked THEATRE and some were marked HOTEL.

But no more checkups now. No more making his way quickly
around to the alley, after this dame closed the front door behind
her, and watching her windows as she turned on the lights. And
timing her movements. Shades down. Lights off. Shades up.
Window up. No more—

She was rounding the corner of Washington Square now. He
kept her well in view. And went on philosophizing.

This beauty with the black hair should be an easy victim. In
fact, the first one of those who had gone before had also been a
woman. A blonde woman. She had died with but a few impotent
thrusting motions of her soft white arms. The next three, however, had been men. They had required a little more skill, a little
more coolness, especially that huge bastard of a German bar-

tender out in Englewood. Wowie—what a fight that Heine had put up! Ivan was honestly convinced that the bartender really hadn't died at all of actual strangulation. The Heine's fat-laden heart, Ivan felt regretfully, had simply given out. But anyway—there'd been too big a run of men. Ivan felt that a little femininity would even things up more. This handsome creature would make the score two to three—and another woman later would balance it.

And even someday, he mused, as he too rounded the corner of Washington Square, he might even strangle a—well, one of those loathsome creatures, with high mincing voices, who call themselves men, but who powdered their faces and used lipstick.

Ugh—such men!

However, all these diversified plans were for the future. A slender, dark-haired woman of twenty-eight should be the strangulation fare for tonight. And tonight was a night, Ivan reflected, when he had just everything he needed to handle her with. Skill and nerve, coolness and practice—four successful stranglings, now! He had—well—everything. He was a strangler who had all that the gods could give—to a strangler.

As the girl tonight ascended the front steps of the red-brick house and shut the street door behind her, Ivan drew to a stop. All O.K.! She'd gone straight home, as always before. That was all he wanted to know. He shrugged his shoulders and laughed curtly. Long before this time tomorrow, the capitalistic newspapers would be out with their glaring headlines reading: THE STRANGLER WORKS AGAIN! and ACTRESS FOUND MURDERED IN BED—VALUABLES MISSING! And he, Ivan, the cause of these extra editions, would be at peace in mind and body, and snug in his attic room in the cottage on Goose Island owned by Grandma Malakovsky—deaf, half blind, and half lame—would be counting currency, and estimating the carat weight of a few diamonds, plucked entirely from their incriminating settings. Preparatory to selling them, after a few months or so, to a certain bearded Bulgarian fence, on Blue Island Avenue—a fence who asked no questions whatsoever. Lest he be asked plenty himself. And in a hangman's court at that!

Swiftly, now that the street door was closed, Ivan circled half around the block and into the dark alley back of the red-brick house, where he secured a position of vantage between two ash-

cans and watched the girl, already entering her room and lighting
the electric bulb. A minute later, she drew down the shades of
the two tall old-fashioned windows. Everything "oke"! That
always meant that she was turning in. A "frog"—as sure as shooting. Or else an early-to-bed dame, making up for all the beauty
sleep she'd lost by hitting countless tank towns on countless tank
railroads. Or else—but what did it matter, anyway? He continued
to roost patiently. Perhaps twenty minutes. Then, the lights
went suddenly out. The shades were raised. And one window
was opened wide, by a silk-nightgowned figure, momentarily in
view, to admit the cool fresh breeze from the lake. Good old lake!
It had obviated four times now the use of either putty and glass
cutter, or jimmy. Ivan leaned much on the lake—because it made
for wide-open windows.

An hour passed.

He was as patient as he was immobile. Almost a human ashcan
himself!

And now, he concluded, the right moment must be at hand.
In fact, Ivan had read somewhere that the first half hour in sleep
was a bit restless; but that that was followed by a profound sleep
which generally lasted three hours. And then—light sleep again.

As a matter of fact, that German bartender had even been
snoring after but twenty minutes of sleep.

Ivan went over the low board fence silently, and crossed the
soft dirt of the yard without a sound. And stood silently next the
equally low fence that separated the two back yards. For that was
the fence, level about with the very sill, that gave in to the open
window!

But before removing his shoes and climbing up on it, Ivan
exercised his fingers vigorously for a few minutes. There was a
little coolness in the air. And one's fingers must not be stiff at the
crucial moment.

It required but a few seconds to climb catlike up on the fence,
and from there, being now in stocking feet, to pass to the sill of
the tall open window, and thence to step lightly in through the
window itself to the floor of the room. Quickly he moved off a few
feet sidewise from the line of the window, and then, for a very
short while, stood motionless, listening to the regular breathing
of the sleeper. Perhaps because there was the slightest trace of a

red glow in the sky tonight from the steel mills of South Chicago and Gary, or perhaps only because of the tall streetlights on Chestnut Street, the next cross-street to the south, their effulgence streaming a bit above the roofs of the dark houses silhouetted against that slightly reddened sky, he could partly make the girl out in the big bed next one wall.

All right! Now to give her the works! Strange shivers of delicious anticipation began to circulate up and down his spine.

He started toward her.

But stopped short.

For he heard footsteps. Up the hall a considerable way—some narrow hall, or perhaps even the great hall, that lay outside the room. Footsteps as of two people. And the faint murmur of their voices. A man, one of them. The other, a woman—yes. Ivan did hope, as he scratched his chin dubiously, that the pair of fools wasn't intending, by any chance, to knock on this very door. And thereby awaken the girl on the bed. And thus ruin everything. What an exit, then, for a professional strangler to have to make! Scuttling out like a flea-bitten cat sent scurrying by a thrown tin can. Humiliating!

Whoops! He wasn't sure he could even stand such a thing. Particularly if the son-of-a-bitch who knocked—and thus frustrated him—was the man, and was, moreover, a tall man.

The footsteps continued, however, to approach the room, rather than to recede from it. Though quite leisurely. More talking, really, than walking. Hm! Lucky, at that, Ivan reflected, that his fingers weren't clamping flesh right now—much as they itched fearfully so to do. He wondered curiously—and for the first time in his professional life as a strangler—just what an interrupted strangulation would be like. The victim, for one thing, would recover. Maybe to identify him!

He looked hastily about him in the semidarkness. No use to scuttle out just because people strolled and walked about in the outside hall. No need, in fact, for everything to be ruined—even if they *should* knock. For there must be a closet somewhere in the room. His eyes swung about in the half gloom.

And stopped.

Then with catlike tread—and extra long steps—he crossed the floor to the opposite wall.

Good!

It was exactly what he had made it out to be in the murk. Not a closet, to be sure, but a huge trunk. He tried the lid. It was unlocked. For it raised. Though he was conscious of a small block of wood tumbling from under it to the floor. He raised it noiselessly the rest of the way up. With his hand he groped far down within. Excellent! The tray had been removed. He felt clear to the bottom. Perfect! For the trunk was empty as well. This would be as good a refuge as any closet while those fools outside should either come to the door and knock, or go on about their business.

He stepped in one end of the trunk with his right foot, and followed with his left. Then he sunk quickly to his knees and allowed the cover to drop slowly with his lowering shoulders till an opening of only an inch in height remained.

Through which he listened.

And—by Godfrey!—he'd guessed right!

"Rap-rap-rap," came from the panel of the door. Though gently. Experimentally. Then the sound of a man's voice, coming seemingly more through a glass transom above the door, than the wooden door itself; and a transom, moreover, painted—as such so frequently were in rooming houses—opaquely black, since no light came through it. "Mimi?" the man exclaimed. "Are you asleep yet? I've a girl friend here who'd like very much to—" But the speaker broke off, as one waiting.

And no answer came to his request. The girl in the bed was, indeed, a sound sleeper.

"Well, she *is* asleep all right," continued the man's voice, to his companion. "She always turns in very early when she isn't putting on the act. And sleeps the sleep of the seven sleepers, too! Well, we won't disturb her. Come downstairs to the basement with me, Nell—and I'm sure she won't object to my showing you what I can—of the props."

The two callers left the region of the door. Entirely. In fact, their footsteps seemed to be creaking now basementward. On some rear stairway. Becoming ever fainter. "But better to wait two or three minutes," thought Ivan, "till everything's quiet again, before giving the dame the works. Those fools *might* change their minds—and come back." He let the heavy lid rest on his shoulders and altered his position a trifle.

"Click!"

It was the sound of the spring fastening on the "trunk," as the upper half of the mechanism, no longer held away from the lower half by that tiny block of wood which had presumably been propping up the cover a half inch or so, came in contact with that lower half and locked the cover shut.

And when, some two and a half hours later, Mademoiselle Mimi LeCompte, professional snake-handler, and known as "Mimi, the Reptile Queen," awoke with a sense of terrible uneasiness, and lighting the lights in her room went to examine her newest acquisition, her Indian Python, she took but one look before she screamed at the top of her voice and fainted dead away. For the python—though safe within his box—was coiled tightly around the neck of a little man whose face was unrecognizable on account of its purplish-black hue, its bulging eyeballs, and its protruding tongue.

JEROME AND HAROLD PRINCE

The Man in the Velvet Hat

INTRODUCTION

Perhaps not this story, but, certainly, a story like it had been swirling around in our minds for a long, long time. It was to be a different kind of story. It wasn't going to be precisely a fantasy, or a mystery, or a psychological drama, or an adventure—and yet it was to be all of these things, and something more. And, because it was a strange kind of story that was rapping at our consciousness, we were going to tell it in a strange kind of way. We were going to devise a style that would not only create the mood of the piece, but also underscore and point up the action, much as music does in the cinema.

This is what we wanted to do. But the truth is: we considered it a hopeless waste of time ever to try to do it. We knew that the slicks would flip it back before they got through the first paragraph, and it was ridiculous even to consider the pulps. But where else was there a market? There just wasn't any.

Then one night, one of us walked into the railroad station in Kingston, New York, and picked up the first issue of a new magazine. By the time he had come home to Manhattan, he was convinced that there was at least one magazine that would give our kind of tale a sympathetic reading. That magazine, of course, was Ellery Queen's.

We decided to go ahead. The plot was spun without any effort at all one evening at Jerry's apartment while we were tossing around the classic horror story theme of "the city in panic." Writing the story wasn't as easy. We were both employed, so the words were put on paper whenever we could: in the morning before the subway, after hours, on weekends, on holidays—six weeks in all. Then we typed the manuscript ourselves, stuffed it in an envelope, and sent it to: The Editor, Ellery Queen's Mystery Magazine.

Two weeks later, the manuscript came back. But with it came a letter from a man named Fred Dannay who, we were surprised to learn, was one-half of Ellery Queen. The letter, which was three pages long, was

142

actually a short lesson on how to write the detective story. "But if you're willing to do some more work," Dannay wrote, "try me with it again. The yarn gripped me."

Try to stop us now! We rewrote, shot the manuscript back. Then we waited. How many years? One hundred? Two hundred? Actually, about three weeks—and this time, Dannay bought "The Man in the Velvet Hat." We received $150 for it—and a long moment of exhilaration that has never quite been matched since.

JEROME AND HAROLD PRINCE

The Man in the Velvet Hat

THERE were no searchlights that night. Far down at the end of the corridor, black, no moonlight through the long open windows, voices, low then loud, slipped through the concrete from the office behind the walls, loud then low, a mumble, a chatter, a senility of sounds. Then a block of light crashed into the hallway—the door of the office was swinging back—and the sounds became laughter, voices, a clarinet's tune—*Come on along, Come on along, Alexander's Ragtime Band*—and the doorknob cracked hard against a retaining wall. Shadows, three dimensional, bulged into the doorway; the block of light was veined with moving strata of black, of gray—*It's the best band in the land*—someone, soprano, was singing; voices were hiccoughing, saying, good-by, Merry Christmas, good-by, Merry Christmas, good-by, good-by. Good-by, a deep voice answered, good-by, good-by, good-by—*played in ragtime, Come on along, Come on along, Alexander's Ragtime Band*—Merry Christmas. Then the shadows stumbled back from the doorway; the man, alone in the corridor, the light upon him, wobbled, grinned, wiped lipstick from his face, straightened his tie, his hat. The office door clicked shut. There was no light now, and only a whispered jazz tune growing fainter; and the man's footsteps sounded loud as they moved up the corridor, sounded louder as they moved more rapidly, seemed one burst of noise as the man began to run. And then there was no sound at all.

When the police found his body in the alley two hours later, there was something ugly where his head had been. The short investigation that followed was decisive. Within an hour, the police had learned that the dead man was a boiler salesman, John Mongon; that he was twenty-six-years old, had no enemies; and that his death could not possibly have resulted from foul play. Both the plain-clothes men assigned to the case and the local uniformed officer agreed that Mongon, drunk, or, at least, strongly under the influence of liquor, had left his company's Christmas party at 11:00 P.M. on Monday, December 17th, during the height of a practice blackout; that, unable to find his way in the dark, he had walked by the elevator shaft, and, then, somehow, had slipped and plunged through an open casement window. It was death by accident, and so far as the police were concerned, the case was closed, despite the morning mail which brought the same letter to Magruder as it did to Reynolds.

Magruder probably never saw the letter that day—it must have been pigeonholed by that clerical machine which is efficient because it has learned not to discriminate—or, if he did see the letter, he had seen so many like it in his long career as a police official that he must have returned it summarily for the clerical machine to pigeonhole. But Reynolds had to see the letter; he had to read it; it was his job. For years now, as a feature writer of that New York daily, as a contributor to the smartest of the slick magazines, he had made a reputation by describing, as Stevenson and Arthur Machen had once done, the romance lurking just beyond the pavement: the unusual, the macabre which rubbed elbows with you in the Polo Grounds, on the B.M.T., along the Bowery, in the middle of Central Park. His early works —he was very young then—were brilliant fantasies, derivatives of James Stephens, Lord Dunsany, Charles Fort, with, if you can imagine it, a strong dose of Ben Hecht and a good deal of O. Henry. But, as he, and his bank account, grew fatter, the rigid discipline which is necessary for the creation of the unreality which is real, was, after a small struggle, forgotten, and his poetry became facts, his dreams, articles. People had come to him— all sorts of queer people—telling him queer tales; and letters, from Massilon, Ohio, and others with strange stamps and stranger script had brought the outré into his study. Most of those yarns —the identity of Hitler's wife, the man who was Crater, the route to Shangrila—were, Reynolds had found, amateurish and scarcely original lies; but he had been surprised to learn that some of the stories were true, and he had been even more surprised to learn that the publication of these stories, whether true or not, earned him more money than he had ever made before. It became his practice thereafter to listen closely to his visitors, to read his mail carefully, and whenever something interested him, to place a large red-crayon check on the relevant documents; and sometimes he would investigate these documents before publication, and sometimes he would not.

Check. *My dear Mr. Reynolds, It was My whim two hours ago to take home with Me to Eternity, My son, known in this life as John Mongon.* Monday, December 18th. It was postmarked 1:00 A.M.

Check. *My dear Mr. Reynolds, In a swift chariot, I have taken Edward Tucker home to Glory.* Tuesday, December 19th.

Check. *My dear Mr. Reynolds, Five have been purified by flames, and are at peace within My heart.* Wednesday, December 20th.

Check. *My dear Mr. Reynolds, I have said love little children, and so I have taken her from suffering to Eternal Happiness.* Thursday, December 21st.

Check. *My dear Mr. Reynolds, Let he who is without sin cast the first stone, so she, too, now knows her God.* Friday, December 22nd.

Check. *My dear Mr. Reynolds, I saw Peter Savitcky today and I knew he was a good man. Peter Savitcky is no longer with you, but with Me in Celestial Happiness; and you must not, John Reynolds, hope that I shall come for you, for I have not willed it, and your time is not yet come. Nor will I be pleased if you seek me out, even though you cannot. You cannot find Me, John Reynolds, and do not ask your police to help you. They find criminals, John Reynolds, here they must find a crime.* By special delivery, Saturday, December 23rd.

Check. *And on the Seventh Day He rested.* By telegram, Sunday, December 24th.

It was with the arrival of the seventh message on Christmas Eve that the events crystallized for Reynolds—and this he reported later—into a Mendeleyev chart of crime, with gaps in the future for events that must occur, with gaps in the past for events that had occurred but had not been observed. It was then that he decided to investigate the incidents of the last week and to find the unknown that he knew must exist. He acted immediately. A telephone call to the office of Western Union brought him no results: the telegram had been dictated from a pay station in the Borough Hall section of Brooklyn; yes, it was a man; no, I couldn't identify the voice; yes, I'm sure. Another call to the local police station wasted a nickel. And the woman who answered the telephone at Magruder's apartment was polite, but nothing could make her admit Magruder was at home. Reynolds dialed another number.

Then without shaving: from lounging pajamas into tweed, a camel's-hair coat, the Hudson on his left, cold wind against his cheeks, the lights of George Washington Bridge growing nearer, behind him now, the screech of his tires on dirty snow, snowflakes on his collar as he stepped from the car. The man was waiting for him, wanting to hear more; but when he heard what Reynolds had to say, he laughed quietly; and when Reynolds continued, excited now, insisting, the man was impatient; and when Reynolds began to argue, his red hair falling over his eyes, constantly being brushed back with a ticlike gesture, the man said, "Listen, mister, I don't know if you are who you say you are, and I don't care. But get this straight. Peter Savitcky was my brother. If anybody knows anything about him, I know, and I'm telling you this for the last time: my brother died of pneumonia and nothing else."

Then the car again, down a Broadway slippery with ice, across town, under an El, over car tracks and cobblestones, dark tenements on both sides of him, then a small brownstone house, shades pulled down on the windows, stained curtains over a large glass door. She answered the bell—her kimono was clinging tightly to her body—"What you want, white man?" she said; and Reynolds talked, as he had to Peter Savitcky's brother, as he knew he must talk; but she just laughed, "Ain't worth worrying about, mister," she said; and when Reynolds muttered something in a low voice, "I ain't afraid. She was a no-good woman and she got what was coming to her. I saw the streetcar cut her in two, and it was nobody's fault but her own. I swear to God—" she kissed the tip of her small finger and held it high in the air—"I swear to God."

He walked now, a few blocks south to a four-story building

of the old type. There was black crepe, already dirty and torn, hanging in the vestibule; the stairs were rotten, insects scurried across the walls; there was black crepe, dirty, too, and torn, hanging on a wooden door two flights up. Inside, it was cold: there was no steam, no stove. An old woman sat on a wooden box, staring in front of her, moaning, softly. When Reynolds spoke to her she whimpered. A neighbor said, "Don't. She's almost out of her mind"; and when Reynolds turned to him questioning, "You're crazy. Her grandmother told her to stay off the ice. A six-year-old girl don't listen. And what could an old lady do?"

He drove across town again, then down the highway, the snow falling more heavily now, the East River dull white, the sound of his tires a soporific crunch; then slush under his wheels as he turned back into the city, pushcarts, delicatessens, slums, a thin red house, skeletal, charred, and a fireman bending his face down to the car window, talking rapidly, and Reynolds answering, arguing, trying to win his point by logic, curses, until the fireman laughed and Reynolds heard him say what the others had said, "But don't you understand," Reynolds still insisted, "that a man smoking in bed could *not* have caused this fire"; but the fireman only smiled, "I don't know anything about that," he said. "Maybe the five guys who were toasted in this little barbecue could tell you more"; and Reynolds shifted gears, cried, "Merry Christmas."

If he were to have continued his journey back into time, his next stop would have been the Coliseum in the Bronx; but the case of Edward Tucker who had made his living driving midget racing cars and who had met his death in one, was more blatantly accidental than any of the others; and, besides, it was now nearly eleven. Instead, Reynolds drove west, stopping at a drugstore near Fulton Street and Broadway. He waited until a phone booth cleared, then spoke into the mouthpiece for several minutes. When he came out, he was sweating, and the night air made him shudder, but he walked up the block to the book-store on the corner, slumped, tired, against the wall of the building, waited. In five minutes, a boy-sized young man wearing an incipient mustache of indeterminate color—pants pegged tightly about his ankles, topcoat hugging his waist, mushrooming widely

over his shoulders, low-crowned, all-brim hat perching on the
back of his head—approached Reynolds uneasily, finally held
out his hand.

"Mr. Reynolds? I'm Larry."

Reynolds took his hand, made the customary remarks, then
spoke rapidly.

"Gee, no, Mr. Reynolds. Gee whiz, no!"

For the next few minutes, his back turned to Larry, Reynolds
read a hundred titles in the bookstore window and remembered
none; then, facing Larry again, he said quietly,

"Larry, this is more important to you than it is to me, or anybody else. Tell me, on the night Mongon fell through the window
did you take anybody up to the party who didn't belong there?"

"No, sir."

"Larry, are you sure?"

"Sure, I'm sure."

"Now, listen, Larry, you know who I am, don't you? That's
right. I can make you a pretty famous fellow, Larry—your picture
in the paper everybody talking about you—if you can remember
what you saw last Monday night."

"I don't get you, Mr. Reynolds. I told you I saw nobody else."

"Are you sure, Larry? Could you swear to it if you had to in
court—particularly if somebody else knew you were mistaken.
Larry, our memories are curious things; they play us tricks. Larry,
try to remember if you brought anybody else up in the elevator
that night—somebody you never saw before."

"Mr. Reynolds, you got me all mixed up. I don't know what
you mean."

"Larry! You know what I mean. Oh, all right, we'll pay you
fifty dollars for your story. Now tell me, what happened when
you saw him?"

Larry said, "Maybe you mean the tall guy who came in at a
quarter to eleven?"

Reynolds said, "Of course. Now let's have it."

Larry moistened his lips.

"He comes in—it's pretty late. I say, 'Floor, please?' He says,
'Twelve' I say, 'There ain't nobody on twelve.' He don't say a
word. I say, 'The party's on sixteen.' He just ignores me. So I
take him up."

"You never saw him before?"

"Never."

"Now what did he look like, besides being tall?"

"You got me there, Mr. Reynolds. I—"

"You must have seen his face. That's a pretty bright light in your elevator. Unless . . . he had his hat pulled down so you couldn't see his face. Was that it, Larry? Did he have his hat pulled down over his face?"

"Sure. That's what it was. He had his hat pulled down over his face."

"What kind of hat was it?"

"Black."

"Black? That's all?"

"Well, an ordinary hat. Old, though. Fuzzy."

"Fuzzy? Like old velvet?"

"If you say so."

"Not if I say so. Was it?"

"O.K., Mr. Reynolds, O.K. It was like you say—velvet. He wore a raincoat," Larry added.

"Good. What color?"

"Pretty dark. Brown. Dark brown."

"That's fine, Larry. Now one thing more, and be very careful that you remember this properly: what time did he come down?"

Larry's face was expressionless.

"He never did come down," he said.

Reynolds opened his wallet.

The remainder of that night was, as Reynolds reported it, an adventure in Freudian psychology: an attempt to restore to the consciousness the memory of the man in the velvet hat which was lost in the hinterland of many minds. (*Now, relax, Bessie. Put your head back on the pillow. Close your eyes—and talk, Bessie. Talk about anything that comes into your mind, Bessie, anything at all. How she walked, Bessie. How she walked when the streetcar hit her. Anything, Bessie, anything that comes into your mind.* a tall man black *Anything, Bessie, no matter how small it is, no matter how silly it sounds.* velvet raincoat a tall man black *No matter how silly it sounds, Savitcky let me know.* a tall man a velvet hat *No matter how silly.*

tall black a velvet hat *Here, grandmother, let me fix the pillow under your head. Just relax, rest, rest, rest.* tall black a velvet hat. *Rest.* atallman a brownraincoat avelvethat *Head back on the pillow.* abrownraincoatavelvet. *Slowly. Slowly.* atallmanatallatallmanabrownraincoat a velvet hat. . . . *A dozen people have sworn that they saw this man talking to the doctor during your brother's crisis. Savitcky, I don't give a damn one way or another, but the police are going to be mighty unpleasant if you deny that you saw him. That suits me, Bessie, but I don't have to remind you that the police and my newspaper might be interested in the business you do. A hundred dollars now; the rest, grandmother, when you find that picture of your daughter. The others swore that they saw this man, surely you're not going to be the only exception?*) And by the morning of Christmas day, Reynolds had in his possession the written testimony of seven witnesses; and by the evening of Christmas day, he said later, he had completed his pattern, and had finished what was to be the first of a series of articles.

In that story which appeared early on the afternoon of December 26th, Reynolds sketched the death scenes of the eight men, the woman, the child, introduced the contents of the letters, stressing the apparent God-substitution schizophrenia; and then made it impossible for the reader to doubt the existence of some agency behind each of the noncriminal acts. How he had searched for that agency and how he had finally identified it as the man in the black velvet hat, he then told in a sequence of exclamation points, culminatitng in an accusation of murder. "But if murder has been done, and if this man is a murderer—" and now Reynolds was writing as he had a hundred times before—"he is a murderer such as the world has never known, or, perhaps, such as the world has always known, but never seen. There is no motive for any of his crimes, no evidence of lust or of envy, of passion or of gain. He kills by caprice, through kindness, by whim, or by some deep underlying necessity. Certainly, if this man is not a God, he has not only succesfully adopted the posturings of one, but the psychic attributes as well. Where he walks, death walks—and this man may be Death himself."

There was no comment on the yarn from Magruder, nothing about it in the later editions of the other evening papers, just a casual reference to it by an obscure radio newscaster; but dozens of people came to see Reynolds, others telegraphed or telephoned, and each swore that he had seen the man in the black velvet hat just before or just after a death by accident or by suicide or by disease. Reynolds remembered particularly, an old Italian woman—her face was a tangle of hard gray threads—who crossed herself as she talked, about her son: dying, slowly, screams clinging to the house, the Blessed Saint and prayer, kissing a silver crucifix as he talked, prayer on bony knees in damp churches, again and again and again, then convalescence in the sunlight, laughter in the sunlight, a blanket over his knees, gay in a wheelchair, laughing, she laughing, too, then a tall man walking in the sunlight, a brown raincoat close to his rib-thin body, a black velvet hat pulled down hard over his eyes, we, laughing in the sunlight, Holy Mother how we laughed in the sunlight, a lean shadow down the street, a lean shadow falling on her son, a silent passing—she kissed the crucifix again —and death. Others remembered that story, too: it was dramatized on several radio news programs almost immediately after its publication under Reynolds' byline; it appeared, rewritten in several current news magazines, in every other paper in New York; it served to introduce the man in the black velvet hat to seven million New Yorkers, and to create, if nothing else, a sense of expectation which was the prelude to the change which came over the city after the eighth letter was made public on Thursday night.

My dear Mr. Reynolds, it read, *Do not deceive yourself. I have been silent, but I have not rested, nor have I ever rested. I shall continue to choose as I have always chosen, as the whim strikes me; and as the whim strikes me, so shall I tell. You will not always know, John Reynolds, how merciful I have been.*

On the following morning, many newspapers began the practice of publishing a daily list of accidental—they printed it "accidental"—deaths in a black-lined box on their front pages; but there was, apparently, no excitement, except in the voices of radio announcers; no panic, except for those few who had seen the man in the velvet hat; no fear, except for the quasi-supernatural warnings of Reynolds and the paraphrases of his colleagues. New York seemed to go about its affairs with its customary indifference; but on that Friday night business began to boom in the night clubs, and flop shows dusted off the standing-room-only signs. The Broadway area during the next few days was so crowded that it often took an hour to walk from Fifty-ninth to Forty-second Street. At the Stork Club, at the Famous Door, at 21, at Fefe's Monte Carlo more people were turned away in one week than had been admitted in the previous six. Eight new jazz bands were imported: six from Chicago, two from New Orleans. The waiting lines to the larger motion picture houses were often as long as two city blocks. There were no cabs to be had at all in the midtown area. At Macy's, in five other department stores, the Bible topped all book sales. Restaurants placed their chairs back to back; and a local comic added to his act a sketch of Casper Milquetoast trying to drink a brimming glass of milk at Dinty Moore's. But on January 5th, all that stopped.

By curtain time of that day, four men and two women had already died, and of the six others at the Polyclinic Hospital, only two were to survive. Most reporters, including Reynolds, credited the first scream ("I did it to warn the others," she said) to a small upholstered woman of about forty; others placed the blame on a middle-aged male neurasthenic, on an unemployed salesman, on a high school girl. But the official report submitted to Magruder spoke of the cause of the panic as a simultaneity of shouts and screams, and of the impossible task of fixing responsibility on any known person: by the time the police had arrived, there was no trace of the man in the black velvet hat, and no one had seen him enter the Radio Building, and no one had seen him leave. But more than two hundred people of the studio audience swore that they had rushed by him just after the first screams—and all New York knew that Reynolds must have received that ninth letter, even though he did not publish it. His column of the next day, denying receipt of the letter, stridently proving—and this was not at all in Reynolds' style— that there could be no connection between the incidents at the radio station and the man in the velvet hat, was met by New York with the same cynicism with which it meets all mollifying propaganda—and it was after that, late on Sunday night, that Reynolds and Magruder came face to face for the first time.

They sat opposite each other, across a small round table, lamplight hushing the ugliness of the room, steam hissing fitfully from a radiator, an old electric clock wheezing, ticking loudly, Reynolds, Magruder, watching each other, listening to the Mayor's footsteps as he walked on the thinly carpeted floor, Magruder a bludgeon, a roll of fat curving over the Mayor's high white stiff collar like a half-baked doughnut, walking, Reynolds sweating, the Mayor talking on and on, pacing up and down, Magruder's eyes hard on Reynolds, on and on, Magruder *Listen, Reynolds, I've been a policeman for forty years. I've seen them come and go. Tricks don't fool me.* The Mayor across the room, his hands behind his back, mop of hair in his eyes, shouting, hands on the table, his face close to theirs, walking again, Magruder saying nothing, Reynolds blinking the sting of a sweatdrop from his eye, Magruder *I've walked beats on nights so cold that fat body of yours would have shrivelled. I have a bullet buried somewhere in my chest.* The steam screeching from the radiator, the Mayor's words drowned in it, weather strips along the windows, fog liquefying against the panes, the Mayor smashing his pudgy fist on the table, asking a question, quiet now.

"Maybe there isn't any murderer," Magruder said. "Not in the ordinary sense."

Reynolds tried to say, then said, "I believe there is."

Magruder went on talking. "The letters that Reynolds got came to us, too. You know that. We checked each one—different typewriter, different stationery, no fingerprints. I don't know if one man wrote them. Or, if he did, he's the cleverest crank I've ever come across. And even if it is the work of one man, there's nothing to connect the writer of the letters with murder. Except for that little picnic at the radio station, every death was accidental or natural as sure as we three are in this room."

The Mayor dragged a small armchair from a corner of the room, forced himself into it, formed a triangle around the table. The clock was ticking more loudly than ever.

Magruder said, "I'd like to put the screws on some of these people who saw the man in the velvet hat. I'd like to bet he'd disappear just like—" He snapped his fingers.

Reynolds stood up. The Mayor talked directly to Magruder.

"Forget it." His shrill voice was always pitched to a key of anger. It hid, perhaps, what may have been other emotional states. "You couldn't prove it if you had until Doomsday to do it, and if you did no one would believe you. To them, the man in the velvet hat is real, and there's a panic."

Magruder lit his pipe, blew out the match. "That's not so. Not in New York. There never will be panic in New York."

"Magruder! Magruder, you think a panic is what happened at the radio station. Somebody screams. 'He's here!' and people lose their heads and trample each other to death. You can't imagine the whole city acting like that. I can't either. But a panic in New York is a cold thing. Listen to me. How's show business? Did you ever see Times Square as empty as you did last night? What was the attendance at the basketball carnival? People are avoiding crowds. They won't admit it. They won't even think of it, but what happened at the radio station, they're afraid will happen again. And they're just afraid. They're scared blue, Magruder."

Reynolds sat down, unbuttoned his vest, straightened his tie, then buttoned his vest. He said,

"Why don't you catch him?"

The Mayor grasped Magruder's coat lapel. "I want to stop all this. Show them that we can stop it—if there is no man in the velvet hat, invent one, and get him."

"That won't help," Reynolds' voice was louder than the ticking of the clock. "He'll murder again. It will be worse."

"I won't do it," said Magruder. "That's not my style."

The Mayor drummed with his child-sized fingers on the liquor-stained, coffee-stained surface of the table; Reynolds looked from one to the other, trying to catch an expression on their averted faces; the steam began to hammer and sizzle in the risers. Magruder knocked ashes from his pipe, a dying cinder glowing on the rug.

"The way I see it," Magruder's tone was speculative, his voice low, "the thing is either a hoax, or there is a man in the velvet hat—perhaps a crank, perhaps a murderer. If we can prove the hoax, or catch our man, the panic, such as it is, disappears. I think we can do it—with Reynolds's co-operation. . . . I'm going to challenge the man in the velvet hat—and Reynolds is going to publish that challenge. I'm going to say that I don't think he's a god, and I don't think he's a good criminal. I'm going to say, I don't even think he *is* a criminal—anybody can boast of a murder after it's happened, but only a master criminal can boast of a murder before it's happened—and get away with it."

The Mayor smiled; his whole face became a series of semicircles curving upward.

"You see the implications," Magruder went on, as slowly as before. "If he doesn't accept the challenge, or if he does accept the challenge and doesn't show up—" He made a gesture indicating finality. "And if he accepts the challenge and tries to succeed, we'll nab him. In either case, the thing is done. Can I count on Reynolds' help?"

The Mayor said, "Yes."

Reynolds had picked up his hat and cane. He was on his feet, walking to the door. He stopped, turned about.

"My own guess is," he was trying to make himself heard above the banging of the steam, the ticking of the clock, "that he will accept the challenge, and that when he does, you will not nab him."

And then it was night again, the Times Building a pale shadow across the street, sounds centrifuged at him, amœba-forms of clouds tasting and disgorging a full white moon, hints of rain slapping his cheeks, jazz from the dance hall overhead, a drunken clown shouting, "Nine o'clock and all's well. Nine o'clock and all's well." *Come on along, Come on along, Alexander's Ragtime Band.* The illuminated dial of his watch told Magruder that it was only three minutes to nine, three more minutes, three minutes to nine. *it's the bestest band what am* Simon and Thompson were in front of the Times Building. Burke and LaMantia were in the lobby. Rowan was across the street on Seventh Avenue. The homicide squad was scattered over the theatrical district. He wanted to, but he didn't dare increase the uniformed police force. No one else knew—only Reynolds, himself, his assistant, Kuchatsky, and the man who wrote the note— written this time in medieval script, delicate colors on yellow parchment. *if you want to hear the Swanee River* Two minutes, two minutes more, two minutes. Anyway, it's over with. After tonight . . . *At nine o'clock, precisely, on Wednesday night, January tenth, a man will die, poisoned, in front of the Times Building. After this I will move again in silence, for only those without faith need signs.* There was a glinting sheet of rain in front of him now. *honey lamb honey lamb* Kuchatsky slipped under the awning dripping wet, a stream of water running from his hat. We thought we had him, Chief. In front of the Majestic, fit the description to a T, turned out to be one of our own boys from Staten Island. They laughed. Another minute, one more minute, less now, less than a minute. *Alexander's Ragtime Band.* Keep your eyes open. Cars were sliding on the water-smooth asphalt. The traffic cops cursed. I see by the clock, Chief, that it's nine o'clock. Done. We'll stick around, maybe his watch is slow. They laughed. Another plain-clothes man elbowed his way through to the awning. He was sweating, but he was grinning. Overhead they were beginning to jam it, bass fiddle throbbing, traps coughing out hoarse subliminals. A man was standing on the Seventh Avenue curb, watching the cars. *ragtime ragtime ragtime* The man was wearing no hat; he was carrying a coat under his arm. He was watching the sliding cars carefully. *come on come on come on along* A trumpet pleading.

The man leapt. Magruder started forward. The man was avoiding the cars, weaving like a basketball player, running hard. Somebody called him a damn fool. He was running toward the wedge end of the Times Building, drenched to the skin.

come on along bugle call in the land in the land

The man was more than halfway across. The traffic cop was shouting at him. Magruder was waving at Simon and Thompson in the lobby of the Times Building. They didn't see him. The man's coat in the dim-out-blackness could have been any color, but it was cloth, tweed.

The man had reached the sidewalk in front of the Times Building. There was some light on him. He was tall and thin. He fumbled in his pocket.

It was the clarinet's lick now. He was warming up, playing it straight for a few bars. *it's the best band in the land   if you want to hear* The man was raising his hand to his mouth, gulping out of a tiny bottle—and then he began to crumble, liquidly, like a trick shot from a motion picture.

Magruder began to sprint. Kuchatsky blew his whistle. Thompson and Simon were already bending over the man. The others were running, too. The traffic cop was trying to hold off the crowd.

Magruder said, "Take him to a hospital."

Simon said, "He's dead as a doornail."

Then Magruder looked at the man. He knew he had never seen that pain-distorted face before, drops of water pounding on open eyes. He knelt and closed the eyelids. Then he picked up the man's coat, held it in his hand. It was light, too light. He shook it. Oilskin glistened where lining should have been. He turned the coat inside out. It was a raincoat, now, and brown. Out of one pocket crumpled, jutted a black velvet hat.

Kuchatsky tugged at Magruder's sleeve. "Look, Chief, the boys say he dropped it just before he kicked off." Folded vellum, tied with a string; Magruder, automatically untying the string, blocked Gothic letters, in red, in blue, rain covering them with a wavering film—*And God*, it read, *so loved this world that He gave His only begotten Son.*

Traffic had stopped; there was an excited crowd whisper all about, but across the street, the jazz men were taking a rest. Magruder began to whistle softly. The tune was, "Alexander's Ragtime Band."

Then the Mayor said, seesawing on the swivel chair behind Magruder's desk, "This is thanks—" winter sunlight breaking against Venetian blinds, the room soft shadows, Magruder leaning under a photograph, Reynolds grinning—"man to man, this is thanks." And Magruder, irritated, playing with the tassels of the blinds, sucking on a long-cold pipe, saying, "Yes, yes, we have a good deal to thank Reynolds for." And Reynolds, easy on the leather lounge, his red hair parted, smooth, the points of his white handkerchief distinct against the brown covert of his suit, bland, happy, saying the proper things—"So, Reynolds," the Mayor said, "this is thanks, but you surprised me. When he died that way, even *I* thought the thing was supernatural. 'Don't have to give me odds,' I said, 'that Reynolds will play it up for all he's worth, and leave us in a worse mess than we were before.' Not surprised?" Magruder's head pivoting in negation.

"Why should you be surprised?" asked Reynolds. "I admit, I'd fancy a supernatural ending to a natural one. After all, that's my trade. But when Magruder told me about the suicide—about his being insane, I mean, what could I think? It was clear then that he couldn't have been associated with the crimes in that inexplicable manner I dreamt of. Actually, there were no crimes; he must have attached his mad ego to each death after the fact. How he got the information so quickly, I don't know; but Magruder says it's easy enough. And once he knew, he appeared at or near the scene of the death in that striking costume, and then he posted the letters. That some witnesses swore he appeared before the deaths, well, that's a human failing, isn't it?

"He was a true psychopath; there's no doubt about that. In his own diseased brain, he was a death-dealing but merciful god, taking to rest those who were 'heavy laden,' or rewarding the good of the earth with the joys of Paradise; and even to the end, he was madly consistent, sacrificing himself rather than admit his inability to meet Magruder's challenge. . . . There was no other way to see it, agreed? That's what I wrote."

"It was enough," said the Mayor. "It brought us back to normalcy." And Magruder striding to his desk, standing over the Mayor, "I have work to do," he said. They, arising, making apologies, the Mayor, his back to Magruder, chuckling, the Mayor, walking to the door, outside in the corridor, Reynolds still in the room, at the door, the Mayor turning to Reynolds, winking, Reynolds adjusting his scarf, the Mayor poking Reynolds in the ribs with his elbow, shouting, "Listen, Magruder. Congratulations to you, too. That challenge idea—it was briliant," laughing silently; and Magruder, head bent over his desk, reports scattered about him, answering softly, "Was it? It amazes me that a hundred lunatics didn't show up, not just one." The Mayor laughing freely now, Magruder head low, footsteps fainter, the glass door closing with a quiver, Magruder busy, reading, annotating, scribbling on a small white pad, yawning, stretching, looking up. Reynolds was standing in front of him.

"Yes?"

Staccato, "It was a queer case, Magruder, wasn't it? Not really knowing . . . All that . . ."

"Yes?"

"I had the right hunch from the beginning. . . . Kept it to myself, you know. . . . Interesting study . . . Lunacy . . ."

"Yes."

"Funny thing, though. About the lunatic, I mean. You never did find out who he really was, did you?"

"Look here, Reynolds, I had you pegged from the start." He turned again to his paper-disarrayed desk.

Reynolds stood where he was. "What do you mean," he asked, " 'pegged from the start?' "

Magruder looked up.

"Interested?"

"Yes."

"Why?"

"I don't know precisely. Curiosity. Was it because you thought I had easy access to the information—my being a newspaperman, I mean?"

"Maybe."

"Do you think I gave the information to the man in the velvet hat?"

"No. . . . I never thought there was a man in the velvet hat. I thought you wrote the letters."

"I? *You* had as easy access to the information as I had. Why didn't *you* write the letters?"

"I had no motive."

"Motive! What motive could I have?"

Magruder said, "I'm an old-fashioned cop, Reynolds, and I always ask, 'Who gains?' You gained—in more ways than one. Do you remember what you wrote after that Orson Welles broadcast. 'If he had done that deliberately,' you said—oh, I don't know if I'm quoting you exactly—you said, 'then it would have been the grimmest but the most satisfactory of literary achievements.' "

"That!"

"Not only that. You had access; you had motive; and it was you who supplied the witnesses and interviewed them before anyone else. It would have been easy for you to have fixed the details of the man in the velvet hat in their minds by suggesting by coercion, by bribery—"

Magruder said, "Maybe we found the typewriters. Maybe we didn't; but if we didn't you can be sure that we will. Maybe I was so sure because I knew beforehand what you'd do after the panic at the radio station. You never could have anticipated the screams of an exhibitionist female—and homicide frightened you. I knew you'd claim there was no letter; I knew you'd deny any connection between the man in the velvet hat and the deaths at the radio station, because the game was getting out of hand, and your wind was up."

Reynolds said, "So that was what you thought."

"That is what I think."

And Reynolds, wiping his face with his pocket handkerchief, "A beautiful theory, Magruder, but spoiled by an ugly fact—" Magruder tilting back in his swivel chair, Reynolds waving good-by, "There was a man in the velvet hat, Magruder—" Magruder filling his pipe, Reynolds, back to Magruder, walking to the door —"and you have him," scarf adjusted, hat set right, hand on the doorknob.

Magruder saying, "But we haven't the man in the velvet hat."

And Reynolds stopping, turning on one foot, facing Magruder, Magruder puffing on his pipe, Reynolds walking slowly again toward the desk, "How do you know?" Magruder laughing.

"Because the man we found dead was released from an asylum *only two days before* you published my challenge. He couldn't have been the man in the velvet hat all those other times—not while he was *in* the asylum."

And Reynolds sober, then frantic, his palms flat on Magruder's desk, his body leaning over the desk, Magruder swinging forward to meet him, Reynolds, Magruder, faces inches apart, Magruder shouting, "You wrote your script. Then you got some poor diseased brain—bribery, coercion, again—to play your principal role."

Reynolds trying to say something, the door opening behind him, a little fat man, perspiring Kuchatsky, happy, shoving the little man in front of him, Kuchatsky, "Here he is, Chief. From a second-hand typewriter store in Flatbush."

Then Kuchatsky pointing to Reynolds, the second-hand dealer squinting, nodding, "That's him!" nodding, nodding, "That's the man, that's the man!"

And Reynolds blurting, "For God's sake, Magruder, listen to me. When I began, I never dreamt—"

Magruder spoke slowly. "I talked to the D.A. this morning," he said "He didn't think we could make a charge of homicide stick. . . . But that was this morning, Reynolds, that was this morning."

AUGUST DERLETH

The Adventure of the Black Narcissus

INTRODUCTION

"The Adventure of the Black Narcissus" was written in 1928, an out-growth of a desire for more stories in the manner of Sherlock Holmes. It was written as the first of an ambitious series of pastiches, after a note from Sir Arthur Conan Doyle conveyed the doubt that he would write more stories about the Master of Baker Street. I was attending the University of Wisconsin at the time, and, on receipt of the letter from Sir Arthur, I drew over my desk calendar, opened it at random, and wrote, "In re—Sherlock Holmes," determined that on that day I would write a pastiche of Sherlock Holmes.

Though I had read and reread Sherlock Holmes and was steeped in the atmosphere of the London of the stories, I knew nothing of London and its environs of the 1920's. When the appointed day came, however, I armed myself with Baedeker's Handbook for London, *and set to work on as "different" a plot as a youth of nineteen could conceive. Thus* The Adventure of the Black Narcissus *came into being in a rooming house on West Johnson Street in Madison, Wisconsin, one spring day of 1928.*

While the market for the pastiche even then was not large, and the story was rapidly returned by a group of established magazines to which it was submitted, it was my good fortune that at the time Harold Hersey was starting a string of new magazines. One of them was The Dragnet. *Hersey had no prejudice against pastiches, and bought* The Adventure of the Black Narcissus *for forty dollars. It made its appearance in print late in 1928 in the issue of the magazine for February, 1929.*

AUGUST DERLETH

The Adventure of the Black Narcissus

IT HAS often been said that truth is stranger than fiction, and I know of no better evidence in support of that statement than the facts attending the adventure of the Black Narcissus, as the crime is listed in my notes. There was little real deduction in Solar Pons's typical vein connected with the case; that is to say, the discovery of the murderer was in itself a comparatively simple problem, but the clue that presented itself was so curiously different that Pons was struck by it at once.

At five-thirty o'clock on a rainy May evening, Mr. Jackson Deming, a stock broker, was found slain in his offices in Paternoster Row. Pons and I had been comparatively inactive that day; we read and wrote; I had little business, for my practice had not at that time taken on much significance. Initial knowledge of the affair reached us at seven o'clock, through the medium of the *News of the World,* which carried two small photographs, one showing the scene of the murder, the other the victim, taken from life. Between the two pictures, in rather well inked print, was a "Wanted":

Wanted for Murder!
A young man of medium height (five feet, seven inches), black hair, dark eyes (supposed brown), full black mustache on upper lip, thin firm lips, long arms; when last seen dressed in gray waterproof and number seven shoes.

It was superscribed "Police Order" and signed Seymour R. Jamison, the Scotland Yard Inspector in charge of the case, and one of Pons's most critical admirers, who very often brought his problems and difficulties to Pons's attention.

Pons, I remember, made some commonplace remark about the matter, and put the paper aside. Rain fell outside, and the twilight was still with that hush which falls along Praed Street just before darkness, so that the distant rumble of the Underground at Paddington made a muted hum in the room.

It could not have been half an hour later when there came a sudden ring at the bell and, before either of us could move to answer it, there followed a wild clatter on the stairs. Pons, who was standing near the window, pulled aside the curtain and looked out. A cab stood below in the driving rain. A moment later the door flew open, and a wild-eyed young man, with a cap pulled low over his forehead, burst into the room.

"Which of you is Solar Pons?" he demanded, looking anxiously from one to the other of us.

Pons stepped away from the window, manifestly identifying himself.

"I am James T. Rudderford," said our visitor, flowing his words together in an agony of haste and obvious fright.

"Wanted for murder, I observe," said Pons. "Please sit down and compose yourself."

The young man pulled his cap from his head and stood staring at Pons with a mixture of fear and perplexity in his eyes, as if he did not know whether he had better turn in flight now or carry on. He did not move to take the chair Pons indicated.

Pons, however, was reassuringly casual. "But for the mustache that you shaved off somewhat awkwardly not long ago—cutting yourself in three places, incidentally—you might fit Jamison's 'Wanted' description as well as any of a thousand or more other young men now in London."

Our visitor collapsed into a chair and covered his face with his hands. "Mr. Pons, I didn't do it."

"I should not have thought you came here to confess," said Pons quietly.

Rudderford raised his head and stared at Pons. "You believe me!" he cried in wide-eyed astonishment. "You don't know then. Every bit of evidence is against me, Mr. Pons—every bit!"

"Suppose you tell us just what happened," suggested Pons.

"Mr. Pons, I am a ruined man. Until yesterday I was moderately wealthy. Today I haven't a halfpenny. I have lost everything through speculation. I do not usually speculate, sir, but I took Deming's word. I had known him for some time, and I had no reason to believe that he was not honest." He shook his head, and his not unhandsome features clouded with sudden anger. "I confess I went up to his office this afternoon to kill him. I'd have done it, too—but someone had got there before me."

"Ah!" exclaimed Pons, his interest manifestly quickening. "Let us start from the beginning, Mr. Rudderford."

"It wasn't until four o'clock that I discovered Claybar Mine had gone under. At first, I couldn't believe it; Deming had assured me that it was a dead certainty to go up. When I saw I was done for, I just simply lost my head. I know I took my revolver, put on my waterproof, and ran out of the house without my hat. I believe I ran all the way to Deming's office. There was no one on the main floor in the halls, and the elevator was not running; so I had to go up the stairs. On the first flight I met an old charwoman descending. There was no one else.

"I got to the fourth story and opened Deming's door slowly, just in case someone were in the outer office. But no one was. I crossed to the inner office, which stood open. I got halfway across that room when I moved into line with the desk in the inner office, and the first thing I saw was Deming's head on its side on the desk, mouth and eyes wide open. For a moment I didn't know what to think; I hesitated; then I went boldly on. I was so angry that it didn't seem to matter what he was doing, and I think I had the idea he was having me a little by some kind of act. But at the threshold I saw what I hadn't been able to see before. Deming was dead. He had been stabbed in the back. Well, sir, when I saw that, I saw it was only by a miracle I had been saved from doing that very thing, and I turned and went back the way I had come.

"When I got down to the main floor, there was a newsboy in the hall—took refuge from the rain, I think. He stepped in front of me and flourished a paper. I brushed him aside and ran out into the street. At seven o'clock I saw the *News of the World,* with my description. I saw then what a net I was in, shaved my mustache, and came directly here."

"Obviously the newsboy described you to Jamison—an observant lad. And your footprints were taken on the stairs. Those are the circumstances of the evidence Jamison has to offer. You have a strong motive, you acted on impulse, you had the intention of committing the crime—yes, you have put yourself into a difficult position. But not a hopeless one."

"What shall I do, Mr. Pons?"

"Since you are doubtless being earnestly sought all over London, I suggest you stay here. I think Dr. Parker and I will go over to Deming's office and have a look around."

Pons doffed his smoking jacket, and put on a light coat and his waterproof. Waiting for me at the door, he turned to our still agitated client and reassured him. "I should not trouble myself too much if I were you, Mr. Rudderford. Let us just see what I can do. Meanwhile, there are books here, if you care to read."

We descended to Praed Street and walked rapidly toward Paddington Station. The rain by this time had deteriorated into a heavy mist, which shrouded everything; wherever one glanced, heavy drops of moisture clung, reflecting light dimly in the murky atmosphere; all sounds were muffled and strange, and there lay in the air from time to time a stray scent of flowers or foliage, as if something of the country air had managed to invade London. We took the Underground at Paddington, rode to Newgate, and walked rapidly over to Paternoster Row.

The building in question was a recently erected office building, five stories high. The constable at the door was young Mecker, still comparatively new to his work, but, as Pons had noticed earlier, rather observant for his limited experience.

He greeted us with a polite "Good evening," adding, "I have orders to let no one pass; but I daresay you may go up. Inspector Jamison's there with the police coroner."

Pons paused to shake some of the moisture from his waterproof and light his pipe. "No doubt the murderer has already been apprehended. I could not help seeing Jamison's remarkably clear description of him in the *News*."

"We've already got thirty suspects," answered Mecker morosely.

Pons smiled dryly. "You should have at least two hundred more by midnight."

"Oh, surely not if they measure his shoes, Mr. Pons; sevens aren't that common."

"Not at all; but that won't be done at once in most cases; and the rest of the man is alarmingly prosaic."

We went up the stairs, seeing at different places sections blocked off, clearly indicating that footprints had been taken there.

"Jamison is thorough," said Pons.

Jamison was walking through the outer office as we entered: a bluff, hearty man, with a closely clipped mustache; the police coroner could be seen in the inner room, though it was obvious that his work had been completed.

"Pons!" exclaimed Jamison. "Whatever brought you down here tonight? I'm afraid this little matter has nothing of interest to offer. Simple vengeance by a swindled investor. We'll have our man in a few hours."

"I wish you luck Jamison. You don't feel, then, that the description you offer through the papers is—shall we say, a little general?"

"Not at all. Taken over-all, not at all general, no sir!"

"Ah, well, a difference of opinion adds zest, eh, Jamison?"

"You'll want to see the body, I suppose?" asked Jamison a little stiffly.

"I did have that in mind."

Jamison led the way into the inner office just as the police coroner came out.

The body of the dead man lay in the position Rudderford had described to us. Projecting from his back was the handle of a common carving knife, driven to the hilt into Deming's body. Pons walked around the body and came back to stand looking at it. It was clear that the knife had been driven into the victim with great force, and I thought of Rudderford, who could easily have had strength enough to use the weapon so forcefully.

"It is not clear who discovered the body," said Pons.

"The charwoman."

"At about what time does the coroner place the murder?"

"At or near five o'clock."

"Where was the charwoman at that time?"

Jamison made an impatient movement. "She was upstairs, cleaning the floor above. She had a good alibi, if you are thinking of her in connection with this. Deming's secretary left at half after four, and stood in the hall talking with the char, who had just come in and was going on upstairs; they talked until quarter of five. When she left, the char went upstairs. The char, incidentally, offers a good alibi for the secretary, for she says she saw Deming at work through the half open door. The broker upstairs, a fellow by the name of Welkins, was still in his office and vouches that the char got there at about quarter of five. She cleaned his office and then the hall; Welkins says he saw her cleaning the hall and stairs as late as twenty past five. Then she came down, cleaning as she went. When she came in here, she found Deming like this. That was about half after five. Welkins was still in his office then, working late, and he called us at once when he discovered why the char had screamed."

During this résumé Pons had been looking around without comment. He had examined the body to his satisfaction, and was now scrutinizing the desk, which was occupied by books, papers, a desk pad, and the various accouterments to be expected there. However, there remained unaccounted for a rather singular object which lay behind a book at the rear of the desk. Pons leaned over and picked it up; it was a single black narcissus, still rather fresh, for it gave off a faint perfume.

"Where was this when the body was found?"

"Near the head."

"So?" Pons placed the flower parallel to the head and stepped back. Jamison nodded thoughtfully.

"Yes, about like that. A little closer to his head, if anything."

"It was moved then. By whom?"

"The coroner, I think."

"Interesting. What do you make of it?"

Jamison was a little taken aback. "Why, nothing. Nothing at all." He hesitated and gazed at the flower again. "However, if you think it significant, I should be obliged to know why."

"Are you aware that a black narcissus is a rare and costly flower, and somewhat out of place in a situation like this? Surely you are not accustomed to finding black narcissi beside your corpses, Jamison! I should place this at about one pound ten."

Jamison made a sound of disgust. "Oh, rot, Pons! Deming was rich enough to buy a carload of the things. Why shouldn't he bring one of them to his office?"

"Ah, and if so, why shouldn't he put it into water, if not in his lapel? No, I'm afraid that will not wash, Jamison. Observe: it is still quite fresh. As a matter of fact, it was removed from the florist's not later than four o'clock this afternoon and reached this desk at approximately five, leaving, as you might have noticed, spots on the desk blotter—raindrops, I submit."

"What you mean is that the murderer brought it."

"Surely it would seem so? Why not just telephone Deming's secretary and ask her if Deming himself brought it after luncheon? Or if it was here in his office when she left for the day, I'll wager she will admit to knowing nothing whatever of this curious flower."

Jamison looked at Pons in bafflement, his inability to follow the trend of Pons's thought quite discernible on his bluff features.

There was, too, a suggestion of aggressive defiance. He turned just as Mecker, having been relieved by another constable below, came into the room, and gave the constable an order to telephone the secretary, who had been asked to remain at her home pending conclusion of the initial phase of the investigation.

Pons now returned to the body and bent to examine the hilt of the knife, looking at it from all sides.

"You noticed this legend burned into the handle, I daresay?" he asked thoughtfully.

"Yes. 'From Emily.' "

"Does it not suggest to you that Deming knew someone named Emily?"

"Oh, that is possible, but surely you don't propose that the murderer left a calling card?"

Pons smiled grimly. "I should hardly need to suggest so obvious a fact. I gave that to you."

"Look, Pons—the knife . . ."

"I am not speaking of the knife," interrupted Pons. "But of the black narcissus."

"Oh, that . . ." Jamison sighed.

At this moment Mecker appeared on the threshold. "Deming's secretary says that Deming did not like flowers, and there was certainly no flower of any kind in either office when she left late this afternoon."

"I put it to you, Jamison," said Pons, "that the significance of the black narcissus cannot any longer be avoided. I earnestly suggest that you concern yourself with discovering the meaning of the flower. I commend to your attention especially the files of the newspapers, which might possibly reveal a connection between Deming and the flower."

Thereupon Jamison burst into a flood of remonstrances, to the effect that, since the murderer was already being sought by the police, surely there was no need to trouble oneself about the appurtenances which had in any case only a dubious relation to the crime. Pons paid little attention to him; he walked to the outer office, seated himself at the secretary's desk, and took up pencil and paper.

Jamison watched him write, silent now, and biting his heavy lips in vexation.

Pons looked up presently, after having written rapidly for a few moments.

"If you have some knowledge I do not have, I think it only fair that you tell me," said Jamison then.

"Quite right. In the first place, then, the young man for whom you are advertising did not commit the murder."

"I am somewhat familiar with your methods, Pons, but I don't follow you."

"There is for one thing, the matter of footprints," said Pons. "I doubt the possibility of tracing them through to the inner office, however wet the shoes were, but if by chance the prints could be traced, I think you would find that they stopped at the threshold. It may be possible to so trace them, and I suggest you try to find the print of a number seven shoe in the inner office anywhere beyond the threshold. That should settle the matter to your satisfaction since the knife could not have been hurled from the threshold."

"Mecker took the prints on the stairs, after we had the news-boy's story. But how do you suspect that? I confess I see nothing to indicate it."

"Obviously, because the man you want told me so himself."

Jamison looked the astonishment he felt.

"And by reason of the fact that he should seek my help, he is innocent; he would never otherwise have done so. From him, too, I learn that at the time he made entry to the building, he encountered a woman he took to be a char coming down—an old woman wearing a shawl over her head."

"We have a record of her."

"Ah, who was she?"

Jamison shrugged. "We don't know."

"Ah, well, I will tell you. It was she who murdered Deming."

"Fantastic!"

"Slowly, slowly, Jamison. You proceed from the theory that the young man committed the crime. I proceed from the premise that he did not. We are thus left with no alternative but the old woman. However implausible or impossible that may sound, I think you will find it to be the ultimately correct explanation. And to facilitate that end, I have here prepared two notices, which ought to appear in all the papers tomorrow. I have taken the liberty of attaching your name to one of them, Parker, and yours to the other, Jamison."

He passed over to Jamison the two notices he had written, and I read them over the Inspector's burly shoulder.

"Found: a large kitchen knife, of the type commonly used for carving fowl, with 'From Emily' burned on the handle near the blade. Owner will please apply to Dr. Lyndon Parker, Number Seven, Praed Street, Apartment 2B." The second notice was more concise: "Will the florist who yesterday, between opening hours and five P.M., sold a single black narcissus to an elderly lady wearing a shawl, please communicate at once with Inspector Jamison at New Scotland Yard."

Jamison looked up, perplexed. "Still going on about that narcissus, Pons."

"I believe it holds the key to our puzzle." Pons smiled. "You'll see that these notices reach the papers, I hope. And if you do set Mecker to looking for footprints of a size seven shoe in the inner office, I would appreciate having a report of his findings in the morning. Furthermore, you can oblige me by coming around when your notice is answered."

"Very well. I'll do it."

Pons touched a match to his pipe, which had gone out. "I think we've done all we can. Ready, Parker?"

We found young Rudderford in an agony of apprehension on our return, but Pons had no great difficulty disposing of him, telling him only that he must be prepared to make a truthful deposition about his part in the matter, and delivering himself of a few remarks about the potential murderer and the fear of punishment. Following Rudderford's return to his own home, Pons spent some time going through a bulky compendium of newspaper accounts of his own compilation—a collection of scrapbooks containing many thousands of stray bits of information relative to frauds, murders, larcenies and other offenses against the law. He was still at this long after I went to bed.

In the morning Pons examined the papers for the notices he had written. He found them easily, and observed to Jamison's credit that the evening's "Wanted" had vanished. We prepared ourselves to await an answer to the advertisement for the knife's

owner, though Pons was not at all sure that such an answer would
be forthcoming, admitting the possibility that the owner of the
knife may not have missed it, or may quite probably have been
the murderess herself.

At shortly over an hour after noon, Jamison appeared.

"Well, Jamison?" asked Pons, looking at the Inspector through
the haze of smoke in the room, though the expression on Jamison's face told its own story.

"You were right, Pons," said Jamison, sitting down. "Mecker
did manage to trace footprints to the threshold, but there they
stopped. There were nines and tens in the inner office, and that's
all we found, though we looked half the night. The weather made
it possible even after the prints had dried."

Pons nodded cursorily. "It is the notice in which I am interested. Any answer?"

"A florist on Cheapside telephoned at noon to say he had sold
a black narcissus to the woman you described. Cost: one pound.
It was sold at around four o'clock yesterday afternoon."

"Capital!" exclaimed Pons.

"I'm not so sure, Pons. Admitting that the young man for
whom we advertised did not commit the crime, we are confronted
with the fact that an old woman—an old woman, mind you, who
yesterday bought a black narcissus, for what reason I have still
not been able to ascertain—stabbed Deming with a common
carving knife, and with such strength that the knife went into
him up to the hilt. Is that tenable?"

"That is the situation as I see it, Jamison. You need only ask
yourself what peculiar conditions need to be satisfied to make it
posible." He reached down among a stack of papers near his
armchair, and, after rummaging among them, he came forth with
one and pointed to a photograph. "Could this person, for instance, have done it?"

Jamison favored the photograph with a long, cold stare, and
I did likewise. The photograph, in a paper of two days past, was
that of an old woman. Beneath it appeared her name: Emily
Riswall, and above, in black-letter: ESCAPED FROM STRATHBONE
ASYLUM FOR THE INSANE.

Whatever Jamison might have said was cut short by a sharp
ring at our bell.

A few moments later, Mrs. Johnson ushered in a thin, slatternly woman, who stood hesitantly on the threshold.

"Come in, come in, my good woman," said Pons.

Thus invited, she ventured three steps—just far enough to permit the door to close behind her—and stood looking from one to another of us.

"You are looking for Dr. Parker, I presume," continued Pons.

"Yes, sir," she said nodding.

"You've come for your knife," continued Pons, in his role.

She nodded, and Pons went into his laboratory and brought out an exact duplicate of the knife which had been used to kill Deming; he had evidently prepared this after I had gone to bed the previous night. He handed it to her and waited while she looked it over, turned it to where "From Emily" was burned on the handle, and nodded with a satisfied, if somewhat worried, air.

"It's mine, all right."

"May I ask how you came to lose it?"

"It was stolen from me."

"Ah! Only the knife?"

For a moment our visitor hesitated. "Well, sir, I guess the same person what took the knife took the two pound I had hid in the teapot."

"Took a knife and two pounds, eh?" Pons looked at her earnestly. "Someone who knew the house, I take it, and knew where you kept your money."

The woman nodded emphatically. "Yes, sir, and so I thought. I kep' an eye on 'Enery—that's my 'usband—because I thought he'd done it, 'specially when he called home that he couldn't get home on account of the rain yesterday. The night of the same day the money was took—that was yesterday, after I come back from a neighbor's house—I found 'alf a pound back in the teapot. Then I knew 'twasn't 'Enery, because he'd have used it all." She looked at the knife. "And this knife, now—I wouldn't care much for it, but seeing as it was a present from my dear sister Emily, I took a fancy to it."

"And your name?" asked Pons.

"Clymer. Mrs. 'Enery Clymer."

"Your sister's?"

"Hers was Riswall. She married a god-for-nothing who shot

'imself and she went out of her 'ead, poor thing." She sniffled a little. "She's been in the asylum these ten years."

"I think you've proved your right to the knife, Mrs. Clymer. You may keep it."

"Thank you, sir." She backed toward the door, a little suspiciously. "Good day, sir." And she was gone.

Jamison stared after her in bewilderment. By this time the Inspector was convinced that Pons was correct, but he had not yet discovered the essential explanation of the mystery. However, he was not to be kept long in ignorance.

"A curious affair," mused Pons, sitting down again, with one volume of his encyclopedia of clippings. "I take it you spent very little time on the black narcissus, Jamison."

"Mecker is looking the matter up."

"Well, we have it here." He was leafing through the pages as he spoke, and now stopped. "It would appear—this is from the *News of the World* of about a decade ago—that the Black Narcissus was the name of a spurious mine, through which Deming, who promoted it, mulcted investors of a good many thousand pounds. Among stockholders suffering the greatest losses when it crashed in 1918 were Sir Evelyn Mansfield, Selwyn Carington, Thomas Gainbridge, and James Riswall. Riswall lost his entire savings and shot himself on the same day. Observe the similarity of the pattern, for that was your young man's experience; his name, by the way, is James T. Rudderford, and he is prepared to make a deposition as soon as you call on him. Shortly after this event, mention of the Black Narcissus so enraged Riswall's widow that she made a murderous attack on Deming, inflicting some injuries. As a result, she was confined to Strathbone Asylum for the Insane, laboring under an obsession to revenge her husband by killing Deming. You will observe, Jamison, the outcome of the obsession, and the singular significance of the flower left on Deming's desk."

"It's clear now, Mr. Pons—or reasonably clear, at any rate," said Jamison, with some trace of bewilderment still in his eyes. "But we haven't got the murderer, after all."

Pons shrugged. "Technically, there is none. The woman will be found, I think, somewhere about the home of her sister, whose statements you will have to take. You might watch for her there."

DAVID ALEXANDER

And On the Third Day

INTRODUCTION

One day when I was a boy of seven my dog Spot and I were playing in the yard. Suddenly it seemed the entire male populace of Shelbyville, Kentucky, was thundering by our house at a dead run. Being a boy and a dog, we followed. We came to a clearing in a woods. A Negro was being hanged from a tree. Folks said he was a "bad nigger." I knew him as a fellow who whittled toy pistols out of wood for me and who always paused to play with Spot. Some of the men who were hanging him belonged to my family's church.

Years later I was a reporter in Lexington, Kentucky. A whiskey-crazed Negro named Ed Harris killed a farmer and his two children with an ax and raped the farmer's wife. Harris killed three human beings, but they didn't try him for murder. They tried him for rape. In Kentucky they hanged for rape and electrocuted for murder. Folks wanted Harris hanged. The sheriff was publicity-conscious. He announced that his son, who was a Boy Scout, would tie the knot. Boy Scouts don't tie very good hangman's knots. Harris choked to death for twenty-seven minutes with the rope in his mouth.

"And on the Third Day" is about lynching, the worst form of murder, because it's mass murder. There may be only one victim, but there's a whole town full of murderers when there's a lynching. The story was written seventeen years ago. I gave it to Willard Huntington Wright, better known as S. S. Van Dine. He thought it was great. He dashed right down to Scribner's Magazine with it and I heard he and Max Perkins nearly had a fist fight when the latter refused it on the grounds it would offend too many readers. Other editors said the same thing. They said it was fine—"But." In the intervening years the story was lost and found twice. Once it reappeared among some canceled checks and receipted bills that came out of storage in a shoe box. Once a friend's wife found it in a notebook full of recipes after he'd insisted he'd returned it. It has never been published before.

The last letter I received from Willard Wright before he died said, "That piece of yours about lynching is the best I've read on the theme. It must be published. An anthology, maybe?" Well, it's in an anthology and I'm very happy. I think Willard would have been happy, too.

One more word: Had I been asked to submit my best story instead of my first story about murder, I'd have sent this one just the same. I don't think I've ever done a better piece of writing. I'm rather afraid I never will.

DAVID ALEXANDER

And On the Third Day

MISS MARY KATE BASCOM lived in a little frame cottage down toward the railroad tracks in Clayville, where the brick pavement ended and the old, slightly rotted plank sidewalk that led to the outskirts of town began. Miss Mary Kate's cottage had been left her, along with a little insurance money, by her father, who had died many years before. At one time it had been painted a yellowish brown, but most of the paint had peeled away and the color was now just the dirty gray of weathered wood. The small front yard was usually overrun with weeds in the summertime. The steps to the porch were rickety and the porch itself was held up by stiltlike supports in the places where it sagged the most. Some of the older townsfolk, in passing the cottage, would say, "Land's sake, it's just a shame the way that place looks. Old Mrs. Bascom used to keep it so trim and neat, with flower beds and all. Like a new pin, she kept it, right up to the time she passed away. But poor Mary Kate, of course . . ."

For everybody knew that Miss Mary Kate was a little touched in the head. Had been a little touched in the head ever since the day word came to Clayville that Ben Willis, who was a lieutenant in the First World War, had been killed at some place over in France called Belleau Wood. Miss Mary Kate was already getting along toward spinsterhood when the war was declared, and you could have knocked most folks over with a feather when she and Ben Willis started courting after Ben had joined the army. He looked fine in his uniform and he was the only boy from Clayville who was an officer, so he probably could have walked out with prettier and younger girls if he'd wanted to. Not that Miss Mary Kate had been bad looking in those days, if you like those small, nervous, little wishy-washy kind of women who don't talk much but that just sort of sit and look at you with their eyes wide open. Anyway, Ben Willis had liked Miss Mary Kate all right, because he and she had got engaged before Ben went over to France.

Miss Mary Kate lived alone in the little, dirty-gray cottage now except for the old Negro, John. Some folks shook their heads when they thought of her being there all by herself except for the old Negro, but usually they wound up saying, well, maybe it was the best thing after all, because John had worked for Miss Mary Kate's father, and he kept the fires going in the wintertime and cleaned up after a fashion and cooked Miss Mary Kate's food for her. If it wasn't for him, Miss Mary Kate might become a public charge, and the good Lord knew folks in Clayville had plenty enough to worry about already. They said old John was a little touched in the head himself, and sometimes they caught him stealing vegetables or chickens from the back yards of the neighboring houses. But old John would always grin when they accused him of such things and say he was only borrowing the vegetables or the chickens because he and Miss Mary Kate were a little short that day and that besides he was an elder of the colored Presbyterian Church. Everybody was inclined to pass such things off with old John because he was good to Miss Mary Kate and kept her from becoming a public charge.

Miss Mary Kate spent most of her days sitting in an old rocking chair by the front window and knitting. She always knit the same things—baby clothes. That was one of the things that proved Miss Mary Kate was touched in the head. She never gave the baby clothes to anybody who might need them, but just locked them away in an old trunk in the attic, and she had the key to the old trunk hidden away somewhere. Once in a while, but not very often, some of the ladies of the town would visit Miss Mary Kate and bring her jelly and things, and they would try to get her to give the baby clothes to the Ladies Aid Society for the poor children. But she'd just shake her head and wouldn't answer them and would keep right on rocking and knitting.

The Negro, John, was getting pretty old and he spent a lot of his days in the house, squatting down on the floor by the iron grate and watching Miss Mary Kate knit. Sometimes he'd talk to her, but she seldom answered him and if she did, she'd just repeat what he'd said or her words wouldn't make much sense. One day in early spring, old John was hunched down by the grate where a low fire was burning and Miss Mary Kate was sitting over by the front window rocking and knitting. Old John had been watching her for a long time, looking as if he wanted to say something. He began to poke up the fire and mumbled, more to himself than to her, "Hyah 'tis spring and still so col' the misery ain' lef' mah bones." He seemed to be mumbling to himself, but he kept glancing out of the corner of his eye at Miss Mary Kate to see if she'd heard him.

"Spring don' come early down South like it usta. Lawsy, hyah 'tis most on to Eastah, and still buhnin' a fiah in the grate." He glanced pointedly at Miss Mary Kate. "You know it's most on to Eastah, Miss Ma'y Kate?"

Miss Mary Kate didn't say anything, but just kept on rocking and knitting.

"Look hyah, Miss Ma'y Kate," said old John, "you know what folks a-doin' nowadays? They givin' away Eastah presents to each other, jes like they do on Chrismus."

He looked at her to see if she'd heard him, but couldn't tell.

"What you goin' give me foah Eastah, Miss Ma'y Kate?"

"Easter," said Miss Mary Kate in a voice that was toneless. "Give you?"

"Yes, ma'm. Folks all give each othah Eastah presents nowadays, jes like Chrismus. Lawsy, Miss Ma'y Kate, I sholly would like to have that Sunday tailcoat yoah daddy will me when he pass away. Ole Mistah Bob, he always say to me, 'John, when I die I will you my Sunday tailcoat,' an' now you bin keepin' it locked up in that old trunk up to the attic all these yeahs and hidin' away the key so I caint find it."

Miss Mary Kate didn't say anything. She just kept on rocking and knitting.

Old John thought she had heard what he said, though, so he kept on talking.

"That jes what old Mistah Bob say to me afore he passed away.

And hyah 'tis Eastah comin' on three-foah days and me an elder in the chu'ch and jes the poah rags on my back. What good that Sunday tailcoat doin' up to the attic in that trunk?" He moved close to her. "Look, hyah, Miss Ma'y Kate, whyn't you give ole John that tailcoat foah a Eastah present?"

Miss Mary Kate dropped her knitting and looked startled, like someone who has heard a sudden noise and is listening for it to be repeated. She quit rocking. Old John knew she was going to say something, so he kept quiet.

"Easter?" she said. "Present?"

"Yes, ma'm. Ole John goin' to give you Eastah present. You want 'nother one of them doll babies lak I git you that time from out that li'l guhl's baby caidge back in the alley? What you want foah Eastah, Miss Ma'y Kate?"

Miss Mary Kate sat very still, with her head cocked to one side, as if she were listening for something. Finally she answered him.

"I want a little baby girl with curly gold hair," she said, almost in a whisper.

"You wanna *live* li'l guhl?" old John asked. "Miss Ma'y Kate, you know ole John caint git you no *live* li'l baby guhl."

"That's all I want," said Miss Mary Kate, her voice still very low.

Old John slumped back to his place by the fire, shaking his head. Several times he seemed about to speak, but didn't. Shadows began to crawl over the threadbare rug of the sitting room. Old John sat watching them despondently, occasionally casting a glance toward Miss Mary Kate, who was not rocking or knitting now, but sitting very still. When the shadows touched the edge of the big white flower in the center of the rug, old John heard a train whistle blow.

"Gittin' on toad six," he muttered to himself. "Freight from up Nawth comin' through."

Old John rose slowly to his feet and walked over toward Miss Mary Kate. He stood there for a minute without saying anything, then when he spoke his words came blurting out.

"Look hyah, Miss Ma'y Kate. If ole John git you that li'l guhl baby, you give him that tailcoat?"

"Yes," said Miss Mary Kate very softly.

Old John left the sitting room and went out through the kitchen toward the alley.

II

The two light colored Negroes from up North scrambled up the cindery bank from the railroad tracks and onto an alley. They stood there for a minute watching the freight they'd left until it had got up steam again and was out of sight around the bend.

"You know where we're at?" asked the little one.

"Naw," said the bigger one. "Somewhere down South."

"Still cold, even if 'tis South," said the little one. "I'm cold, and goddam, man, I'm hongry."

"Yeah," said the bigger one. He walked a few yards up the alley. "Houses 'round here."

The two light-colored Negroes from up North began walking up the alley like they weren't going any place in particular. They kept looking around them. The little one kept rubbing his hands together. His hands were stiff and cold. They walked quite a piece up the alley, the cinders crunching under their feet. They passed the back yards of several houses and saw no signs of life except at one. A little girl was playing alone in the backyard of that one. They went on farther up the alley, then they heard someone behind them. They turned around and looked, but all they could make out was a dim figure about fifty yards back. It was getting pretty dark. The two Negroes kept on walking.

Farther up the alley, the big Negro grasped the little one's arm.

"You see what I see?"

"Chackens!"

The coop was right against the back fence. The gate was half open and only had one hinge. The two Negroes could look into the coop and see the chickens roosting.

"Chackens is right," said the bigger Negro. "And nobody a-tall around."

"Somebody up the alley minute ago," said the little Negro. "White men down South don't like niggers from up North."

The big Negro turned around and looked back of him. He couldn't see or hear anything now.

"Nobody back there now," he said. "Come on."

III

Old John opened the gate and went out to the alley in back of Miss Mary Kate's cottage. He kept muttering to himself: "Miss Ma'y Kate jes doan talk sense sometime."

He walked up the alley slowly. He thought he heard somebody walking along in front of him. He couldn't see very well, for the southern dusk was purpling things up pretty fast. He thought it was a couple of fellows, but he couldn't tell whether he knew them or not. Too far off.

He walked on slowly and when he passed the back yard to Mr. Mel Shelby's house up the alley a ways, a little squeaky voice said, " 'Lo." Old John stopped and looked over the fence.

It was little Sue Alice Shelby. She was sitting down in the back yard pulling up weeds.

"What you doin' theah all by yo'self, honey?" Old John asked.

"Pickin' roses," said the little girl, pulling up another weed.

Old John cackled. "Lawsy, lawsy," he said. "Doan you know roses ain't a-growin' this time a yeah? You jes pullin' up ragweed foah yoah daddy, thassall."

"They're roses," said the little girl. She scraped a bunch of the weeds she'd pulled together and bunched them up in a tight fist. She got up off the ground and came walking over toward him. "You want some roses?"

Old John cackled again. "What'd I do with that old ragweed?" he asked. He put his hand on her head and looked down at her. "Sho have got purty gold haih," he said.

Suddenly the old man's body became stiff and he just stood there looking down at the upturned face of the child. Then he said slowly, talking to himself, "*Curly* gold haih."

"You want some roses?" the little girl asked.

Old John took the weeds with a motion that was mechanical, still standing stiff and looking down at her.

Finally he spoke to her, his hand smoothing her curly head. "You want to see some real purty roses?" he asked. "Miss Ma'y Kate, she got some roses in a jah up on the mantel what keep the whole yeah 'round. Wax roses. You evah see any purty wax roses?"

"No," said the little girl.

"You wanna see Miss Ma'y Kate's purty wax roses?"

"Yes," said the little girl.

"You come along with me," said old John.

Old John walked back down the alley with the little girl trotting along beside him, her hand in his.

"Ain' no ha'm in borryin'," he muttered to himself.

IV

It was a little after eight o'clock.

Six or eight fellows were at the bar of Dan Squires' saloon, drinking corn whiskey and talking. Doc Hardy said to Kelsay Bolton, who ran the Clayville Clothing Store, "Well, Kells, I guess your business is looking up now Easter's coming." It was Kelsay's turn to buy.

"*You* ain't bought any clothes off me," said Kelsay.

"Well," said Doc Hardy, "you ain't bought any pills off me."

Everybody laughed. Doc Hardy was the town druggist.

Acey Farrell, a big, red-handed farmer up at the end of the bar, wanted to buy everybody a drink. The rest of them looked at him suspiciously. Acey was a tough customer when he got drunk, but none of them wanted to take a chance on not drinking with him. He could get mighty ugly when he wanted to.

Just then the door opened and Sheriff Charley Estes came in with his deputy, Coates Williams. There was a chorus of "Hi, Sheriff," "Evenin', Coates."

"Heard you got them two nigger tramps from up North that robbed Arthur Redd's chicken coop, Charley," said Kelsay Bolton.

"Sure," said Charley Estes. "They're over in the hoosegow now. Me and Coates caught 'em down in the holler by the railroad tracks, building themselves a fire and fixing to have a nice chicken dinner."

"Goddamn niggers from up North," said Acey Farrell, banging his fist down on the bar. "Every Goddamn nigger from up North ought to have his guts cut out with a pitchfork. Goddamn bastards live with white women."

Charley Estes took a drink.

"Well, they ain't getting away with nothing down in these parts," he said. "Not them two niggers, anyhow."

Just then the door opened again and Mel Shelby came in. His

face was white and he looked kind of sick all over. He didn't say anything to anybody, but went right up to the Sheriff.

"You got two niggers over in the jail that stole Arthur Redd's chickens tonight, Charley?"

"Sure I got 'em," said Charles Estes. "What's the matter with you? You look like you need a drink, Mel."

"Strange niggers?" asked Mel.

"Why, yeah," said Charley. "They're a couple of tramps from up North somewhere come in on the freight tonight.

Everybody stopped talking and drinking and just stood there looking at Charley and Mel. They could tell something was happening.

"Listen here, Charley," said Mel, "my baby's missing. She's missing and she can't be found, because we've been looking everywhere for over two hours. She ain't in any of the neighbors' houses and she's nowhere around the railroad tracks or any place else she could have wandered. She's just five years old and she couldn't have got far by herself because her mother saw her out in the backyard just ten minutes before she called her and when she called her, Sue Alice wasn't anywhere around."

"Goddamn," said Charley. "You mean she's been kidnapped?"

"That's what I mean," said Mel. "Those niggers stole Arthur's chickens just about the time my baby disappeared. And Arthur Redd's house is just a few doors up the street from mine."

"But look here, Mel," said Charley Estes, "Coates and I caught them niggers down in the holler by the railroad tracks no more'n an hour ago, and they didn't have Sue Alice with them then."

"Kidnapped!" said Doc Hardy.

Acey Farrell gulped down a drink.

"Those niggers have got my baby and they've hid her somewhere," said Mel. "Charley, you got to go over and beat it out of them where she is."

"By God, I'll go," said Acey Farrell.

"I'm Sheriff here and I can attend to my own business," said Charley. He opened up his coat and showed a gun in a shoulder holster. "Come on, Coates," he said. "You others form a searching party and meet me back here in an hour. Scout the town and all the country you can."

"We ought to form a necktie party," said Dan Squires, the saloon owner.

"Goddamn nigger bastards," said Acey Farrell.

V

Miss Mary Kate sat by the window, rocking the sleeping child in her lap and stroking her curly hair. Old John was squatting over the fire grinning happily. He was wearing an old frock coat that needed pressing very badly. He looked at Miss Mary Kate, and it made him feel good somehow to look at her. "Ain't seen Miss Ma'y Kate smile lak that sence that young gemmun went off to wah," he mumbled to himself.

It was very quiet except for the occasional crackle of the fire and the squeaking of Miss Mary Kate's rocking chair. You could hear the child breathing.

Must be late, old John thought. But he didn't want to go to bed and he guessed Miss Mary Kate didn't. Sure did perk her up a lot to have that little baby girl in her lap. Mighty glad he'd borrowed her. And that Sunday tailcoat of old Mr. Bob's would be as good as new with a little flat-iron pressing. Sure glad he'd got it in time for Easter.

Miss Mary Kate sat rocking and stroking the head of the child in her lap. Old John squatted in his corner, feeling of his coat with a caressing hand now and then, and grinning.

The sleeping child had a wax rose clutched tightly in her little fist.

VI

It was going on ten o'clock when the first of the searching parties began to drift back to Dan Squires' Saloon. Coates Williams, the Deputy Sheriff, was there waiting for them. The first men who came in were with Acey Farrell. Acey had picked up several fellows from over in the south end of town. That was the tough neighborhood of Clayville. Acey and the boys from the south end of town had taken a jug of corn along with them and you could tell they'd had several swigs from it. They were looking kind of mean.

Besides the boys from the south end, Kelsay Bolton and Doc Hardy were with Acey's bunch. Acey didn't say anything to

Coates Williams. He just gave him a kind of dirty grin as much as to say, "Well, you ain't got nothing out of them niggers yet, mister." Coates didn't say anything either.

Dan Squires could tell they hadn't found Mel Shelby's baby, so he didn't ask any questions. He just set one up on the house. It was about that time that Mel Shelby came in. Other men kept arriving, too, a lot of them in automobiles. It looked as if half of Clayville was jamming into Dan Squires' Saloon.

Mel Shelby hadn't gone out with the searching parties. He'd gone home to his wife who was having hysterics so bad they had to call a doctor for her. He looked pretty bad himself, all white and shaking and sweating like a trooper, even though the night was cold. He looked sick. For a minute he just stood there and stared at everybody and nobody seemed to know what to say to him. There was a big crowd there by now, but it was so quiet the tinkle of a glass sounded like a loud noise. Finally Mel started asking questions, and his voice was high and piercing like a woman's.

"Did you find anything?" he asked. "Anything at all?"

Doc Hardy tried to soothe him. "Not yet, Mel," he said, "but the night ain't over yet. You get a-hold of yourself now, Mel."

Mel Shelby turned to Coates Williams. "Why, Goddamn you," he said, "why ain't you over there sweating those niggers that stole my baby? Goddamn you, how're you going to find my baby standing up here at the bar and drinking?"

"Take it easy, Mel," said Coates. "I been over there and Charley's still with them. He sent me over here to meet you fellows. Charley and I did everything we knew to do to 'em and if they know anything, they just won't talk."

Acey Farrell came blustering up and stuck his jaw out at Coates. "Yeah," said Acey, "you done everything *you* knew to do. Maybe you slapped 'em on the wrist right hard."

Coates didn't back off an inch and he looked calm. "Charley slapped that little nigger on the wrist so hard he broke his arm," he said. "We gave 'em the gun butt an' we gave 'em the boot and the little one fainted twice. But they're still swearing they don't know nothing about Mel's kid."

Acey turned around to the rest of the boys and there was an ugly look on his face. "What do you say, boys?" he asked. "Looks like the law can't do nothing."

One of the toughs from the south end pulled a thick looped-up rope from under his coat. "I say let's go talk to them niggers," he said.

Coates went for his gun, but he just took hold of the butt. He didn't draw it. "You ain't pulling nothing like that in this town while Charley Estes is Sheriff," he said. "Charley's getting in touch with the state police and the government agents. He's doing all he can."

"Oh, Christ," cried Mel Shelby, "don't hang those niggers. Oh, Christ, men, we'll never find out where my baby is if you do that."

Everybody began talking at once, so you could hardly understand anything. Mel began sobbing.

"I think Acey's right," said Dan Squires. "Look here, Mel, them niggers will be more afraid of a lynching than anything else. We don't have to really hang 'em, but if we get 'em out under a tree and work on 'em a little, they'll talk."

"Oh, Christ," moaned Mel. "Oh, Jesus Christ." He was so white he looked like he was going to faint.

"Why, Goddamn it," said Acey, "you're that baby's dad and you're sobbing about them niggers. Why, you ought to be the one that ties the knot. You don't know what them nigger bastards done to your little girl. Them Goddamn Yankee niggers would do anything."

"Oh, Christ," Mel said. He was shaking so his teeth rattled.

"And you," Acey said to Coates, "ain't going to stop us, you Goddamn . . ."

Coates pulled his gun, but it was too late. One of the toughs from the south end of town slugged him from behind and he went down as limp as a burlap bag.

There was almost complete silence for a minute. Then everybody started talking and it was an ugly sound. Everybody seemed to get his blood up all of a sudden. You could tell they were all behind Acey now. Even Mel had quit sobbing, and was cursing the Goddamn niggers. Dan Squires took off his apron and came out from behind the bar. He picked up a blackjack from the back bar and brought that with him.

"All of you as have cars, go get 'em and rush back to the jail," said Acey. "Rest of you come on with me."

They started across the street to the jail, with Acey and his toughs in front of them. Acey had taken Coates Williams' gun and he was carrying it in his right hand. Everybody was talking. They were excited, but they were talking low.

Charley Estes didn't try to stop them. He saw them coming and he looked like he'd been expecting them. Charley Estes knew when he was licked and he figured there wasn't any use in shooting a couple of men he knew on account of two nigger tramps.

The big Negro was dripping blood from his mouth and he had a swollen eye. He was hunched over in a corner holding onto his groin when the boys came in to get him. He didn't scream or yell. He just kept moaning. Even when they slugged him a few times, he just moaned.

The little Negro with the broken arm seemed to be unconscious. Acey tried to bring him to by twisting his broken arm but he just gave one sharp scream and that was all.

They hustled the Negroes into a car and Acey and a couple of toughs from the south end of town got in with them. There were quite a few cars there by now and everybody got a ride, although some of the boys had to stand on the running board.

They headed for a clearing on the edge of town, down past Miss Mary Bascom's cottage. Kelsay Bolton took Doc Hardy and Mel Shelby in his roadster. When they got to the outskirts of town, Kelsay said, "Let's stop off and get Arthur Redd. He ought to go along, even if he is a deacon in the church. After all, those niggers stole his chickens."

Mel Shelby gave a kind of crazy laugh. "They stole his chickens," he said. "They stole his chickens and they stole my baby."

But they stopped off and got Arthur Redd. He seemed willing enough to go along.

The things that happened out in the clearing made some of the boys kind of sick. There were three big trees right at the edge of the clearing, where the woods began. They put ropes around the Negroes' necks and threw the other ends of the ropes over limbs, but they didn't string the Negroes up for a long time. That's why some of the boys got sick. Acey and the toughs from over in the south end of town did everything they could to make the Negroes answer questions. They sharpened sticks to a fine point and did things to the Negroes with them. The big Negro started screaming instead of moaning then, but he didn't even seem to hear the questions they were asking him. The little Negro wasn't making any sound at all. They took off the Negroes' shoes and lit matches, but still the big Negro just screamed and the little Negro just swayed against the tree. The noose around the little Negro's neck seemed to be all that was holding him up. One of the fellows from the south end of town even took some twigs and started a fire around the little Negro's feet. But he decided the little Negro was dead, so he stomped the fire out. No use in attracting unnecessary attention by a fire.

After a while they knew the Negroes weren't going to answer any questions, no matter what they did to them, so they strung them up and got done with it. Acey Farrell kept cursing the Negroes even after they were strung up. Everybody just kind of stood around for a while and looked at the two Negroes hanging there. Acey pulled out Coates Williams' gun and took a pot shot at the little Negro just for luck. Hit him, too.

The echo of the shot had no more than died away when a woman screamed. Everybody was startled. Even Acey jumped. The woman came running into the clearing, screaming at the top of her voice. She had nothing on but a night gown and a quilted kimono. It was Ethel Shelby, Mel's wife.

"Mel!" she was yelling. "Mel! They found her! She's back home, Mel!"

A bunch of the men jumped in front of her so she wouldn't see the Negroes hanging there, and Mel, looking a lot worse than a dead man, ran up and threw his arms around her. It was hard to tell who was shaking the most, Mel or his wife.

"Where'd you find her, Mrs. Shelby?" Doc Hardy asked.

Mrs. Shelby was so excited she could hardly talk. But she finally told them that one of the town Negroes had been passing Miss Mary Kate Bascom's house and had seen Miss Mary Kate through the window with a little girl in her lap. Just then the cars that had headed for the clearing came by, so the town Negro got scared and hid. But he'd heard about the missing baby, so he finally came over to the Shelby house and told them. Mrs. Shelby and her mother had rushed right over and it was Sue Alice all right. And that crazy old Negro, John, had said he'd just borrowed the baby for a while.

"That nigger John of Miss Mary Kate's?" Acey asked that.

Just then Mrs. Shelby saw the two Negroes hanging from the trees and she fainted. They hustled her and Mel into an automobile and drove them off as fast as they could.

Everybody stood around. Nobody said anything. Acey pulled out a bottle and took a drink. He looked over toward the edge of the clearing. The two Negroes were hanging from trees about ten yards apart, and there was another tree between them.

"Well," said Acey, "there's another tree."

"God, man," said Arthur Redd, "you're not thinking of stringing up old John, too?"

"Listen here," said Acey, "old John's a nigger, ain't he? And so are them two over there niggers. Maybe old John knew them two and they fixed it up between them to kidnap this baby and make that half-crazy old woman keep her. I say old John's guilty as hell and we can't back out on this thing now we started it."

They all thought over what Acey had said. They'd be in a pretty jam all right if they'd strung up a couple of niggers who were nothing more than chicken thieves. They'd have a lot of explaining to do if they let those two hang there and let old John go and be tried by law. Likely enough old John had been in on the thing with these two niggers anyway.

So after a while they started back to town.

Miss Mary Kate was sitting in a chair, her eyes kind of glazed, her head bent over, rocking fast. She seemed to be humming to herself, but it wasn't much of a tune. Old John was sitting on the floor by the fire, wearing a wrinkled frock coat when they came in.

Miss Mary Kate didn't even seem to know they were there. She just kept rocking and humming and looking at nothing at all with her eyes wide open.

"Git up, nigger," said Acey.

"Yassuh," said old John. He didn't know what it was all about but the white folks had always said he was a good nigger, so he wasn't scared. He scrambled to his feet.

"You steal the Shelby baby?" asked Acey.

"Steal?" said old John. "Why, nossuh, indeed. Jes borried huh, thassall."

Acey hit old John in the mouth. The Negro staggered back and put his hand to his lip and wondered what was happening.

Nothing like this had ever happened before, but still old John wasn't scared. He was a good nigger and an elder in the colored church. Rough hands were laid on him and they shoved him out of the house. Miss Mary Kate still sat there, rocking and humming and looking at nothing at all.

There was a wax rose on the floor at her feet.

"Don't teah mah new Sunday tailcoat, white boss," old John begged.

They didn't do any fancy business with old John. They just strung him up to the middle tree as fast as they could and got it over with. Old John never did seem to know what was happening to him. He didn't resist at all and even when they put the rope around his neck he still had a sort of silly grin on his face.

Everybody was anxious to get back to town. So they took one look at him hanging there and left. Old John looked kind of funny. A wind had come up and it blew his tailcoat up around him. He looked like a big buzzard flapping its wings.

Everybody hurried off. Hurried off and left old John hanging there—between two thieves.

Kelsay Bolton, the clothing merchant, drove Arthur Redd back to town in his roadster. Neither spoke for a while but Kelsay whistled softly through his teeth. Finally he said, "Arthur, you better come around to my place tomorrow and buy a new suit. Just got some mighty fine stuff in."

"Not interested," said Arthur Redd shortly.

"Not interested?" said Kelsay. "And you a deacon in the church!"

"What's that got to do with it?" asked Arthur.

"What's that got to do with it?" said Kelsay. "Why, man, don't you know it's just three days before Easter?"

RUTH WILSON

Too Many Brides

INTRODUCTION

The broad red-brick road where I have my peace-seeking roots with Alex Sr., Alex Jr., and a small, orange-and-white, demoniac gent named Buttercup is decked with sycamores and maples, japonica and althea, and ivy from the churchyard at Stoke Pogis, England. On it I have been held up at gunpoint by a knot of teen-age thugs, I have been attacked by a psychopathic woman, I have fought off the violence of two battling gangs wrecking my house in an invasion of hoodlum warfare. It has been staked out by the F.B.I., scouted by the police, inhabited by actors, painters, musicians, a paranoiac, two would-be suicides, and an unsuccessful murderer. On it is also a small house with a seven-sided parlor and a ballroom-sized chandelier. What more inevitable than that I should write a story like "Too Many Brides"?

That was not its original title. It began as five thousand words called "One After Another." But editors, bless their little hearts, have a way with them.

Speaking of editors: Ellery Queen, one of MWA's anthology board this year, suggested that an odyssey of each story be included. Tell me, cher M. Queen, should you have asked me that question? You were the only editor who turned this story down and then it landed in the arms of Mike Tilden, editor of 15 Mystery Stories. But no doubt there is, in some far bad lands beyond the reach of plane or burro, at least one wandering editor who may have turned down a script which came from you. In any case, since you were one of the board of acceptance for this book, how could it be other than that now all is forgiven and forgotten?

RUTH WILSON

Too Many Brides

ANOTHER one!
     Hetty Clinger, peering from under her eyelids, hardly felt she could give a good old-time greeting to her brother's bride.

When it had been just Mamma and Hetty and Felix, everything had been fine. She was so much older than Felix—twenty-one years older—that there had been no bad feelings between them. Mamma and she had been almost like partners, and Mamma was always so pleased because Hetty had her saving ways. Everything about Mamma had been just perfect; she was the smartest person in the world. All Hetty ever had to do was just follow along and everything came out fine.

It was strange to think that she was fifty-three now, and Mamma had been gone ten years. Hetty could still hear her say, "Now mind, Hetty, after I pass off, mind you take good care of all the things; mind you see they look as if they had a summer cleaning every week."

When Felix went off on one of his trips, Hetty would go from room to room, looking at the knickknacks and antiques, the bric-a-brac and curios, the pictures hung edge to edge from ceiling to window sill all over the walls, and especially her chief treasure, the big crystal chandelier with the thousand prisms that hung in the middle of the little seven-sided parlor.

Those were the times she could take all the china out of one of the dining-room cabinets and wash it right, although nowadays she got kind of bothered in her chest when she got too tired. The little house sat off by itself like a sleepy dog, outside an out-of-the-way suburb; no nosy neighbors anywhere to kill time.

It was after Mamma had "passed off," as they said, that Felix had begun taking the trips. Always restless; and now he'd brought this mousy wife home.

Jane was her name. Plain Jane for sure—her fingers were limp as she shook Hetty's hand.

"Pleased to meet you," Jane said.

She looked just like the kind of dull wallflower who'd fall for Felix. Why did a man thirty-two need to keep trying to be a

Prince Charming? Or did the new Mrs. Clinger have money maybe? And how had he done it this time—oh yes, a sightseeing tour on a river boat. You started out with a thin purse and a change of shirts, and you came back with a sack of soiled laundry and a wife. Smooth talking and scenery was all it took.

"I'm awfully glad to know you, Hetty." Jane was trying hard to please. "Felix and I want to say first thing that we hope you'll stay on here and make your home with us."

That was a laugh! Hetty could hardly keep it from showing. Of course that would be what Felix would tell her. Instead of the truth, which was that the house and the things, down to the last mustache cup and seal-skin tippet, belonged to Hetty. To say nothing of the little income, which came from Mamma's careful investments of insurance and savings. All Hetty's. She was sure Felix had not told Jane that he had hardly worked a day in his life. Just kept looking for the right deal. But Felix was a one for making himself biggety.

Felix puffed out his chest and put an arm around Jane. "What do you think of my little squaw?"

That was another thing about Felix. He could find such a roundabout way to rub you the wrong way. Hetty no longer let the rubbing show. But Jane didn't know how to act; she tried to smile.

It didn't take Hetty long to find out what there was to know about her. Just a country schoolteacher who had never had a beau. Made to order for Felix's tricks. But if she had no oilwells, no rich grandfather in Australia, no Wall Street securities—why had Felix married her?

Well, there was a stepuncle, and he had an invention that looked more than promising, and because Jane had financed the invention she had a contract that would give her seventy-five per cent of the profits as soon as the deal now in process was concluded. The contract was in her lawyer's safe, where it would be likely to stay for a while. The deal might take at least several months or more to be fixed up satisfactorily. Hetty guessed Felix would be able to stand Jane for that long. He'd have to; the financing had used up all her savings. And of course she no longer had her teaching position.

She wasn't any bother around the house. A quiet little thing who tried to help with the chores when Hetty would let her, and kept out of the way other times. Hetty saw how her eyes followed Felix when Felix was home, but it didn't take too long before Felix at home was something that happened less and less often. Hetty wondered how many lonely, foolish, thoughtless women, even those who were not special because they had an agreement in a lawyer's strongbox, slipped so easily into the hands of a fellow like Felix.

One day Hetty noticed that she seemed more underfoot than usual. Finally Jane remarked, "Felix says he is busy with offers for a fine position. That's why he has to be away from home so much."

Hetty only nodded. She had heard it all before. Then Jane said, "Felix seems to have forgotten to leave me any money."

Hetty looked at her curiously. "What do you need money for? You haven't been anywhere since you've been here. You haven't even written a letter. Don't you have any folks?" She was sure she knew the answer to that.

Jane shook her head. "Just that stepuncle I told you about. But I—I never have been before where I didn't have a penny to my name."

"Well, I guess it's mean not to even have two cents to knock together on a coffin." Hetty hesitated. "But what would you do if I—if you had any money? I buy all the groceries and tend to everything."

Jane turned a sallow red. "I figured I might get a few trimmings and try to fix myself up a new hat and—and things like that. Just—just in case, you know."

"In case of what?"

"Just in case," Jane repeated.

The silly! She thought if she dolled herself up in some new duds she'd be able to stir up a little of Felix's fading interest. Hetty thought of a little tickle she could play on Felix, which might make up a little for all the foolishness she'd had to take from him since Mamma had passed off.

Suppose, from one of the extra storage trunks, she dug out an old feather or two and some of the lace-trimmed flimsies that had belonged to Eileen? Hetty knew as sure as shooting that Felix hadn't mentioned Eileen to Jane.

Eileen had been Mrs. Felix Clinger Number One. That had been a real blowup to Hetty. She had never dreamed of a stranger in the house, and so soon after Mamma died. But that was Felix for you—left Hetty lonely and sadhearted packing away Mamma's hand-embroidered pillow shams and the three fur coats Mamma bought when she got married, and went off on a boat trip with the first installment of the insurance. That was before Hetty took hold.

Felix had come back with Eileen, a steady eater with a loud voice and a hanker for fresh air and long walks. She had a line of monkey-chatter and a nice little nest egg, and she led Felix around like a caged cat. He was wild to be rid of her. It was Eileen who nosed out the means for her own passing off.

It was she, on one of the hikes she dragged Felix on, who came on the abandoned well surrounded by tilt-stones, in the deep patch of lonely wood far beyond the sight of any house now standing. After it had gone dry, it had seemingly been made over into a shaft for unwanted rubbish. You set an object on one of the tilt-stones and it shot down lost forever into the deeps of the earth, faster than a buttered pig on a greased slide. And you'd never guess the well was there if you didn't come across it by accident, it was so overgrown with weeds and vines. Of course Eileen's discovery was by accident; she stepped on one of the tilt-stones. She never even had time to yell.

"You know, Hetty," Felix said, "I don't know why I should speak to anybody about it. It's not as if Eileen had people who cared to make a fuss. And to have rubbernecks come snooping around asking questions, you wouldn't like that. First thing you know, they'd be poking through the house and opening trunks and things—why, they'd be saying finally I *pushed* her in. You can see that."

Hetty was never one for inviting strangers or trouble. Much better to pack away Eileen's loud finery and let Felix spend the rest of Eileen's money. That took a year or two, before he got restless again. Hetty could tell when that time was coming, because Felix started talking, as he always did, about the three knocks he had heard the night Mamma had passed off. It was as if he were running away from something that scared him.

Hetty never saw any reason to argue him out of it. Three

knocks were three knocks, if they came from the spirit world or
from a defective flush ball in the bathroom tank that Hetty
mended later. If Felix were handier around the house he'd have
known more of what went on. Hetty knew how much stock
Mamma would have put in any stuff about three knocks. But it
was one more thing to tuck away in your mind.

In a couple of years Felix found himself a new wife, Birdie.
He met her in a railroad station. This time he picked her out
pretty carefully. Not bright, not pretty, not related, and with a
nice amount of loose cash. Two weeks was all she lasted. And
Felix was sure he had worked out the know-how of getting along
in the world. Besides, it was romantic to get your wife to go
walking at night in the woods.

Hetty could hardly peeve, since she had such long stretches
of time when she didn't have to give Felix money. But having
four wives, and getting rid of them so handily—Della had been
the third—had surely gone to Felix's head.

He never brought a wife home until he had gone through all
the money he could, and how many women he had done out of
a little here and a little there, Hetty would never know. But he
was getting bossy around the house, acting as if the things in it
were there to be used up, worked on—even sold!

Now, Jane's stepuncle still hadn't started on the big money-
making and times were looking down in the mouth for Felix.
That was bad, though he still would go off for weeks at a time.
He was away now.

Thinking it over, Hetty tipped her head for Jane to come up
while she found her a few pretties.

"I've never seen you open any of the trunks before," Jane told
her, as Hetty picked out a key or two from the line of them hung
inside the storeroom closet.

"These are Mamma's trunks." She looked around the second-
story back, where trunks were piled on top of one another and
the camphor smell never left. "But I've a couple here that—well,
I'll find you something."

Eileen had had an orange ostrich feather that went well with
the tan velvet hat shape that had belonged to Della. These, combined with the foulard shirtwaist that Birdie had thought so
stylish, gave Jane the beginnings of a costume.

"Now don't show it to Felix till you're all ready to wear it," Hetty suggested.

"I hope he comes home soon," Jane said thoughtfully. "He never writes on these trips and I get so lonesome. I don't guess all this finery was your Mamma's."

Hetty grinned. Might as well at least let Eileen's name come into the picture by mentioning it now.

She had planned to surprise Felix by sending Jane shopping in the new costume. Perhaps the storekeeper would remember the orange feather; that might embarrass Felix and maybe cool off his high-handed notions about Mamma's things.

She puffed a little, after she sent Jane down, and closed and stacked the trunks. Funny how that tightness squeezed in around her chest, but she didn't hold with all this doctoring. She'd go downstairs and see what Jane was doing.

Hetty could travel the padded stairs softer than a mouse. Jane was sitting on the love seat in the parlor, with the things on her lap, looking at a hand-colored oleo of Mamma at the age of sixteen. Tears were sliding down her face.

"Why, Jane!" Hetty had to ask. "What's got into you?"

Jane just sat there, smoothing the feather-stitched galloon edging around Mamma's favorite stamped Turkish pillow.

"No cause for you to let your feelings leak all over the place. It's no skin off your nose if Felix was married before."

"I don't care too much about that," Jane said. "Though he might have told me. But I was pretty sure I wasn't the first in his life, anybody as good-looking as he is." She sighed. "No, it's not that."

"Well, dry up the sniffles and let's have it," said Hetty. "What's the big grief?"

"It's your mother."

"Mamma?" Hetty felt a slow burning inside.

"Yes. She was so pretty. No matter how I'd try I could never get to look anywhere near as pretty as that. She looks just like a calendar picture."

Hetty left her sitting there while she brought a cup of tea. Jane almost couldn't drink it.

"You shouldn't go to all this trouble for me," she said. "First all these pretty things, and now tea."

"I guess there must be a few more odds and ends up in the trunks that you could see," Hetty said.

It didn't take Jane long to get the sewing started. When Felix turned up a few days later, Hetty was all prepared.

"I've had to try sending Jane over to the store. My chest felt a little funny the last day or two."

Felix didn't seem as much bothered as Hetty had hoped. "She oughtn't to get friendly with people, though. It's not like you not to be smart."

More of his sarcasms. "But if you're not here and I don't feel up to snuff . . ." Hetty told him. "Anyway, it's just lately she's been going."

Felix turned at the sound of the door opening. The feather on the hat was outlined against the outside sky.

"What on earth . . ." Felix turned on Hetty. "What kind of a trick is that?"

"Aren't you glad to see me?" Jane asked Felix hopefully.

"What way is that to rig yourself out? Where did you get that feather—and that hat—and—"

"I found them in the boxes upstairs when I was cleaning. I didn't think you'd mind. Why let good clothes go to waste?"

"And you've been gallivanting in them, have you?" He was careful not to show how he felt.

Jane was not fussed. "Not a soul gave me a second look. They had no bluing like you wanted, Hetty, but the man said to wash the chandelier crystals with vinegar and salt—they'll shine better. Though I still think ammonia water is best."

Jane was turning out not at all the way Hetty had first sized her. Was it her clothes that had changed her?

Felix hardly said a word while Hetty put the supper on the table. But as they were eating the Lady Baltimore cake Hetty had baked the day before, Felix remarked, "Now, Jane, don't get any ideas in your head. You can't show off those clothes any place, because there's no money for high times."

"I just made them over for something to do," she said.

Hetty was more and more taken by what a cool one Jane was turning out to be.

Then Felix asked, "Have you heard anything yet about that invention from the lawyer?"

There was a slight wait before Jane shook her head. Could she have been meeting the mailman, Hetty wondered. Maybe she was fooling both of them. But Jane wasn't treading on Hetty's toes. To Hetty's surprise, she could feel more than a little sorry for Jane.

Pretty cute, too, how Jane had not given away Hetty's trick to Felix. And it was an earful to hear all the things she said about Mamma, asking about Mamma's ways and how she looked and all.

All of Mamma's clothes, down to the last pair of clocked lisle stockings and double-front corset-covers, were up there, aired and freshened by Hetty twice a year, and folded so that they kept like new. It might be a pastime to show them to Jane. Before anything happened.

Jane was saying, "I don't know when I'll hear from him. Maybe nothing'll ever come of it."

Hetty didn't even know what the invention was. Could Jane have make-believed it? To catch Felix? Hetty could hardly keep from laughing.

Felix's face wasn't something to laugh at. Jane mightn't notice, but it signaled Hetty that there had better be some money coming from that invention, or Felix would reclassify Jane for the Dead Letter Office.

Fall showed signs of setting in earlier than usual. High winds and leaves flying thick and fast, and bright sunsets lighting up the skies and then getting dark quickly. Hetty took notice that Felix kept to himself for a while, as if he were fixing for a change.

She herself couldn't get it clear if she really wanted to have it on her mind about Jane.

Funny, how that tired feeling seemed to keep catching up with her since the day she'd piled and unpiled the trunks to get Jane the feather.

And it seemed that a few times, when she was up in her room resting, with the door tight shut, that Felix had company. She was sure each time she had heard somebody come in and keep talking for a few minutes. That wasn't like Felix. He never asked anyone in.

It got Hetty so stirred that one day she crept down the stairs in her stocking feet. Sure enough, around the bend of the landing she could hear a strange voice.

This voice was saying, "I couldn't give you more than five hundred for that chandelier, especially if I have trouble getting your sister to agree. I don't care if Harris offered you fifteen hundred. You'll have to get your sister to agree—I won't risk trouble. I'm a peaceable dealer with a good reputation and I aim to stay that way."

Hetty felt a slow burning inside. Felix trying a trick like that! Could you match it? Anything to line his pockets! The women in the well—that had nothing to do with Hetty. But Mamma's chandelier! The nerve of Felix! Next thing, he'd be selling the silverware Mamma'd eaten with, the linens she'd stitched, the clothes she'd worn! Those three fur coats, real Russian sable one of them was—maybe he'd gotten somebody to price those too!

Thinking about it made Hetty so tired she could hardly get up to the bedroom again.

At supper that night Hetty saw Felix paying little attentions to Jane, things he hadn't done since he'd first brought her home. That didn't look good. No word from the lawyer on the invention, either. Hetty guessed Felix had made up his mind.

She waited for Felix to take a twilight walk in the woods with Jane. But Felix didn't mention it.

Hetty took a little longer in the bathroom that night. There was a way she could bend one of the little hollow lengths of pipe in the tank that would float the flush ball up against the lid of the tank three times, and three times only, as the water rose and stopped. She heard it, later in the night, give its three knocks, and she fell asleep smiling.

Felix looked pretty hollow-eyed at breakfast. He said, out of a clear sky, "I always want to be sure I know what I'm doing." Hetty was certain Felix wouldn't talk about the three knocks with Jane around, but they had been heard, all right.

"How do you know, to be sure of what you're doing?" Jane asked.

"I know," Felix said. Hetty wondered if Jane could tell when Felix was scared.

Hetty had bent back the little length of pipe to its regular shape when she straightened up the bathroom early that morning. No need to overdo things.

"Felix was telling me he gets messages sometimes from the spirit world," Jane told Hetty a few days later.

"He did?"

"Yes. Did you know about it?"

"He mentions them sometimes before he goes on a trip." Hetty was feeling pretty tired that day. It would be a good day to lie down.

"Didn't he go on trips quite a few times before he met me?" Jane asked.

"He always was a traveler."

"The dresses in the brown trunk are three different sizes," Jane said after a while.

"I heard you moving things around in the storeroom yesterday, after I said you could take a look."

"I closed everything up tight after I got through. Your mother didn't have anything of hers in the brown trunk, did she?"

"No."

"Hetty," Jane asked, "did Felix truly love your mother? Like you do?"

"Well . . ." Hetty tried to think back. It was hard to remember. Or maybe, about that there was nothing to remember.

"I thought that might be how it was." Jane sighed. "She looks so pretty on all her pictures. Like a calendar."

"It's a shame you never knew her." Hetty felt sad.

"Hetty—have you noticed how Felix has been sort of making up to me lately?"

"Looks like it, doesn't it?"

"He's even started me meeting him out in the woods. As if we were courting."

Hetty felt a little jerk in her chest. She would have to rest more. Well, she soon would not have to think much longer about poor Jane.

"Felix likes to walk far out in the woods. There's one special place he likes to walk out to see. Way out. Kind of a dreamy place. But lonely."

"Is it?"

"It's cold to walk out there in just my thin coat in this

weather. A couple times I went out and met him out there. It got awful cold, waiting."

Without believing it, Hetty heard herself saying, "I guess you could take whatever you need from upstairs."

"Thank you."

Jane'd take good care of Mamma's things; she handled them so ladylike.

Mostly Hetty was glad now to spend time lying down. The stairs began to be such a drag. She could hear Jane rummage around in the storeroom every once in a while; she could smell the camphor off and on. But somehow Jane could look after things. Not like Felix. Hetty never let Felix in the storeroom. Felix didn't even know the half of what was in the trunks. Well —poor Jane.

Hetty'd be lying down every day now when they got back from the walks. Every time she heard the squeaky bottom hinge on the front door, she'd know they had come back this once more. Funny, she'd get the queerest feeling these days. As if Mamma were telling her things; only, she couldn't make out what it was. What was right and what wasn't, and yet it was all mixed up.

Mamma had always had the say of it when she was here, and Hetty'd never had to think. Just go along with her, sure that she'd put right where right belonged. Now there seemed to be some feel to it that things were moving in Hetty's direction so they were going to be up to her. Yet that couldn't be. She'd never had a part of it and she wanted no part of it. She'd never been what Felix called smart. And if Felix thought that trying to sell the chandelier was smart—well, Mamma wouldn't like it. Thinking about it made her tired so she had to go and stay on the bed a long time.

It was good and dark when she woke up. Had they come back again yet? That squeak must be the front door. Felix must be by himself this time, it felt so late. Well on in the night. She waited for Felix to call up for supper.

Felix'd be going off now, if that's how it was. She listened; then she had to know. "What time is it?" she called down.

"Ten o'clock."

Jane's voice! She could hardly get her slippers on fast enough to get downstairs.

Jane was just walking from the lighted dining room into the dark kitchen. Her outline stood out like a calendar picture. As much like Mamma as a double! The way she'd fixed her hair, the sable coat with the stand-out bustle back and the leg-o'-mutton sleeves—it all made Hetty's skin do little jumps. Like Mamma all over again. She'd even put on a pair of those tight gloves Mamma used to wear. Hetty couldn't help but admire her. Then she remembered. She didn't want to ask. But . . .

"Where's Felix?"

Jane wasn't being rushed. "It was truly cold out in the woods today. You were so thoughtful to let me wear these things." She began to take off the gloves, very thoughtfully.

Hetty couldn't think what to say. She could tell that somehow it was all different. She went in the kitchen and set the kettle on to boil.

"I waited for Felix quite a spell today," Jane said. "I got out there pretty early. But he couldn't find me for quite a while when he did come."

"Hide-and-seek was always a game Mamma liked." Hetty thought how exciting this was. "Did you ever make Felix look for you before?"

"Once or twice," Jane admitted.

"He didn't like it, though, did he?"

"Not to speak of. The woods are pretty thick there and you could lose your way easy when it starts getting darker."

"Then what happened?" Hetty left the kettle boiling.

"The leaves and vines around the whole place are knee-high. You couldn't tell where you're stepping even in a good light if you get a little excited. If in the dusk you think you see somebody all of a sudden from in back of a tree who you think is somebody else, it's pretty easy to forget just where you know is the only way it's safe to be walking."

Hetty stood and thought. Somehow her thoughts kept going back to Mamma. Wearing Mamma's coat, it was as if Jane had Mamma's knowing ways. She had done just what Mamma would have worked out for herself if it had been Mamma inside the coat instead of Jane. Hetty always knew if she left things to

Mamma they would work out. Felix had made one misstep too many, this time.

Finally Hetty said, "I don't guess there'll be any that'll be interested in any mishap that might have come to Felix."

"I'd agree with you there, Hetty," Jane said. She was folding up the sable coat very carefully and now she put it on a chair. "He'd been so restless lately, almost as if he had something on his mind."

"You don't say."

"Talking in his sleep and all. I can't feel he had been himself at all. I couldn't even bring myself to tell him about the invention."

"The invention? What about it?"

"I'll have money every month from now on." She smoothed the sleeves of the coat. "There was a letter from the lawyer, a while back. I couldn't decide whether to show it to Felix or not."

"You don't say," Hetty repeated. "I never knew Felix ever talked in his sleep."

Jane nodded slowly. "Just lately, these last couple of weeks. He never did before. One thing after another, he kept talking about. Things you would never believe. Just one after another."

That was one way, Hetty thought, of putting it.

JEROME BARRY

The Fourth Degree

INTRODUCTION

"The Fourth Degree" was my first crime story and the first piece of fiction of mine that appeared in a slick magazine. Hitherto I had had some straight adventure stuff in the pulps.

While I was scraping my brain raw in search of a story germ I remembered that somewhere I had read that if one just looks about at the ordinary objects in sight and tries to imagine how one of them could be of supreme interest to some person, he has a story idea. At this point, either because of intense concentration or because I was about to fall asleep, my eyes were closed. "This is fortunate," I said to myself, "because now I will write a story about the tremendous importance to someone of the first thing I see when I raise my lids."

A few moments later I waked from a sound doze when my face fell into the typewriter keys. All that saved me from a nasty cut on the bridge of the nose was my right hand, which had been resting on UIOP, waiting for the big idea to start it going at sixty words a minute. Naturally the first thing I saw, badly out of focus, of course, was the back of the hand.

"Very well," I told myself. "I am now committed to write a story about this hand that is here before me."

So at once there began evolving a story about a hand that wasn't there at all. Can I help it if that's the way my mind works?

The story was submitted to Collier's. Kenneth Littauer, then fiction editor, made a few cogent suggestions for improving it. He did not buy the revised version, however, and it sold to Liberty on the next trip out—for $100. In those days, when writers were even more from hunger than they are now (depression being even more depressing than inflation), Liberty followed the practice of some other magazines in buying all rights—and meaning it. A year or two after "The Fourth Degree" was published, I was surprised when I tuned in by chance to

hear the story being dramatized on the radio. Not only had no addi-
tional payment been made to me and no permission requested, but I
had not even been notified that my story would be on the air.

JEROME BARRY

The Fourth Degree

"I THOUGHT I'd better frisk him first," Sergeant Friedman said deferentially. "He looks mean. But there ain't a gun or knife anywhere on him."

Chief Mangan nodded. The Sergeant stepped out, and Potter entered the room. He was forty-five, with the eyes of a fox and the square, sensitive hands of the skilled worker. One hand, that is. The other was a wooden stump ending in a hook. He took the chair to which Mangan nodded and laid the wooden wrist on the desk.

"Look at that," he said. His eyes had a feverish shine.

"Well?" The Chief was a broad block of a man, with a steady gray gaze.

"I made it myself."

"You were always clever with your hands, Potter. Especially on bank-note plates."

"I didn't have enough scratch left after Jim's trial to buy a regular artificial duke. So I put this one together out of odds and ends. I managed it with one hand and a bench vise and a few tools. Look at it. It's as much your work as mine."

Mangan frowned. "What? Oh—you fell downstairs during the examination, didn't you?"

"That's what they said in court. They broke that wrist making me tell where Jim was! My own son! . . . Gangrene set in afterward. It was taken off in the hospital. And you know who'd given the orders for the third degree, Mangan. It was you."

The Chief shook his head. "Not for that, Potter. The boys were crazy to get Jim after the way he killed Hallahan. Surrendered and then shot him through the belly with a sleeve gun. They didn't care much for orders."

"And what did they do to Jim when they got him?" Potter

cried savagely, unlistening. "It wasn't the first time they worked him over, either. He wasn't used to it. I never lifted a hand to him since he was a little kid."

"No," the Chief said levelly. "You trained him to pass the queer bills you engraved. And when we took you up, you handed him over to Red Guszki to train as a punk in his mob. You took care he was in fine hands while you did your stretch! If you'd given him a good cuffing or two as a kid he mightn't have come —Why, isn't it today?"

"Yes," said Potter, watching Mangan sidewise. "They hanged Jim this morning. . . . And do you think I blame a few flatfeet for what's happened to him and me? One man's been after us— hunting us down."

"It's my job, Potter," the Chief answered patiently. "I'm sorry for you today."

Potter's voice dropped to a harsh whisper. "You've seen Jim hanged. But you did worse to me when you had them beat me up till I told where he was, like—like a Judas. But I'll make up for it. See this, Mangan? See it?"

He put his hands together in a grotesque and curious gesture. The real hand clasped the wooden stump, and he held the two out before him as if begging for something. "Look at it! What do you see, Mangan? Just below the hook."

The chief said slowly, "There's a small hole."

"Big enough for a bullet, Mangan. When I press this— spring—" his fingers shifted their grip deftly—"that bullet is going to crash through your brain."

Hard gray eyes and feverish wide ones were fixed intently on one another.

"Jim was in the death house for weeks," Potter went on in a vicious whisper. "I want you to see the end coming at you that way—gradually. I'm going to start counting—Wait. You have a gun in that side drawer. Take it out. Very slow. Lay it on the desk. I don't think this thing will miss fire, but I'll take no chances. I want to be sure you haven't a weapon in reach."

Mangan laid the revolver on the desk and withdrew his hand from it slowly, reluctantly. That tiny black opening, like the eye of a snake, looked unwaveringly into his face.

But instead of moving the chief's gun farther away, Potter

disregarded it and in a fierce ecstasy leaned forward and caressed the wooden wrist.

"I'm going to count to a hundred," he whispered. "Sit and wait for the end, like Jim did. At a hundred I press the spring."

He counted slowly, tasting the numbers one by one on his tongue. Mangan's fingers lay on the desk, helpless, unmoving. At fifty Potter was rocking slightly from haunch to haunch, caught up in the delectable rhythm of his vengeful tally. At eighty, his eyes half closed with delight, he swayed just enough so that for a brief moment the wooden hand wavered off line.

Mangan's fingers darted, twitched up the revolver as the artificial hand swung back. A sharp report shook the air.

In the outer room Friedman was talking stiffly with Mr. Horace Gaillard, leader of the reform faction, who had been making capital of police brutality.

At the sound of the shot, Friedman ran into Mangan's office, and close on his heels followed the crusading lawyer, Gaillard. The Chief stood beside the desk, the revolver smoking in his hand. On the floor lay Potter.

"Good Lord!" the lawyer said. "So it's come to outright murder!"

Mangan's eyes darted at him. "What are *you* doing here?"

"Potter begged me to come. You had summoned him, and he feared for his safety, his life. With reason, it seems."

"I hadn't summoned him. He threatened to shoot me. Friedman, see if there's a gun built into that wooden hand."

The sergeant stooped, probed, flashed a torch. "No, sir. There's just a hole drilled in it that don't lead anywheres. The rest of it's solid."

"The old police trick!" Gaillard taunted acidly. "Trying to plant a weapon, and I've never seen a stupider or more barefaced attempt. It's lucky I'm here, Mangan. I'll see you hanged for this!"

"It was a job," the Chief said slowly. "The poor, crazy devil wanted to die, and he wanted to see me suffer the way his son did in the death house."

"And you'll go there," Gaillard stated icily. "A more cold-blooded killing—"

"Killing?" Mangan said. "I knew there was something wrong

when he left that gun in my reach. I took a chance and wasted a shot to find why he wanted me to use it. The bullet's up there in a ceiling beam. When he saw he'd failed, he came at me with the hook, and I knocked him cold.

"His eyes are opening now. . . . Friedman, show both these gentlemen out."

LILLIAN DE LA TORRE

The Second Sight of
Dr. Sam: Johnson

INTRODUCTION

"Detective stories," said my husband, "are the bunk."

I had heard it before.

"What a preposterous bunch, detectives," said he, warming to his theme. "Foreigners! Old maids! Cute brides! First thing you know, there'll be a police dog."

"There's been a police dog."

My husband snorted.

"What makes the bad ones bad," said I, "is thin character drawing. Now what you need for a detective is a real, foursquare, believable character like—like Dr. Sam: Johnson in Boswell's great Life."

It came out of my mouth before it crossed my mind; but when I heard myself say it, I knew in a flash that the thing was inevitable. Here was a natural-born detective, full of curiosity, common sense, and courage, living in an age of raffish crime and logical thinking, equipped moreover with history's most perfect Watson, his inquiring biographer, James Boswell. I had been studying Johnson for eighteen years. Now he flashed before my mind's eye in an exciting kinetograph of real-life scenes: breaking the case of the Cock Lane Ghost, detecting and defying "Ossian" McPherson, standing off four footpads with a cudgel, investigating the "second sight" in the Hebrides.

I had never written a detective story, but this was an idea too good to neglect. I turned to Boswell's Tour to the Hebrides, *and my first story practically wrote itself—or rather, James Boswell in person had practically written it for me. His book provided the description of Dr. Johnson, his friends on the Isle of Raasay, their conversation about the second sight, the ramble to the cave, the mysterious fox, and the couch of fern. Around them I wove my first mystery story, as related by James Boswell and solved by "The Second Sight of Dr. Sam: Johnson."*

Where to market it? I tried it on the long-hairs. No, indeed—far too frivolous. Then I did what I should have done in the first place—I sent it to Ellery Queen. This was in 1943.

LILLIAN DE LA TORRE

The Second Sight of Dr. Sam: Johnson

SIR,' said the learned Dr. Sam: Johnson to the Laird of Raasay, 'he who meddles with the uncanny, meddles with danger but none the less for that, 'tis the duty of the philosopher, diligently to enquire into the truth of these matters.'

All assented to my learned friend's proposition, none dreaming how soon and how terribly his words were to be verified, and his intrepidity put to the test.

No premonition of events to come disturbed the pleasure with which I saw my learned companion thus complacently domesticated upon the Isle of Raasay. Our long-cherished scheam of visiting the Western Islands of Scotland was now a reality; and it was in acknowledgement of the plans of the Laird for exploring the wonders of the isle that the respectable author of the *Dictionary* uttered these words.

As he did so, he gazed with complacency upon his companions by the Laird's fireside; a group of Highland gentlemen, shewing in face and bearing that superiority which consciousness of birth and learning most justifiably supplies. Of the family of MacLeod were the Laird himself, a sensible, polite, and most hospitable gentleman, and his brother, Dr. MacLeod, a civil medical man of good skill. These gentlemen shewed a strong family resemblance, being tall and strongly made, with firm ruddy countenances; genteelly apparelled in sad-coloured suits with clean ruffles.

Their companions in the ingle-nook by the glowing peat fire were two brothers, Angus and Colin MacQueen, sons of the incumbent rector of the parish of Snizoort on Skye. They resembled one another, being lean, light, and active, with bony dark faces; wearing suits of scholarly black, and their own heavy dark hair cut short.

The elder, Mr. Angus MacQueen, was a learned young man, a close observer of the natural phænomena of the island. He filled the trusted post of tutor to Raasay's heir. The younger son, Colin, new returned from the University, had all his elder brother's wide and curious learning, but displayed withal an ill-regulated instability of mind and a hectick behaviour, poorly held in check by respect for Raasay and my learned companion.

Dr. Samuel Johnson's character—nay, his figure and manner, are, I believe, more generally known than those of almost any man, yet it may not be superfluous here to attempt a sketch of him. His person was large, robust, I may say approaching to the gigantick, and grown unwieldy from corpulency. His countenance was naturally of the case of an antient statue, but somewhat disfigured by the scars of that evil which it was formerly imagined the royal touch would cure. He was now in his sixty-fourth year, and was become a little dull of hearing. His sight had always been somewhat weak, yet so much does mind govern and even supply the deficiency of organs that his perceptions were uncommonly quick and accurate. His head and sometimes also his body shook with a kind of motion like the effect of a palsy; he appeared to be frequently disturbed by cramps or convulsive contractions, of the nature of that distemper called St. Vitus's dance. He wore a full suit of plain brown cloathes with twisted-hair buttons of the same colour, a large bushy greyish wig, a plain shirt, black worsted stockings, and silver buckles. He had a loud voice and a slow deliberate utterance, which no doubt gave some additional weight to the sterling metal of his conversation. He had a constitutional melancholy the clouds of which darkened the brightness of his fancy and gave a gloomy cast to his whole course of thinking; yet, though grave and awful in his deportment when he thought it necessary or proper, he frequently indulged himself in pleasantry and sportive sallies. He was prone to superstition but not to credulity. Though his imagination might incline him to a belief of the marvellous, his vigorous reason examined the evidence with jealousy.

Such was my learned friend during our visit to the Western Islands; and thus it was that on this first evening of our sojourn on Raasay our talk turned on the topography, the antiquities, and especially the superstitions of the Isle of Raasay.

Dr. Johnson had professed himself eager to enquire into our Highland phænomenon of second sight.

'Sir,' said Angus MacQueen, 'I am *resolved* not to believe it, because it is founded on no principle.'

'Then,' said Dr. Johnson, 'there are many verified facts that you will not believe. What principle is there why the lodestone attracts iron? Why an egg produces a chicken by heat? Why a tree grows upward, when the natural tendency of all things is downward? Sir, it depends on the degree of evidence you have.'

Young Angus MacQueen made no reply. Colin MacQueen rolled his wild dark eyes on the awe-inspiring figure of my friend as he asked: 'What evidence would satisfy you?'

'Whist, then, Colin,' interposed his brother, 'let past things be.'

'I knew a MacKenzie,' Dr. MacLeod said cheerfully, 'who would faint away, and when he revived again he had visions to tell of. He told me upon one occasion, I should meet a funeral just at the fork of the road, and the bearers people I knew, and he named them, too. Well, sir, three weeks after, I did meet a funeral on that very road, and the very bearers he named. Was not that second sight?'

'Sir,' said my friend, 'what if this man lay a-dying, and your MacKenzie and the whole town knew who his friends would be to carry him to the grave?—Ay, and by the one nearest way to the graveyard?'

'What do you say then to the women of Skye,' said the honest Laird, 'who stopped me on the road to say that they had heard two *taisks*, and one an English one—'

'What is a *taisk*?' I ventured to enquire. It is the part of a chronicler to omit no opportunity to clarify his record.

'A *taisk*, Mr. Boswell, is the voice of one about to die. Many of us in the Highlands hear *taisks* though we have not the second sight.'

'Sir,' said Dr. Johnson, 'it is easy enough for the women of Skye to say what they heard. Did *you* hear it?'

'I have not the gift,' said the Laird of Raasay, 'but returning the same road, I met two funerals, and one was of an English-woman.'

'Is there none in the Isle of Raasay with the second sight?' enquired my learned friend.

'There is indeed,' replied Colin MacQueen in a low voice. 'There is an old wife on the other side the island with the second sight. She foresaw my brother's murder.'

'How, sir!' exclaimed Dr. Johnson. 'Murder! I had no intent to distress you.'

"I will tell you the story.' Young MacQueen's eyes glittered in the firelight. 'Rory was younger than I, and meddled with the lasses where he had no concern. Old Kirstie comes one night to Angus and me, and falls to weeping, crying out that she has heard Rory's *taisk*, and seen him lying dead with his head broke. Wasn't it so, Angus?'

'It was so,' said the young tutor sombrely.

'And did it fall out so?' I enquired.

'So it fell out, for Angus was there and saw it,' replied young Colin, 'and if 'twas a grief to us, it broke old Kirstie's heart; for it was her own son killed him. A strapping surly ghillie he was, Black Fergus they called him, and he broke Rory's head for him over the bouman's lass.'

'Did the villain suffer for his crime?' enquired Dr. Johnson, profoundly struck by this tale of moral obliquity.

'He did, sir, though we have neither court nor judge upon Raasay since the troubled days of the '45; but rather than be took he flung himself into the sea; and his mother saw him in a dream rising up out of the sea dripping wet, with his face rotted away.'

' 'Twould interest me much,' said Dr. Johnson, 'if I might meet with this aged Sybil.'

'Nothing is easier,' replied Dr. MacLeod, 'for to-morrow I propose to shew you the strange caves of our eastern coast, and the old woman lives hard by. You shall interrogate her to your heart's content.'

'Sir,' said Dr. Johnson, 'I am obliged to you. What is the nature of the caves you mention?'

'They are sea caves,' replied Dr. MacLeod, 'of great age and extent. No one has ever explored all their ramifications.'

'My young friend MacQueen,' added the Laird, bowing to Angus, 'who is botanist, lapidarian, and antiquary of our island, knows them better than any man; but even he has never penetrated to their depths.'

'He fears the Kelpie,' said young Colin recklessly.

'The Kelpie?' I echoed.

'A water demon,' said Colin. 'He lives in the Kelpie Pool under the Kelpie's Window, and he eats men.'

'Such is the belief of the islanders,' assented Angus MacQueen. 'In their superstition they connect this supernatural being with a certain natural orifice in the cave wall, giving upon a deep pool of the sea.'

'The pool is bottomless,' struck in Colin, 'and under it sits the Kelpie and hates mankind.'

'It is impossible,' pronounced Dr. Johnson, 'by its very nature, that any depression which contains water should lack a bottom.'

'This one does,' muttered Colin.

' 'Tis perfectly true,' said Raasay, 'that the Kelpie Pool has never been sounded.'

'Thus do we see the credulity of ill-instructed men,' cried Dr. Johnson, with a glance of fire at young Colin, 'who because a thing *has never been done*, conclude illogically that it *cannot be done*.'

'To-morrow you shall see the Kelpie Pool,' said the learned young tutor, 'and judge for yourself. I can promise you also some interesting petrifications; and you shall see there a device which I have constructed to measure the rise and fall of the tides.'

'I shall be happy to be instructed,' replied Dr. Johnson civilly.

'Pray tell me,' I enquired, 'is the Isle of Raasay rich in fauna?'

'We have blackcock, moorfowl, plovers, and wild pigeons in abundance,' replied Dr. MacLeod.

JOHNSON: 'And of the four-footed kind?'

MACQUEEN: 'We have neither rabbits nor hares, nor was there ever any fox upon the island until recently; but now our birds are hunted, and one sees often the melancholy sight of a little heap of discarded feathers where the brute has supped.'

BOSWELL: 'How came a fox to Raasay? By swimming the channel from the mainland?'

MACLEOD: 'We cannot believe so, for a fox is a bad swimmer. We can only suppose that some person brought it over out of pure malice.'

JOHNSON: 'You must set a trap for him.'

MACQUEEN: 'I think to do so, for the remains of his hunting betray where he runs.'

BOSWELL: 'Now had you but horses on the island, we should give Reynard a run.'

This said, by mutual consent we all arose. Dr. Johnson and the Laird stolled off with Angus MacQueen to behold the stars of these northern latitudes. Dr. MacLeod, yawning, sought his bed; young Colin disappeared from my side like a phantom into the night; and I was left alone to the pleasing task of arranging my notes of the evening's discourse.

The morrow dawned wet and stormy, being one of those Hebridean days of which Dr. Johnson complained that they presented all the inconveniences of tempest without its sublimities. Our enforced confinement was made pleasant by the learned discourse of the Reverend Donald MacQueen and his no less learned son; till, the storm abating, the younger man left us near sundown, to inspect his sea-gauge at the edge of the island. He parted from Dr. Johnson on terms of mutual respect, and promised to bring him some specimens of petrifications.

The night came on with many brilliant stars; and we congratulated ourselves on the prospect of a fair dawn for the promised ramble about the island.

Colin was at my bedside next morning between five and six. I sprung up, and rouzed my venerable companion. Dr. Johnson quickly equipped himself for the expedition, and seized his formidable walking stick, without which he never stirred while in Scotland. This was a mighty oaken cudgel, knotted and gnarled; equipped with which the doughty philosopher felt himself the equal of any man.

We took a dram and a bit of bread directly. A boy of the name of Stewart was sent with us as our carrier of provisions. We were five in all: Colin MacQueen, Dr. MacLeod, the lad Stewart, Dr. Johnson, and myself.

'Pray, sir, where is Mr. Angus MacQueen?' enquired Dr. Johnson.

'Still on the prowl,' said his brother carelessly.

'Observing the stars, no doubt,' said Dr. MacLeod. 'No matter, we shall surely encounter him in our peregrinations.'

We walked briskly along; but the country was very stony at first, and a great many risings and fallings lay in our way. We had a shot at a flock of plovers sitting. But mine was harmless. We came first to a pretty large lake, sunk down comparatively with the land about it. Then to another; and then we mounted up to the top of Duncaan, where we sat down, ate cold mutton and bread and cheese and drank brandy and punch. Then we had a Highland song from Colin, which Dr. Johnson set about learning, *Hatyin foam foam eri*. We then walked over a much better country, very good pasture; saw many moorfowl, but could never get near them; descended a hill on the east side of the island; and so came to a hut by the sea. It was somewhat circular in shape, the door unfastened.

We called a blessing on the house and entered. At the far end an old woman was huddled over a peat fire. As we entered, she dropped the steaming breeks she had been drying before the glowing peat, and redded up for company by shuffling them hastily under the bedstead.

'Well, Kirstie,' Colin MacQueen greeted her, 'here's Dr. Johnson come all the way from London to ask you about your gift of the second sight.'

To our utter astonishment the wizened old creature dropped to her knees and began to keen in a dreadful voice, rocking herself to and fro and wringing her hands.

'Come, come my good creature,' said the humane Doctor, 'there's no occasion for such a display, I'm sure,' and he benevolently insinuated half a crown into her clenched clawlike hand.

The aged Sybil peeped at it briefly, and stowed it away about her person; but she continued to keen softly, and presently her words became audible: 'Alas, 'tis no gift, but a curse, to have seen what I have seen, poor Rory gone, and my own son drowned, and now this very day—' The keening rose to a wail.

'We are causing too much distress by our enquiries,' muttered my friend.

But the aged crone caught him by the wrist.

'It is laid on me to tell no less than to see.'

'What have you seen to-day, then?' enquired Dr. MacLeod soothingly.

'Come,' said Colin roughly, 'there is nothing to be gained by lingering.'

'*Angus! Angus! Angus!*'

'What of Angus?' asked Dr. Johnson with apprehension.

'I have heard his *taisk!* I have seen him lying broken and dead! He's gone, like Rory, like my own son that's drowned. Ai! Ai!'

'Come away,' cried Colin, and flung out at the door. My friends complied, and I followed them, but not before I had bestowed some small charity upon the pathetic aged creature.

Colin led the way, walking heedlessly and fast. My friend and I perforce dropped behind.

'This is most remarkable,' said Dr. Johnson. 'If we should indeed find that the young man has met with a misfortune—which Heaven forfend—'

'We may speak as eyewitness of this often-doubted phænomenon,' said I, concluding his statement.

'Nevertheless, sir,' pronounced the learned philosopher, 'man's intellect has been given him to *guard against credulity*. Let us take care not to fall into an attitude of superstitious belief in the old dame's powers. As yet her allegation is unsupported.'

By this time we were come to the cave. It lies in a section of the coast where the cliffs mount up to a threatening height, with a deep sound under, for a reef of jagged rocks some way out takes the pounding of the sea.

Dr. Johnson shewed especial curiosity about the minerals of the island. Ever solicitous for the improvement of human comfort, he enquired whether any coal were known on the island, 'for,' said he, 'coal is commonly to be found in mountainous country, such as we see upon Raasay.'

'See,' he continued, 'this vein of black sand, where otherwise the sand is white.'

He gathered a handful; it stained his hand, and he cast it away.

'It is surely powdered coal,' concluded my learned friend, punching at the deposit with his sturdy stick.

'Sir,' I ventured, 'it more nearly resembles charcoal.'

'Coal or charcoal, 'til all one,' returned my friend. 'Did I live upon Raasay, I should try whether I could find the vein, for there's no fire like a coal fire.'

'Come, let us enter the cave,' cried Colin MacQueen impatiently.

To my surprise the ghillie who carried our provisions unconditionally refused to enter the cave, alleging it to be haunted; **a** circumstance which was confirmed to his untutored mind by a strange echo from within, as of footsteps walking, that seemed to sound over the breakers.

'I'll not go in,' said the lad stubbornly, ' 'tis full of wildfire these days, and something walks there.'

' 'Tis your fox that walks there,' observed Dr. Johnson, poking at a pile of feathers hard by the entrance.

'Well, my lad, if you won't come you may e'en stay here,' said Colin MacQueen impatiently. 'I fear neither fox nor fox fire, and I'm for the cave. Come, gentlemen.'

He led the way up a sloping incline and through a low entranceway. Dr. Johnson had to stoop his great frame as he crowded through. Within, our footsteps rattled on the pebbly path. Colin carried a torch, which gleamed upon the rising roof and upon the petrifications that hung from it, formed by drops that perpetually distil therefrom. They are like little trees. I broke off some of them.

The cave widened and grew lofty as we progressed. Dr. Johnson was much struck by the absolute silence, broken only by the noise of our advance, which re-echoed ahead of us.

I drew Colin's attention to certain places on the floor, where partitions of stone appeared to be human work, shewing indeed the remains of desiccated foliage with which they had once been filled.

'In the days of the pirates,' he explained, 'this cave was a place of refuge. These are what is left of the beds. Here,' he continued, 'the cave divides. The left-hand arm slopes down to the sea, where a wide opening provided shelter for boats and a hiding-place for oars. Halfway down, there is a fresh spring. We take the right-hand turning, gentlemen.'

'In times past,' contributed Dr. MacLeod as we ascended the right-hand slope, 'the cave sometimes served as a refuge for malefactors; but it invariably proved a trap.'

'How so, sir,' I asked, 'with a fresh spring, escape by sea or land, and the unexplored fastnesses of the cave to lurk in?'

There was a puff of air, and the torch with which Colin was leading the way was suddenly extinguished. At first the blackness was pitchy.

'You may proceed without fear,' spoke Colin out of the darkness, 'provided you always keep the wall of the cave at your left hand. I will endeavour to restore the light.'

'Colin knows this cave as he knows his own house,' Dr. Mac-Leod assured us.

We groped our way forward.

'Thus it was, in darkness on this ascent, that men waited to take or destroy the outlaw,' Dr. MacLeod took up his narrative 'Just around this bend we come into light.'

He spoke truly, for already a faint ray was diluting the darkness. As we rounded the bend we saw, ahead and close at hand, an irregular opening through which we could glimpse the sky.

'Whoever takes shelter in the innermost recesses of this cave,' said Dr. MacLeod, 'must pass by that opening whenever thirst drives him down to the spring below. A marksman stationed at the bend can pick him off as he passes against the light.'

'That's the Kelpie's Window,' said Colin at my elbow. I started, and then in the uncertain light perceived him where he leaned in a little recess striking a light with flint and steel.

'Press on,' said Colin, 'I'll come behind with the torch.'

I own it oppressed me with gloomy thoughts to climb in the darkness this path where savage and lawless men of the past had died. My venerable companion is of more intrepid mould; he and Dr. MacLeod pressed forward undismayed.

'I was on this path not three months since,' pursued the physician, 'when Black Fergus the murderer took shelter in these caves.'

'Did you take him?' enquired Dr. Johnson with interest.

'We did not,' said Dr. MacLeod. 'We waited here in the dark, off and on by relays, for three days and three nights.'

'Did not he come down?'

'When he came, he came running, and before we could take aim, he had flung himself into the sea.'

I was powerfully struck by this narration. I seemed to see the hunted figure, driven by thirst to a watery grave.

We attained the top of this sinister incline, and stood in the Kelpie's Window, a sheer one hundred feet above the black waters of the Kelpie Pool. Height makes me flinch; I retreated behind a rock which jutted out beside the opening.

Dr. Johnson stood firm and viewed the craggy descent with

curiosity. The cliff fell away almost perpendicularly, but much gashed and broken with spires and chimneys of rock.

'From this point Black Fergus flung himself into the sea,' mused Dr. Johnson. ' 'Tis a fearful drop. His body must have been much battered by those jagged rocks below.'

'We never recovered his body,' replied Dr. MacLeod. 'He had sunk before we reached the window, and he rose no more.'

Colin came behind us with the torch alight.

'He must rise to the surface in the evolution of time,' said Dr. Johnson. 'What is that at the edge of the Kelpie Pool?'

The physician stared fixedly below.

'It is certainly a body,' he pronounced.

' 'Tis Black Fergus,' cried I, peeping in my turn.

Colin leaned boldly out to see.

'That is never Black Fergus,' he said. 'Good God! 'Tis my brother!'

He turned and plunged down the dusky slope, carrying the torch with him.

'Wait, sir!' cried Dr. Johnson.

'I fear he is right,' said Dr. MacLeod quietly, 'that broad sunhat is certainly Angus's. I must go to him.'

He in turn ran down the slope, following the diminishing gleam of Colin's torch.

It was indeed the unfortunate young tutor. His grief-stricken brother drew the body gently to land, and we made shift among us to bear it to the mouth of the cave. The terrified ghillie wrung his hands and babbled about the Kelpie; but Dr. MacLeod bade him hold his tongue and run to the big house for bearers.

'Poor lad,' said Dr. MacLeod, 'those petrifications have been the death of him. He must have overbalanced and fallen from the Kelpie's Window.'

'I don't understand it,' cried poor Colin. 'Angus had no fear of height; he could climb like a cat.'

'Nevertheless, he fell from the Kelpie's Window and drowned in the Kelpie Pool,' I said with a shudder.

'Not drowned,' said the physician. 'He was dead when he hit the water. He must have struck his head as he fell; his skull is shattered.'

The bearers arriving, we carried the unfortunate young man to his patron's house and laid him down.

This sad occurrence, as may be imagined, cast a pall over Raasay; all retired early, with solemn thoughts of the mutability of human affairs.

The night was advanced when I awoke with a start and was astounded to behold my venerable companion risen from bed and accoutered for walking in his wide brown cloth greatcoat with its bulging pockets, his Hebridean boots, and his cocked hat firmly secured by a scarf. I watched while he stole forth from the chamber, then rose in my turn and made haste to follow.

Lighted by a fine moon, the sturdy philosopher crossed the island at a brisk pace. I caught him up as we neared the opposite coast. As I came up with him he whirled suddenly and threw himself in an attitude of defence, menacing me truculently with his heavy staff.

'Sir, sir!' I expostulated.

'Is it you, you rogue?' exclaimed he, relaxing his pugnacity.

'What means this nocturnal expedition, sir?' I ventured to enquire.

'Only that I have a fancy to interrogate old Kirstie farther about the second sight,' responded he.

'You do well,' I approved, 'for we have had a convincing if tragic exhibition of her powers.'

'Have not I warned you against an attitude of credulity?' said the learned Doctor severely. 'I must understand more of her powers before I may say I have seen a demonstration of the second sight.'

'What more can you ask?' I replied.

By now we were within sight of old Kirstie's hut. Without replying, Dr. Johnson astounded me by striking up an Erse song in a tuneless bellow.

'Sir, sir, this is most unseemly!' I expostulated.

'*Hatyin foam foam eri*,' chanted Dr. Johnson lustily, striding along vigorously.

A boat was drawn up in a cove; Dr. Johnson rapped it smartly with his stick as we passed it. Then with a final triumphant '*Tullishole!*' he thundered resoundingly on the door of the hut.

The little old crone opened for us without any delay, and

dropped us a trepidatious curtsey. The close apartment reeked of the remains of the cocky-leeky standing at the hearth. We had interrupted breakfast, for a half-consumed bowl of the stewed leeks and joints of fowl stood on the rude table.

'So, ma'am,' said Dr. Johnson bluntly, 'Angus MacQueen is dead like his brother.'

The old beldame began to wail, but Dr. Johnson most unfeelingly cut her short.

'We found him dead in the Kelpie Pool with his head broke.'

'He should never have gone in the cave!' whispered the aged Sybil. 'He had my warning!'

'There's Something lives in that cave,' said Dr. Johnson solemnly.

'Ay! Ay!'

'There's Something wicked lives in that cave, that comes forth to kill the blackcock by night, and hides in the upper reaches by day.'

'Ay!'

'Have you seen it in your visions?'

'Ay, a mortal great ghostie that eats the bones of men. . . . Alas! Alas!' the keening broke forth afresh.

'Then, ma'am,' said the intrepid philosopher, 'I have a mind to see this ghostie.'

Hefting his heavy stick, Dr. Johnson left the hut. The woman burst forth into a clamour of warning, admonition, and entreaty, to which my friend paid little heed. Having bestowed a small gratuity, which served to intermit the old dame's ululations, I hurried after the venerable Doctor.

I caught him up at the cove. The declining moon was bright and clear.

'That is MacQueen's boat.' I recognized it. 'Who has brought it here?'

My only answer was a touch on the arm.

'Be quiet,' said my friend in my ear. 'Take this—' he pressed a pistol in my hand, 'and when we come to the cave—'

'You will never go into the cave at this hour!' I gasped.

'You need only go as far as the fork. Watch what I do, but take care not to reveal your presence. I have a mind to conjure up the Kelpie.'

There was no gainsaying my learned friend. So it was done. I own it was rather a relief than otherwise, after the pitchy blackness of the first ascent, to come in sight of the moonlight streaming through the Kelpie's Window. I shrank gratefully into the shelter of the shoulder of rock where Colin had stood that morning. I thought no shame to breathe a prayer for the intercession of St. Andrew, patron of Scotland.

My lion-hearted friend mounted steadily, till at last I saw him stand in bold relief against the moonlit sky in the ill-omened Kelpie's Window. He stood foursquare without shrinking, his cocked hat tied firmly to his head, his heavy stick lost in the voluminous skirts of his greatcoat. What incantation he recited I know not.

Whatever incantation the intrepid initiate recited, it served to raise the Kelpie. There was a slip and slither of stealthy footsteps in the cave above; and then he came down with a rush and a rattle of pebbles. I saw his bulk dimly in the half light, with the great club raised; then my friend wheeled nimbly into the shelter of the rock that had served me that morning. At the same time he struck down strongly with his heavy stick, and with a horrible cry the threatening figure overbalanced and tumbled headlong.

I hastened up the slope. At the top, my friend stood motionless and grave. At the foot of the cliff the fallen figure lay horribly still at the pool's edge.

'If he appear to his mother this time,' muttered Dr. Johnson, 'I'll know that she has the second sight.'

'It mazes me,' I remarked when once more we sat together at the Laird's fireside, 'how in a record of second sight thrice confirmed, you, sir, managed to read the unsupernatural truth.'

'Man's power of ratiocination,' returned Dr. Johnson, 'is his truest second sight.'

'Doubtless,' remarked Colin MacQueen, 'old Kirstie, poor thing, was just as amazed at the learned Doctor's perceptions as we were at hers.'

'Pray explain, then, how ratiocination led you to the truth.'

'Sir, 'tis my earnest endeavour to instruct myself in your

Highland phaenomenon of second sight, of whose existence I have heard so much. I repeat, I am willing to be convinced; but of each demonstration I remain a skeptick. I ask: Is second sight possible? And I reply in the affirmative. Of each separate occurrence I then ask: Is *this* second sight? Could not it be something else? I have yet to hear of the case that would not admit of some other explanation. Such was my frame of mind when first I heard of old Kirstie and her feats of second sight.'

'She prophesied Rory's death,' said Colin.

JOHNSON: 'Nay sir, she *warned* you of his danger. Her reputation for second sight enabled her to do so without betraying her son. She foresaw what happened, not by second sight, but by her knowledge of her son's murderous frame of mind.'

BOSWELL: 'Then her story of her son rising out of the sea before her in the night was a pure invention.'

JOHNSON: 'Nay, sir, 'twas pure truth, save for the one detail that he was alive.'

MACQUEEN: 'How knew you that?'

JOHNSON: 'Sir, I had concluded before I heard of this second apparition that the first one was a lie. If the second was a lie, it had one of two motives: if her son was dead, to add to her reputation for second sight; if alive, to contribute to his safety by confirming his supposed death. Thus far had ratiocination carried me when we visited her hut and heard her third prophecy. I had no faith in this third apparition, which I took, wrongly, to be a second warning.'

BOSWELL: 'Why a warning?'

JOHNSON: 'Because, sir, I saw in the hut that which convinced me that Black Fergus was alive and on the island.'

BOSWELL: 'What?'

JOHNSON: 'Why, sir, the great pair of breeks which we caught her drying at the fire, that she quickly hid under the bedstead. Think you that that poor wizened body had been wearing them, even were the women of Raasay given to masculine attire?'

'But with my own eyes I saw him leap into the sea and rise no more,' objected Dr. MacLeod.

'You saw him leap,' returned Dr. Johnson. 'I saw when I stood in the Kelpie's Window how a strong and intrepid swimmer could leap outward and take no harm, for the Kelpie Pool is deep and calm, and for his life a man can swim a long stretch under water. Had you looked along the cliffs instead of down into the pool, Dr. MacLeod, you might have seen his head breaking water, like a seal's, to breathe. So it was that he came dripping to his mother out of the sea by night, and she comforted him, and hid him in the cave, and they plotted how he should reappear disguised when the nine-days' wonder had died down.'

'Did ratiocinating on a single pair of sodden breeches tell you all this?' I rallied my learned friend.

'Not so,' replied Dr. Johnson. 'I concluded only to keep a sharp eye for signs of where she had hidden him. By the cave I saw the remains of his hunting—we have scotched your fox, Dr. MacLeod—and the charcoal of his fire ground into the sand; and in the cave we saw the fern he had couched on. From Dr. MacLeod I learned of the fresh spring and the chambers above; and I saw the Kelpie's Window and the pool below. Then we found the unfortunate young Angus, and the thing was certain. I knew at once how he had met his death.'

'Why? Why did Black Fergus wish to harm him?' burst forth Colin MacQueen bitterly.

'Your brother ventured into the cave, torch in hand, to fetch those specimens of petrifications he promised me. There he came face to face with his brother's murderer, and knew him. So much is certain. I think he fled, and was struck down from behind.'

'How came he in the Kelpie Pool, then?'

'Ratiocination tells me,' replied Dr. Johnson, smiling slightly, 'that guilt and terror obscured the man's reason. Instead of hiding the body where it might never have been found, he endeavoured to simulate an accident, by flinging the body from the Kelpie's Window. He then swam or waded by night to his mother's hut and implored her to facilitate his flight. There he lay hid while the old beldame dried his garments.'

'Was he then, in the very house when the old woman "prophesied" Angus's death?'

'Was he, elsewhere, without his breeches?' countered Dr. Johnson. 'When I saw Angus lying murdered, I knew who had done it, I knew what he must do next. I resolved to stop his flight.'

'Why you? Why single-handed?'

'Since the '45, there is no law on Raasay, save what is brought from the mainland. I, an Englishman, a stranger, might most safely take justice upon myself. By night, I returned to the hut.'

'How dared you seek him out on his own ground?'

'I preferred to face him on ground I had chosen. By the ostentatiousness of my arrival I gave such warning as drove him from the hut to his hiding-place in the cave. Mr. Boswell will confess that though I am scarce fit for Italian opera, my rendition of an Erse song has a peculiar carrying power. For the same purpose I thundered, sir—' turning to Colin—'upon your boat, which the murderer had stolen and beached, ready for his flight. Having thus assured the murderer's presence in the cave, I entered in search of him.'

'Good heavens, sir!' cried Colin impetuously, 'to venture thus into the lair of a wild beast, and hope to surprize him ere he can surprize you!'

'I had no such hope,' replied my intrepid friend. 'He was sure to perceive me and attack me first. I permitted him to do so, only choosing my ground with some care.'

'The Kelpie's Window hardly seems like favourable ground.'

'On the contrary,' replied Dr. Johnson. 'If I was to bait my own trap, I had to have visibility, a quality provided in the whole cave only by the Kelpie's Window. There also shelter is provided, as Mr. Boswell found.'

'Do you mean to say, sir,' cried Dr. MacLeod, 'that you stood in that orifice, contemplating such a declivity, and permitted a desperate murderer to creep up on you in the dark?'

'I expected him; I detected his approach; I was able to evade him at the crucial moment. That he fell from the Kelpie's Window was no part of my plan, for I had counted on taking him with my pistol.'

'Sir, sir,' I cried, 'you took a grave risk thus staking your life on your hearing.'

'Nor did I so,' replied Dr. Johnson, half smiling. 'You forget that Black Fergus had been supping on cocky-leeky. It takes neither ratiocination nor second sight, sir, to detect the proximity of your pervasive Scottish leek!'

JOSEPH FULLING FISHMAN

Old Calamity Tries a Bluff

INTRODUCTION

During the years I was Inspector of Prisons for the United States Government, I watched with astonishment the outstanding detective ability displayed by Loney J. Fletcher, Deputy Warden of the Federal Penitentiary at Atlanta, in solving mysteries which arose in the prison.

These included the smuggling of guns and narcotics, the making of various weapons, plots to escape which had not yet come to fruition, knifings by inmates and other things of the kind.

With little to go on—sometimes but a vague anonymous note—and with an almost hundred-per-cent-chronic-liar population with which to contend, Fletcher achieved extraordinary success in checkmating the plots, counterplots, double-crossings, intrigues and framings which are as much a part of every big penitentiary as the walls and gun towers.

It was my observation of the detection methods of "Old Calamity"— prison slang for the Deputy Warden, probably because he's the officer who holds "court call" for rules infractions and dishes out the punishments—which suggested to me the idea of stories of a "Dep" who solves all kinds of evildoings inside a penitentiary.

I wrote many of them for Munsey's Detective Fiction *magazine, all entitled "Old Calamity" (does this, that or the other). The plots suggested themselves in the hundreds of investigations which I made of all phases of prison administration in various types of penal institutions in the United States, Alaska, and Puerto Rico.*

I don't know how many years ago this story was written, as I haven't the exact date, but it's probably twenty-six or twenty-seven. I sent it initially to Detective Fiction, *and it was bought by them. I think they paid me sixty dollars, although it may have been seventy or seventy-five.*

Whatever it was, I'm certain I spent at least half of it buying the magazine to hand to friends and to mail anonymously to enemies. I don't know if, after reading the story, it made the latter regret they hadn't remained friendly with me, or if it confirmed them that my friendship wasn't worth having.

Anyhow, they're still enemies.

JOSEPH FULLING FISHMAN

Old Calamity Tries a Bluff

HAD it not been for the walls and the towers which from a distance so much resembled a Chinese coolie's hat, the prison yard would have looked like almost any public recreation park. In one corner, with a natural backstop formed by the wall, a baseball game was in progress between the white and the colored inmates. In the bleachers, back of the base line, a howling crowd of convicts shouted unheeded advice to the players. Back of the three fielders a straggling group of gray-clad men watched the game with a casual interest, one occasionally leaving here and there and walking back to other parts of the yard where more interesting diversion was promised.

In another part of the field a group of men were playing handball. In still another a perspiring crowd was engaged in pushball. Here a few played checkers. There one strummed on a banjo or other musical instrument, each surrounded by a small group of ardent admirers or equally ardent critics.

Suddenly, by that invisible telegraph system which scientists call mob psychology, practically every one of the more than three thousand prisoners in the yard became conscious of something unusual going on in the welter of activity. Almost simultaneously their eyes were directed to a point near that part of the field which was devoted to basketball. And even before they themselves were aware of it, half of them were running toward this spot without the slightest idea of what was going on but convinced that something was happening which would lift, if only for a moment, the blanket of monotony which made up their lives.

And they were not disappointed. It was a fight, that most welcome spectacle in all prisons, that great lightener of spirits which made them forget for the moment where they were and gave them the feeling of aliveness which all human beings welcome, inside walls and out.

But this was more than a fight between two individuals, the kind generally staged, which were usually stopped by the officers almost before they had begun. This was a fight between groups. And such a fight as even the oldest convict in the Cosmopolis Penitentiary had never seen. There must have been twenty five or thirty prisoners taking part in it. When the leaders of the eager spectators arrived panting at the scene the basketball field was a cursing, shouting, struggling mass of men who, with fists, sticks, pieces of brick or anything else which they could put their hands on, were laying about them with a total disregard of their own skulls and those of their opponents. Three men were lying on the ground, one of them totally unconscious and with blood streaming from an open cut in his head, while two others, semi-conscious, struggled on their hands and knees to crawl out of the fighting ring to escape being trampled to death. The over-wrought, highly inflammable spectators soon added to the delirium. Shrieks of advice and encouragement, shouts of "The Dockers!," "The Alleys!," "Attaboy, Blinky!," "Look out, Mike, he's got a shiv!," and a jumbled mass of incoherent sounds resounded throughout the prison yard.

Then there was a break in the surrounding mass of men and four blue-coated guards, sticks in hand, pushed their way into the fighting circle and with swinging clubs threw themselves into the fight. It was like trying to sweep the ocean back with a broom. Outnumbered five or six to one, their clubs were wrested from their hands, they were thrown to the ground to be trampled on by the fighters, now warming to their work and determined to see the thing through to a finish.

Then there came an ominous crack, followed by another and another. As one man the prisoners, fighters as well as spectators, whirled and stared at the point from which the ominous sound came. On the platform outside of his tower stood Guard Todd, rifle in hand, a thin mist of white smoke curling from the muzzle. For a second the prisoners stared uncertainly, then slowly turned and looked dubiously at each other while the fighters paused uncertainly. Then came the voice they all knew so well, quiet, commanding, "That'll be about all, boys."

In a fleeting second or two Deputy Warden Fletcher, or "Old Calamity" as he was known to all the prisoners in the institution, took in the scene before him, the prisoners lying on the ground, three trying feebly to rise, the one standing on his feet but swaying dizzily from side to side. The several with blood streaming from their heads, but, from the look on their faces, still in a decidedly belligerent mood. The rest, not particularly marked, but with mussed hair and torn clothing, stared at the Deputy and tried to figure out just what their next move should be. Five or six more guards, out of breath from their long run from the other end of the yard, had now come puffing up. Old Calamity took command immediately.

"All right, boys," he said to the spectators, "back to the ball game. Do you hear me?" he added as several hesitated muttering.

"I don't want to see no ball game," one of them said insolently.

Like a flash Old Calamity shot out his fist and sent the protesting one sprawling. It was just the show of force needed. The other prisoners waited but a second to see if the one who had been struck would show fight. When he slowly pulled himself to his feet and, feeling his jaw, walked mumbling over to the ball game, the others followed leaving Old Calamity and the five or six guards with the fighting group of prisoners. He nodded to the guards.

"Get their sticks and things," he directed. "All right, boys," he went on, turning to the prisoners, "drop your weapons, keep your hands up straight. You, Mike," to a red-haired cruel-looking prisoner who was evidently the leader of one of the groups, "come over here and bring your mob with you. You, Stitch, get your mob and stand over there. I thought something like this might happen," he said, turning to Ackerson, one of the guards, "I warned them down at the Central Office it was foolish to send two big mobs like this to the same prison. They should have split them up and sent one mob over to Springfield. But you can't tell them anything down there. If they had to run the prison they'd see it differently."

"Yes, sir," said Ackerson, "they're two of the worst mobs I've ever seen. God, how they hate each other! It was good that Todd fired a few shots over their heads to scare them. The whole yard would have been fighting in no time if he hadn't."

"Yes," said the Deputy, "I was in Rogers' office and I heard the shots. Henley," he called out to one of the guards, "you and Ackerson and Coltrane take Mike and his mob up to the cell house and lock them in. The rest of you take Stitch and his woolies."

Many times during the ensuing weeks Fletcher almost wished that he had let the two gangs exterminate each other and thus rid him of the most perplexing mystery which had confronted him during his more than thirty years as a prison official. It was scarcely three days after the fight that things began to happen. The telephone rang.

"Deputy, this is the doctor talking. You know that little Levine kid, don't you? You know, he's one of the Dock gang."

"Yes," said the deputy, "what about him?"

"Something rather funny. They found him unconscious in his cell this morning. Just finished examining him and find he's taken cyanide."

"That's funny," said the deputy, "he didn't seem to me like the kind who'd commit suicide."

"Me either," said the doctor. "He'll have to try again because he didn't take enough to kill him. But he'll be a pretty sick boy for a few weeks to come."

"Where did he get the poison?" the deputy inquired.

"I'm sure I don't know."

"O.K.," said the deputy, "I'll see what I can find out."

A search of Levine's cell revealed nothing. There was not the slightest sign of poison in his tin cup or in any other part of the cell. A few days later, when Levine became conscious, he denied as vociferously as he could in his weakened condition that he had taken poison and said that all he remembered was that he suddenly felt sick with terrible pains in his head and stomach and then, the next thing he knew, he awakened in the prison hospital.

Old Calamity, although puzzled and upset by the occurrence, finally decided that Levine was lying and that he had endeavored to kill himself. But about ten days later the prison doctor walked into his office and stood waiting for a second while Fletcher finished reading and signing a letter. When he looked up he could tell from the doctor's manner that something was amiss.

"Another cyanide case, Deputy," he said.

For a moment Fletcher stared without speaking. "You mean," he said finally, "that another prisoner has taken cyanide?"

The doctor nodded. "Yes, sir, Wiley Callahan. The curious thing is, he won't die either. Didn't take enough to kill him."

"He didn't take it at all," said Old Calamity. "It was given to him."

"Given to him!" the doctor exclaimed. "How could it be given to him? He would know who gave it, wouldn't he?"

"Not necessarily," said Old Calamity. "Levine didn't."

"You don't mean to say," said the doctor, "that somebody gave it to him and he didn't know it? You know that you take cyanide through the mouth."

"I know it," said Old Calamity, "and I still think that somebody gave it to him. They both belong to the Dock mob."

"But how could they give it to him without his knowing it?"

"I'm sure I don't know," Old Calamity replied. "That's what we'll have to try and find out."

After the doctor had gone Old Calamity sent for Mr. Mellish, Mr. Lewis, and Mr. Henry, the three guards on duty in cell house B.

"You have ten of the Dock gang in your cell house, haven't you?" he inquired.

"Yes, sir," said Mr. Lewis.

"Well," went on Old Calamity, "I think attempts are being made to kill all of them and I want you to keep your eyes particularly on their cells. On second thought, you'd better change their cells. Put one next to the other in the cells nearest your desk so that you can watch them at all times. Don't let anybody go in or out of their cells except on the regular business of the institution and even then I want you to watch anybody who goes in."

The following week Blouser Hicks, the trigger man of the Dock gang dropped to the floor unconscious as he was standing at the door of his cell while the count was being taken. "Cyanide poisoning," he doctor reported once again. "This time it was enough to kill him."

Old Calamity was thoroughly aroused. He sent for Mr. Lewis who was on the first night shift.

"Didn't I tell you," he roared at that thoroughly frightened official, "not to let anybody go in or out of any of the Dock mob cells and to watch them every minute of the time?"

"I did," Mr. Lewis stammered. He had seldom seen the even-tempered Old Calamity in a rage and he admitted to himself that he didn't like the spectacle at all. "I watched those cells every minute of the time I was on duty. Nobody went in or out except on prison business."

"How about the orderlies?" the deputy demanded.

"I stood by and watched them when they went in to clean," Mr. Lewis said. "Nobody else went in the cells the entire time I was on duty except the man who delivers the books from the library, and that little dip Alberson and that bird from the record office who delivers paper and pencils. You know it was Friday, writing day yesterday.

"All right," said Old Calamity, somewhat mollified, "I want you to get that chemist up in the doctor's office. You know, that fellow doing the five spot. Take him down to Hicks' cell with you and go over everything in it to see if you can find any signs of cyanide."

Three hours later Mr. Lewis reported that nothing whatever had been found to indicate the presence of the poison.

Now thoroughly aroused, the deputy summoned one by one all the members of what had once been the scourge of Cosmopolis, the thugs and gangsters known as the "Alley Cats" who for years had terrorized merchants on the East Side by levying on them assessments for "protection" which they did not dare refuse to give. A thorough grilling of each one accomplished nothing. From "Stitch" down they insisted earnestly and vociferously that they had not the slightest knowledge of any poison and that they did not know who apparently was trying to kill off the members of the Dock mob.

A week later the doctor again told Old Calamity what was getting to be a routine story. A fourth man had "taken cyanide" and was so sick that he might even die.

"I'm over in the cell house," said the doctor. "I've given him an antidote but haven't moved him yet. You know you told me you wanted to see the next one immediately, if there was a next one."

"O.K.," said the deputy. "I'll be right over.

He hurried over to cell house B, said a sharp word or two to disperse the cell house cleaning gang gathered in the corridor outside the stricken prisoner's cell and walked in to where the doctor and the cell house guard were bending over a man on the cot. As he went in the deputy glanced at the little card in the metal slot just outside the cell. "Mitchell Evans" it read. Another member of the Dock gang! The prisoner lay on the cot breathing heavily, his face flushed and uneasy moans escaping from his lips.

"Unconscious, Deputy," said the doctor briefly. "Better look at him quick so we can take him to the hospital."

Old Calamity nodded. He bent over the unconscious figure and examined the face and particularly the lips of the poisoned prisoner. Then he turned to one of the guards.

"Hold his mouth open a second," he directed.

The guard did as instructed and Old Calamity pulled a magnifying glass from his pocket and swept it carefully over the mouth of the unconscious man. The other guard smiled grimly to himself. It was axiomatic among the guards that when Old Calamity started using his magnifying glass things were getting hot. But his face was as unreadable as usual when he finally straightened up.

"All right, doctor," he said. "Take him upstairs. I want to search the cell myself," he said briefly to the two guards who saluted and stepped back into the corridor and walked away.

After they had gone Old Calamity ransacked every corner of the cell. He looked on the underside of the table, he examined the perforated ventilator with his magnifying glass, ran a button-hook down the drainpipe to see if anything were attached to the cross bar and drew a small quantity of water from the spigot into the prisoner's cup. Then he carefully smelled it but could detect no odor. He remembered the case on which he had worked for another warden some months before in which cyanide potassium had been stuffed into the spigot so that the prisoner in the cell would drink it with the first cup of water he drew. But there was not a sign of poison here. A further search of the hems of the sheets and blankets, of the pillow case and mattress and of the upper part of the crossbars (which could not be seen from the floor) also revealed nothing. In deep thought Old Calamity walked slowly back to his office. He checked up the dates on which the other prison episodes had occurred. Then a grim smile came over his face. Every one of the attempted killings had occurred on a Friday.

The deputy sent for Mike, the leader of the Dock gang."

"Mike," he said when the prisoner appeared, "what do you think about these poisonings?"

"I don't know, sir." Hard-boiled as he was, it was plain to be seen that he was worried and frightened and glad of the opportunity to talk. "I don't know," he went on, "I ain't afraid of nobody when I can see them. But this business that's going on now, and not knowing who will be next. It's some of the 'Cats' doing it. You know we ain't friends exactly and since that battle in the yard when we put it all over them they been pretty sore. I'd like to get moved over to the Western Prison, sir, and so would the other boys in the mob. I ain't afraid of nothin'—"

"Yes, I know," said Old Calamity stopping a flood of words, "I'll tell you what I want you to do. I want you to tell your mob that next Friday they're not to do any writing at all till they hear from me. You understand? Don't tell anyone else but them what I'm telling you and tell them to keep their mouths shut. If you do that I think I may be able to find out what it's all about."

Stitch looked mystified. "You mean," he said, "you don't want them to write any letters home or nothin' until you give the O.K.?"

"Yes," said Old Calamity, "that's exactly what I mean."

"All right, sir," the prisoner replied, adding a heartfelt "I hope you find out who it is."

The following Friday afternoon there was the usual routine in cell house B. After supper and a short period of exercise in the yard the long gray snakelike line marched four abreast up the long central corridor, those who celled in B swinging to the right as they came to its entrance. The line divided again as it approached the steps at the end of the cell block, some of the prisoners swinging to the right and left on the ground floor "flats" and the others mounting the stairs which led to the four upper tiers. They stood in front of the cell doors while the count was being taken. Then, as the clanging bell at the end announced the count checked, they stepped back in their cells. The trusty at the end of the block wound the locking device which sent the cell doors clanging shut. There were the usual noises as the prisoners got settled for the evening and then, four minutes later, two prisoners pushing a cart in front of them entered with the books for the weekly distribution. They were followed by two others prisoners from the chief clerk's office, both with leather pouches swinging over their shoulders, one carrying paper and the other pencils. The books were distributed to the men who had ordered them. A pencil and three sheets of paper went to every cell.

The four prisoners had scarcely passed out of the cell house when Old Calamity entered. The night guard, who had been instructed in advance, swung the indicators of the locking device from one to ten and pulled the lever. The doors of the first ten cells swung open while the others remained locked.

"Come out in the corridor, boys," the Deputy said to those in these cells.

The ten did as directed and Old Calamity entered one of the cells and made a careful inspection of the things which the four prisoners had just left. The ten noticed that when Old Calamity came out of one of the cells he carried something in his hand which he apparently did not want them to see as he kept his hand up against his sleeve.

"All right, boys," he said briefly, "you can go on back."

The ten members of the Dock gang, with fear-stricken faces, stepped hesitantly back into their cells. The instructions which their leader had given them on the order of the Deputy had caused them to reflect on the mysterious happenings. The inevitable had happened. They, too, had noticed that the poisonings had all taken place on Friday. Who knew which one would be next?

The Deputy noticed their appearance. "Don't be afraid, boys," he said confidently, "there won't be any more poisonings." His face was grim and there was a glint of anger in his eyes which both prisoners and guards knew from long experience meant that somebody was in for a decidedly bad time of it.

Old Calamity went to the guard's desk at the end of the corridor. "Send McLain in the chief clerk's office in here at once," he directed the telephone operator. In a few moments there was a ring at the cell house door and a prisoner entered, accompanied by a guard.

"All right, Niles," said Old Calamity, turning to the guard, "you may go."

He turned to the prisoner and looked him over slowly and coolly and appraisingly. McLain was good-looking, well-educated and smart. He had a pleasant and disarming smile and an inoffensive look. But Old Calamity was not at all fooled. In his thirty years of intimate contact with every kind of prisoner he had met many of the "mildest mannered men that ever scuttled a ship or cut a throat."

"Sit down at the desk, McLain," the Deputy said, eyeing him closely, a set, and what the guards called a "wicked," expression around the corner of his mouth. "I want you to write a letter by hand for me."

"A letter?" McLain repeated. If he was at all nervous he didn't show it. Old Calamity scarcely thought that he would. He had sized him up as being cool and well poised.

"Yes," the Deputy repeated, "a letter."

"You mean you want me to do it in the chief clerk's office on the machine?"

"You heard what I said," replied Old Calamity evenly. "I want you to write it by hand."

"By hand, sir? Wouldn't it be quicker on the typewriter?"

"Yes," said Old Calamity, "it might be but that isn't the way I want it done. Sit down at the desk there."

McLain did as he was directed. Try as he would to hold himself in check he was somewhat flustered.

"Shall I use a pen, sir?" he said, picking up the pen from the guard's desk.

"No," said Old Calamity, "I want it written with a—" he paused for a minute—"pencil."

McLain reached into his inside pocket.

"No," said Old Calamity, "not that pencil." He suddenly thrust one in front of the now white-faced prisoner. "This one!"

McLain took the pencil, his hands shaking despite all his efforts to control himself.

"All right," said Old Calamity, "direct it to John McLain."

The prisoner, keeping his face averted, started to put the pencil against the paper. There was a scratching sound but no mark appeared.

"Why don't you," inquired Old Calamity softly, "wet the pencil with your lips?"

"I—can sharpen it, sir, if you will lend me your—your knife."

"I know you can," said Old Calamity. There was a steely glitter in his eye. "But I want you to wet it with your lips. Here," he suddenly reached over across the desk and pulled the prisoner to his feet, at the same time wrenching the pencil out of his hand and bringing it close to the prisoner's lips. "Hold his hands," he directed the guard.

"Don't!" McLain screamed. "My God, don't!"

"Why not?" said Old Calamity. "What are you afraid of? It's only a pencil, isn't it?"

McLain did not answer. Completely unnerved, he struggled to shake himself loose from Old Calamity's iron grip and from that of the guard who was now holding him by the wrists. But it was no use. Despite his efforts he was borne slowly to the stone floor, the guard kneeling on one side and Old Calamity on the other. Suddenly Old Calamity jammed the pencil between the prisoner's lips who, in a frenzy, was rolling his head from side to side trying to escape it. Then, nodding to the guard, both he and the guard arose. McLain staggered to his feet, clutching at this throat, his face a sickly green.

"My God," he gasped, "you've—you've poisoned me."

"Well, why not?" said Old Calamity. "You poisoned four others, didn't you?"

The prisoner rolled his head from side to side in an agony of apprehension.

"Didn't you?" insisted Old Calamity. "All right," he added when the prisoner did not answer, "you won't get any treatment from the doctor until you tell me."

"Yes," said McLain hoarsely, wetting his dry lips, "I did it. For God's sake call the doctor. I did it, don't you hear? I tell you I did it. Get the doctor, won't you?"

"Just one second," said Old Calamity with a callousness which amazed the guard who had always looked upon him as a rather kindly man, "I want to know first just exactly what you did."

"Can't you see I'm dying?" McLain screamed.

"What did you do?" Old Calamity repeated.

"Glue—I put glue—a little glue—on the pencil point and sprinkled cyanide on it and let it dry. For God's sake, can't you —won't you get the doctor?"

"You don't need the doctor," said Old Calamity calmly. "There was nothing on the pencil but granulated sugar."

"Thank God you found out who it was," said the doctor a few hours later in the Deputy's office. "McLain's one of the Alley Cats, isn't he?"

"Yes," said Old Calamity, "he was the brains of the gang. He has a nice appearance and good manners, so he fronted for them."

"How did you ever get on to it?" asked the doctor.

"By examining the mouth of that last bird with a magnifying glass. I found black pencil marks on his lips. You see, the pencil wouldn't write with the small cyanide crystals on it, so naturally a prisoner, not being allowed to have a knife in his possession with which he could sharpen a pencil, would put it in his mouth to wet it. I changed pencils and fixed one up with sugar to scare a confession out of him. Just a piece of good luck that I got the first clue."

"Maybe," said the doctor, "but it's luck plus."

"Plus what?" said Old Calamity.

"Brains," replied the doctor briefly.

DAY KEENE

A Great Whirring of Wings

INTRODUCTION

Fishing back into a none-too-retentive memory for the details of a birth taking place ten years ago is apt to be akin to dipping into a booby-trapped Pandora's box, but as I recall "A Great Whirring of Wings" was born of two newspaper clippings with economic necessity acting as midwife.

I had for some years been very profitably engaged in lowering the intelligence quotient of the American housewife via the radio soap opera route when in the words of Wakeman's huckster I awakened one morning to the firm conclusion "there wasn't that much money." Having purchased a home in Florida while in the chips (soap) I promptly repaired there only to be awakened a second morning, by the good wife this time, with the cryptic statement it was nice to have some money.

As I recall the morning paper contained two items, one concerning the first of the so-called Cleveland torso murders, the other an item datelined Chicago re a flock of jays that had pre-empted a householder's back yard and were viciously attacking anyone attempting to dispossess them. Combined, they sounded like story material. Having always been a devout reader of pulp yarns I had plenty of magazines on hand in which to study format, editorial likes and dislikes, and general policy. I cracked open a half-dozen stories by such men as T. T. Flynn, Merle Constiner, Dale Clark, D. L. Champion, Peter Paige, William Brandon, Tod Ballard, saw how they handled their subject material and sat down and attempted to do likewise in a style natural to myself.

Such an easy thing to do. Just sit down and write a story. Some buckets of sweat, gallons of blood, and reams of paper, later, the thing did come out fairly well. Learned then and there that in a good many cases it's not what you put into a story but what you leave out that makes it good or bad. Again, as I recall, Ken White was then editing Dime Detective *and the story sold on its first trip out, for a penny a point. That was in 1943.*

Rereading the yarn from the viewpoint of a few millions of words later, I would like very much to rewrite it as I now think it should be written. But then I can say the same of every yarn I've ever done, including the last one out of the machine, so probably it's best to let spent checks alone. Have never claimed to be a writer, preferring to consider myself a teller of tales. Had I been born in ancient Baghdad I know I would have had a hell of a time sitting cross-legged in the market place collecting copper coins for relating—"There was no moon. There were no stars. The houri was a slave girl from Kashmir. She was blonde. She was beautiful. She was dead. . . ."

DAY KEENE

A Great Whirring of Wings

JULY 13TH

I T WAS a sight that I shan't soon forget. Even as much as I have hated Isaac for these last twenty years, I knew a moment of pity. He, who had been such a power, looked so pathetically helpless lying there in the middle of the flame-vine-covered patio calling on his Savior to help him as the hundreds and hundreds of blue jays pecked viciously at his nose, his eyes, his scalp. I reached him shortly after Caldwell had fired and the birds had been frightened away. He had stopped screaming. I felt for his pulse. It was faint. By the time that the others had reached him, he was dead. I shan't pretend that I am sorry. I feel, and justifiably so, that he robbed me of my career.

There is not much excitement in Coveport, especially during the summer months, and Isaac's death will be a godsend to the community, as well as to those of us of his family who are mentioned in his will. I suppose that Martha's son will inherit the bulk of his millions, although I admit that I never could see why Isaac should favor Caldwell over me, his own flesh brother. Both life and death are so difficult to understand at times.

JULY 14TH

The coroner's inquest, a tiresome affair, was held this afternoon on the spot where Isaac died. He would have died a second time, of apoplexy, if he had been alive to see the invasion of his privacy. Literally hordes of people used a pretended interest in the manner of his death—God knows that it was bizarre—as an excuse to prowl the grounds that for so long have been forbidden to the general public. Nothing that the Coveport Chamber of Commerce could have conceived would have had the same stimulating effect on local business as did his death. Although Isaac retired from active business years ago, he was still a figure of national importance, the last of the old robber barons of another day. All the great newspapers of the country, as well as the various press associations, have sent their representatives to cover the inquest and the cremation. Most of them came by plane from spots as far distant as Los Angeles and Montreal.

The manner of his death seems to have intrigued the public fancy, no easy thing to capture in this age of war and sudden death. One moment he had been alive, a very old but still a very wicked and lecherous old man. The next moment he was clay, his face and the top of his bald skull well scarred by angry beaks. He, who had stolen a quarter of a continent and had looted it of its oil and other mineral resources with impunity, he who had played with and broken men's lives as one might snap a match, had been assaulted by a screaming formation of blue jays on the grounds of his own spacious Gulf-front estate. It is, to quote one of the younger reporters, a laugh.

A good many religious leaders and parlor pinks are regarding his death openly, and I presume to their profit in print, as a divine manifestation of a just and a vengeful God. This belief was further bolstered by the testimony given at the inquest by Isaac's two male nurses, in reality two solid, unimaginative men from one of New York's most reputable agencies which has supplied Isaac's bodyguard for years, and, I suppose, by Caldwell and myself.

The agency men's names are Morrison and Carter. They had accomanied Isaac from New York, the three of them arriving in Coveport only a few hours before his death.

I quote Carter's testimony verbatim: "The old man and Mr. Caldwell had been having an argument about the birds, see? Caldwell said that they had been raising hell for three days and he had phoned the sheriff's office for permission to shoot them but he hadn't been able to contact the sheriff."

Here, Sheriff Cobb admitted that he had been on a four day fishing trip, sudden death and crime being a rarity in Coveport, and he not being clairvoyant enough to have foreseen that his services might be needed. A soft spoken, middle-aged man, Cobb looks and acts like a fool. I believe that his looks are deceptive. He reads too much to be a fool. Such men are always dangerous to those who need to fear the law. His sole contribution to the inquest, however, was to ask Carter if Caldwell had warned Isaac about the birds before he went into the patio.

Carter answered, "Yes, sir. He said that the jays were dangerous and warned Mr. Hargrove not to go out until something had been done about them. But the old man was bull-headed as usual. He said that he had faced guns, mobs, and Congressional investigating committees all of his life and he was damned if he would be intimidated by a bunch of birds."

At this point there was such a howl of laughter that the coroner was forced to inform the spectators that they would preserve the decorum commensurate with the occasion or he would be forced to bar the public from the inquest.

Carter continued, "Mr. Isaac Hargrove walked out of the French windows into the patio. Then, suddenly, before any of us could do anything about it, there was a great whirring of wings and maybe a couple of hundred of screaming birds swooped down out of the trees and began to peck hell out of the old man. While we are standing there like fools, he grabs at his heart and falls. His brother, Doctor Hargrove, with me right behind him, runs out to try and scare the birds away when I hear a shotgun let loose behind us. Mr. Caldwell is the only one who keeps his head, see? He grabs a shotgun and blasts right into the middle of the birds and they scram. We count them afterward and he gets seventy jays with the two shots."

Caldwell was called next. I must say that he made a good appearance on the stand. He gave his profession as an explorer and a writer, and admitted openly that he had reason to expect he would inherit the bulk of Isaac's fortune. More, he admitted frankly that he felt no sorrow over Isaac's passing. He was glad that the old man was dead, but regretted the manner of his death. He confirmed the previous testimony that he had phoned the sheriff's office for permission to shoot the birds. Cobb, I noted, eyed him thoughtfully all the time that he was on the stand.

As Isaac's examining and attending physician, I was the next and the last witness. There was little I could tell them. I testified briefly as to the condition of the body and to the fact that I had certified the death, in nontechnical terms, as heart failure, and had so signed the death certificate.

The jury brought in their verdict promptly—death by misadventure. The case is closed. Only Sheriff Cobb and the young reporter, whom I previously mentioned, seem disappointed. Both expressed a belief that Isaac had been murdered. Such a theory is, of course, ridiculous. There was a great whirring of wings—and Isacc died. *Sic semper tyrannis.* And *sic transit gloria mundi*, for that matter.

JULY 15TH

Isaac's will was read this afternoon. It is needless to write here that I am disappointed. Outside of a few minor bequests, Caldwell inherits his millions. I, his own brother, who gave up a brilliant career to serve as Isaac's personal physician for years, have been cut off with a paltry ten thousand dollars annuity, even this inadequate sum to be stopped if I attempt to resume my long interrupted practice or leave Coveport. There is no longer any doubt in my mind. Isaac was insane. Even in death his bony fingers have reached out from the grave to stay my arm from perfecting the many marvelous benefits to mankind that I once had planned. I am to be no better than a well treated prisoner here on the estate. The only ray of hope that I have left is that Caldwell may die before I do, or before he marries and begets legally. In that event, I would inherit, I being the last of the Hargroves.

The little local Methodist Church and the municipality both did much better than I did. Isaac left them one hundred thousand dollars apiece, all taxes paid, and no strings tied to their acceptance. I could have done a lot with one hundred thousand dollars. I could have returned to Boston, fitted up a surgery and laboratory and continued with my experiments that Isaac so brusquely, so inhumanly, and so selfishly interrupted.

Tomorrow the cremation.

JULY 16TH

Isaac is gone. All of his pomp of yesterday, is as Rudyard Kipling wrote in his *Recessional,* "one with Nineveh and Tyre!" The services were really quite impressive. The local minister, thinking of Isaac's bequest, could scarcely speak for sniveling. Senator Hooper did much better. He traced Isaac's career of theft from its beginning, but of course gilded it with the respectability of big business. Outside the crematorium, solid ranks of reporters, the hoi polloi, and nationally known congressmen, senators, and industrialists, stood, bareheaded under the midsummer Florida sun. The latter, I presume, attended the simple rites not so much out of respect to the deceased as to assure themselves that the old devil was really dead, and died without leaving any notes or records that might prove incriminating to them.

I must go through Isaac's personal papers tomorrow and burn any that might harm anyone. I doubt, though, that I will find a thing. Isaac belonged to the school of men who believe in carrying anything incriminating in their heads, knowing that they cannot be forced to testify against themselves.

The boom to the town is remarkable. There have never been so many people in Coveport at one time since its origin. All of the small hotels and the boarding houses are filled. They have even opened the large luxury hotel that customarily is open only during the three or four most severe winter months. The sidewalks and the beaches teem with people. I would give a pretty penny, if I had one, to continue my work right here. Perhaps I shall. There is so much to be done. The more that a man of my profession sees of mankind, the more he realizes the crudities and incompetency of nature.

Sheriff Cobb and the young reporter, whose name, it develops, is Mason, and who is with the Associated Press, were snooping in the house when we returned from Isaac's funeral. In fact they were searching through his desk and had it littered with his papers and news clippings. Caldwell was forced to speak to them sharply. He contends, and rightly, that one can't very well arrest a scattered flock of blue jays for murder, and that if Sheriff Cobb had been at his post as he should have been, it is very unlikely that the whole thing would have happened.

Cobb accepted the rebuke calmly and turned the subject matter so deftly into other channels, mainly Caldwell's various expeditions of the Guianas, and the Matto Grosso, (he had read both of Caldwell's poorly written books) that the pompous young fool was not only mollified, but actually invited both Cobb and Mason to join us in a supper of speckled trout that he had caught from Isaac's, or rather his own private pier that morning.

The table conversation was boring, being mainly by Caldwell about Caldwell. I made my excuses and retired to my room early to read a new medical treatise and to think, leaving Caldwell with considerably more wine than was good for him under his belt and talking excitedly. Sometimes I wonder if anyone in the family but myself is really sane. All that Isaac thought of was money. All that Caldwell thinks of is women. His escapades and peccadillos cost Isaac thousands of dollars in the past, and I noted tonight at supper that the youngest and prettiest of the serving maids is beginning to show signs of his handiwork. It is fortunate, very fortunate for Caldwell that Isaac died when he did. We are, I fear, a very sticky family.

MUCH LATER,
ALMOST DAWN

There is something very horrible happening in this house. I am tired, but I do not dare to sleep. Tonight someone, or something, tried to kill me. I had barely begun to doze when I heard a great whirring of wings, felt fingers on my throat, flexing, choking. I tried to scream. I couldn't. I struggled with the frenzy of a madman in the dark. Then a scream burst from my lungs. The fingers on my throat relaxed. The whirring of wings faded through the open window. But it was no illusion. There still are dull red fingermarks upon my throat. I must consult the sheriff in the morning. Perhaps Sheriff Cobb is right. Perhaps my brother was murdered. Perhaps it was Caldwell who killed him. In that case, and if it can be proven, the money will be mine. But no. It is too fantastic to consider. I know. I was there. I saw the birds attack Isaac. I was the first one to reach him. No one touched him but myself. Still . . .

JULY 17TH

In the clear light of day what I have written seems fantastic. My mind was overtired. It was merely something that I dreamed. Still, I thought it best to follow my first impulse and phone the sheriff. He was, as usual, not in his office, but young Mason who seems to have elected himself the sheriff's secretary kindly made an appointment for me for later in the day.

I spent the morning, before Caldwell had arisen, with Isaac's papers in which we had found the sheriff snooping. There had been no need for anyone to worry. There was nothing of a confidential business nature. Isaac's desk was, to me at least, a revelation. It revealed a soiled side of his character that I had not known existed. He had been a student of the morbid and the gruesome. There were reams of newspaper clippings and press photographs, all of them dealing with murder, and most of them concerning the so-called "Butcher Killings" that took place in Boston's swank Back Bay district some twenty years ago. I remembered the killings well. I had been at the height of my fame as a surgeon in those days, and quite as well known in my field as Isaac had been in the world of finance. I had been overworked, and harassed by the inadequacies of nature to be sure, but I had been happy in my work until Isaac overpersuaded me to give up my private practice and become his personal physician. I began to hate him then, I think, but I did not realize it at the time. But to return to the "Butcher Killings." Most of them had been vagrants and street women, but I had known one of them quite well. She had been a young patient of mine. The police had questioned me concerning her, but there had been nothing that I could tell them. I had been as shocked as they when her nude, mutilated body had been found wrapped in bloody burlap in a manhole.

For a moment, staring at the clippings, I knew fear. Isaac had been extremely nervous at about that time, and had shown symptoms of it since. He, for example, was very sensitive about anything concerning flowing blood and would suffer a boil to burst rather than allow me to lance it and ease his sufferings. Was it possible that he, his mind straining under the tremendous financial burden of mergers and corporations that it carried, had sought relief in an atavistic orgy of murder? Was that why he had wanted me with him? It was something to consider. He had retired from active business at about that time and had announced his firm determination never to leave Coveport. Nor had he ever left it except for his recent trip up to New York.

On the other hand, there was Caldwell. He had just turned forty. He would have been nineteen or twenty then—and most of the victims had been women. Still, so far as I could tell by skimming through the clippings, the murders had not been sex crimes and the "Butcher" had gained little but sadistic pleasure. Still, there were two sides to Caldwell. He was definitely the victim of a split personality, or technically speaking, schizophrenia. And for some reason Isaac had seen fit to keep the clippings.

It was all very confusing. I determined to burn the clippings, and I did. The last of them was turning to ashes in the fireplace when Caldwell entered. His hair was tousled. His face was puffed with drink. His good morning was, as usual, both profane and abrupt.

"What the hell are you doing?" he demanded.

"Protecting the family name," I told him curtly, and left to keep my appointment with the sheriff.

Cobb was waiting, and sympathetic. I told him what had happened, or what I thought had happened on the night before, and he asked me to demonstrate the hold that the fingers had upon my throat, which I did using my own hands.

He asked, "And you still think that there *was* someone in your room?"

I told him that I had been positive the night before, and had so written in my diary, but I admitted that my doubts had grown with the morning, and that if it hadn't been for the whirring of the wings I would be inclined to think that it was merely something that I had dreamed.

Mason wanted to know then if I had ever heard the whirring of the wings before. I told him that I had, on the day that Isaac died.

"And you are how old, Doctor?" Cobb asked me.

I told him. "Sixty-eight. I was seven years younger than Isaac."

Mason grinned. "His baby brother, eh?" and we all laughed.

They were really very pleasant men and I enjoyed conversing with them. That was why when Mason asked if I minded answering some questions that might clear up the case, I told him, "Not at all."

To the best of my recollection, the questions and my answers were as follows:

"You have been your brother's personal physician for how long, Doctor Hargrove?"

"Almost twenty years."

"He was ill often during that time?"

"Not often," I admitted. "That is one of the reasons that I feel so hemmed in, futile. I feel that I am wasting my life."

Mason nodded. "I can understand how you feel. You see, I have looked up your record in Boston, Doctor, and the older surgeons there still speak of your skill with a scalpel with awe."

I liked the young man immensely. Age is so easily pleased.

"All of them are agreed, however," he continued with a smile, "that due to that very skill you were greatly overworked. Have you—er—ever considered resuming your practice, Doctor?"

I told him in no uncertain language that I had and both Cobb and Mason were most sympathetic when I explained that the terms of Isaac's will had very definitely ended that. For the experiments that I had meant to make a lot of new equipment and money would be needed.

Then the sheriff handed me a clipping. "You happen to see this in the local paper, Doc? Say, about two months ago."

The clipping read:

Chicago—Mack Beemer has designated his tree-shaded backyard a danger zone—in possession of a flock of blue jays.

Since the jays moved into the some dozen trees growing in his back yard, Beemer has ventured out a few times but each time he was attacked by a screaming formation of jays that attempted to take chunks out of his head. His wife won't go past the back door and their four-year-old son has temporarily lost his playground.

Beemer wants police permission to shoot the birds and the police have promised to investigate.

"Yes," I nodded, returning the clipping. "It was in the morning *Times* or in the evening *Independent*. I don't remember which."

"And your nephew Caldwell saw it?"

"He did," I answered truthfully. "We discussed the coincidence when the jays took possession of the pepper trees in Isaac's patio."

"And that was two or three days before your brother's return from New York?"

I informed him that that was correct and Sheriff Cobb thumbed through an *Esquire* on his desk dated May, 1940. "And what," he asked, "if anything, do you know about *neku*, Doctor Hargrove?"

I asked him to spell the word and when he had, I told him, "Not a thing. I have never even heard the word before."

"That's fine, just fine," he told me. "Now you go on back home, Doctor. We'll be along in a few minutes to arrest your nephew Caldwell for the murder of your brother. But don't you worry about a thing. We are going to take good care of you."

The relief that I felt was intense. *It had been Caldwell who had murdered Isaac, however fantastic it might sound.*

"You can prove that?" I demanded.

"I can prove it," he said grimly.

I shook hands with Cobb and Mason. I had never known two men whom I liked better.

DECEMBER 20TH

So much has happened since I last made an entry that I scarcely know where to start. In a way, I feel sorry for Caldwell. But he brought it all on himself, and my new assistants, here in the spacious laboratory that I have purchased with a portion of Isaac's money, have promised faithfully to remind me of the day that he goes to the electric chair in Raiford (the Florida State Penitentiary) in the event that I should be so engrossed in an experiment that I overlook the date. It was a terrible thing that he did, and I hope that Isaac speaks to him most severely when the two men meet in the afterworld.

I, however, have my own bone to pick with Isaac. Why didn't he tell me that the minor stomach pains of which he had complained shortly before his last trip to New York was really acute appendicitis? Why did he go to another doctor to have such a simple operation performed? God knows he had no reason to fear my skill! I have performed many an appendectomy in less than eleven minutes. And my incisions are clean and neat. I am no butcher as some of these younger doctors are. In my day speed was essential and to hell with all this antisepsis nonsense. You see, the longer that the internal cavity of the body is exposed to— but I must not get started on that. To go back to my return from the sheriff's office.

Caldwell was nastily drunk. You are in for it, young man, I thought. But not so much as by a look or a word did I even intimate what Sheriff Cobb had told me. I had a certain little matter of my own that I wanted to attend to before Cobb's arrival.

I would have passed him by without a word, but drunkenly he stopped me. "Where you been, you old loon?" he demanded. "Out carving up a few cadavers?"

"I know one that I'd like to carve," I told him, and went directly to my room.

Cobb arrived almost on my heels. Mason, and four men whom I didn't know were with him. I learned later that they were county officers.

Caldwell offered them a drink, but they refused it.

Cobb came directly to the point. "This is a business call. I have come to arrest you, Caldwell Hargrove, for the murder of your uncle."

I never saw a man sober so fast. "You are insane and absurd!" Caldwell spat. "Uncle Isaac died of a heart attack after being assaulted by a vicious flock of blue jays."

Cobb said, patiently, "The jays worked in just fine. They probably gave you the idea. But if they had moved on by the time he had returned, you would have found some other way to have had a bird peck at him. Maybe you might have bought a parrot. As it turned out, you didn't have to."

The four men left the room to search the house under his instructions. He took a vine-like plant from his pocket which I had noticed Caldwell cultivating assiduously in one corner of the hothouse.

"That's *neku*," Cobb told me. "Caldwell must have brought a plant or slip back from the Guianas. Birds or other animals can eat it. They can even peck their beaks into pans of grain that have been saturated with it. But you as much as scratch a man, or beast, or fish with it, and it is as sudden as prussic acid. The natives use it as a poison on their arrows."

I told the truth. "And he did feed those jays. I saw him. It was after Isaac had phoned from the station."

Caldwell turned deathly white.

Cobb continued, "You see, the murder business being kind of slow in Coveport, I get quite a bit of time to read and fish. And when old Isaac died, I just happened to remember an article that I had read in *Esquire* and put two and two together. Maybe you read it. Maybe not. What with one thing and another, including Fanny May's condition, I don't think that little things are going to make much difference to a jury."

Caldwell blustered, "You're bluffing."

Cobb shook his head. "We dug them seventy jays that you shot and washed enough stuff off their beaks to wipe out the whole town of Coveport. Moreover it matched up exact with the foreign substance that the county coroner found in old Isaac Hargrove's blood."

"Then—er—my death certificate wasn't accepted?" I asked. "There was an autopsy?"

Young Mason patted my shoulder. "I am happy to say that there was. But don't you let it worry you, Doctor. You brother was dead when he hit the ground and the overdose of digitalis you jabbed in him didn't do him a bit of harm. You can't, of course, kill a dead man."

I felt better than I had in days. Fratricide is so distasteful a thing, even if Isaac had stood in the way of all of the big things that I wanted to do. "But the birds! The ones who flew away?" I worried.

"I've been holding my breath," Cobb told me. "But it's a kind of a volatile stuff and it sure as hell must be washed and pecked off their beaks by now."

One of the officers returned with the syringe I had hidden in Caldwell's room.

"I'll just keep this, Doc," Cobb told me. "That is, if you don't mind."

I told him that I didn't. I was beginning to feel like a fool. Here, I had felt like a murderer for days and I had been perfectly guiltless.

Caldwell had come to some decision. He looked a lot like Isaac, cold, and hard, and ruthless. "O.K. You think that you have a case. I have forty million that says that you haven't. And it might be that I'll win."

"It might be," Cobb admitted. "Juries are sometimes stupid as hell."

Caldwell hesitated, said, "I am admitting nothing. But I would like to ask one question. What made you suspect me?"

"The fish," Cobb told him promptly.

"What fish?" Caldwell demanded.

The sheriff grinned and scratched his ear. "The speckled trout that you served me for supper on the night of your uncle's funeral. You know and I know that there is a closed season on trout from the fifteenth of June to the fifteenth of July. You boasted that you had caught them that morning. Breaking one game law didn't mean a thing to you. *But still you wouldn't shoot a flock of blue jays because you were hoping to use them in a little murder.*"

Two of the officers took Caldwell out, struggling, and cursing profanely. Mason and Cobb stayed with me.

"It—it was an awful thing that he did," I said.

"An awful thing," Cobb agreed. He hesitated, added, "But how about you, Doc? Now that you will come into the money have you any immediate plans?"

I had. And I told him so. I told him that I wanted to get back to work as soon as I possibly could. He seemed to think that was a good idea, but suggested that I stay in Florida. He said that he knew just the sort of a place for me.

"I'll tell you what, Doc," he suggested, spreading a legal paper of some sort on Isaac's desk. "You just sign this paper for me, giving up a sort of a power of attorney like, and I'll fix you right up with one of the nicest laboratories that you ever saw."

That was just splendid with me, and here I am. This really is a most delightful place, and my assistants are most helpful. I put on a gauze mask and a fresh clean white operating apron every day and am busy all day in my surgery planning the things that I always intended to do. I have so many things to try. For one thing, the nasal appendage is in such a silly place, exposed to cold and to bacteria. Now, if a really clever surgeon like myself could cut off a man's nose and graft it onto his hand, and make it grow and function, it would be such a vast improvement on nature. And take the internal organs. How many hundreds and thousands of doctors have labored and sweated and cursed as they cut through the layers of flesh and fat and muscle that forms the abdominal wall? Now, if all of the internal organs that are apt to need repair could be carried in a little convenient flesh sac grafted under one's left armpit say, how much simpler, convenient, and humane it would be to get at the seat of most troubles.

All I need now is patients on whom I may experiment. My assistants are scouring the countryside for them. And they tell me that I may expect to begin work daily. I can hardly wait for that first clean cut of the scalpel with the blood oozing over the edges of the wound.

There is just one little thing that worries me at times. And it is then that I beat at these bars that we have put on the windows to keep the curious out. It is then that I hear the whirring of the wings and feel the phantom fingers at my throat.

Why did Isaac save those clippings of twenty years ago? Why did he interrupt my practice so abruptly as he did? Who do you imagine was the "butcher"? Was it Isaac, or was it Caldwell?

ANTHONY BOUCHER

Threnody

INTRODUCTION

Strictly speaking, I made my first professional sale when I was sixteen: a short ghost story so abominably written that I now feel that the editor who bought it must have had a sadistic grudge against his readers. Fortunately it was not a murder story and thus did not impair the particular maidenhead under consideration in this anthology.

My professional murder writing dates from 1937, when Lee Wright accepted my first novel, and my murder short stories from 1942, when Ellery Queen bought the first Nick Noble puzzle. But the story here printed was written in January of 1936, when I still thought that I was going to be a playwright.

I was writing unnumbered (and unproduced) plays then, and every so often a few short stories. And when, in morbid moments, I now go back and reread them, I'm ashamed of my exceedingly slow development as a writer.

As an editor, I've bought highly attractive and polished stories from authors as young as sixteen. Most of my colleagues in science fiction (which seems oddly to mature its writers earlier than the mystery field) were well established in print before they could vote. Yet I, a dull and muddy-mettled rascal, went on well into my middle twenties producing stuff for which "unprofessional" is the kindest epithet.

So I have complaint about the harshness or imperceptiveness of the editors who kept sending back those printed forms without even a penciled note; the only mistake an editor made with me in my youth was buying that first ghost story. With maybe one exception, and that's this "Threnody." I've always had a weakness for it; and whatever it is in the absolute it's at least incomparably better, in both plot and writing, than anything else I did around that time.

It's strictly of its period, the '30's. Alexander Woollcott no longer sways mass enthusiasms; Granville Hicks no longer contributes to The

New Masses; Corey Ford (damn it!) no longer writes brilliant parodies.
In these respects it does seem dated—which is, at that, proper for such
a retrospective anthology. In others I hope it may still prove readable,
and justify me in the belief that every author must cherish: that he was
at least once unjustly rejected.

At any rate, appearing as it does for the first time in print, it's as
hymenally intact as a maiden murder can be.

ANTHONY BOUCHER

Threnody

IN THE spring of that year they were both completely unknown. They said good-by in a cheap beer joint. There was a
red and white checked cloth on the table, and the pianist was
playing a Rodgers and Hart tune of six months past. Lawrence
Winton looked at his departing friend, felt low, and ordered
another beer.

Al Hanford had never seemed more hale nor blithe. His coming wanderings in Mexico inspired him, and he talked gaily and
unceasingly. But Winton felt a self-conscious sense of foreboding.
It was, he supposed, because he was a poet and imagined some
sort of damned obligation to spread a blob of lyric sadness over
any suitable occasion. For one clear analytical moment he looked
at Hanford and wondered why they were friends. He was acute
enough, in these rare instants of clear vision, to see through
Hanford's surface charm to the weakness beneath it. But the
fresh round of beer came, Al began to speak of the volume of
verse which Winton had submitted to the Caxton Printers, and
the rare instant passed.

The Caxton Printers were reaching a conclusion on that volume
on the day in July when Lawrence Winton learned of his friend's
death at the hands of Mexican bandits. He was seated at his desk
when the wire came (a letter with his return address had been
found on the body), and his world folded. There was no clear
instant in this grief, only the knowledge that his friend was dead.
For a moment he held in his hand the paper cutter—a small
dagger which Al Hanford had picked up somewhere in the East.

It was still sharp and would serve. But he threw it down and took up his pencil instead.

It was midnight before he had stopped writing, erasing, rewriting, and shaping. He was hungry and his hand was cramped; but on his desk lay the final draught of "Threnody—for Alaric." His mind was unable to judge the poem then. His only thought was a vague surprise at the realization that he had never written out Al's full name before. He looked at the threnody for a little while and then went to the kitchen to fry an egg.

The letter from the Caxton Printers came two days later. The editors were mildly enthusiastic about his verse, but found the quantity submitted slight. If he had some longer work to round out the volume . . . So he typed out a good copy of "Threnody" and sent it on.

Saturn in Sables, by Lawrence Winton, was published in due time. It got passable notices and, for verse, nearly passable sales, and that was all. Winton went on teaching night school and lucky to have that. And then someone gave a copy of the book to Alexander Woollcott.

So impressed was he by "Threnody," although the other poems left him unmoved, that he devoted an entire radio program to sugared ecstasies on the greatest elegy of our times, ending by reading, with orchestral accompaniment, extensive excerpts. With unerring taste he chose exactly those portions which Winton, on reading the printed volume, had decided should be cut if the thing ever saw another edition.

The next day every librarian, public or rental, found himself besieged by customers who demanded the book that had "Threnody" in it. The title of the book and the name of the author were generally unknown. Those librarians who had heard the Woollcott broadcast had already, and wisely, ordered copies. The others lost no time in identifying the desired book.

Within a week Lawrence Winton was famous and "Threnody" had become a byword. Much to his own surprise, he discovered that in this expression of his purely personal grief and hope he had written a comforting panacea for America's sorrows. The ever narcotic assurance that death is, after all, a beautiful thing had never before been expressed in words so suited to the understanding of the American public.

In its own lyric way "Threnody" became a public menace, in the manner of "Yes, We Have No Bananas" or a "Music Goes Round and Round." Bing Crosby scored an even greater hit than usual as the introducer of a new song entitled "Threnody." (It ended: "for this melody is my threnody of love.") Benjamin Z. Fineberg bought the film rights to the title and handed the poem to five writers in turn, with injunctions to turn out a story treatment on this by Monday. Of the five writers, only three were shortly removed to sanitariums for acute alcoholism.

Lestrois Parish compiled a two-page article for Hearst's *American Weekly* on the world's great elegies. The literati succumbed to the craze, and argued violently as to whether "Threnody" bore more resemblance to "Lycidas" or to "Adonais." A minority held out for "Thyrsis." The *Journal of English and Germanic Philology* published a carefully annotated essay on "Lawrence Winton's 'Threnody': a comparative study in the influences of Milton, Shelley, Arnold, and Jorge de Manrique." Manrique, whom Winton had never read, was an easy winner.

James Hilton, who had himself endured an almost equally amazing mass enthusiasm, referred in a radio talk to Mr. Winton's admirable "Threenody." This sent thousands scurrying to the Oxford English Dictionary, and set other thousands writing indignantly to their pet radio editors. Fifty-three per cent of these managed an indirect reference to England's war debt.

Corey Ford wrote an ingenious parody on the poem, which was refused by his publishers as being in questionable taste. Mr. Ford consoled himself with a brilliant burlesque of all raves on "Threnody."

Only the *New Masses* remained immune to the epidemic; and even there Granville Hicks contrived to mention Lawrence Winton's obvious subconscious fascism.

And Chico Marx, in a Kaufman-Ryskind political satire, described himself as a threnody people.

Lawrence Winton, meanwhile, gave up his teaching job two weeks after the Woollcott broadcast. Mr. Fineberg's check for the film rights was in itself enough to keep him comfortable for years, to say nothing of the royalties on the book itself and the numerous incidental rights which he had acquired. He realized that this wild popularity was bound to blow up in time. Consequently he lived quietly as always and saved the greater part of his fabulous income.

He had begun the new narrative poem for which his publishers were so eager when he received a telegram from Mr. Fineberg begging him to come to Hollywood at once on his own terms. "Threnody" was causing a tragic depletion in the ranks of Fineberg writers, and the genius of screen production had decided to let the author do his own adaptation.

The prospect fascinated and terrified Lawrence Winton. He had never written anything in the least dramatic, and yet he had the feeling common to all who ever attend the films that, by God, he could do better than that. He was still in lonely indecision when the doorbell rang.

It was some minutes before he recognized in this bearded, shabby tramp his friend Al Hanford. When recognition came, he seized Al warmly by the hand. Hanford answered the grip indifferently and walked into the house. First he asked for a drink, and then congratulated Winton on his success. Not until after the second drink could he be made to tell how he happened to be alive.

It was simple enough. He had had pressing reasons (which he left purposely vague) for disappearing. He stumbled across the corpse of a victim of bandits, planted all his identification on it, and vanished. When at last he heard of the success of "Threnody," he could not rest until he had thanked his friend for that magnificent tribute.

Throughout his narrative he smiled absently as though thinking of what he was leading up to. Soon he began to point out what would happen if his continued life became known. He chose his words sharply. Winton writhed as he outlined the country's reaction. People would think the whole thing a hoax in bad taste. Not only would money stop coming in, but Winton's further writings would prove quite unsalable. It was a convincing picture.

He ended with the obvious proposition. Fifty per cent of

Winton's income paid to him through specified channels and he would remain dead.

Winton looked at him a long while. He saw what he would be damned to—utter servile dependence on this weakling cheat. All his former moments of clear vision were concentrated now in one blazing light. But he saw more. He saw that Hanford had changed, changed so much that he himself could scarcely recognize him. He saw that the clothes looked like those of any cheap tramp, and that nothing about the man could suggest to anyone the object of the famous "Threnody."

He slipped the paper-knife in his pocket unobserved. After a moment's silence he gave a nod of assent and rising walked behind Al Hanford's chair.

On the way back from his long automobile drive to the outskirts of town, where tomorrow an unidentified vagabond would be found dead, Winton stopped at a telegraph office to send his acceptance to Benjamin Z. Fineberg. Death was, he thought as he signed the blank, an even more beautiful thing than he had ever realized.

ELLERY QUEEN

The Adventure of the One-Penny Black

INTRODUCTION

Looking backward, it is hard to believe that we wrote no less than seven detective novels before we tackled the exceedingly difficult medium of the short story. One would think we had undergone sufficient basic training, yet after five novels under the pseudonym of Ellery Queen and two under the alter-pseudonym of Barnaby Ross, our first venture in the short-story field was almost a total failure.

It was some time in 1932 (twenty years ago!) that our literary agent suggested we broaden our base of operations and attack the magazine market. It was a lucrative field, he said, and we couldn't miss. The word "lucrative" is one we have never been able to resist.

Well, first, as always, we needed a plot—the writing man's burden. Since we were both rabid philatelists at the time, we decided on stamp collecting as the theme of our first short story. In due course the manuscript was delivered to our agent, who promptly sent it out on the road to fame and fortune.

The high-priced "slicks" turned it down, one after another. All right, we consoled ourselves, so we wouldn't get a fat check for our first short story. Then the medium-priced "slicks" showed the same indifference. We reconciled ourselves to a leaner check. Finally, the low-priced "pulps" sent their regrets, and by this time we had resigned ourselves to no check at all. Our first short story was obviously a complete bust, and we wrote it off to that grand old sanity saver, experience.

At the end of 1932 Will Levinrew started a new magazine called Great Detective. *Will phoned our agent and said he was looking for originals—cheap. Our agent remembered our "maiden murder." He sent it to Will, who said he liked the story and made our agent an offer —$25. Our agent relayed the offer to us. We had known that Will wanted originals cheap—but we didn't think* that *cheap.*

How our short-story hopes had fallen! From dreams of $1,000 to a mere one-fortieth *of that! It was too much to bear. We instructed our agent to reject the offer. But Will was persistent: he said he might just possibly be able to raise the price. By slow stages it reached the astronomical figure of $35. At this point our agent made the classic remark: "I admit there's no money in it—for any of us—but there's always the publicity value."*

We capitulated. Perhaps we just couldn't resist the prospect of seeing our first story in the pages of a magazine—any magazine. So our agent earned himself a big $3.50, and we struck magazine pay dirt to the tune of a fabulous $15.75 each.

The story finally appeared in the April, 1933, issue (Volume 1, Number 2) of Great Detective. *Oh, frabjous day! It was worth it after all! For Will Levinrew, that wily editor, had this to say on the contents page: "The Distinguished American Writer Brings the Science of Deduction to the nth Degree." Caps, mind you—especially in "Distinguished American Writer."*

Who cared about money? True, it was the only medium of exchange butchers and bakers would accept—but wasn't that of piddling significance compared with prestige and editorial praise? And consider the illustrious company we found ourselves in: for in that issue of "Great Detective" there were stories, among others, by Dorothy L. Sayers, Earl Derr Biggers, Sax Rohmer, Edwin Balmer and William MacHarg.

All the same, we can't help wondering to this very day: Just how much did the others *receive?*

ELLERY QUEEN

The Adventure of the One-Penny Black

"A CH!" said old Uneker. "It iss a terrible t'ing, Mr. Quveen, a terrible t'ing, like I vass saying. Vat iss New York coming to? Dey come into my store—*polizei*, undt bleedings, undt whackings on de headt. . . . Diss iss vunuff my oldest customers, Mr. Quveen. He too hass hadt exberiences. . . . Mr. Hazlitt, Mr. Quveen. . . . Mr. Quveen iss dot famous detectiff feller you read aboudt in de papers, Mr. Hazlitt. Inspector Richardt Quveen's son."

Ellery Queen laughed, uncoiled his length from old Uneker's

counter, and shook the man's hand. "Another victim of our crime wave, Mr. Hazlitt? Unkey's been regaling me with a feast of a whopping bloody tale."

"So you're Ellery Queen," said the frail little fellow; he wore a pair of thick-lensed goggles and there was a smell of suburbs about him. "This *is* luck! Yes, I've been robbed."

Ellery looked incredulously about old Uneker's bookshop. "Not *here?*" Uneker was tucked away on a side street in mid-Manhattan, squeezed between the British Bootery and Mme. Carolyne's, and it was just about the last place in the world you would have expected thieves to choose as the scene of a crime.

"Nah," said Hazlitt. "Might have saved the price of a book if it had. No, it happened last night about ten o'clock. I'd just left my office on Forty-fifth Street—I'd worked late—and I was walking crosstown. Chap stopped me on the street and asked for a light. The street was pretty dark and deserted, and I didn't like the fellow's manner, but I saw no harm in lending him a packet of matches. While I was digging it out, though, I noticed he was eyeing the book under my arm. Sort of trying to read the title."

"What book was it?" asked Ellery eagerly. Books were his private passion.

Hazlitt shrugged. "Nothing remarkable. That best-selling non-fiction thing, *Europe in Chaos;* I'm in the export line and I like to keep up to date on international conditions. Anyway, this chap lit his cigarette, returned the matches, mumbled his thanks, and I began to walk on. Next thing I knew something walloped me on the back of my head and everything went black. I seem to remember falling. When I came to, I was lying in the gutter, my hat and glasses were on the stones, and my head felt like a baked potato. Naturally thought I'd been robbed; I had a lot of cash about me, and I was wearing a pair of diamond cuff links. But—"

"But, of course," said Ellery with a grin, "the only thing that was taken was *Europe in Chaos*. Perfect, Mr. Hazlitt! A fascinating little problem. Can you describe your assailant?"

"He had a heavy mustache and dark-tinted glasses of some kind. That's all. I—"

"He? He can describe not'ing," said old Uneker sourly. "He iss like all you Americans—blindt, a *dummkopf*. But de book, Mr. Quveen—de book! Vhy should anyvon vant to steal a book like dot?"

"And that isn't all," said Hazlitt. "When I got home last night —I live in East Orange, New Jersey—I found my house broken into! And what do you think had been stolen, Mr. Queen?"

Ellery's lean face beamed. "I'm no crystal gazer; but if there's any consistency in crime, I should imagine another book had been stolen."

"Right! And it was my second copy of *Europe in Chaos!*"

"Now you do interest me," said Ellery, in quite a different tone. "How did you come to have two, Mr. Hazlitt?"

"I bought another copy from Uneker two days ago to give to a friend of mine. I'd left it on top of my bookcase. It was gone. Window was open—it had been forced; and there were smudges of hands on the sill. Plain case of housebreaking. And although there's plenty of valuable stuff in my place—silver and things— nothing else had been taken. I reported it at once to the East Orange police, but they just tramped about the place, gave me funny looks, and finally went away. I suppose they thought I was crazy."

"Were any other books missing?"

"No, just that one."

"I really don't see . . ." Ellery took off his pince-nez eyeglasses and began to polish the lenses thoughtfully. "Could it have been the same man? Would he have had time to get out to East Orange and burglarize your house before you got there last night?"

"Yes. When I picked myself out of the gutter I reported the assault to a cop, and he took me down to a nearby station house, and they asked me a lot of questions. He would have had plenty of time—I didn't get home until one o'clock in the morning."

"I think, Unky," said Ellery, "that the story *you* told me begins to have point. If you'll excuse me, Mr. Hazlitt, I'll be on my way. *Auf wiedersehen!*"

Ellery left old Uneker's little shop and went downtown to Centre Street. He climbed the steps of Police Headquarters, nodded amiably to a desk lieutenant, and made for his father's office. The Inspector was out. Ellery twiddled with an ebony

figurine of Bertillon on his father's desk, mused deeply, then
went out and began to hunt for Sergeant Velie, the Inspector's
chief-of-operations. He found the mammoth in the Press Room,
bawling curses at a reporter.

"Velie," said Ellery, "stop playing bad man and get me some
information. Two days ago there was an unsuccessful man-hunt
on Forty-ninth Street, between Fifth and Sixth Avenues. The
chase ended in a little bookshop owned by a friend of mine
named Uneker. Local officer was in on it. Uneker told me the
story, but I want less colored details. Get me the precinct report
like a good fellow, will you?"

Sergeant Velie waggled his big black jaws, glared at the reporter, and thundered off. Ten minutes later he came back with
a sheet of paper, and Ellery read it with absorption.

The facts seemed bald enough. Two days before, at the noon
hour, a hatless, coatless man with a bloody face had rushed out
of the office building three doors from old Uneker's bookshop,
shouting, "Help! Police!" Patrolman McCallum had run up,
and the man yelled that he had been robbed of a valuable
postage stamp—"My one-penny black!" he kept shouting. "My
one-penny black!"—and that the thief, black-mustached and
wearing heavy blue-tinted spectacles, had just escaped. McCallum had noticed a man of this description a few minutes before,
acting peculiarly, enter the nearby bookshop. Followed by the
screaming stamp dealer, he dashed into old Uneker's place with
drawn revolver. Had a man with black mustaches and blue-
tinted spectacles come into the shop within the past few minutes? "*Ja*—he?" said old Uneker. "Sure, he iss still here." Where?
In the back room looking at some books. McCallum and the
bleeding man rushed into Uneker's back room; it was empty. A
door leading to the alley from the back room was open; the man
had escaped, apparently having been scared off by the noisy entrance of the policeman and the victim a moment before. Mc-
Callum had immediately searched the neighborhood; the thief
had vanished.

The officer then took the complainant's statement. He was,
he said, Friederich Ulm, dealer in rare postage stamps. His office
was in a tenth-floor room in the building three doors away—the
office of his brother Albert, his partner, and himself. He had

been exhibiting some valuable items to an invited group of three stamp collectors. Two of them had gone away. Ulm happened to turn his back; and the third, the man with the black moustache and blue-tinted glasses, who had introduced himself as Avery Beninson, had swooped on him swiftly from behind and struck at his head with a short iron bar as Ulm twisted back. The blow had cut open Ulm's cheekbone and felled him, half-stunned; and then with the utmost coolness the thief had used the same iron bar (which, said the report, from its description was probably a "jimmy") to pry open the lid of a glass-topped cabinet in which a choice collection of stamps was kept. He had snatched from a leather box in the cabinet an extremely high-priced item—"the Queen Victoria one-penny black"—and had then dashed out, locking the door behind him. It had taken the assaulted dealer several minutes to open the door and follow. McCullum went with Ulm to the office, examined the rifled cabinet, took the names and addresses of the three collectors who had been present that morning—with particular note of "Avery Beninson"—scribbled his report, and departed.

The names of the other two collectors were John Hinchman and J. S. Peters. A detective attached to the precinct had visited each in turn, and had then gone to the address of Beninson. Beninson, who presumably had been the man with black mustaches and blue-tinted spectacles, was ignorant of the entire affair; and his physical appearance did not tally with the description of Ulm's assailant. He had received no invitation from the Ulm brothers, he said, to attend the private sale. Yes, he had had an employee, a man with black mustaches and tinted glasses, for two weeks—this man had answered Beninson's advertisement for an assistant to take charge of the collector's private stamp albums, had proved satisfactory, and had suddenly, without explanation or notice, disappeared after two weeks' service. He had disappeared, the detective noted, on the morning of the Ulms' sale.

All attempts to trace this mysterious assistant, who had called himself William Planck, were unsuccessful. The man had vanished among New York City's millions.

Nor was this the end of the story. For the day after the theft old Uneker himself had reported to the precinct detective a

queer tale. The previous night—the night of the Ulm theft—
said Uneker, he had left his shop for a late dinner; his night
clerk had remained on duty. A man had entered the shop, had
asked to see *Europe in Chaos,* and had then to the night clerk's
astonishment purchased all copies of the book in stock—seven.
The man who had made this extraordinary purchase wore black
mustaches and blue-tinted spectacles!

"Sort of nuts, ain't it?" growled Sergeant Velie.

"Not at all," smiled Ellery. "In fact, I believe it has a very
simple explanation."

"And that ain't the half of it. One of the boys told me just
now of a new angle on the case. Two minor robberies were reported from local precincts last night. One was uptown in the
Bronx; a man named Hornell said his apartment was broken
into during the night, and what do you think? Copy of *Europe
in Chaos* which Hornell had bought in this guy Uneker's store
was stolen! Nothin' else. Bought it two days ago. Then a dame
named Janet Meakins from Greenwich Village had *her* flat
robbed the same night. Thief had taken her copy of *Europe in
Chaos*—she'd bought it from Uneker the afternoon before.
Screwy, hey?"

"Not at all, Velie. Use your wits." Ellery clapped his hat on
his head. "Come along, you Colossus; I want to speak to old
Unky again."

They left Headquarters and went uptown.

"Unky," said Ellery, patting the little old bookseller's bald
pate affectionately, "how many copies of *Europe in Chaos* did
you have in stock at the time the thief escaped from your back
room?"

"Eleffen."

"Yet only seven were in stock that same evening when the thief
returned to buy them," murmured Ellery. "Therefore, four
copies had been sold between the noon hour two days ago and
the dinner hour. So! Unky, do you keep a record of your customers?"

"*Ach,* yes! De few who buy," said old Uneker sadly. "I addt to
my mailing lisdt. You vant to see?"

"There is nothing I crave more ardently at the moment."

Uneker led them to the rear of the shop and through a door

into the musty back room from whose alley door the thief had escaped two days before. Off this room there was a partitioned cubicle littered with papers, files, and old books. The old bookseller opened a ponderous ledger and, wetting his ancient forefinger, began to slap pages over. "You vant to know de four who boughdt *Europe in Chaos* dot afternoon?"

"*Ja.*"

Uneker hooked a pair of greenish-silver spectacles over his ears and began to read in a singsong voice. "Mr. Hazlitt—dot's the gentleman you met, Mr. Quveen. *He* boughdt his second copy, de vun dot vass robbed from his house. . . . Den dere vass Mr. Hornell, an oldt customer. Den a Miss Janet Meakins—*ach!* dese Anglo-Saxon names. *Schrecklich!* Undt de fourt' vun vass Mr. Chester Singermann, uff t'ree-tvelf East Siggsty-fift' Street. Und dot's all."

"Bless your orderly old Teutonic soul," said Ellery. "Velie, cast those Cyclopean peepers of yours this way." There was a door from the cubicle which, from its location, led out into the alley at the rear, like the door in the back room. Ellery bent over the lock; it was splintered away from the wood. He opened the door; the outer piece was scratched and mutilated. Velie nodded. "Forced," he growled. "This guy's a regular Houdini."

Old Uneker was goggle-eyed. "Broken!" he shrilled. "Budt dot door iss neffer used! I didn't notice not'ing, undt de detectiff—"

"Shocking work, Velie, on the part of the local man," said Ellery. "Unky, has anything been stolen?" Old Uneker flew to an antiquated bookcase; it was neatly tiered with volumes. He unlocked the case with anguished fingers, rummaging like an aged terrier. Then he heaved a vast sigh. "*Nein,*" he said. "Dose 'ire vons . . . Not'ing stole."

"I congratulate you. One thing more," said Ellery briskly. Your mailing list—does it have the business as well as private addresses of your customers?" Uneker nodded. "Better and better. Ta-ta, Unky. You may have a finished story to relate to your other customers after all. Come along, Velie; we're going to visit Mr. Chester Singermann."

They left the bookshop, walked over to Fifth Avenue and turned north, heading uptown. "Plain as the nose on your face," said Ellery, stretching his long stride to match Velie's. "And that's pretty plain, Sergeant."

"Still looks nutty to me, Mr. Queen."

"On the contrary, we are faced with a strictly logical set of facts. Our thief stole a valuable stamp. He dodged into Uneker's bookshop, contrived to get into the backroom. He heard the officer and Friederich Ulm enter, and got busy thinking. If he were caught with the stamp on his person . . . You see, Velie, the only explanation that will make consistent the business of the subsequent thefts of the same book—a book not valuable in itself—is that the thief, Planck, slipped the stamp between the pages of one of the volumes on a shelf while he was in the back room—it happened by accident to be a copy of *Europe in Chaos,* one of a number kept in stock on the shelf—and made his escape immediately thereafter. But he still had the problem of regaining possession of the stamp—what did Ulm call it?—the 'one-penny black,' whatever *that* may be. So that night he came back watched for old Uneker to leave the shop, then went in and bought from the clerk all copies of *Europe in Chaos* in the place. He got seven. The stamp was not in any one of the seven he purchased, otherwise why did he later steal others which had been bought that afternoon? So far, so good. Not finding the stamp in any of the seven, then, he returned, broke into Unky's little office during the night—witness the shattered lock—from the alley, and looked up in Unky's Dickensian ledger the names and addresses of those who had bought copies of the book during that afternoon. The next night he robbed Hazlitt; Planck evidently followed him from his office. Planck saw at once that he had made a mistake; the condition of the weeks-old book would have told him that this wasn't a book purchased only the day before. So he hurried out to East Orange, knowing Hazlitt's private as well as business address, and stole Hazlitt's recently purchased copy. No luck there either, so he feloniously visited Hornell and Janet Meakins, stealing their copies. Now, there is still one purchaser unaccounted for, which is why we are calling upon Singermann. For if Planck was unsuccessful in his theft of Hornell's and Miss Meakins' books, he will inevitably visit Singermann, and we want to beat our wily thief to it if possible."

Chester Singermann, they found, was a young student living

with his parents in a battered old apartment house flat. Yes, he still had his copy of *Europe in Chaos*—needed it for supplementary reading in political economy—and he produced it. Ellery went through it carefully, page for page; there was no trace of the missing stamp.

"Mr. Singermann, did you find an old postage stamp between the leaves of this volume?" asked Ellery.

The student shook his head. "I haven't even opened it, sir. Stamp? What issue? I've got a little collection of my own, you know."

"It doesn't matter," said Ellery hastily, who had heard of the maniacal enthusiasm of stamp collectors, and he and Velie beat a precipitate retreat.

"It's quite evident," explained Ellery to the Sergeant, "that our slippery Planck found the stamp in either Hornell's copy or Miss Meakins'. Which robbery was first in point of time, Velie?"

"Seem to remember that this Meakins woman was robbed second."

"Then the one-penny black was in her copy. . . . Here's that office building. Let's pay a little visit to Mr. Friederich Ulm."

Number 1026 on the tenth floor of the building bore a black legend on its frosted-glass door:

ULM

Dealers in

Old & Rare Stamps

Ellery and Sergeant Velie went in and found themselves in a large office. The walls were covered with glass cases in which, separately mounted, could be seen hundreds of canceled and uncanceled postage stamps. Several special cabinets on tables contained, evidently, more valuable items. The place was cluttered; it had a musty air astonishingly like that of old Uneker's bookshop.

Three men looked up. One, from a crisscrossed plaster on his cheekbone, was apparently Friedrich Ulm himself, a tall gaunt old German with sparse hair and the fanatic look of the confirmed collector. The second man was just as tall and gaunt and old; he wore a green eyeshade and bore a striking resemblance to Ulm, although from his nervous movements and shaky hands he must have been much older. The third man was a little fellow, quite stout, with an expressionless face.

Ellery introduced himself and Sergeant Velie; and the third man pricked up his ears. "Not *the* Ellery Queen?" he said, waddling forward. "I'm Heffly, investigator for the insurance people. Glad to meet you." He pumped Ellery's hand with vigor. "These gentlemen are the Ulm brothers, who own this place. Friederich and Albert. Mr. Albert Ulm was out of the office at the time of the sale and robbery. Too bad; might have nabbed the thief."

Friederich Ulm broke into an excited gabble of German. Ellery listened with a smile, nodding at every fourth word. "I see, Mr. Ulm. The situation, then, was this: you sent invitations by mail to three well-known collectors to attend a special exhibition of rare stamps—object, sale. Three men called on you two mornings ago, purporting to be Messrs. Hinchman, Peters, and Beninson. Hinchman and Peters you knew by sight, but Beninson you did not. Very well. Several items were purchased by the first two collectors. The man you thought was Beninson lingered behind, struck you—yes, yes, I know all that. Let me see the rifled cabinet, please."

The brothers led him to a table in the center of the office. On it there was a flat cabinet, with a lid of ordinary thin glass framed by a narrow rectangle of wood. Under the glass reposed a number of mounted stamps, lying nakedly on a field of black satin. In the center of the satin lay a leather case, open; its white lining had been denuded of its stamp. Where the lid of the cabinet had been wrenched open there were the unmistakable marks of a "jimmy," four in number. The catch was snapped and broken.

"Amatchoor," said Sergeant Velie with a snort. "You could damn near force that locked lid up with your fingers."

Ellery's sharp eyes were absorbed in what lay before him. "Mr. Ulm," he said, turning to the wounded dealer, "the stamp you call 'the one-penny black' was in this open leather box?"

"Yes, Mr. Queen. But the leather box was closed when the thief forced open the cabinet."

"Then how did he know so unerringly what to steal?" Friederich Ulm touched his cheek tenderly. "The stamps in this cabinet were not for sale; they're the cream of our collection; every stamp in this case is worth hundreds. But when the three men were here we naturally talked about the rarer items, and I opened this cabinet to show them our very valuable stamps. So the thief saw the one-penny black. He was a collector, Mr. Queen, or he wouldn't have chosen that particular stamp to steal. It has a funny history."

"Heavens!" said Ellery. "Do these things have histories?"

Heffly, the man from the insurance company, laughed. "And how! Mr. Friederich and Mr. Albert Ulm are well known to the trade for owning two of the most unique stamps ever issued, both identical. The one-penny black, as it is called by collectors, is a British stamp first issued in 1840; there are lots of them around, and even an uncanceled one is worth only seventeen and a half dollars in American money. But the two in the possession of these gentlemen are worth thirty thousand dollars apiece, Mr. Queen—that's what makes the theft so doggone serious. In fact, my company is heavily involved, since the stamps are both insured for their full value."

"Thirty thousand dollars!" groaned Ellery. "That's a lot of money for a little piece of dirty paper. Why are they so valuable?"

Albert Ulm nervously pulled his green shade lower over his eyes. "Because both of ours were actually initialed by Queen Victoria, that's why. Sir Rowland Hill, the man who created and founded the standard penny-postage system in England in 1839, was responsible for the issue of the one-penny black. Her Majesty was so delighted—England like other countries, had had a great deal of trouble working out a successful postage system—that she autographed the first two stamps off the press and gave them to the designer—I don't recall his name. Her autograph made them immensely valuable. My brother and I were lucky to get our hands on the only two in existence."

"Where's the twin? I'd like to take a peep at a stamp worth a queen's ransom."

The brothers bustled to a large safe looming in a corner of the office. They came back, Albert carrying a leather case as if it were a consignment of golden bullion, and Friederich anxiously holding his elbow, as if he were a squad of armed guards detailed to protect the consignment. Ellery turned the thing over in his fingers; it felt thick and stiff. It was an average-sized stamp rectangle, imperforate, bordered with a black design, and containing an engraving in profile of Queen Victoria's head—all done in tones of black. On the lighter portion of the face appeared two tiny initials in faded black ink—V. R.

"They're both exactly alike," said Friederich Ulm. "Even to the initials."

"Very interesting," said Ellery, returning the case. The brothers scurried back, placed the stamp in a drawer of the safe, and locked the safe with painful care. "You closed the cabinet, of course, after your three visitors looked over the stamps inside?"

"Oh, yes," said Friederich Ulm. "I closed the case of the one-penny black itself, and then I locked the cabinet."

"And did you send the three invitations yourself? I noticed you have no typewriter here."

"We use a public stenographer in Room 1102 for all our correspondence, Mr. Queen."

Ellery thanked the dealers gravely, waved to the insurance man, nudged Sergeant Velie's meaty ribs, and the two men left the office. In Room 1102 they found a sharp-featured young woman. Sergeant Velie flashed his badge, and Ellery was soon reading carbon copies of the three Ulm invitations. He took note of the names and addresses, and the two men left.

They visited the collector named John Hinchman first. Hinchman was a thick-set old man with white hair and gimlet eyes. He was brusque and uncommunicative. Yes, he had been present in the Ulm's office two mornings before. Yes, he knew Peters. No, he'd never met Beninson before. The one-penny black? Of course. Every collector knew of the valuable twin stamps owned by the Ulm brothers; those little scraps of paper bearing the initials of a queen were famous in stampdom. The theft? Bosh! He, Hinchman, knew nothing of Beninson, or whoever it was that impersonated Beninson. He, Hinchman, had left before the thief. He, Hinchman, furthermore didn't care two raps in Hades who stole the stamp; all he wanted was to be let strictly alone.

Sergeant Velie exhibited certain animal signs of hostility; but Ellery grinned, sank his strong fingers into the muscle of the Sergeant's arm, and herded him out of Hinchman's house. They took the subway uptown.

J. S. Peters, they found, was a middle-aged man, tall and thin and yellow as Chinese sealing-wax. He seemed anxious to be of assistance. Yes, he and Hinchman had left the Ulms' office to gether, before the third man. He had never seen the third man before, although he had heard of Beninson from other collectors. Yes, he knew all about the one-penny blacks, had even tried to buy one of them from Friederich Ulm two years before; but the Ulms had refused to sell.

"Philately," said Ellery outside to Sergeant Velie, whose honest face looked pained at the word, "is a curious hobby. It seems to afflict its victims with a species of mania. I don't doubt these stamp-collecting fellows would murder each other for one of the things."

The Sergeant was wrinkling his nose. "How's she look now?" he asked rather anxiously.

"Velie," replied Ellery, "she looks swell—and different."

They found Avery Beninson in an old brownstone house near the River; he was a mild-mannered and courteous host.

"No, I never did see that invitation," Beninson said. "You see, I hired this man who called himself William Planck, and he took care of my collection and the bulky mail all serious collectors have. The man knew stamps, all right. For two weeks he was invaluable to me. He must have intercepted the Ulms' invitation. He saw his chance to get into their office, went there, said he was Avery Beninson . . ." The collector shrugged. "It was quite simple, I suppose, for an unscrupulous man."

"Of course, you haven't had word from him since the morning of the theft?"

"Naturally not. He made his haul and lit out."

"Just what did he do for you, Mr. Beninson?"

"The ordinary routine of the philatelic assistant—assorting, cataloguing, mounting, answering correspondence. He lived here with me for the two weeks he was in my employ." Beninson grinned deprecatingly. "You see, I'm a bachelor—live in this big shack all alone. I was really glad of his company, although he *was* a queer one."

"A queer one?"

"Well," said Beninson, "he was a retiring sort of creature. Had very few personal belongings, and I found those gone two days ago. He didn't seem to like people, either. He always went to his own room when friends of mine or collectors called, as if he didn't want to mix with company."

"Then there isn't any one else who might be able to supplement your description of him?"

"Unfortunately, no. He was a fairly tall man, well advanced in age, I should say. But then his dark glasses and heavy black mustache would make him stand out anywhere."

Ellery sprawled his long figure over the chair, slumping on his spine. "I'm most interested in the man's habits, Mr. Beninson. Individual idiosyncrasies are often the innocent means by which criminals are apprehended, as the good Sergeant here will tell you. Please think hard. Didn't the man exhibit any oddities of habit?"

Beninson pursed his lips with anxious concentration. His face brightened. "By George, yes! He was a snuff-taker."

Ellery and Sergeant Velie looked at each other. "That's interesting," said Ellery with a smile. "So is my father—Inspector Queen, you know—and I've had the dubious pleasure of watching a snuff-taker's gyrations ever since my childhood. Planck inhaled snuff regularly?"

"I shouldn't say that exactly, Mr. Queen," replied Beninson with a frown. "In fact, in the two weeks he was with me I saw him take snuff only once, and I invariably spent all day with him working in this room. It was last week; I happened to go out for a few moments, and when I returned I saw him holding a carved little box, sniffing from a pinch of something between his fingers. He put the box away quickly, as if he didn't want me to see it—although I didn't care, Lord knows, so long as he didn't smoke in here. I've had one fire from a careless assistant's cigarette, and I don't want another."

Ellery's face had come alive. He sat up straight and began to finger his pince-nez eyeglasses studiously. "You didn't know the man's address, I suppose?" he asked slowly.

"No, I did not. I'm afraid I took him on without the proper precautions." The collector sighed. "I'm fortunate that he didn't steal anything from me. My collection is worth a lot of money."

"No doubt," said Ellery in a pleasant voice. He rose. "May I use your telephone, Mr. Beninson?"

"Surely."

Ellery consulted a telephone directory and made several calls, speaking in tones so low that neither Beninson nor Sergeant Velie could hear what he was saying. When he put down the instrument he said, "If you can spare a half-hour, Mr. Beninson, I'd like to have you take a little jaunt with us downtown."

Beninson seemed astonished; but he smiled, said, "I'd be delighted," and reached for his coat.

Ellery commandeered a taxicab outside, and the three men were driven to Forty-ninth Street. He excused himself when they got out before the little bookshop, hurried inside, and came out after a moment with old Uneker, who locked his door with shaking fingers.

In the Ulm brothers' office they found Heffly, the insurance man, and Hazlitt, Uneker's customer, waiting for them. "Glad you could come," said Ellery cheerfully to both men. "Good afternoon, Mr. Ulm. A little conference, and I think we'll have this business cleared up to the Queen's taste. Ha, ha!"

Friederich Ulm scratched his head; Albert Ulm, sitting in a corner with his hatchet knees jack-knifed, his green shade over his eyes, nodded.

"We'll have to wait," said Ellery. "I've asked Mr. Peters and Mr. Hinchman to come, too. Suppose we sit down?"

They were silent for the most part, and not a little uneasy. No one spoke as Ellery strolled about the office, examining the rare stamps in their wall cases with open curiosity, whistling softly to himself. Sergeant Velie eyed him doubtfully. Then the door opened, and Hinchman and Peters appeared together. They stopped short at the threshold, looked at each other, shrugged, and walked in. Hinchman was scowling.

"What's the idea, Mr. Queen?" he said. "I'm a busy man."

"A not unique condition," smiled Ellery. "Ah, Mr. Peters, good day. Introductions, I think, are not entirely called for . . . Sit down, gentlemen!" he said in a sharper voice, and they sat down.

The door opened and a small, gray, birdlike little man peered in at them. Sergeant Velie looked astounded, and Ellery nodded gaily. "Come in, Dad, come in! You're just in time for the first act."

Inspector Richard Queen cocked his little squirrel's head, looked at the assembled company shrewdly, and closed the door behind him. "What the devil is the idea of the call, son?"

"Nothing very exciting. Not a murder, or anything in your line. But it may interest you. Gentlemen, Inspector Queen."

The Inspector grunted, sat down, took out his old brown snuff box, and inhaled with the voluptuous gasp of long practice.

Ellery stood serenely in the hub of the circle of chairs, looking down at curious faces. "The theft of the one-penny black, as you inveterate stamp fiends call it," he began, "presented a not uninteresting problem. I say 'presented' advisedly. For the case is solved."

"Is this that business of the stamp robbery I was hearing about down at Headquarters?" asked the Inspector.

"Yes."

"Solved?" asked Beninson. "I don't think I understand, Mr. Queen. Have you found Planck?"

Ellery waved his arm negligently. "I was never too sanguine of catching Mr. William Planck, as such. You see, he wore tinted spectacles and black mustachios. Now, any one familiar with the science of crime detection will tell you that the average person identifies faces by superficial details. A black mustache catches the eye. Tinted glasses impress the memory. In fact, Mr. Hazlitt here, who from Uneker's description is a man of poor observational powers, recalled even after seeing his assailant in dim street light that the man wore a black mustache and tinted glasses. But this is all fundamental and not even particularly smart. It was reasonable to assume that Planck wanted these special facial characteristics to be remembered. I was convinced that he had disguised himself, that the mustache was probably a false one, and that ordinarily he does not wear tinted glasses."

They all nodded.

"This was the first and simplest of the three psychological signposts to the culprit." Ellery smiled and turned suddenly to the Inspector. "Dad, you're an old snuff addict. How many times a day do you snuff that unholy brown dust up your nostrils?"

The Inspector blinked. "Oh, every half-hour or so. Sometimes as often as you smoke cigarettes."

"Precisely. Now, Mr. Beninson told me that in the two weeks

during which Planck stayed at his house, and despite the fact that Mr. Beninson worked side by side with the man every day, he saw Planck take snuff only *once*. Please observe that here we have a most enlightening and suggestive fact."

From the blankness of their faces it was apparent that, far from seeing light, their minds on this point were in total darkness. There was one exception—the Inspector; he nodded, shifted in his chair, and coolly began to study the faces about him.

Ellery lit a cigaret. "Very well," he said, expelling little puffs of smoke, "there you have the second psychological factor. The third was this: Planck, in a fairly public place, bashes Mr. Friederich Ulm over the face with the robust intention of stealing a valuable stamp. Any thief under the circumstances would desire speed above all things. Mr. Ulm was only half-stunned—he might come to and make an outcry; a customer might walk in; Mr. Albert Ulm might return unexpectedly—"

"Just a moment, son," said the Inspector. "I understand there are two of the stamp thingamajigs in existence. I'd like to see the one that's still here."

Ellery nodded. "Would one of you gentlemen please get the stamp?"

Friederich Ulm rose, pottered over to the safe, tinkered with the dials, opened the steel door, fussed about the interior a moment, and came back with the leather case containing the second one-penny black. The Inspector examined the thick little scrap curiously; a thirty-thousand-dollar bit of old paper was as awesome to him as to Ellery.

He almost dropped it when he heard Ellery say to Sergeant Velie, "Sergeant, may I borrow your revolver?"

Velie's massive jaw seesawed as he fumbled in his hip pocket and produced a long-barreled police revolver. Ellery took it and hefted it thoughtfully. Then his fingers closed about the butt and he walked over to the rifled cabinet in the middle of the room.

"Please observe, gentlemen—to expand my third point—that in order to open this cabinet Planck used an iron bar; and that in prying up the lid he found it necessary to insert the bar between the lid and the front wall four times, as the four marks under the lid indicate.

"Now, as you can see, the cabinet is covered with thin glass. Moreover, it was locked, and the one-penny black was in this closed leather case inside. Planck stood about here, I should judge, and mark that the iron bar was in his hand. What would you gentlemen expect a thief, working against time, to do under these circumstances?"

They stared. The Inspector's mouth tightened, and a grin began to spread over the expanse of Sergeant Velie's face.

"But it's so clear," said Ellery. "Visualize it. I'm Planck. The revolver in my hand is an iron 'jimmy.' I'm standing over the cabinet . . ." His eyes gleamed behind the pince-nez, and he raised the revolver high over his head. And then, deliberately, he began to bring the steel barrel down on the thin sheeting of glass atop the cabinet. There was a scream from Albert Ulm, and Friederich Ulm half-rose, glaring. Ellery's hand stopped a half-inch from the glass.

"Don't break that glass, you fool!" shouted the green-shaded dealer. "You'll only—"

He leaped forward and stood before the cabinet, trembling arms outspread as if to protect the case and its contents. Ellery grinned and prodded the man's palpitating belly with the muzzle of the revolver. "I'm glad you stopped me, Mr. Ulm. Put your hands up. Quickly!"

"Why—why, what do you mean?" gasped Albert Ulm, raising his arms with frantic rapidity.

"I mean," said Ellery gently, "that you're William Planck, and that brother Friederich is your accomplice!"

The brothers Ulm sat trembling in their chairs, and Sergeant Velie stood over them with a nasty smile. Albert Ulm had gone to pieces; he was quivering like an aspen leaf in high wind.

"A very simple, almost an elementary, series of deductions," Ellery was saying. "Point three first. Why did the thief, instead of taking the most logical course of smashing the glass with the iron bar, choose to waste precious minutes using a 'jimmy' four times to force open the lid? *Obviously to protect the other stamps in the cabinet which lay open to possible injury,* as Mr. Albert Ulm has just graphically pointed out. And who had the greatest concern in protecting these other stamps—Hinchman, Peter,

Beninson, even the mythical Planck himself? Of course not. Only the Ulm brothers, owners of the stamps."

Old Uneker began to chuckle; he nudged the Inspector. "See? Didn't I say he vas smardt? Now me—me, I'd neffer t'ink of dot."

"And why didn't Planck steal these other stamps in the cabinet? You would expect a thief to do that. Planck did not. But if the *Herren* Ulm were the thieves, the theft of the other stamps became pointless."

"How about that snuff businss, Mr. Queen?" asked Peters.

"Yes. The conclusion is plain from the fact that Planck apparently indulged only once during the days he worked with Mr. Beninson. Since snuff addicts partake freely and often, Planck wasn't a snuff addict. Then it wasn't snuff he inhaled that day. What else is sniffed in a similar manner? Well—drugs in powder form—heroin! What are the characteristics of a heroin addict? Nervous drawn appearance; gauntness, almost emaciation; and most important, tell-tale eyes, the pupils of which contract under influence of the drug. Then here was another explanation for the tinted glasses Planck wore. They served a double purpose—as an easily recognizable disguise, and also to conceal his eyes, which would give his vice addiction away! But when I observed that Mr. Albert Ulm—" Ellery went over to the cowering man and ripped the green eyeshade away, revealing two stark, pin-point pupils—"wore this shade, it was a psychological confirmation of his identity as Planck."

"Yes, but that business of stealing all those books," said Hazlett.

"Part of a very pretty and rather far-fetched plot," said Ellery. "With Albert Ulm the disguised thief, Friederich Ulm, who exhibited the wound on his cheek, must have been an accomplice. Then with the Ulm brothers the thieves, the entire business of the books was a blind. The attack on Friederich, the ruse of the bookstore-escape, the trail of the minor robberies of copies of *Europe in Chaos*—a cleverly planned series of incidents to authenticate the fact that there was an outside thief, to convince the police and the insurance company that the stamp actually was stolen when it was not. Object, of course, to collect the insurance without parting with the stamp. These men are fanatical collectors."

Heffly wriggled his fat little body uncomfortably. "That's all very nice, Mr. Queen, but where the deuce is that stamp they stole from themselves? Where'd they hide it?"

"I thought long and earnestly about that, Heffley. For while my trio of deductions were psychological indications of guilt, the discovery of the stolen stamp in the Ulms' possession would be evidential proof." The Inspector was turning the second stamp over mechanically. "I said to myself," Ellery went on, "in a reconsideration of the problem: what would be the most likely hiding-place for the stamp? And then I remembered that the two stamps were identical, even the initials of the good Queen being in the same place. So I said to myself: if I were Messrs. Ulm, I should hide that stamp—like the character in Edgar Allan Poe's famous tale—in the most obvious place. And what is the most obvious place?"

Ellery sighed and returned the unused revolver to Sergeant Velie. "Dad," he remarked to the Inspector, who started guiltily, "I think that if you allow one of the philatelists in our company to examine the second one-penny black in your fingers, you'll find the *first* has been pasted with noninjurious rubber cement precisely over the second!"

STANLEY ELLIN

The Specialty of the House

INTRODUCTION

The people and events in "The Specialty of the House" are, in the words of the fine old disclaimer, entirely imaginary. The restaurant, however, is real. Its name is Gage and Tollner's, and it may be found not far from Brooklyn's Borough Hall where it has stood for the past seventy-three years. The management solemnly affirms that the installation of electric lighting is the only real change in the room during those years. I can solemnly affirm that the food is superb, and that what God hath wrought in an oyster, clam, or lobster, Gage and Tollner's will never undo.

"The Specialty of the House" was born in that restaurant one evening in October, 1946, when my wife and I were eating dinner there, and talking about stories and storytelling. It was her contention that not only were there sermons in stones, and books in running brooks, but an anthology of stories in the old room around us. That stout gentleman, for example, remarking that as an amateur chef he'd enjoy visiting the kitchen, and the waiter explaining that it would be difficult to arrange during dinner hour, but perhaps some other time . . .

I started the story the next day and finished it three weeks later. The New Yorker rejected it promptly, and again my incomparable wife played a key role by suggesting Ellery Queen's Mystery Magazine as the best possible market. One week later Fred Dannay, the editor, phoned me and announced his decision to buy the story, and his desire to have me enter it in the magazine's annual contest. It won the prize as Best First Story in the contest that year, 1947, and brought me three hundred dollars, plus the peculiar distinction of always being introduced in company as "the one who wrote 'The Specialty of the House,'" although I have had a number of stories published since then, and a couple of novels as well.

I have not yet decided whether it is an asset or not to travel always with Mr. Sbirro saddled, like an Old Man of the Mountain, to my back. I leave that decision to you.

STANLEY ELLIN

The Specialty of the House

"AND THIS," said Laffler, "is Sbirro's." Costain saw a square brownstone façade identical with the others that extended from either side into the clammy darkness of the deserted street. From the barred windows of the basement at his feet, a glimmer of light showed behind heavy curtains.

"Lord," he observed, "it's a dismal hole, isn't it?"

"I beg you to understand," said Laffler stiffly, "that Sbirro's is the restaurant without pretensions. Besieged by these ghastly, neurotic times, it has refused to compromise. It is perhaps the last important establishment in this city lit by gas jets. Here you will find the same honest furnishings, the same magnificent Sheffield service, and possibly, in a far corner, the very same spider webs that were remarked by the patrons of a half century ago!"

"A doubtful recommendation," said Costain, "and hardly sanitary."

"When you enter," Laffler continued, "you leave the insanity of this year, this day, and this hour, and you find yourself for a brief span restored in spirit, not by opulence, but by dignity, which is the lost quality of our time."

Costain laughed uncomfortably. "You make it sound more like a cathedral than a restaurant," he said.

In the pale reflection of the street lamp overhead, Laffler peered at his companion's face. "I wonder," he said abruptly, "whether I have not made a mistake in extending this invitation to you."

Costain was hurt. Despite an impressive title and large salary, he was no more than clerk to this pompous little man, but he was impelled to make some display of his feelings. "If you wish," he said coldly, "I can make other plans for my evening with no trouble."

With his large, cowlike eyes turned up to Costain, the mist drifting into the ruddy, full moon of his face, Laffler seemed strangely ill at ease. Then "No, no," he said at last, "absolutely not. It's important that you dine at Sbirro's with me." He grasped Costain's arm firmly and led the way to the wrought-iron gate of the basement. "You see, you're the sole person in my office who seems to know anything at all about good food. And on my part, knowing about Sbirro's but not having some appreciative friend to share it, is like having a unique piece of art locked in a room where no one else can enjoy it."

Costain was considerably mollified by this. "I understand there are a great many people who relish that situation."

"I'm not one of that kind!" Laffler said sharply. "And having the secret of Sbirro's locked in myself for years has finally become unendurable." He fumbled at the side of the gate and from within could be heard the small, discordant jangle of an ancient pullbell. An interior door opened with a groan, and Costain found himself peering into a dark face whose only discernible feature was a row of gleaming teeth.

"Sair?" said the face.

"Mr. Laffler and a guest."

"Sair," the face said again, this time in what was clearly an invitation. It moved aside and Costain stumbled down a single step behind his host. The door and gate creaked behind him, and he stood blinking in a small foyer. It took him a moment to realize that the figure he now stared at was his own reflection in a gigantic pier glass that extended from floor to ceiling. "Atmosphere," he said under his breath and chuckled as he followed his guide to a seat.

He faced Laffler across a small table for two and peered curiously around the dining room. It was no size at all, but the half dozen guttering gas jets which provided the only illumination threw such a deceptive light that the walls flickered and faded into uncertain distance.

There were no more than eight or ten tables about, arranged to insure the maximum privacy. All were occupied, and the few waiters serving them moved with quiet efficiency. In the air was a soft clash and scrape of cutlery and a soothing murmur of talk. Costain nodded appreciatively.

Laffler breathed an audible sigh of gratification. "I knew you would share my enthusiasm," he said. "Have you noticed, by the way, that there are no women present?"

Costain raised inquiring eyebrows.

"Sbirro," said Laffler, "does not encourage members of the fair sex to enter the premises. And, I can tell you, his method is decidedly effective. I had the experience of seeing a woman get a taste of it not long ago. She sat at a table for not less than an hour waiting for service which was never forthcoming."

"Didn't she make a scene?"

"She did." Laffler smiled at the recollection. "She succeeded in annoying the customers, embarrassing her partner, and nothing more."

"And what about Mr. Sbirro?"

"He did not make an appearance. Whether he directed affairs from behind the scenes, or was not even present during the episode, I don't know. Whichever it was, he won a complete victory. The woman never reappeared nor, for that matter, did the witless gentleman who by bringing her was really the cause of the entire contretemps."

"A fair warning to all present," laughed Costain.

A waiter now appeared at the table. The chocolate-dark skin, the thin, beautifully molded nose and lips, the large liquid eyes, heavily lashed, and the silver white hair so heavy and silken that it lay on the skull like a cap, all marked him definitely as an East Indian of some sort, Costain decided. The man arranged the stiff table linen, filled two tumblers from a huge, cut-glass pitcher, and set them in their proper places.

"Tell me," Laffler said eagerly, "is the special being served this evening?"

The waiter smiled regretfully and showed teeth as spectacular as those of the major-domo. "I am so sorry, sair. There is no special this evening."

Laffler's face fell into lines of heavy disappointment. "After waiting so long. It's been a month already, and I hoped to show my friend here . . ."

"You understand the difficulties, sair."

"Of course, of course," Laffler looked at Costain sadly and shrugged. "You see, I had in mind to introduce you to the greatest treat that Sbirro's offers, but unfortunately it isn't on the menu this evening."

The waiter said: "Do you wish to be served now, sair?" and Laffler nodded. To Costain's surprise the waiter made his way off without waiting for any instructions.

"Have you ordered in advance?" he asked.

"Ah," said Laffler, "I really should have explained Sbirro's offers no choice whatsoever. You will eat the same meal as everyone else in this room. Tomorrow evening you would eat an entirely different meal, but again without designating a single preference."

"Very unusual," said Costain, "and certainly unsatisfactory at times. What if one doesn't have a taste for the particular dish set before him?"

"On that score," said Laffler solemnly, "you need have no fears, I give you my word that no matter how exacting your tastes, you will relish every mouthful you eat at Sbirro's."

Costain looked doubtful, and Laffler smiled. "And consider the subtle advantages of the system," he said. "When you pick up the menu of a popular restaurant, you will find yourself confronted with innumerable choices. You are forced to weigh, to evaluate, to make uneasy decisions which you may instantly regret. The effect of all this is a tension which, however slight, must make for discomfort.

"And consider the mechanics of the process. Instead of a hurlyburly of sweating cooks rushing about a kitchen in a frenzy to prepare a hundred varying items, we have a chef who stands serenely alone, bringing all his talents to bear on one task, with all assurance of a complete triumph!"

"Then you have seen the kitchen?"

"Unfortunately, no," said Laffler sadly. "The picture I offer is hypothetical, made of conversational fragments I have pieced together over the years. I must admit, though, that my desire to see the functioning of the kitchen here comes very close to being my sole obsession nowadays."

"But have you mentioned this to Sbirro?"

"A dozen times. He shrugs the suggestion away."

"Isn't that a rather curious foible on his part?"

"No, no," Laffler said hastily, "a master artist is never under the compulsion of petty courtesies. Still," he sighed, "I have never given up hope."

The waiter now reappeared bearing two soup bowls which he set in place with mathematical exactitude, and a small tureen from which he slowly ladled a measure of clear, thin broth. Costain dipped his spoon into the broth and tasted it with some curiosity. It was delicately flavored, bland to the verge of tastelessness. Costain frowned, tentatively reached for the salt and pepper cellars, and discovered there were none on the table. He looked up, saw Laffler's eyes on him, and although unwilling to compromise with his own tastes, he hesitated to act as a damper on Laffler's enthusiasm. Therefore he smiled and indicated the broth.

"Excellent," he said.

Laffler returned his smile. "You do not find it excellent at all," he said coolly. "You find it flat and badly in need of condiments. I know this," he continued as Costain's eyebrows shot upward, "because it was my own reaction many years ago, and because like yourself I found myself reaching for salt and pepper after the first mouthful. I also learned with surprise that condiments are not available in Sbirro's."

Costain was shocked. "Not even salt!" he exclaimed.

"Not even salt. The very fact that you require it for your soup stands as evidence that your taste is unduly jaded. I am confident that you will now make the same discovery that I did: by the time you have nearly finished your soup, your desire for salt will be nonexistent."

Laffler was right; before Costain had reached the bottom of his plate, he was relishing the nuances of the broth with steadily increasing delight. Laffler thrust aside his own empty bowl and rested his elbows on the table. "Do you agree with me now?"

"To my surprise," said Costain, "I do."

As the waiter busied himself clearing the table, Laffler lowered his voice significantly. "You will find," he said, "that the absence of condiments is but one of several noteworthy characteristics which mark Sbirro's. I may as well prepare you for these. For example, no alcoholic beverages of any sort are served here, nor for that matter any beverage except clear, cold water, the first and only drink necessary for a human being."

"Outside of mother's milk," suggested Costain dryly.

"I can answer that in like vein by pointing out that the average patron of Sbirro's has passed that primal stage of his development."

Costain laughed. "Granted," he said.

"Very well. There is also a ban on the use of tobacco in any form."

"But good heavens," said Costain, "doesn't that make Sbirro's more a teetotaler's retreat than a gourmet's sanctuary?"

"I fear," said Laffler solemnly, "that you confuse the words, *gourmet* and *gourmand*. The gourmand, through glutting himself, requires a wider and wider latitude of experience to stir his surfeited senses, but the very nature of the gourmet is simplicity. The ancient Greek in his coarse chiton savoring the ripe olive; the Japanese in his bare room contemplating the curve of a single flower stem—these are the true gourmets."

"But an occasional drop of brandy, or pipeful of tobacco," said Costain dubiously, "are hardly overindulgences."

"By alternating stimulant and narcotic," said Laffler, "you see-saw the delicate balance of your taste so violently that it loses its most precious quality: the appreciation of fine food. During my years as a patron of Sbirro's, I have proved this to my satisfaction."

"May I ask," said Costain, "why you regard the ban on these things as having such deep esthetic motives? What about such mundane reasons as the high cost of a liquor license, or the possibility that patrons would object to the smell of tobacco in such confined quarters?"

Laffler shook his head violently. "If and when you meet Sbirro," he said, "you will understand at once that he is not the man to make decisions on a mundane basis. As a matter of fact, it was Sbirro himself who first made me cognizant of what you call 'esthetic' motives."

"An amazing man," said Costain as the waiter prepared to serve the entrée.

Laffler's next words were not spoken until he had savored and swallowed a large portion of meat. "I hesitate to use superlatives," he said, "but to my way of thinking, Sbirro represents man at the apex of his civilization!"

Costain cocked an eyebrow and applied himself to his roast

which rested in a pool of stiff gravy ungarnished by green or vegetable. The thin steam rising from it carried to his nostrils a subtle, tantalizing odor which made his mouth water. He chewed a piece as slowly and thoughtfully as if he were analyzing the intricacies of a Mozart symphony. The range of taste he discovered was really extraordinary, from the pungent nip of the crisp outer edge to the peculiarly flat yet soul-satisfying ooze of blood which the pressure of his jaws forced from the half-raw interior.

Upon swallowing he found himself ferociously hungry for another piece, and then another, and it was only with an effort that he prevented himself from wolfing down all his share of the meat and gravy without waiting to get the full voluptuous satisfaction from each mouthful. When he had scraped his platter clean, he realized that both he and Laffler had completed the entire course without exchanging a single word. He commented on this, and Laffler said, "Can you see any need for words in the presence of such food?"

Costain looked around at the shabby, dimly lit room, the quiet diners, with a new perception. "No," he said humbly, "I cannot. For any doubts I had I apologize unreservedly. In all your praise of Sbirro's there was not a single word of exaggeration."

"Ah," said Laffler delightedly. "And that is only part of the story. You heard me mention the special which unfortunately was not on the menu tonight. What you have just eaten is as nothing when compared to the absolute delights of that special!"

"Good Lord!" cried Costain; "What is it? Nightingale's tongues? Filet of unicorn?"

"Neither," said Laffler. "It is lamb."

"Lamb?"

Laffler remained lost in thought for a minute. "If," he said at last, "I were to give you in my own unstinted words my opinion of this dish, you would judge me completely insane. That is how deeply the mere thought of it affects me. It is neither the fatty chop, nor the too solid leg; it is, instead, a select portion of the rarest sheep in existence and is named after the species—lamb Amirstan."

Costain knit his brows. "Amirstan?"

"A fragment of desolation almost lost on the border which

separates Afghanistan and Russia. From chance remarks dropped by Sbirro, I gather it is no more than a plateau which grazes the pitiful remnants of a flock of superb sheep, Sbirro, through some means or other, obtained rights to the traffic in this block and is, therefore, the sole restaurateur ever to have lamb Amirstan on his bill of fare. I can tell you that the appearance of this dish is a rare occurrence indeed, and luck is the only guide in determining for the clientele the exact date when it will be served."

"But surely," said Costain, "Sbirro could provide some advance knowledge of this event."

"The objection to that is simply stated," said Laffler. "There exists in this city a huge number of professional gluttons. Should advance information slip out, it is quite likely that they will, out of curiosity, become familiar with the dish and thenceforth supplant the regular patrons at these tables."

"But you don't mean to say," objected Costain, "that these few people present are the only ones in the entire city, or for that matter, in the whole wide world, who know of the existence of Sbirro's!"

"Very nearly. There may be one or two regular patrons who, for some reason, are not present at the moment."

"That's incredible."

"It is done," said Laffler, the slightest shade of menace in his voice, "by every patron making it his solemn obligation to keep the secret. By accepting my invitation this evening, you automatically assume that obligation. I hope you can be trusted with it."

Costain flushed. "My position in your employ should vouch for me. I only question the wisdom of a policy which keeps such magnificent food away from so many who would enjoy it."

"Do you know the inevitable result of the policy *you* favor?" asked Laffler bitterly. "An influx of idiots who would nightly complain that they are never served roast duck with chocolate sauce. Is that picture tolerable to you?"

"No," admitted Costain, "I am forced to agree with you."

Laffler leaned back in his chair wearily and passed his hand over his eyes in an uncertain gesture. "I am a solitary man," he said quietly, "and not by choice alone. It may sound strange to you, it may border on eccentricity, but I feel to my depths that this restaurant, this warm haven in a coldly insane world, is both family and friend to me."

And Costain, who to this moment had never viewed his companion as other than tyrannical employer or officious host, now felt an overwhelming pity twist inside his comfortably expanded stomach.

By the end of two weeks the invitation to join Laffler at Sbirro's had become something of a ritual. Every day, at a few minutes after five, Costain would step out into the office corridor and lock his cubicle behind him; he would drape his overcoat neatly over his left arm, and peer into the glass of the door to make sure his Homburg was set at the proper angle. At one time he would have followed this by lighting a cigarette, but under Laffler's prodding he had decided to give abstinence a fair trial. Then he would start down the corridor, and Laffler would fall in step at his elbow, clearing his throat. "Ah, Costain. No plans for this evening, I hope."

"No," Costain would say, "I'm footloose and fancy free," or "At your service," or something equally inane. He wondered at times whether it would not be more tactful to vary the ritual with an occasional refusal, but the glow with which Laffler received his answer, and the rough friendliness of Laffler's grip on his arm, forestalled him.

Among the treacherous crags of the business world, reflected Costain, what better way to secure your footing than friendship with one's employer. Already, a secretary close to the workings of the inner office had commented publicly on Laffler's highly favorable opinion of Costain. That was all to the good.

And the food! The incomparable food at Sbirro's! For the first time in his life, Costain, ordinarily a lean and bony man, noted with gratification that he was certainly gaining weight; within two weeks his bones had disappeared under a layer of sleek, firm flesh, and here and there were even signs of incipient plumpness. It struck Costain one night, while surveying himself in his bath, that the rotund Laffler, himself, might have been a spare and bony man before discovering Sbirro's.

So there was obviously everything to be gained and nothing to be lost by accepting Laffler's invitations. Perhaps after testing the heralded wonders of lamb Amirstan and meeting Sbirro, who thus far had not made an appearance, a refusal or two might be in order. But certainly not until then.

That evening, two weeks to a day after his first visit to Sbirro's, Costain had both desires fulfilled: he dined on lamb Amirstan, and he met Sbirro. Both exceeded all his expectations.

When the waiter leaned over their table immediately after seating them and gravely announced, "Tonight is special, sair," Costain was shocked to find his heart pounding with expectation. On the table before him he saw Laffler's hands trembling violently. "But it isn't natural," he thought suddenly. "Two full grown men, presumably intelligent and in the full possession of their senses, as jumpy as a pair of cats waiting to have their meat flung to them!"

"This is it!" Laffler's voice startled him so that he almost leaped from his seat. "The culinary triumph of all times! And faced by it you are embarrassed by the very emotions it distills."

"How did you know that?" Costain asked faintly.

"How? Because a decade ago I underwent your embarrassment. Add to that your air of revulsion and it's easy to see how affronted you are by the knowledge that man has not yet forgotten how to slaver over his meat."

"And these others," whispered Costain, "do they all feel the same thing?"

"Judge for yourself."

Costain looked furtively around at the nearby tables. "You are right," he finally said. "At any rate, there's comfort in numbers."

Laffler inclined his head slightly to the side. "One of the numbers," he remarked, "appears to be in for a disappointment."

Costain followed the gesture. At the table indicated a gray-haired man sat conspicuously alone, and Costain frowned at the empty chair opposite him.

"Why, yes," he recalled, "that very stout, bald man, isn't it? I believe it's the first dinner he's missed here in two weeks."

"The entire decade more likely," said Laffler sympathetically. "Rain or shine, crisis or calamity, I don't think he's missed an evening at Sbirro's since the first time I dined there. Imagine his expression when he's told that on his very first defection, lamb Amirstan was the *plat du jour*."

Costain looked at the empty chair again with a dim discomfort. "His very first?" he murmured.

"Mr. Laffler! And friend! I am so pleased. So very, very pleased. No, do not stand; I will have a place made." Miraculously a seat appeared under the figure standing there at the table. "The lamb Amirstan will be an unqualified success, hurr? I myself have been stewing in the miserable kitchen all the day, prodding the foolish chef to do everything just so. The just so is the important part, hurr? But I see your friend does not know me. An introduction, perhaps?"

The words ran in a smooth, fluid eddy. They rippled, they purred, they hypnotized Costain so that he could do no more than stare. The mouth that uncoiled this sinuous monologue was alarmingly wide, with thin mobile lips that curled and twisted with every syllable. There was a flat nose with a straggling line of hair under it; wide-set eyes, almost Oriental in appearance, that glittered in the unsteady flare of gaslight; and long, sleek hair that swept back from high on the unwrinkled forehead— hair so pale that it might have been bleached of all color. An amazing face surely, and the sight of it tortured Costain with the conviction that it was somehow familiar. His brain twitched and prodded but could not stir up any solid recollection.

Laffler's voice jerked Costain out of his study. "Mr. Sbirro. Mr. Costain, a good friend and associate." Costain rose and shook the proferred hand. It was warm and dry, flint-hard against his palm.

"I am so very pleased, Mr. Costain. So very, very pleased," purred the voice. "You like my little establishment, hurr? You have a great treat in store, I assure you."

Laffler chuckled. "Oh, Costain's been dining here regularly for two weeks," he said. "He's by way of becoming a great admirer of yours, Sbirro."

The eyes were turned on Costain. "A very great compliment. You compliment me with your presence and I return same with my food, hurr? But the lamb Amirstan is far superior to anything of your past experience, I assure you. All the trouble of obtaining it, all the difficulty of preparation, is truly merited."

Costain strove to put aside the exasperating problem of that face. "I have wondered," he said, "why with all these difficulties you mention, you even bother to present lamb Amirstan to the public. Surely your other dishes are excellent enough to uphold your reputation."

Sbirro smiled so broadly that his face became perfectly round. "Perhaps it is a matter of the psychology, hurr? Someone discovers a wonder and must share it with others. He must fill his cup to the brim, perhaps, by observing the so evident pleasure of those who explore it with him. Or," he shrugged, "perhaps it is just a matter of good business."

"Then in the light of all this," Costain persisted, "and considering all the conventions you have imposed on your customers, why do you open the restaurant to the public instead of operating it as a private club?"

The eyes abruptly glinted into Costain's, then turned away. "So perspicacious, hurr? Then I will tell you. Because there is more privacy in a public eating place than in the most exclusive club in existence! Here no one inquires of your affairs; no one desires to know the intimacies of your life. Here the business is eating. We are not curious about names and addresses or the reasons for the coming and going of our guests. We welcome you when you are here; we have no regrets when you are here no longer. That is the answer, hurr?"

Costain was startled by this vehemence. "I had no intention of prying," he stammered.

Sbirro ran the tip of his tongue over his thin lips. "No, no," he reassured, "you are not prying. Do not let me give you that impression. On the contrary, I invite your questions."

"Oh, come, Costain," said Laffler. "Don't let Sbirro intimidate you. I've known him for years and I guarantee that his bark is worse than his bite. Before you know it, he'll be showing you all the privileges of the house—outside of inviting you to visit his precious kitchen, of course."

"Ah," smiled Sbirro, "for that, Mr. Costain may have to wait a little while. For everything else I am at his beck and call."

Laffler slapped his hand jovially on the table. "What did I tell you!" he said. "Now let's have the truth, Sbirro. Has anyone, outside of your staff, ever stepped into the sanctum sanctorum?"

Sbirro looked up. "You see on the wall above you," he said earnestly, "the portrait of one to whom I did the honor. A very dear friend and a patron of most long standing, he is evidence that my kitchen is not inviolate."

Costain studied the picture and started with recognition. "Why," he said excitedly, "that's the famous writer—you know the one, Laffler—he used to do such wonderful short stories and cynical bits and then suddenly took himself off and disappeared in Mexico!"

"Of course!" cried Laffler, "and to think I've been sitting under his portrait for years without even realizing it!" He turned to Sbirro. "A dear friend, you say? His disappearance must have been a blow to you."

Sbirro's face lengthened. "It was, it was, I assure you. But think of it this way, gentlemen: he was probably greater in his death than in his life, hurr? A most tragic man, he often told me that his only happy hours were spent here at this very table. Pathetic, is it not? And to think the only favor I could ever show him was to let him witness the mysteries of my kitchen, which is, when all is said and done, no more than a plain, ordinary kitchen."

"You seem very certain of his death," commented Costain. "After all, no evidence has ever turned up to substantiate it."

Sbirro contemplated the picture. "None at all," he said softly. "Remarkable, hurr?"

With the arrival of the entrée Sbirro leaped to his feet and set about serving them himself. With his eyes alight he lifted the casserole from the tray and sniffed at the fragrance from within with sensual relish. Then, taking great care not to lose a single drop of gravy, he filled two platters with chunks of dripping meat. As if exhausted by this task, he sat back in his chair, breathing heavily. "Gentlemen," he said, "to your good appetite."

Costain chewed his first mouthful with great deliberation and swallowed it. Then he looked at the empty tines of his fork with glazed eyes.

"Good God!" he breathed.

"It is good, hurr? Better than you imagined?"

Costain shook his head dazedly. "It is as impossible," he said slowly, "for the uninitiated to conceive the delights of lamb Amirstan as for mortal man to look into his own soul."

"Perhaps," Sbirro thrust his head so close that Costain could feel the warm, fetid breath tickle his nostrils, "perhaps you have just had a glimpse into your soul, hurr?"

Costain tried to draw back slightly without giving offense. "Perhaps," he laughed, "and a gratifying picture it made: all fang and claw. But without intending any disrespect, I should hardly like to build my church on *lamb en casserole*."

Sbirro rose and laid a hand gently on his shoulder. "So perspicacious." he said. "Sometimes when you have nothing to do, nothing, perhaps, but sit for a very little while in a dark room and think of this world—what it is and what it is going to be— then you must turn your thoughts a little to the significance of the Lamb in religion. It will be so interesting. And now," he bowed deeply to both men. "I have held you long enough from your dinner. I was most happy," he nodded to Costain, "and I am sure we will meet again." The teeth gleamed, the eyes glittered, and Sbirro was gone down the aisle of tables.

Costain twisted around to stare after the retreating figure. "Have I offended him in some way?" he asked.

Laffler looked up from his plate. "Offended him? He loves that kind of talk. Lamb Amirstan is a ritual with him; get him started and he'll be back at you a dozen times worse than a priest making a conversion."

Costain turned to his meal with the face still hovering before him. "Interesting man," he reflected. "Very."

It took him a month to discover the tantalizing familiarity of that face, and when he did, he laughed aloud in his bed. Why, of course! Sbirro might have sat as the model for the Cheshire cat in *Alice!*

He passed this thought on to Laffler the very next evening as they pushed their way down the street to the restaurant against a chill, blustering wind. Laffler only looked blank.

"You may be right," he said, "but I'm not a fit judge. It's a far cry back to the days when I read the book. A far cry, indeed."

As if taking up his words, a piercing howl came ringing down the street and stopped both men short in their tracks. "Someone's in trouble there," said Laffler. "Look!"

Not far from the entrance to Sbirro's two figures could be seen struggling in the near darkness. They swayed back and forth and suddenly tumbled into a writhing heap on the sidewalk. The piteous howl went up again, and Laffler, despite his girth, ran toward it at a fair speed with Costain tagging cautiously behind.

Stretched out full-length on the pavement was a slender figure with the dusky complexion and white hair of one of Sbirro's servitors. His fingers were futilely plucking at the huge hands which encircled his throat, and his knees pushed weakly up at the gigantic bulk of a man who brutally bore down with his full weight.

Laffler came up panting. "Stop this!" he shouted. "What's going on here?"

The pleading eyes almost bulging from their sockets turned toward Laffler. "Help, sair. This man—drunk—"

"Drunk am I, ya dirty—" Costain saw now that the man was a sailor in a badly soiled uniform. The air around him reeked with the stench of liquor. "Pick me pocket and then call me drunk, will ya!" He dug his fingers in harder, and his victim groaned.

Laffler seized the sailor's shoulder. "Let go of him, do you hear! Let go of him at once!" he cried, and the next instant was sent careening into Costain, who staggered back under the force of the blow.

The attack on his own person sent Laffler into immediate and berserk action. Without a sound he leaped at the sailor, striking and kicking furiously at the unprotected face and flanks. Stunned at first, the man came to his feet with a rush and turned on Laffler. For a moment they stood locked together, and then as Costain joined the attack, all three went sprawling to the ground. Slowly Laffler and Costain got to their feet and looked down at the body before them.

"He's either out cold from liquor," said Costain, "or he struck his head going down. In any case, it's a job for the police."

"No, no, sair!" The waiter crawled weakly to his feet, and stood swaying. "No police, sair. Mr. Sbirro do not want such. You understand, sair." He caught hold of Costain with a pleading hand, and Costain looked at Laffler.

"Of course not," said Laffler. "We won't have to bother with the police. They'll pick him up soon enough, the murderous sot. But what in the world started all this?"

"That man, sair. He make most erratic way while walking, and with no meaning I push against him. Then he attack me, accusing me to rob him."

"As I thought," Laffler pushed the waiter gently along. "Now go on in and get yourself attended to."

The man seemed ready to burst into tears. "To you, sair, I owe my life. If there is anything I can do—"

Laffler turned into the areaway that led to Sbirro's door. "No, no, it was nothing. You go along, and if Sbirro has any questions send him to me. I'll straighten it out."

"My life, sair," were the last words they heard as the inner door closed behind them.

"There you are, Costain," said Laffler, as a few minutes later he drew his chair under the table, "civilized man in all his glory. Reeking with alcohol, strangling to death some miserable innocent who came too close."

Costain made an effort to gloss over the nerve-shattering memory of the episode. "It's the neurotic cat that takes to alcohol," he said. "Surely there's a reason for that sailor's condition."

"Reason? Of course there is. Plain atavistic savagery!" Laffler swept his arm in an all-embracing gesture. "Why do we all sit here at our meat? Not only to appease physical demands, but because our atavistic selves cry for release. Think back, Costain. Do you remember that I once described Sbirro as the epitome of civilization? Can you now see why? A brilliant man, he fully understands the nature of human beings. But unlike lesser men he bends all his efforts to the satisfaction of our innate natures without resultant harm to some innocent bystander."

"When I think back on the wonders of lamb Amirstan," said Costain, "I quite understand what you're driving at. And, by the way, isn't it nearly due to appear on the bill of fare? It must have been over a month ago that it was last served."

The waiter, filling the tumblers, hesitated. "I am so sorry, sair. No special this evening."

"There's your answer," Laffler grunted, "and probably just my luck to miss out on it altogether the next time."

Costain stared at him. "Oh come, that's impossible."

"No, blast it." Laffler drank off half his water at a gulp and the waiter immediately refilled the glass. "I'm off to South America for a surprise tour of inspection. One month, two months, Lord knows how long."

"Are things that bad down there?"

"They could be better." Laffler suddenly grinned. "Mustn't forget it takes very mundane dollars and cents to pay the tariff at Sbirro's."

"I haven't heard a word of this around the office."

"Wouldn't be a surprise tour if you had. Nobody knows about this except myself—and now you. I want to walk in on them completely unsuspected. Find out what flimflammery they're up to down there. As far as the office is concerned, I'm off on a jaunt somewhere. Maybe recuperating in some sanatorium from my hard work. Anyhow, the business will be in good hands. Yours, among them."

"Mine?" said Costain, surprised.

"When you go in tomorrow you'll find yourself in receipt of a promotion, even if I'm not there to hand it to you personally. Mind you, it has nothing to do with our friendship either; you've done fine work, and I'm immensely grateful for it."

Costain reddened under the praise. "You don't expect to be in tomorrow. Then you're leaving tonight?"

Laffler nodded. "I've been trying to wangle some reservations. If they come through, well, this will be in the nature of a farewell celebration."

"You know," said Costain slowly, "I devoutly hope that your reservations don't come through. I believe our dinners here have come to mean more to me than I ever dared imagine."

The waiter's voice broke in. "Do you wish to be served now, sair?" and they both started.

"Of course, of course," said Laffler sharply, "I didn't realize you were waiting."

"What bothers me," he told Costain as the waiter turned away, "is the thought of the lamb Amirstan I'm bound to miss. To tell you the truth, I've already put off my departure a week, hoping to hit a lucky night, and now I simply can't delay any more. I do hope that when you're sitting over your share of lamb Amirstan, you'll think of me with suitable regrets."

Costain laughed. "I will indeed," he said as he turned to his dinner.

Hardly had he cleared the plate when a waiter silently reached for it. It was not their usual waiter, he observed; it was none other than the victim of the assault.

"Well," Costain said, "how do you feel now? Still under the weather?"

The waiter paid no attention to him. Instead, with the air of a man under great strain, he turned to Laffler. "Sair," he whispered. "My life. I owe it to you. I can repay you!"

Laffler looked up in amazement, then shook his head firmly. "No," he said. "I want nothing from you, understand? You have repaid me sufficiently with your thanks. Now get on with your work and let's hear no more about it."

The waiter did not stir an inch, but his voice rose slightly. "By the body and blood of your God, sair, I will help you even if you do not want! *Do not go into the kitchen, sair.* I trade you my life for yours, sair, when I speak this. Tonight or any night of your life, do not go into the kitchen at Sbirro's!"

Laffler sat back, completely dumfounded. "Not go into the kitchen? Why shouldn't I go into the kitchen if Mr. Sbirro ever took it into his head to invite me there? What's all this about?"

A hard hand was laid on Costain's back, and another gripped the waiter's arm. The waiter remained frozen to the spot, his lips compressed, his eyes downcast.

"What is all *what* about, gentlemen?" purred the voice. "So opportune an arrival. In time as ever, I see, to answer all the questions, hurr?"

Laffler breathed a sigh of relief. "Ah, Sbirro, thank heaven you're here. This man is saying something about my not going into your kitchen. Do you know what he means?"

The teeth showed in a broad grin. "But of course. This good man was giving you advice in all amiability. It so happens that my too emotional chef heard some rumor that I might have a guest into his precious kitchen, and he flew into a fearful rage. Such a rage, gentlemen! He even threatened to give notice on the spot, and you can understand what that would mean to Sbirro's, hurr? Fortunately, I succeeded in showing him what a signal honor it is to have an esteemed patron and true connoisseur observe him at his work first hand, and now he is quite amenable. Quite, hurr?"

He released the waiter's arm. "You are at the wrong table," he said softly. "See that it does not happen again."

The waiter slipped off without daring to raise his eyes and Sbirro drew a chair to the table. He seated himself and brushed his hand lightly over his hair. "Now I am afraid that the cat is out of the bag, hurr? This invitation to you, Mr. Laffler, was to be a surprise; but the surprise is gone, and all that is left is the invitation."

Laffler mopped beads of perspiration from his forehead. "Are you serious?" he said huskily. "Do you mean that we are really to witness the preparation of your food tonight?"

Sbirro drew a sharp fingernail along the tablecloth, leaving a thin, straight line printed in the linen. "Ah," he said, "I am faced with a dilemma of great proportions." He studied the line soberly. "You, Mr. Laffler, have been my guest for ten long years. But our friend here—"

Costain raised his hand in protest. "I understand perfectly. This invitation is solely to Mr. Laffler, and naturally my presence is embarrassing. As it happens I have an early engagement for this evening and must be on my way anyhow. So you see there's no dilemma at all, really."

"No," said Laffler, "absolutely not. That wouldn't be fair at all. We've been sharing this until now, Costain, and I won't enjoy this experience half as much if you're not along. Surely Sbirro can make his conditions flexible, this one occasion."

They both looked at Sbirro who shrugged his shoulders regretfully.

Costain rose abruptly. "I'm not going to sit here, Laffler, and spoil your great adventure. And then too," he bantered, "think of that ferocious chef waiting to get his cleaver on you. I prefer not to be at the scene. I'll just say good-by," he went on, to cover Laffler's guilty silence, "and leave you to Sbirro. I'm sure he'll take pains to give you a good show." He held out his hand and Laffler squeezed it painfully hard.

"You're being very decent, Costain," he said. "I hope you'll continue to dine here until we meet again. It shouldn't be too long."

Sbirro made way for Costain to pass. "I will expect you," he said. *"Au 'voir."*

Costain stopped briefly in the dim foyer to adjust his scarf and fix his Homburg at the proper angle. When he turned away from the mirror, satisfied at last, he saw with a final glance that Laffler and Sbirro were already at the kitchen door; Sbirro holding the door invitingly wide with one hand, while the other rested, almost tenderly, on Laffler's meaty shoulders.